The Tale of
Applebeck
Orchard

THE TALE OF
APPLEBECK
ORCHARD

The Cottage Tales of
BEATRIX POTTER

Susan Wittig Albert

BERKLEY PRIME CRIME, NEW YORK

THE BERKLEY PUBLISHING GROUP
Published by the Penguin Group
Penguin Group (USA) Inc.
375 Hudson Street, New York, New York 10014, USA
Penguin Group (Canada), 90 Eglinton Avenue East, Suite 700, Toronto, Ontario M4P 2Y3, Canada
(a division of Pearson Penguin Canada Inc.)
Penguin Books Ltd., 80 Strand, London WC2R 0RL, England
Penguin Group Ireland, 25 St. Stephen's Green, Dublin 2, Ireland (a division of Penguin Books Ltd.)
Penguin Group (Australia), 250 Camberwell Road, Camberwell, Victoria 3124, Australia
(a division of Pearson Australia Group Pty. Ltd.)
Penguin Books India Pvt. Ltd., 11 Community Centre, Panchsheel Park, New Delhi—110 017, India
Penguin Group (NZ), 67 Apollo Drive, Rosedale, North Shore 0632, New Zealand
(a division of Pearson New Zealand Ltd.)
Penguin Books (South Africa) (Pty.) Ltd., 24 Sturdee Avenue, Rosebank, Johannesburg 2196,
South Africa

Penguin Books Ltd., Registered Offices: 80 Strand, London WC2R 0RL, England

This book is an original publication of The Berkley Publishing Group.

Copyright © 2009 by Susan Wittig Albert.
Cover illustration by Peggy Turchette.
Cover design by Lesley Worrell.
Interior map created by Peggy Turchette.

FIRST EDITION: September 2009

Library of Congress Cataloging-in-Publication Data

Albert, Susan Wittig.
  The tale of Applebeck Orchard : the cottage tales of Beatrix Potter / Susan Wittig Albert. — 1st ed.
    p. cm.
  ISBN 978-0-425-22977-4
  1. Potter, Beatrix, 1866–1943—Fiction. 2. Women authors—Fiction. 3. Women artists—
Fiction. 4. Country life—England—Fiction. I. Title.
  PS3551.L2637T343 2009
  813'.54—dc22

                                                                                    2009012791

PRINTED IN THE UNITED STATES OF AMERICA

10   9   8   7   6   5   4   3   2   1

To Peggy Moody,
Webmistress, helper, and friend,
with thanks for all
you do

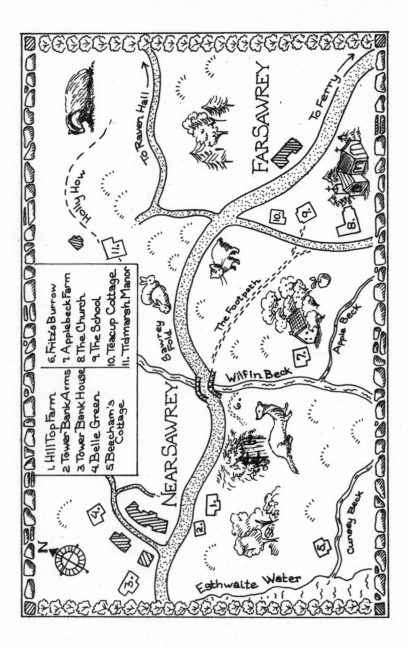

FarSawrey

To Raven Hall →

To Ferry →

Holly How

NearSawrey

Sawrey Fold

The Footpath

Wilfin Beck

Apple Beck

Cunsey Beck

Esthwaite Water

1. Hill Top Farm
2. Tower Bank Arms
3. Tower Bank House
4. Belle Green
5. Beecham's Cottage
6. Fritz's Burrow
7. Applebeck Farm
8. The Church
9. The School
10. Teacup Cottage
11. Tidmarsh Manor

N

Cast of Characters

(* indicates an actual historical person or creature)

People of the Land Between the Lakes

Beatrix Potter* is best known for the series of children's books that began with *The Tale of Peter Rabbit*. She lives with her parents, *Helen and Rupert Potter*, at Number Two, Bolton Gardens, in London, but spends as much time as possible at her farm, Hill Top, in the Lake District village of Near Sawrey. *Mr. and Mrs. Jennings* and their three children live in their part of the Hill Top farmhouse.

Will Heelis* is a solicitor who lives in the nearby market town of Hawkshead. Well-known to everyone in Sawrey, he helps Miss Potter with her property purchases.

Adam Harmsworth is the owner of Applebeck Farm at the edge of Far Sawrey. His wife, *Ernestina*, keeps the house, helped by Mr. Harmsworth's fourteen-year-old orphaned niece, *Gilly*.

Thomas Beecham (known to the villagers as Auld Beechie) is a former employee of Mr. Harmsworth's. He now works as odd-jobs man at the Tower Bank Arms.

Major Roger Ragsdale is president of the Claife Heights Ramblers, an association of fell-walkers. A retired military man, he lives in Teapot Cottage, Far Sawrey.

Sarah Barwick operates the Anvil Cottage Bakery in Near Sawrey.

Captain Miles Woodcock, who lives in Tower Bank House, is justice of the peace for Sawrey District and a trustee of Sawrey School. *Elsa Grape* cooks and keeps house for him.

Vicar Samuel Sackett is the vicar of St. Peter's Church in Far Sawrey. *Mrs. Hazel Thompson* (a cousin of Agnes Llewellyn) keeps house for him.

Margaret Nash is head teacher at Sawrey School. She lives in one of the Sunnyside Cottages with her sister, *Annie Nash*, a piano teacher.

Bertha Stubbs and her husband, *Henry*, live in the Lakefield Cottages. Bertha, a tempestuous character, cleans Sawrey School; Henry operates the Windermere ferry.

Dimity Woodcock Kittredge, Captain Woodcock's sister, is married to *Major Christopher Kittredge*, of Raven Hall. The Kittredges have two children, little *Flora* and baby *Christopher*.

Mathilda Crook boards visitors at Belle Green. Her husband, *George*, is the village smith.

Agnes and Dick Llewellyn live next door to Belle Green, at High Green Gate.

John Braithwaite is the constable for Near and Far Sawrey; he and his wife, *Hannah*, live at Croft End Cottage.

Caroline Longford, sixteen, lives with her grandmother, *Lady Longford*, at Tidmarsh Manor. Caroline has set her heart on becoming a musician and composer. Also at Tidmarsh Manor: Caroline's governess, *Miss Cecily Burns*, a friend of Miss Potter's.

Creatures of the Land Between the Lakes

Tabitha Twitchit, president of the Village Cat Council, is a calico cat with an orange and white bib. Tabitha's rival, *Crumpet*, is a handsome gray tabby cat. *Max the Manx* is once again between assignments and looking for steady work.

Rascal, a Jack Russell terrier, lives at Belle Green but spends his time making sure that the daily life of the village goes according to plan.

Fritz the ferret has a reputation as a disagreeable hermit. Escaped from captivity, he now lives alone near the bridge over Wilfin Beck.

Bosworth Badger XVII keeps The Brockery, an animal hostelry on Holly How. *Parsley* serves up fine meals from The Brockery kitchen, while *Primrose* manages the housekeeping, ably assisted by her daughter, *Hyacinth*. Her son, *Thorn*, has been traveling since January.

Professor Galileo Newton Owl, D.Phil., is a tawny owl who conducts advanced studies in astronomy and applied natural history from his home in a hollow beech at the top of Cuckoo Brow Wood. As far as he is concerned, his is the final say on any important matter in the region.

Kep the collie is top dog at Hill Top Farm. Other notable barnyard animals include *Winston* the pony; *Aunt Susan* and *Dorcas*, the Berkshire pigs; *Kitchen* the Galway cow; and *Blossom*, her calf.

THE TALE OF
APPLEBECK ORCHARD

PROLOGUE

Before the Beginning

Every story has a beginning. Ours opens on a bright August morning in 1910, in the Lake District of England. The sun, eager to be about his day's work, has already waded through the layer of cottony mist that blanketed Lake Windermere, clambered up the steep eastern slope of Claife Heights, and launched himself with a cheer into the clear blue sky above the Land Between the Lakes, a vantage point from which he can beam down upon the leaf-green and lake-blue earth.

But before every story there is . . . well, another story. For this is not the first time the sun has made his daily journey across the Land Between the Lakes. A great deal of time—a vast immensity of time, an unthinkable infinity of time, human and otherwise—has transpired before the beginning of our story. In fact, you might think that the sun is already quite tired of his day-in and day-out routine, for he has climbed Claife Heights more times than you or I could possibly count.

But if you asked the sun, I'm sure he would tell you that every day brings something interesting and intriguing to observe. He has seen mountains rise beneath him, volcanoes erupt in his face, and seas ebb and flow. For a long time he watched icy glaciers advancing and retreating as they carved the ancient rock, scooping out convenient places for lakes and dropping enormous boulders here and there as if they were pebbles carelessly falling through a hole in a boy's pocket. All this ice made the earth shiver and even the sun felt a little chilly and remote and not terribly interested in what was going on below.

But then the weather warmed. The sun took off his overcoat and mittens, the ice thawed, and rivers and streams took over the job of pushing rocks here and moving mountains there, and generally rearranging the furniture. The lakes brimmed and green things made themselves at home, putting down roots and thrusting up leaves—mosses and lichens at first, then heather and bilberry and fern and willow and alder and finally oak and beech and yew and juniper and the lovely hawthorn. Animals set up housekeeping in the dales and fells, fish filled the lakes, birds took to the skies, and the sun was happy for the company.

And then the animals had to move over, because people had arrived. First came the clans who worked with stone, then iron and bronze. These people did not travel much farther than they could walk in a day, having nearly everything they needed and wanted right in front of their noses. But then the Romans landed in the south of England. Since they had already traveled a considerable distance from Rome, you'd think they'd be ready to settle down. But they weren't, so they built a network of military roads and a massive wall of stone and turf right across England, east to west, to separate the civilized from the barbarians (although the sun was hard-pressed to tell which was which).

But things didn't exactly turn out as the Romans planned, and a few centuries later, they packed up and journeyed back to Rome. The Celts carried on until they were joined by the Angles and the Saxons, and they continued carrying on as the Norsemen arrived and settled around the lakes, farming in the dales and pasturing sheep in the fells. The old Roman roads conveyed wayfarers from one market town to another, whilst the villages and farms were linked by cartways suited to oxen and carts, bridleways suited to horses, and narrower footways suited to people. These were a great convenience, permitting people who lived in one valley to travel over the mountain to the next valley. Everyone went from cottage to market and church and field by the most direct and shortest route, and all got on quite famously.

But then people began buying and selling the land and constructing stone walls around the parts of it they owned, miniature versions of the Roman Wall. Hills were enclosed and divided, woodlands were fenced, fields hedged. The Age of Enclosure had arrived, and the land that was once used by many in common—for picking fruit, pasturing livestock, gathering wood or bracken or peat or stone—became the private and exclusive property of a few. More than seven million acres of England's fields, forests, pastures, and uplands were turned over to private ownership and enclosed.

The sun was baffled by this, and failed to see how all those walls, fences, and hedges made life better for anyone, except possibly for the few rich people who owned the land. In fact, it looked to him as if all these barriers were a frightful nuisance, getting in the way of people and animals and requiring the bother of gates and stiles so people could continue to do their ordinary business, going along the by-ways they had used since longer than any could remember.

Time passed, as time has a way of doing. A young girl named Victoria became England's queen, and then grew to a very old and much loved lady. The kingdom prospered, and railways and roads were built to carry newly manufactured goods to seaports and cities. By this time, there were a great many more people in the Land Between the Lakes. They came afoot, on horseback, by carriage and coach and bicycle, and even by motor car, an occasional brash *toot-toot!* frightening the birds into flight. A ferry made regular (more or less) trips across Lake Windermere and the railroad arrived at the edge of the district. It was kept by public opinion from going farther than Windermere Station, so there it had to stop and turn around and go back to London, sulking all the way.

The railroad and ferry brought even more people, of course, so that the more-traveled lanes became turnpikes and the less-traveled lanes became roads, and some of the paths became lanes, and others—well, they kept to being footpaths, for the convenience and pleasure of those who still, by choice or otherwise, went on foot. And because they had been footpaths for a very, very long time, everyone thought it quite reasonable that they all should go on being footpaths, forever, no matter who might own the property over which they crossed.

But that did not happen.

And that is where our story begins, on an August morning in 1910, in the Lake District of England.

1

The Village Animals Confront
a Crisis

It was the sort of bright, dry day when farmers in the Land Between the Lakes could cut their hay and stook their barley and oats without fear that their crops would get wet and spoil. The sun had just scrambled to the top of Claife Heights and was preparing to coast across the sky in the direction of Coniston Old Man, the great, broad-shouldered fell that loomed against the western horizon. The Sawrey Village animals were gathered on the grass in front of Belle Green, the house at the top of Market Street, to discuss a just-discovered and exceedingly disturbing problem.

"Will somebody please tell me what's going on?" asked Tabitha Twitchit crossly, curling the tip of her tail over her front paws. *"What is all the fuss about?"* A calico cat with a fluffy orange and white bib, Tabitha was getting on in years and had become (I am sorry to say) rather stout. But while the increase in girth had somewhat slowed her mousing abilities, it had not dulled her curiosity. And as senior cat

and president of the Sawrey Cat Council, she felt it her obligation—and her entitlement—to be fully informed about and completely in charge of everything that went on in the little Lake District village.

"*It's about the footpath,*" Rascal explained. He was momentarily distracted by the sight of Sarah Barwick, owner of the Anvil Cottage Bakery, pedaling her bicycle up Market Street in the direction of Castle Cottage, her wicker basket piled high with morning deliveries of bread and scones. You could set your pocket watch (if you had one) by Miss Barwick, Rascal thought with approval. A Jack Russell terrier with a strong organizational sense, he always felt more comfortable when people went about their business (which was Rascal's business, too, of course) in the usual way, at the usual time, by the usual means. Which was why this affair of the footpath was so unsettling.

"The public *footpath,*" Crumpet said with emphasis. "*Through Applebeck Orchard.*" Crumpet, a handsome gray tabby with a red collar and a gold bell, set a great store by factual precision, having little patience with animals who omitted pertinent details from their reports. As you might guess, this habit did not endear her to everyone, especially because Crumpet's tongue was sharp and she did not hesitate to use it.

"*The problem, you see,*" Max the Manx said glumly, "*is that Mr. Harmsworth has blocked the footpath—at both ends. He took down the wooden stile and built a great barricade of wire and wood in its place.*"

Max was a stocky black cat with a noticeable absence of tail, an hereditary trait that came about (as Max will tell you himself if you give him half a chance) at the time of the Great Flood. The ancestral Manx was the very last animal to board the ark and his tail was accidentally shut in the door by Noah himself, who was in a hurry to get everyone in out of the rain. Max was by nature a gloomy puss, but he was even gloomier lately. He had been without steady work for some months, and was in the market for a new job and a new home. He had yet to find either. The villagers seemed to have a prejudice against cats with no tails.

"At both ends!" cried Tabitha, aghast. *"But that means—"*

"It means that everyone will have to go the long way round to get to Far Sawrey." Crumpet lifted her right paw and looked critically at her claws. She always took special care to keep each in perfect condition. An unwary mouse, a careless vole, an incautious bird—one never knew when a very sharp claw might come in handy. Crumpet believed in being prepared for any eventuality.

"People will have to walk farther to get to church," Rascal added in a practical tone, *"and school. And the butcher shop."*

"Think of the children," Max said gloomily. *"Especially in the winter. And some of them don't have proper boots."*

Now, the closing of a footpath may not seem very important to you and me, since we depend on automobiles to take us here and there. Why, we even drive the two or three blocks to the grocery store! But it was a crisis of great significance to the residents of both Near and Far Sawrey, who mostly walked where they needed to go. To understand why it was so important, you might take a moment to glance at the map at the front of this book. You will see that the path through Applebeck Orchard shortens the distance between the two hamlets by over a half-mile. This is a great improvement in any weather (as I'm sure you'll agree), but especially when people are loaded with baskets or buckets or schoolbooks and when it is raining or snowing or very warm or very cold. For as long as anyone could remember, the Applebeck Footpath had saved people hundreds of extra steps every day. They would not be happy to find it blocked.

"This is a bad bit of business altogether," Rascal said, shaking his head. *"I don't know what the world's coming to."* It had already been an unsettled summer, with good King Edward dying in May and the unseasonable June frost that everyone said was caused by Halley's Comet and the coach accident on Ferry Hill in July and the haystack catching fire. And now the footpath. Not a calamity, perhaps, but certainly an appalling inconvenience.

"Everyone is quite annoyed," said Crumpet. *"Especially Mrs. Stubbs."* Crumpet should know, for she lived in the Lakefield Cottages with Mrs. Stubbs (who cleaned at Sawrey School) and Mr. Stubbs (who operated the ferry). Of course, when Mrs. Stubbs was truly annoyed, everyone in the village knew it. She was not a woman to bridle her tongue.

Max closed his eyes with a morose sigh. *"I don't suppose there's anything to be done about it. People will simply have to get used to walking farther."*

"People will simply tear the barricade down," Rascal barked. *"And in my opinion, they're perfectly entitled. That path belongs to everyone. Mr. Harmsworth has no right to block it."*

"Someone will pick up a rock and heave it through Mr. Harmsworth's window," Crumpet predicted in a knowing tone. She was not going out on a limb, for that was precisely what Mrs. Stubbs had promised to do. Go right to Applebeck Farm and put a rock through Harmsworth's front window.

Tabitha felt it was time to regain control of the discussion. *"I am sure,"* she said firmly, *"that Captain Woodcock will instruct Mr. Harmsworth to take down his barricade. Rascal is right when he says that the footpath belongs to everyone. And since Captain Woodcock is justice of the peace for Sawrey District, he has the proper authority."* Tabitha did not feel it necessary to add that the captain also had the authority to order a path to be stopped if it was no longer in use. This was most definitely not the case with the Applebeck Footpath. It was used every day by all manner of people and animals, coming and going. Tabitha herself had used the path just a few days before, to visit a cousin who lived the other side of St. Peter's.

"But why?" wondered Crumpet. A cat with an analytic mind, she always liked to get to the bottom of every subject. *"Why did Mr. Harmsworth block the footpath?"*

"P'rhaps he is just being cantankerous," Rascal said.

"Or malicious," said Tabitha authoritatively. *"From everything I've heard about him, he's an ill-tempered fellow. His reason is neither here nor there, however. The more important question is what's to be done about it."* She looked around. *"Well, what? Who has a plan?"*

Crumpet flicked her tail. Any cat worth her salt would have already thought of a solution. Tabitha was past her prime. She was not likely to step down from her presidency of her own accord, at least not while everyone continued to look to her for leadership. But if another cat proved herself a more effective organizer, then surely—

"I have a plan," Crumpet announced, raising her voice. She should have to make this up as she went along, but she was both clever and inventive and planning was her forte. Still, even she was surprised by the bold words that came out of her mouth—bold or foolhardy, she was not sure which.

"You all know that Fritz the ferret lives near Wilfin Beck Bridge, not far from our end of the footpath."

Tabitha gave her whiskers a nervous twitch. *"I hope you're not suggesting we involve that ferret,"* she said uneasily. *"He is not a nice animal. Terribly uncivil. Totally lacking in couth."* She shivered. *"From all I've heard, he's likely to tear us limb from limb."*

"Where did you hear that, Tabitha?" Rascal put in with a chuckle. *"From the rabbits? They're his favorite dinner guests, you know. There's nothing a ferret likes better than fresh rabbit."*

"Then what would keep him from sampling a cat?" Tabitha demanded testily. *"I for one do not propose to be dined upon."*

"I suppose there is a certain risk," Crumpet said, ignoring her own apprehension. She didn't like the idea of dealing with the ferret any more than Tabitha did, but leadership has its price. *"However, from what I've heard, Fritz takes a proprietary interest in everything that goes on in the neighborhood. And the footpath begins practically at his front door. He's bound to know something about the situation."*

Max frowned. *"I don't think it would help to—"*

Tabitha interrupted him. *"I'm not sure it's necessary—"*

"I fully understand your trepidation, Tabitha." Crumpet smiled cattily. The silly old thing was playing right into her paws. *"Of course, dear, if you're afraid, you should stay right here where it's safe. You, too, Max."* She stretched herself to her fullest height and added, in a firm, courageous tone, *"I will pay a visit to the ferret, and Rascal can go with me."*

"I'll be glad to go," Rascal said. *"Fritz may be snappish at times, but there's no reason to be afraid of him."*

"Afraid?" Tabitha scoffed. She tried to speak lightly, but Crumpet could hear the tremor in her voice. *"That's ridiculous. Whatever gave you that idea? I'm just not sure what that ferret could tell us that we don't already know."* She cast an appealing look at Max. *"What do you say, Max?"*

But before Max could say that he for one was not anxious to go within reach of that ferret's claws, Rascal broke in.

"I don't know what you're all afraid of," he said. *"Fritz is a shy fellow and he certainly values his privacy. But I have gone rabbit hunting with him on occasion, and he—"*

"He is a ferret," Tabitha said firmly, as if that settled it.

Rascal frowned. *"What's wrong with ferrets?"*

"Ferrets are not to be trusted." Tabitha was emphatic. *"Ferrets would as soon bite off your ears as look at you. What's more, they are born liars. They never tell the truth. So it's not likely that you'd learn anything of consequence."*

"Excuse me," Rascal asked mildly, *"but how do you know all this?"*

There was a silence. None of the three cats could answer, because none was personally acquainted with Fritz. All they knew was what everyone had heard: that the ferret had been so vicious and unmanageable that his owner had finally given up any hope of training him and released him into the wild. The ferret now lived a reclusive life, keeping to his burrow near the bridge and terrorizing the warren in Sawrey Fold, where the rabbits cringed at the very thought of him.

For their part, the village animals were at pains to avoid the area, for Fritz had the reputation of being not only fierce, but a fierce thief.

Didn't he wear a black robber's mask across his face?

Didn't the word *ferret* derive from the Latin *furritas*, meaning "little thief"? He wasn't so little, either—for a ferret, he was quite, quite large.

And didn't all the members of the ferret's extended family have the reputation of being thieves, as well?

Of course they did. Very bad apples, the whole lot of them. The stoat and weasel cousins were despised for their habit of raiding the village chicken coops and the woodland nests of native birds, stealing every egg they could get their filthy paws on. The aquatic branch of the family, the otters, had been trapped into near-extinction because of their appetite for the trout and char that (as everyone knew) belonged exclusively to the fishermen. And the ferret's nearest kin, the polecat (who also wore a black robber's mask), was no longer seen in the Land Between the Lakes, for the simple reason that the farmers and gamekeepers had killed every last one of them. Their name, in French, was *poule-chat*, or chicken-cat, for their cruel habit of eating the farm wives' chickens and the gamekeepers' pheasants.

So it was probably in Fritz's self-interest that he dined out after dark and mostly kept to himself, retreating when any animal came near. As a result, the cats knew only the rumors they had heard about him. And since what they had heard did not make them anxious to meet him face-to-face, it wasn't likely that their unfavorable impression would be corrected.

But Crumpet was not going to let any of this deter her, not when she felt she had the upper paw. She gave Tabitha a condescending smile. *"Well, then, old dear, since you and Max aren't anxious to meet this fellow, Rascal and I will go. We'll report back when we've found out what Fritz knows about——"*

"You'll do nothing of the sort!" Tabitha snapped, quite naturally smarting at the unkind phrase *old dear. "I will go with Rascal, and you and Max will stay here."* She cast a half-beseeching glance at Rascal. *"That is, unless Rascal thinks it isn't safe, in which case——"*

"Oh, it's safe enough," Rascal said with an amused smile. *"Fritz isn't harmless, by any means, and he's certainly fierce with the rabbits. But as far as being a liar or——"*

"I don't care what you say, Tabitha," Crumpet broke in. *"Talking to Fritz was my idea. I'm not going to sit idly by and let you get all the glory."*

"Glory?" Tabitha hooted scornfully. *"I don't know what makes you think there's any glory in exchanging a few words with a nasty, smelly old ferret."* She gave a heavy sigh. *"But as senior cat and president of the Council, I shall not shirk the dirty work.*

If Rascal thinks there's something to be learnt from this ferret fellow, I'm willing to give it a go."

"*I think we should talk to him,*" Rascal said definitively.

Wearing an air of supreme self-sacrifice, Tabitha got up. "*Come along, then, everyone.*"

Crumpet had no choice but to follow. Max, who (as usual) had said almost nothing, brought up the rear.

As the little group set off, Rascal trotted up next to Crumpet. "*Nice try, old girl,*" he said with a chuckle.

"*Oh, shut up,*" Crumpet snarled, perfectly out of temper.

So our friends are off to see the ferret. But since it will take them some little time to locate Fritz and begin their inquiries, we shall turn our attention elsewhere—to Mathilda Crook, who has just come out of the kitchen at Belle Green with a basket of freshly washed laundry.

2

The Crisis Deepens

Mathilda had been up with the washing since well before dawn on this Monday morning, and was hurrying to hang out her sheets and tea towels before Agnes Llewellyn, who lived just next door at High Green Gate, could hang out hers. It was always a contest to see who would be the first to get her Monday morning laundry out of her washing tub and onto the clothesline. Whilst there were no prizes in this weekly competition, the glow of Monday morning's triumph always warmed the winner's heart right through to the following Sunday night.

Agnes had won the previous week, by the patently unfair expedient (or so Mathilda saw it) of washing only half a load of white things and leaving the other half to soak whilst she rushed her half-filled laundry basket out to the clothesline. This week, Mathilda had filled her copper wash boiler and put it on the kitchen range the night before, so when she got up on Monday morning, she did not have to wait for it to heat. When her first load was finished, she wrung it out as fast as she could, dumped it into the basket, and raced out to the clothesline.

But Mathilda's was a hollow victory, for Agnes was nowhere to be seen. Mathilda hung up her sheets and towels, then, killing time while she waited for Agnes to emerge with her laundry, brought out a bowl and began picking blackberries for a pie for George's supper.

Five or so minutes later, Agnes came out of her washhouse at a leisurely pace, carrying her wicker basket. She put it down, took a handful of wooden pins out of her apron pocket, and began pinning up tea towels, carefully smoothing the wrinkles from each one. She did not appear to notice that Mathilda's clothesline was already full.

Mathilda looked up from the blackberry bush, feigning great surprise. "Why, Agnes," she said, in the broad dialect of the Lake folk. "Wot's kept thi this mornin'? Tha'rt verra late with t' washin'."

Agnes took a clothespin out of her mouth. "Oh, aye," she said airily. "I lingered a lit'le long o'er breakfast. Mr. Llewellyn had a reet int'restin' bit o' news to tell. I thought t' washin' cud wait." She shook out the last towel and pegged it to the line. "Doan't nivver hurt to be a wee bit late wi' t' wash noo an' then, do it?"

Mathilda felt a twinge of irritation. "News? Wot news?"

Agnes appeared surprised. "Why, I reckon'd tha'd heard it by now, Tildy. I'd uv laid money on't, informed as tha'rt." She allowed herself a small smile. "Most of t' time."

"Heard wot?" Mathilda demanded, hands on hips. She had gone to help a niece with a new baby on Saturday and hadn't got back until late the previous night. Obviously,

something important had happened while she was gone—
something Agnes knew and she did not. "Heard wot?" she
repeated sharply.

Agnes pursed her lips. "Aboot t' Applebeck Footpath.
Mappen thi doan't know, after all, Tildy."

"Wot aboot t' Applebeck Footpath?" cried Mathilda, by
now feeling desperate. "Tell me, Agnes!"

"Mr. Harmsworth has closed it off," Agnes replied briskly.
"Satiddy mornin', 'twas. Bertha Stubbs and me went to t'
church to do t' flowers fer Sunday, and t' gate was gone. There
was a tangle of barbed wire and wood stakes, all poured o'er
wi' tar, an' laid reet across t' path. 'Twere put there by Mr.
Harmsworth, we reckoned. We had to go t' long way round,
by Church Lane."

"Barbed wire?" Mathilda was aghast. "But he can't. That's
a public footpath!"

"Well, he has. Both ends o' it. Oh, and there's t' Applebeck
ghost, too."

"T' ghost!" Mathilda exclaimed, by now almost beside
herself. "Has somebody seen her again?"

"So says Auld Dolly. Which is a sign o' evil to come, o'
course. T' ghost nivver shows hersel' unless bad times is
comin'. Who knows wot'll be happenin' next? Another fire?
Mebee t' church or t' schoolhouse this time? T' ghost is al-
lus right."

"Now, Agnes," Mathilda said in a comforting tone. Agnes, the village doomsayer, was always imagining one disaster after another. "Likely it won't be that bad."

But Agnes was paying no attention. She was scowling at
Sarah Barwick and her green bicycle, as Sarah whizzed
down Market Street on her way back to her bakery, her
brown hair loose from its pins and flying.

"Jes' look at them trousers and that wild hair," she muttered darkly. "These mod'rn women. 'Tis a disgrace to t' whole village. Near as bad as Grace and t' vicar."

It was tempting to digress to the subject of Grace Lythe-coe and the vicar of St. Peter's, but Mathilda went back to the subject at hand. "Well, I doan't know about t' ghost, but somebody ought to do somethin' aboot t' path. It needs to be opened up, that it does, and straightaway. I'll march reet to t' smithy and ask my George what's best to be done."

Agnes picked up her empty basket. "No cause to bodder yer George aboot it," she said loftily. "My Dick has gone to take Captain Woodcock his milk. They'll manage t' prob-lem, 'tween 'em." She looked over Mathilda's shoulder and widened her eyes. "Why, Tildy," she said, with a mournful relish. "Such a shame. And yer best 'broidered, too. It'll niv-ver be t' same agin, t' poor thing."

Mathilda turned. To her dismay, she saw that her finest embroidered tea towel had fallen from the line and was draped across the blackberry bush, a large, juicy purple stain spreading across its snowy middle.

Dick Llewellyn made it a regular practice to take a bottle of fresh milk from the High Green Gate cows to the Tower Bank House kitchen twice a week, where he gave it to Elsa Grape for Captain Miles Woodcock's breakfast. This morn-ing, however, the kitchen was dark and Elsa was nowhere to be seen. Dick ventured to put his head into the dining room to interrupt the captain, who appeared to be break-fasting on bread and jam and coffee. With him was Mr. Will Heelis, a well-respected local solicitor.

"Elsa's gone away again," Captain Woodcock said, in re-sponse to Dick's question. Dick understood and commiser-ated. He, too, went without hot meals when his Agnes was off visiting her sister in Carlisle. "This time, she's taking care of her niece, who's just had a baby," the captain went on. "What's more, she gave the maid the day off. Just leave the milk in the kitchen, Dick. I'll put it away."

"I've summat to tell thi, Cap'n," Dick said, and told his story. "I saw t' barrier m'self," he added. "Means bus'ness, it do. Noboddy can get on t' path without rippin' it down, an' that woan't be easy, I wager."

"Ah, yes," the captain remarked thoughtfully. "Lester Barrow spoke to me about this last night at the pub. He was quite incensed about it." To Mr. Heelis, he said, "Barrow is a member of the Claife Heights Ramblers Association, y'know. He says there may be trouble over the matter."

"I wudna be s'prised," Dick said wisely. "Summat's got to be done afore sumbody tears t' barricades down or Mrs. Stubbs heaves a rock through Mr. Harmsworth's window, as she's promisin' to do. And cert'nly afore next Sunday, when ever'body'll have to walk t' extra way to church."

"Right," the captain remarked thoughtfully. "Well, it's probably got to be done sooner than that."

Miles had been justice of the peace for Sawrey District for nearly ten years now. He'd lived here longer than that, of course, ever since he had retired from Her Majesty's Army in Egypt in search of a quiet life in a green country under a sun that did not blister the hide off a fellow. He had chosen Sawrey for its peace and quiet, although he had to admit that there hadn't been much of that lately. His position put him into the thick of things, requiring him to certify deaths, deal with disturbances, witness documents, and uphold property rights.

And footpaths were an especially sore subject these days. Almost every time a piece of land changed hands, either the seller or the buyer made a determined effort to close off any footpaths through it, to which the Claife Ramblers—a group of fell-walkers who advocated free access to all the countryside—took immediate offense. There was nothing new about any of this, of course, especially in the Lakes, where walkers flocked to cross the wild moors and climb the fells. The poet William Wordsworth had flung down his pen and destroyed a wall blocking a path between Ullswater and Lowther Castle. And just twenty-three years before, in the summer of 1887, some 500 people stormed a blocked footpath at Fawe Park, near Keswick, not forty miles away. To hearten themselves, they sang their own version of "the Lion of Judah," with the stirring words, "The Lions of Keswick will break every chain, and open the footpaths, again and again!"

The captain was necessarily involved with this sort of thing because Parliament had passed a law, back in 1815, giving the justice of the peace the authority to determine whether the "highway, bridleway, or footway" in question should remain open or be "stopped up and disposed of." In the past three years, Miles had been called to rule on four other footpaths in the district. Since he himself was an advocate of open access to fields and fells, he had in every case but one ruled in favor of keeping the footpath open. It was a devilish tricky business, and it all fell on his shoulders.

"Seems to me you'd better get on it right away," Will Heelis said. A solicitor who lived in the nearby market town of Hawkshead, Will was a tall, athletic-looking man with fine eyes, a strong jaw, and a shock of thick brown hair that fell boyishly across his forehead. He remained a bachelor, in spite of Miles' efforts to pair him with his sister, Dimity. Instead, Dim had defied her brother and married Christopher Kittredge. "It will soon be the anniversary of the Keswick affair," Will added, pouring himself another cup of coffee.

"We might be listening to Ragsdale and his Ramblers singing 'The Lions of Sawrey will break every chain.' "

Miles shook his head glumly. "We certainly don't need that," he agreed.

Will frowned. "I wonder what Harmsworth has in mind by closing the path. So far as I know, Applebeck Farm isn't for sale." In his legal work, he usually happened across all the land transactions in the district. He knew what was for sale or what had recently sold, and for how much.

"This bis'ness will do nothin' but cause hard feelin's," Dick Llewellyn said dourly, as he took his leave. "Thi'll speak wi' Mr. Harmsworth today, Cap'n?"

"As soon as possible," the captain promised. When his neighbor had left, he said to Will, "I don't suppose you'd like to go with me to call on Harmsworth, would you? This afternoon, p'rhaps?" He was not exactly eager to make the call by himself. Not that he was afraid of the man, of course. But Harmsworth was known to be of intemperate moods. He might be less likely to go off the handle if Will came along.

"I would, of course, but I don't think it's my place," Will said seriously. "I'm known to be a supporter of the Freedom to Roam Bill." Member of Parliament James Bryce had first introduced the bill more than twenty years before, with the idea of restoring open access to the countryside for any who wanted to walk there. It was reintroduced every year, and although it wasn't likely to pass anytime soon, its friends kept trying. He paused, adding thoughtfully, "There's no merit in this closure, I don't suppose."

"I'll have to investigate before I can answer that," Miles said grumpily. Longing for his usual bacon and eggs, he buttered another slice of bread. "So far as I know, that path has been in regular use for decades. It saves quite a distance for both churchgoers and schoolchildren. P'rhaps the vicar knows something of it's history."

Will looked thoughtful. "Why don't you think of forming a footpath committee, Miles? The vicar could serve on it, perhaps, and three or four villagers—people with good heads who can be counted on to make a fair recommendation. It would take some of the burden off your shoulders." He grinned. "I shouldn't like to be the one to tell Adam Harmsworth to unstop that path. But if I had the weight of a committee behind me—"

Miles nodded approvingly. "Jolly good idea, Will. I'll see to it right away." He cocked his head. "Will you serve?"

"I shouldn't like to," Will said with a twinkle. "The committee might have to rule on a property that belongs to one of my clients. But you might consider asking Miss Potter. She's one of the steadiest people I know." He took out his watch and glanced at it. "I'd best be off. I'm headed for Windermere this morning." Frowning, he pocketed his watch. "You've heard about the hydroplane factory that's proposed for Cockshott Point, I suppose. A few of the local landowners are trying to find a way to stop it from being built. They've asked me for advice."

The captain stood. "No, I hadn't heard. Cockshott Point, you say?" He frowned. "I'm all for the aeroplane, you know. The machine of the future, in my view. I suppose you heard that Charlie Rolls made a nonstop flight across the Channel and back in only ninety-five minutes. Ninety-five minutes—imagine that!"

"Indeed," Will said, raising one eyebrow. "And then crashed his plane and died just a month later."

Miles nodded regretfully. "I'm all for the aeroplane," he said again, "but I'll be the first to admit that Windermere isn't the place to fly them."

"Agreed," Will replied. He shook his head. "But times are changing, Miles. The king's death, the land tax that's supposed to pay for naval armament, two new German dreadnoughts operational—I fear we're in for difficulties. Without Edward's steady hand at the helm, we'll be lucky to avoid a war."

King Edward VII had died just two months before, after an attack of bronchitis. He had not begun his reign as a beloved monarch. In fact, when he took the throne in 1901, on the death of his mother, Queen Victoria, he had been greatly belittled as a "playboy" king. But in the brief decade of his rule, he had come to be admired and even loved, and his passing was widely seen as the end of a period of strength and stability. Uncertainty about the capabilities of the new king, George V, taken with unrest across the Empire, labor strikes at home, women's suffrage, foreign competition, the constantly increasing German threat—all in all, most people felt that the ship of state was not sailing on an even keel.

"It's not like you to be pessimistic, Will," Miles said, getting up to see his friend to the door. "You know what my sister is always saying to me. 'Take a wife, Miles. It will improve your outlook on things.'"

Will chuckled. "Who would have a crusty old bachelor like one of us, Woodcock?" He paused. "But of course, there's Butters. He's found himself a wife, and a pretty one at that. P'rhaps there's hope for us." He went to the door, then paused and eyed his friend. "Speaking of Miss Potter, I have been hearing that you and she may be—"

"No," Miles said definitively. "That's been settled for some time. We remain good friends, of course, but she's devoted to the memory of her fiancé, who's been dead since before she bought Hill Top Farm. And to her books. And her parents. Oh, and her farms."

Miss Potter was a much-admired children's author and illustrator who lived mostly in London but made frequent visits to the farm she owned—two farms, actually, for she had just last year bought Castle Farm, at the top of the village. Some months before, Miles had got it into his head that Miss Potter might be a suitable wife and mistress of Tower Bank House, and he had made one or two determined efforts in that direction. But to his disappointment, and not a little irritation, the lady seemed determined to remain a spinster for the rest of her life.

This was really too bad. Since his sister had married, his housekeeper, Elsa Grape, considered herself to be the mistress of the house and came and went pretty much as she pleased, sometimes leaving important duties undone—such as had been the case this morning, when the captain discovered that there were no clean collars and cuffs in his shirt drawer. The Tower Bank household would run smoothly again only when there was someone to look after Elsa. The captain was in want of a wife.

Miles pursed his lips. "And you, Heelis? I believe I recently heard that you and Miss Nash—"

"You'll hear all manner of things if you listen long enough." Will shook his head ruefully. "This is the worst village for gossip I have ever seen. I'm an admirer of the way Miss Nash manages Sawrey School, and I helped her and her sister untangle a legal problem last winter, having to do with a little money from their father's estate. But that's as far as it goes. Anyway, Miss Nash has her sister to care for, you know, which complicates her life." He turned the doorknob. "And now I really am off. Cheerio, Woodcock. Good luck with that footpath business."

When his friend had gone, Miles took his coffee and newspaper and went down the hall to the library, where he filled his pipe and settled in for a comfortable morning smoke and the paper. But he found it difficult to concentrate on the *Times*, which was just as well, really, for it seemed to be full of nothing but bad news. He was thinking of Adam Harmsworth, whom he had met only once, during a dispute over a horse. In that case, Harmsworth had been rude and irascible, but even the most petulant of landowners didn't stop a footpath unless he had a very good reason to do so. Usually, it was done only when the landowner thought that no one would notice—which in this case was certainly not true.

Miles sighed. Well, there was no point in speculating. He should simply have to go and see Harmsworth today and find out what the fellow had in mind and what could be done about it. That settled, he went back to the newspaper. But after a moment, his mind had wandered again, and he found himself thinking of Miss Nash.

He was rather surprised to learn that his friend Will Heelis was not interested in the lady, for he had overheard Henry Stubbs telling Lester Barrow all about it. Miles was also quite relieved that there was no romantic entanglement—although he could not admit this, for the simple reason that he did not know it himself. Captain Woodcock, while remarkably astute about a great many things in the worlds of property, finance, and governance, was (like many British gentlemen) usually quite unaware of his feelings, unless they were so strongly negative or positive that they clamored for his notice. Although he knew Margaret Nash to be a competent and attractive young woman and thoroughly enjoyed himself in her company, he was not yet conscious of any deeper feeling for her, and no amount of urging from anyone else—from Dimity, for instance, who had somehow taken it into her romantic head that Miss Nash might make a suitable wife for her brother—would hurry him toward that awareness.

In fact, Dimity's urging was probably having the opposite effect, for Miles prided himself on knowing his own mind and would not be told what should be in it. He had replied to Dimity in no uncertain terms that such a relationship was out of the question, although when pressed for a reason, he could only say that Miss Nash's sister was often ill and required constant looking after, and he preferred a wife who would put him first in her life.

"And that, dear Dim, is that," he concluded emphatically. "Let's hear no more about it, shall we?" I regret to report that if he had looked just a little further into himself, he would have found that he took more pleasure in telling his sister to drop the subject than he did in dropping the subject. Perhaps he might also have seen that the idea of taking a wife who would have no other gods before him was decidedly self-centered. But no, I doubt that. I don't think the captain would be able to see himself with that much critical detachment.

In fact, I am sorry to say that (at this point, at least) you and I know a good deal more about Captain Woodcock than he knows about himself. But that's neither here nor there, at least at the moment. Miles has stopped thinking about Will Heelis and Miss Nash, picked up the newspaper, and begun to read a letter to the editor from someone who feels that the current turbulence in human affairs was caused by the near-earth passage of Halley's Comet, which has been visible in the sky since April.

He wonders briefly if that was the reason that Elsa Grape had granted herself four days off in the past three weeks, and he reminds himself that he must either buy more collars and cuffs or have a very firm talk with her.

But he fails to remember that the milk Dick Llewellyn had brought is still sitting on the kitchen table and, if it is not removed to a cooler place, will sour in the August heat.

Captain Woodcock is most surely in want of a wife.

3

"It's a Conundrum!"

The handsome gray horse lifted his hooves smartly as he pulled Will Heelis' gig out of Near Sawrey, in the direction of Far Sawrey and down Ferry Hill to the ferry landing on the west shore of Lake Windermere.

Near and Far Sawrey—the names have puzzled many people. If you're wondering how these two hamlets came to be so called, I can explain it very simply. Near Sawrey is nearer the market town of Hawkshead, whilst Far Sawrey (which is nearer Lake Windermere) is farther away, but only by a half-mile or so. Near Sawrey prides itself on having a pub, a bakery, a smithy, a joinery, and its own post office. Far Sawrey boasts St. Peter's Church and the vicarage, the school, a post office, the butcher, and the Sawrey Hotel, which also has a pub, of course, as well as a dining room and substantial accommodations for travelers. As you might imagine, there is a great deal of coming and going between the two hamlets, with almost all of the pedestrian traffic being carried by the Applebeck Footpath, which shortens the distance considerably.

As Will crossed the bridge over Wilfin Beck, he looked off to the right. Yes, there it was: the ugly barbed wire barricade, studded with wooden stakes and coated with tar, that Adam Harmsworth had thrown across the footpath. Will frowned, thinking that he did not envy his friend Woodcock the task of ordering Harmsworth to take down the barrier, or telling the villagers (not to mention Roger Ragsdale and the Claife Ramblers) why they should remain, if that were the outcome. Either way, there would be trouble. He was glad that he was not the one who had to deal with it.

Farther along, as he rounded the hill and came along the lake, Will was relieved to see the ferry making slow headway across the choppy waters of the narrow lake, its smokestack belching clouds of black smoke that showered soot on all the passengers. The old thing was doddery and unreliable— one never knew whether it would arrive on time, or at all.

For longer than anyone could remember, a ferryboat had plied the lake between the western Lancashire shore and the eastern Westmorland shore, saving a very long trip around either end of the nearly eleven-mile-long lake, the longest in all of England. The earliest ferries were merely long wooden rowboats rowed by two or more men that crossed the lake in twenty to thirty minutes. The present ferry, a much more elaborate affair, was built in 1870. It was powered by a coal-fired steam engine and was large enough to carry a coach-and-four or even two coaches, if the lead horses were unhitched.

The ferry's design was not a happy one, however, for both the boiler and engine were located on the same side, and the boat had the tendency to list rather dangerously. In stormy weather, when the waves were high, it did not sail, for fear of capsize. Either the engine or the boiler was out of service often, and even in good weather, the crossing took the best part of an hour—more, if there was difficulty loading. Off-comers and day-trippers were known to speak contemptu-ously of the ferry: "Why, we could build a bridge in the time it takes that joke of a boat to go and come back again."

But the local people usually tolerated its idiosyncrasies of speed and lopsided gait, and some could even manage an affectionate laugh at the rickety old ferry. It was said, for instance, that each year on the summer solstice, as the fer-ryman prepared to make his last journey from the east shore to the west, an old woman would come down to the jetty as if to board. Shuddering, she would hide her face in her hands and cry, "Nay, I canna. It's nivver a boat, it's a conundrum!"—and then vanish into the twilight until the next solstice. Whenever anyone complained about the boat, someone else was sure to say, "That's not a ferry, it's a co-nundrum," and everyone would laugh, much to the puzzle-ment of off-comers, of course. They didn't get the joke.

This morning, Will reached the landing just as the ferry pulled into its berth, not far from the Ferry Hotel, an im-posing inn that catered to fishermen and to the yachtsmen whose sailing boats were moored in the nearby cove. Rigg's Coniston Coach was aboard the ferry, so there would be a substantial wait while the horses were hitched up again and the coach could disembark. As well, there were two old-fashioned hooped carts in the queue ahead of him. Will doubted whether he would make this crossing. Where the Windermere ferry was concerned, one learnt to possess one's soul in patience.

So he pulled to a stop behind the second cart, took out his pipe, and began to watch the people getting off, a few day-trippers with their baskets, a bicyclist, an elderly woman in an old-fashioned black bonnet and tippet. And then, to his enormous surprise, Miss Potter—Miss Beatrix Potter, of Hill Top Farm. Will was greatly delighted, more delighted, I must tell you, than he would have been able to acknowledge to himself or to anyone else. It is a sad fact that, like his friend Captain Woodcock, Will Heelis always knew precisely what he thought and could tell you all about it in no uncertain terms. Unfortunately, he rarely had any idea how he *felt*.

But he was beginning to learn. He had taken his first lesson the previous winter, when he and Miss Potter had been alone together and he had found himself, quite impulsively, seizing her hand. (If you have read *The Tale of Briar Bank*, you will undoubtedly recall this rather shocking event—shocking for Will, anyway.) He now had a pretty good idea of how he felt about Miss Potter, and although the awareness made him distinctly uncomfortable, it also (and contradictorily) made him feel quite glad.

And why shouldn't it? Miss Potter was a forthright, thoughtful, and very levelheaded person, with a shy charm and rather old-fashioned reserve. Her quiet conversation especially appealed to Will, for he himself was very shy and often tongue-tied in the presence of brash young ladies like Sarah Barwick, who embarrassed him by flirting and chattered on nineteen to the dozen, giving him no opportunity to speak even if he could think of something interesting to say, which he couldn't. He found Miss Potter quite attractive, too, with her rounded face and figure, bright blue eyes that shone with an alert and interested intelligence, and a fine disregard for fashion that pleased Will, who much preferred plain country dress and sensible shoes to city lace, velvets, and stylish boots.

Today, Miss Potter was dressed for summer. She wore a dark gray gored skirt, a simple white blouse with a blue tie, and a narrow-brimmed straw hat with a blue velvet ribbon. She was carrying a wicker hamper in one hand and a small satchel in the other. And since Lakelanders are perfectly aware that even the finest summer day can turn showery, she prudently carried an umbrella under one arm.

"Miss Potter!" Will pushed his pipe back into his pocket and leapt to his feet, waving excitedly. "Hullo, Miss Potter! Over here!"

"Good morning," Miss Potter said, coming toward him, smiling. Her deep-set blue eyes sparkled. Her brown hair was pulled back and snugged, but a few renegade curls had escaped, framing her pink cheeks, and Will thought how handsome she looked, and how bright the morning (which had darkened considerably when he discovered how long he should have to wait for the ferry) had become. In fact, it suddenly seemed like a whole new day.

"So very nice to see you again, Mr. Heelis," Miss Potter said cheerfully. "You're on your way across?"

"Eventually," Will said, since crossing the lake had just tumbled off his list of immediate priorities. "It's very nice to see you, too." Even in his current limited awareness, he recognized "very nice" to be a substantial understatement and felt that, had he spoken all the truth, he might have said something like, *"I am absolutely, enormously, utterly delighted and thrilled to see you, my very dear Miss Potter."* But of course he couldn't say this, so he didn't. "I had no idea that you were back in the village."

"I've just arrived," Miss Potter said. "My parents have taken Helm Farm for their holiday. Just over there, near Bowness." She nodded toward the eastern shore of the lake. "I've been staying with them for the past week. But I've

been longing to come to Hill Top and see how Mr. Jennings
is getting on with the haying, so I arranged for someone
else to look after them for a few days."

Will suddenly recollected himself. "That's a heavy load,"
he said, jumping down from the gig. Ferry Hill was steep,
and Hill Top Farm was a good hour's walk. What a splendid
accident of fortune, arriving here to the ferry at the exact
moment that Miss Potter disembarked! His good luck
made him feel almost giddy. He snatched up the satchel
and the hamper and stowed them under the seat before she
could say a word.

"Get in, Miss Potter," he said. "I shall drive you to the
farm."

Miss Potter caught her breath, and her cheeks bloomed a
most becoming pink. "Oh, but you're here to catch the
ferry," she protested, trying to retrieve her satchel. "You'll
be delayed in crossing. It's such a pretty day, and not that
far to walk. I would really much rather—"

"Nonsense," he said, with an entirely uncharacteristic
firmness. Smiling down at her, he softened his tone. "You
know how slow that blasted ferry is. I can drive you to Hill
Top Farm and be back here by the time it docks again—
which may be tomorrow or the next day."

Hesitating, she pressed her lips together. She looked as if
she would rather reclaim her luggage and be on her way,
but she chuckled when Will added playfully, "It's nivver a
boat, remember? It's a conundrum."

"It certainly is that," she agreed, still hesitating. "If you
really wouldn't mind—"

"Not in the slightest," Will assured her. He was about to
take her hand to help her into the gig, but she stepped up
quickly, sat down, and settled her skirts. He got in and
turned the horse back up the hill. Normally, he found it

difficult to initiate conversation with a woman, but there was something about Miss Potter that put him at his ease.

"Your parents have taken Helm Farm?" he asked. "I know the place. It's charming, but isn't it just a bit old-fashioned for their tastes?" Wealthy Londoners, the Potters always spent their holiday in the Lake District, but they usually stayed in fashionable holiday villas. Miss Potter had told him that they once rented Wray Castle, a huge stone palace overlooking Lake Windermere. (It's still there, by the way, and you can visit it. If you do, you'll be astonished at its grandeur. I was.) Helm, on the other hand, was a very old farmhouse perched on the top of a very steep hill. There was nothing at all elegant about it.

"I'm afraid it is rather old-fashioned," Miss Potter said ruefully, "and not exactly to their taste. But we delayed in finding a holiday place because my father was not well and didn't want the bother. By the time we began to look, Helm was all there was to be had. Mama and Papa always like to bring the servants, of course—they wouldn't know what to do without the cook and the butler. Mama insists on having the carriage, as well, which means bringing the coachman and his wife, who does the daily work." Her laugh was lightly ironic. "I'm afraid it was the barn at Helm that decided the matter. There's room for carriage and horses both."

"I see," Will said with a chuckle. "Well, at least the horses will be comfortable."

This was one of the things he found so intriguing about Miss Potter. The daughter of wealth, she obviously lived a comfortable, privileged life in London, with a cook, a butler, servants, a coachman. Yet she sometimes spoke ironically of it all. She could even laugh at the idea of her parents' taking their horses and carriage on the railway train when they went away on holiday. And when she came to the

Lakes, she always seemed eager to be away, as if her London life were a very great burden.

She returned his laugh, and he saw with a great deal of pleasure that the blue of her simple tie and the narrow ribbon on her hat matched almost exactly the shade of her eyes. "Very comfortable indeed, considering," she said. "There is a rather steep hill up to the house which makes it inconvenient to drive out, so the horses are likely to enjoy a lazy holiday." Her smile faded. "Mama would much rather I stayed at Helm and kept her and Papa company, I'm afraid."

Will could hear the unhappiness in her voice. "I'm sorry," he said quietly. "I'm very sorry."

From things she had told him, he knew that her parents had opposed the idea of her buying Hill Top Farm in the first place, just as they had strenuously opposed the idea of her marrying her editor and publisher, Norman Warne. The Potters, who had inherited their substantial wealth from hardworking Lancashire calico manufacturers, were exceedingly conscious of their social position, an attitude that Will, a plainspoken countryman who had been raised to believe that honest work was its own reward, considered the worst sort of snobbery. Miss Potter had stood firm against their opposition, accepting Warne's ring in spite of them. In fact, she was wearing the simple gold band at this very moment, as Will could plainly see, a testimony to her enduring devotion. The engagement had come to an abrupt and unexpected end. Warne had died, worse luck for him, just a month after his proposal.

But Will, who was often much more astute about other people's feelings and motives than about his own, understood that Warne's undesirable social standing was only part of the reason for the Potters' opposition. They intended that their daughter should stay home and care for them and manage their house and their servants until both of them were dead—after which time she could marry, of course, if she were not too old.

Now, while you and I might be aghast at such an attitude, it was not at all unusual in those days. Queen Alexandra, wife of the late monarch, kept her spinster daughter, Princess Victoria, as a lifelong companion, never allowing her to marry, not even Lord Rosebery, who was said to be madly in love with her. Will himself knew several Lakeland families in which an unmarried daughter remained at home for her entire life, designated caretaker of her parents and their household. But in his view (as it is certainly in mine and probably in yours), this was a very bleak future for any person, especially for one so talented and energetic and interesting as Miss Potter.

Will couldn't say any of this, of course. It wasn't his place to criticize the Potters, and anyway, it would make Miss Potter uncomfortable. Instead, he only added, with genuine sympathy, "I'm sure it will be a trial for you, having to go back and forth on the ferry."

I'm wondering (and I expect you are, too) how Miss Potter feels about what Mr. Heelis has said—and what he hasn't. Beatrix grew up with a father who completely suppressed his feelings and a mother who overly dramatized hers, and where other people were concerned, she had learnt to be a perceptive observer. She heard the sympathy in Mr. Heelis' voice and caught his glance at Norman's ring. She thought she knew what it meant, and while either you or I might find it flattering to be warmly regarded by as handsome and eligible a bachelor as Mr. Heelis, Beatrix found it deeply troubling—threatening, even.

She and Mr. Heelis had been acquainted now for nearly

five years, since she had bought Hill Top Farm and begun coming regularly to the village. He had helped her to purchase Castle Farm and managed it for her while she was in London, which meant that they traded frequent letters and even occasional telegrams. He was as interested as she in the fate of the Lake District, which was seriously threatened by commercial development and in danger of losing not only its beautiful old farms, but its pastoral way of life. They shared the view that it was entirely possible that, within a few decades, a blight of holiday cottages and villas would spread like an ugly pox across dale and fell, and that somebody ought to be doing something to stop it. This shared passion made for some interesting and spirited conversations when they found themselves together, and Beatrix enjoyed their discussions very much.

But something else was afoot here. While Beatrix couldn't read Mr. Heelis' thoughts, she understood pretty well—or thought she did—what was in his mind. And since she desperately wanted to keep him from putting those thoughts into words, she only said, in a very polite, prim tone, "Coming and going on the ferry is an interesting diversion, and I enjoy the trip across the lake. I'm only sorry that the travel will take time away from the other things I want to do—sketching, and the farm."

Now, if you are thinking that it is rather silly for these two people—grownups, both of them—to pussyfoot around the subject of their relationship (a topic that must have been of very deep interest to both of them), I shall have to agree. But we must try to see the matter as they saw it, and not from our modern point of view.

Will Heelis was beginning to be aware that he was in love with Beatrix, but understood why her parents had rejected Norman Warne and was pretty sure that he would meet the same fate. Even more important, he knew that Beatrix was deeply loyal to Warne's memory. He felt himself to be a fragile cockleshell of a boat, uneasily moored between the implacable Mr. and Mrs. Potter and the steadfast Miss Potter. If he spoke, Beatrix might find it necessary to break off their friendship, to cut him adrift. Better to keep his desires to himself than to risk complete and total rejection.

For her part, Beatrix was beginning to be aware that she was very fond of Will Heelis, a dangerous fondness, as she saw it. In fact, it was so dangerous—rather like walking along the edge of a very steep cliff that threatened to crumble beneath her feet and send her plummeting into an unfathomable abyss—that the only thing she could think to do was to retreat from the edge, and steer the conversation in a safer direction, away from herself altogether.

"And there is some rather nice news, isn't there?" she went on quickly. "Margaret Nash wrote to tell me that Dr. Butters has married." Dr. Butters was the much-beloved doctor who treated all the villagers. Like Mr. Heelis, he lived in Hawkshead and traveled the countryside by horse. And like Mr. Heelis, he was a confirmed bachelor—until he met Miss Mason at Briar Bank House. *The Tale of Briar Bank* relates the circumstances, which (as you may recall) were somewhat unusual.

"Married indeed," Mr. Heelis said. "Miss Mason took a house in Hawkshead after the magistrate decided the case against her was too weak to prosecute. The next thing we knew, Dr. Butters announced that they were to marry, which they did forthwith. The doctor's friends approve," he added cheerfully. "Most of them."

"I don't imagine Captain Woodcock likes the idea very much," Beatrix said, and then bit her tongue. The remark sounded critical.

But Mr. Heelis only nodded, his expression turned serious. "How did you know? Did he tell you?"

Now that she had begun, there was nothing for it but to
go on. "I'm only guessing," she said, "but it seems to me
that the captain prefers people who play by the rules. Miss
Mason broke them. I imagine the captain thinks she should
have been punished." She herself had every sympathy for
Miss Mason, for while it was true that the lady had set out
to deceive poor Mr. Wickstead of Briar Bank, it had not
been with a malicious intention, and she had soon found
herself in a situation she hadn't bargained for—all of which
you will understand if you have read that story. "Personally," she added, "I think Miss Mason—Mrs. Butters, that
is—was a victim of circumstance."

"Well put, Miss Potter," Mr. Heelis said in an approving
tone. "Woodcock wasn't at all keen on the marriage. But
rules or no, Dr. Butters is happier than I've ever seen him.
And I believe Mrs. Butters is quite content, as well. They
seem to suit one another."

"That's all that matters," Beatrix said quietly. "I am very
glad for the both of them."

They had driven through the hamlet of Far Sawrey now.
The hedges were summer-heavy and starred with a few late
wild roses and even later elderflowers, and the roadside grasses,
bleached by the sun, displayed a scattering of summer wildflowers, agrimony and scabious and knapweed. Beatrix loved
this time of year. The hay harvest was under way, the gardens were overflowing with abundant vegetables, and the
orchard trees were heavy with fruit. She glanced to the left,
to Applebeck Orchard, the oldest in the district.

"Why, there's a barricade across Applebeck Footpath!"
she exclaimed in surprise, seeing the tangle of wire and
wooden stakes, covered with tar. "It's been closed off! Did

Mr. Harmsworth do it? Of course he did," she added, half to herself. "He must have. Applebeck Farm is his."

"Yes, Harmsworth did it," Will said grimly, pulling his horse to a stop. "The Claife Ramblers are up in arms and the villagers are quite put out. Captain Woodcock intends to see the fellow today."

Beatrix spoke in a measured tone. "One doesn't like to speak ill of a neighbor, but Adam Harmsworth is not an altogether pleasant person. His property abuts Hill Top, you know. I was out with the sheep one day last spring when I saw him beating a dog." She shivered, remembering what she had seen and how it had made her feel. Cruelty to animals was something she could not abide. "He did not much like it when I told him he must stop, but he did—at least as long as I had him in sight."

"You're a brave lady," Mr. Heelis said, and gave her a glance that made her color. He chuckled. "I suspect that Captain Woodcock would be glad to have you go along when he talks to Harmsworth."

"I'm sure the captain is perfectly capable of handling Mr. Harmsworth all by himself. I'd only get in the way." Uncomfortable with the personal direction of the conversation, Beatrix changed the subject again. "Have you seen Caroline Longford recently?"

Now sixteen, Caroline was the granddaughter of Lady Longford, of Tidmarsh Manor. The girl's father and mother were dead and she had come from New Zealand to live with her grandmother some five years before. The previous winter, Beatrix had persuaded Lady Longford to allow Caroline to take piano lessons with Mrs. King, a well-known London teacher who had settled in Hawkshead. This had not been easy, for her ladyship was one of the most parsimonious people Beatrix had ever met, and piano lessons were costly.

"As a matter of fact, I saw Caroline just last week," Will said. "I called to speak with Lady Longford about Caroline's inheritance."

"Inheritance?"

"The legal knots have finally been untied and the money left to her in her parents' estate has become available. It's a tidy sum, I'm glad to say, and prudently invested. Caroline has enough money to do what she'd like."

"Indeed," Beatrix said thoughtfully.

"Unfortunately, Lady Longford has not seen fit to tell her about the money," Will went on with a frown. He lifted the reins and his horse moved forward. "I pointed out that Caroline will be able to assume responsibility for its management in something less than two years. And at sixteen, she certainly ought to be giving some thought to her future."

"I fully agree," Beatrix said, thinking that it was just like Lady Longford to insist on keeping the information to herself. As long as Caroline believed she was penniless, her ladyship could control her more easily. I daresay that this is not a nice thing for Beatrix to think, but in some ways her ladyship is not a nice person. You might recall that she once tried to install her own candidate as the head teacher at Sawrey School, and was only just prevented from doing so by the determined intervention of the school's overseers— Mr. Heelis, Captain Woodcock, and the vicar—with a little help from our Beatrix. (If you have not read this story, it is told in *The Tale of Holly How*.)

"I am glad to say that Caroline is quite extraordinarily talented," Will added, as they crossed the stone bridge over Wilfin Beck. "She played her own piano composition for me—a nocturne, I believe she said."

"Her own composition," Beatrix murmured. "How very nice. You liked it?"

"I did, indeed. I'm no music critic, of course, but I found it quite lovely. She is gifted."

Beatrix was silent for a moment, thinking of the letter that Caroline had written to her just a few days before, enclosed with a note from her governess, Miss Burns. "Speaking of conundrums," she said, "I have the idea that Caroline is facing an important one."

"Oh?" Will asked curiously. "And what is that?"

Beatrix was about to answer, but at that moment, Will had to pull up sharply on the reins to keep from hitting a black cat that dashed across the road in front of them and scrambled down the grassy bank on the other side, very near the bridge. The gig tipped up on one wheel and nearly went over. Beatrix grabbed at the arm of the seat with one hand and her hat with the other.

"My goodness gracious," she exclaimed breathlessly, and turned to look.

"Steady on!" Handling the reins expertly, Will clucked to his horse. "You're all right, Miss Potter?"

"Just a little surprised, that's all."

Will lifted the reins and they were off again. "A black cat. I hope you're not superstitious."

"It was Max," Beatrix replied, settling her hat firmly on her head. "Max the Manx. You probably don't remember, but he stayed in the Hill Top barn for a time, to help us get rid of a horrible infestation of rats. I don't know where he lives now, but I'm surprised to see him so far from the village. Most of the cats stay close to home."

"You amaze me, Miss Potter," Will said lightly. "You're not only informed about what's going on in the village, but you know the habits of the village cats as well." He shook his head. "Is there anything that escapes you?"

Beatrix suspected that he was teasing her. She wasn't

sure how to respond, and in any case, the conversation was becoming dangerously personal again. She changed the subject once more.

"Speaking of Castle Farm, that reminds me. You and I must have a look at that barn roof, Mr. Heelis. I'm afraid it will need rather a lot of mending. P'rhaps it might be better to replace it entirely."

"I'm glad you brought that up," Will said. "There are several problems with that barn, and quite a few other things that want doing."

So while they drove along the road to the village and Hill Top Farm, they spoke very seriously of barns and fences and drains and sheep, and of all the things that had yet to be done at Castle Farm—so deep in conversation that they scarcely noticed the pedestrians they passed along the way. There was Joseph Skead, the sexton at St. Peter's, his scythe over his shoulder, on his way to the church to cut the grass. There was Agnes Llewellyn, on her way to have a cup of tea and a bite with her cousin Hazel Thompson, the vicar's cook-housekeeper. There was Bertha Stubbs, coming back from the butcher in Far Sawrey, where she had purchased a soup bone and a shoulder of mutton.

But the pedestrians noticed them. And when they got home, they were happy to tell their friends and families that they had seen the village's most famous spinster and the district's most eligible bachelor riding along together, chatting as agreeably and amiably as the very best of friends.

"An' not just friends, neither," Bertha exclaimed to Miss Margaret Nash, her next-door neighbor at Lakeside Cottages. She gave a gusty romantic sigh. "Billin' an' cooin' just like a pair o' turkle-doves. I reckon we can look for a weddin' sometime soon. An' I ain't jumpin' to any contusions, neither." When the soup bone was in the pot, with carrots and potatoes and onions, Bertha popped over to Buckle Yeat to tell Betty Leach what she had seen. Betty told her husband, Tom, when he came home for tea, and Tom told Lester Barrow when he went to the pub that night for his usual half-pint.

"Thick as thieves, they was, t' two o' them," Joseph told his wife, Lucy, the postmistress, when he got home from St. Peter's. Lucy related this to Mathilda Crook, who had come to mail a package of knitted baby bonnets to her cousin in Brighton. Mathilda dropped in at the smithy on her way home to tell her husband, George, who was shoeing Mr. Dixon's big black draft-horse, Petunia. Mr. Dixon took the news home with him to relate to his wife over dinner, where it overtook the closure of Applebeck Footpath as the topic of conversation. And Agnes, of course, told her cousin Hazel.

Oh, dear. Of course, Joseph and Bertha and Agnes ought to have kept their observations to themselves, but that is too much to expect of them, I imagine. They live in a village where there is not much in the way of entertainment except for gossip, tittle-tattle, and tale-telling. As far as they are concerned, there is no such thing as personal privacy, even when it comes to matters of the heart—or perhaps *especially* when it comes to matters of the heart.

Miss Potter and Mr. Heelis may not like this. Indeed, I am quite sure that they would not like it at all, if they knew. But try as they might, there is nothing they can do to change things. It's a conundrum, I should think.

Meanwhile, back at the bridge . . .

4

In Which We Meet an Artistic Ferret and Learn More about a Manx

It's a good thing Max didn't have a tail, for he would certainly have lost it under the wheels of Mr. Heelis' gig.

But he didn't, so he managed to escape any further damage, except to his pride. He skidded on his rump down the embankment next to the old stone bridge, then followed Rascal and the two other cats as they made their way amongst the willows along Wilfin Beck (the word *wilfin* means "willow," and a beck is a stream) to a great clump of trees hanging over a steep bank at the bottom of the rocky hill about twenty yards south of the bridge.

Wilfin Beck was in full spate, on this day, and in a very great hurry and deliriously happy about it, and why not? For the stream was on its way down from the fells to Lake Windermere, and when it had got all the way through this great lake and out the other end, it would be the River Leven. It would scull under Newby Bridge, slide past the pretty village of Greenodd into broad, shallow Morecambe

Bay, and—at last, at last, at last!—glide into the Irish Sea and lose itself in all the great mysteries of the deep. In anticipation of this marvelous journey, the beck was chortling and chuckling between its fern-fringed banks, telling itself stories about the glorious adventure to come, and calling out happily to the water-ouzels fishing from mossy stones, and to the dippers and wagtails, none of them minding at all that they were getting their feet wet.

But Max was not thinking about the beck's splendid journey, for his near miss on the road had made him fall behind, and he was in a breathless hurry to catch up without losing his footing and tumbling into the water. I am sorry to say that, for Max, there was nothing very new about being last, or even being forgotten. When he went off with the other village cats, he always brought up the rear, the last in line, and—to tell the honest truth—felt rather sorry for himself.

This was because Max was different, you see. He had no tail, none at all, not even a short, stumpy stub. All the other cats had beautiful tails—long, luxurious tails that they flicked and flipped and flourished like flags in the breeze. But Max had only a little dimple where his tail ought to have been, which meant that he was much shorter, back to front, than other cats—so short, in fact, that he seemed quite round, an impression that was reinforced by the roundness of his face and cheeks and eyes and his round rump and rounded, muscular thighs. What's more, his hind legs were longer than his forelegs, so that his rear was higher than his head and his spine was a continuous arch, front to back. He was quite a muscular cat and agile, and he could run even faster than the other cats, certainly faster than Tabitha (who was quite old) or Crumpet (who was not as young as she thought she was). But he ran with an odd little hop, like a rabbit, and his fur had a rabbit's softness.

Now, you have lived in the world and have seen a great many strange and unusual things, so I imagine that you have had the advantage of seeing at least one Manx cat, and that you are able to keep an open mind about such things as missing tails. But the Sawrey cats were a parochial lot who had never been more than a mile from the hayloft or cellar or shed in which they were born. They considered Max—lacking a tail, short back to front, and very round—to be an aberration, a regrettable freak of nature. I am sorry to report that they snickered at him behind his back, made fun of him to his face, and left him out of all their group activities. This was very unkind of them, to be sure, but that is the way some cats are, and there is just no getting around it.

I daresay that Max would have felt much better about himself if there had been at least one other cat like him. But since he was the only Manx in the village—in the whole of the Land Between the Lakes, for that matter—he stood out like a very sore thumb. He was intelligent and sensitive and felt the pain of his exclusion more deeply than he could ever have admitted, so that the more he was left out of things, the more he kept to himself, not wanting to endure the humiliation of being left out again. Perhaps you can remember how it felt when you were the last one to be chosen for a game or a dance or a competition, and how you would rather stay home from school than go through the experience again. Well, that is exactly how Max felt, and this dismal cycle had made him very melancholy. He had spent most of his life looking at the dark side of things, until this had become such a habit that he could not change it. Max was a very gloomy cat, indeed.

Now, having at last caught up with the others, Max sat down on his haunches and tried to steady his breath as Rascal knocked at a small wooden door fitted into the curve of the east-facing bank and half-hidden by an overhanging blackberry bush. It had black iron hinges and a large brass door handle, so it was most definitely a door. But there was no welcome mat, no doorplate engraved with the resident's name, no door knocker, not even a bellpull and a bell to notify the animal indoors that someone was waiting on the doorstep. Clearly, the ferret did not encourage callers, which made Max think (nervously) that it might be smarter to go away and not come back.

"Knock again," advised Crumpet. Her voice squeaked.

"And do it louder," urged Tabitha, trying to disguise the tremble in her tone.

"He's probably having a nap," Rascal said, and knocked again, more loudly.

"P'rhaps we oughtn't to disturb him," Max muttered uneasily. He had heard somewhere that ferrets were nocturnal creatures and liked to spend their mornings in bed with the window shades drawn and the covers pulled over their heads.

Now, it wasn't that Max was afraid of this ferret, if that's what you're thinking. He was as brave as the next cat, especially where mice were concerned and even rats. Hadn't he been hired to help clear out that plague of rodents that infested Hill Top Farm? Hadn't he performed commendably? Even Miss Potter had said so, and seemed very sorry when Mrs. Jennings, the farmer's wife, said that cats with no tails made her queasy, and that Max should find another place. No, he wasn't afraid, just cautious. Ferrets were fiercer than rats, he had always heard. Ferrets were—

The door opened on the chain, just wide enough for Max to see a gray-furred creature, a little smaller than himself, glaring out at them. Max had never before seen a ferret, and was taken aback both by his size (Max had imagined he would be much larger) and by the black mask the fellow was wearing, through which shone two beady black eyes, glittering like polished ebony. Beneath the mask was a quivery pink nose in a forest of stout whiskers. Above the mask was a pair of perky ears.

The ferret opened his mouth, showing sharply pointed teeth, like needles. *"What the devil is going on out here?"* he squeaked, in a high, thin voice. *"What do you think you're doing, banging on my door and waking me up in the middle of the morning? How is a civilized animal supposed to get any sleep?"*

"Terribly sorry, Fritz, old fellow," Rascal said apologetically. *"I—"*

"Who's that?" the ferret demanded. He shielded his eyes with his paw against the sunlight that slanted down through the willow trees along the beck. *"Rascal, is that you? Who else is out there?"*

"Yes, it's me, Fritz," Rascal said, in a humble tone. *"I'm really sorry to bother you at this hour. I've brought Crumpet and Max the Manx and Tabitha Twitchit to see you. Tabitha is president of the Village Cat Council and we've—"*

"We've come to ask you a question of some importance," Tabitha said, shoving in front of Rascal.

"It's about the footpath," Crumpet said, crowding past Tabitha.

"Don't push," snapped the ferret. *"It's not civil."*

"P'rhaps we'd better go away and come back some other time," Max said in a low voice. *"If we're disturbing you, that is."*

"Of course you're disturbing me," the ferret growled, showing his teeth again. He began to close the door, but Crumpet put her paw into it.

"The footpath's closed," she said.

"Of course it's closed," the ferret growled. *"Mr. Harmsworth threw a barricade across it."*

"*We're hoping you can tell us why,*" Rascal put in, over Crumpet's shoulder. "*You keep a close eye on what goes on in the neighborhood. We thought you might know—*"

"*And what if I do?*"

"*Why, we'll use the information to get the path opened up again,*" Crumpet said.

"*Three cats and a dog will open the path? Don't make me laugh.*" The ferret eyed them suspiciously. "*Why in thunder are there so many of you? Does it take a whole gang to wake up a fellow and ask him silly questions about a footpath?*"

"*I'm dreadfully sorry,*" Max said, feeling now that this really was an ill-advised errand. No matter the ferret's size, his teeth were undeniably sharp. "*We'll come back another time, when it's more convenient.*" He tugged at Tabitha's tail. "*Let's go,*" he whispered urgently. "*Now!*"

The ferret peered around the others and gave Max a penetrating look. "*Who're you? And where'd you leave your tail?*"

"*I'm Max. I'm a Manx. Manx don't have tails.*"

"*Ah,*" said the ferret thoughtfully. "*I have always wanted to meet a Manx.*" He made a clucking noise. "*Well, since the lot of you are already here, and I'm already awake, I suppose I'll have to hear what this is all about.*" He turned with an undulating, snake-like motion and Max saw that he was very long—longer than a cat, counting his long tail—and very lean and lithe, like a weasel. "*Come on,*" he said over his shoulder. "*But one at a time, mind. Single file, no shoving. Last one in, close the door. We don't need any more callers.*" And with that, he slithered down the burrow.

This was very like a tunnel, so narrow and twisting that the animals could only go single file, ducking their heads, dropping their tails, and sucking in their breaths to squeeze themselves smaller. Rascal led the way, since he was used to creeping into burrows (he was, after all, a fox terrier), and also because he was acquainted with their host. Tabitha and Crumpet came after, and, as usual, Max brought up the rear, closing the door behind him and throwing them into inky darkness. If he could only manage to turn around, Max thought, he would, and let the others go on without him. But the burrow was so narrow that turning was impossible. There was nowhere to go but forward and down. And then up again, and then down and up and around and around until Max was no longer sure which direction they were going.

Just when he had decided that they were doomed to follow the ferret to the very center of the earth, the turning and twisting stopped and the burrow opened up into a surprisingly pleasant parlor, neatly circular in shape, with a high, domed ceiling, and large enough so that three cats and a small dog and a ferret could fit comfortably into it with very little crowding. The room was nicely furnished with one or two thick white fleeces spread on the floor in place of rugs, a fireplace with a carved wooden mantel, a bolstered brown velvet settee, and a ferret-sized lounge chair constructed like a canvas sling. There was a desk against the wall and shelves filled with what looked like pieces of sculpture and a table with a small paraffin lamp.

But this lamp was not burning at the moment, for the room was amply lit by the natural light that spilled in through a window-sash, set into the ceiling for a skylight. Above the skylight, through a screen of leafy green bushes, Max could see a swathe of clear blue sky, so bright it made him blink. But that wasn't all that made him blink, for the walls of this round room were whitewashed, like the walls you have seen in art galleries, and on them hung some very fine water color landscapes, along with beautifully detailed studies of small animals—rabbits, voles, frogs, badgers, foxes—all tastefully framed.

Max stared at the paintings, feeling his pulses quicken. He had never seen such beautiful objects in his entire life. The landscapes glowed with the emerald green of grass and tree and the silver-blue of lake and the scarlet and gold of flowers, and the animal studies—remarkably clever and perceptive—were done with infinite attention to the intricacies of ears and whiskers. The only pictures Max had seen that he liked as much as these were the ones drawn by Miss Potter, in her little book about the rats at Hill Top Farm, which had been much admired by the team of cats who helped get rid of the rats. But these—

"Oh, my," Max breathed, looking from one painting to another and feeling as if they were all just too beautiful and amazing for any other words. *"Oh, oh, my."*

"You like them?" asked the ferret, at his shoulder. Standing on his haunches, he was about half a head taller than Max. *"They're mine, of course, but if you don't like them, don't say you do. I can't abide hypocrisy."*

"Oh, I like them," Max whispered. *"I do, very much."* And then, almost incredulously, *"You don't mean to say that* you *painted them?"*

"I certainly did," said the ferret, sounding put out. *"What do you think all that is over there?"* And with an impatient wave of his paw, he gestured toward an alcove that Max had not yet noticed, containing an easel and a table with paint pots and brushes. An artist's smock was draped over a stool, and an artist's beret hung on the easel.

"I'm sorry," Max said humbly, finding all of a sudden that his view of the ferret had altered. This couldn't be the same ferret who was so wild and unmanageable that his owner

had decided that training him was impossible—or could it? *"I never would have thought."*

"No," said the ferret, giving him a measuring look. *"I don't suppose you would."* He put his head to one side, studying Max. *"I don't suppose you've ever had your picture painted, either. Have you?"*

Max was so taken aback by the question that he almost swallowed his tongue.

Tabitha cleared her throat. *"About that footpath,"* she began.

With a sigh, the ferret turned away from Max. *"Tea first,"* he said. *"I always have tea when I wake up in the morning."* He scowled at the clock on the mantelpiece. *"Although I have to say that I'm not usually awakened so early. And I am not accustomed to entertaining company at this hour—in fact, I am not accustomed to entertaining company at all."* To Tabitha, he said, *"You seem to be in charge. Come and lend a paw, will you? I shall have to see whether there are enough cups to go around."*

While Fritz is rummaging for cups and Tabitha is measuring out the tea and Max is still absorbed in the ferret's art and Crumpet and Rascal are waiting patiently for everyone to get back together again, I will tell you the ferret's story. I am sure you're wondering how an animal with a fine talent for landscapes and portraits found himself under a bank beside Wilfin Beck, especially since we know that there are no ferrets in the Land Between the Lakes.

That is, there are no wild ferrets. Fritz himself was no wilding. In fact, he was quite a civilized ferret, and the true story of his life is nothing at all like the tale the village animals have heard. Before coming to the Lakes, the ferret had belonged to a cultured London gentleman who, like many owners of ferrets (Queen Elizabeth I, for example), took Fritz everywhere he went, to concerts, gala balls and dinners, museums and art galleries, even on holiday abroad. When Fritz and his master walked around the streets of London, the ferret wore a collar and a leash. When they were traveling, he had his own special ferret cage, custom-made and furnished with a comfortable sleeping hammock, a food bowl, and everything that might entertain a ferret on a long journey. And their journeys were frequently very long, for Fritz's master was fond of travel. Fritz had been to Paris, to Rome, to Berlin. He'd been to the Brighton Pier, to the Cornwall Lizard, to the Highlands of Scotland, and to the world-renowned Lake District.

And it was in the Lakes—just here, in fact, near Wilfin Beck, on the road between Far Sawrey and Near Sawrey—that the worst had happened, the very worst. There had come an immense storm of blinding rain and thunder and lightning. Frightened, the horses ran away with the coach in which his master was riding and it overturned. The master was carried off to the Sawrey Hotel, where he died the next day. Fritz himself was not injured, but when the coach overturned, his cage was thrown into the brambles. The door popped open and Fritz, frightened nearly out of his ferret wits, slithered through the prickles and down a muddy bank, where he hid in an abandoned weasel's burrow under the bridge. He waited patiently for his master to come and rescue him, but as the days went by and no one came, it dawned on him that he was now on his own. No human was going to provide his meals, a place for him to sleep, and entertainment. If he were to survive, he should have to pay strict attention to the basics—food, water, shelter. And he should have to depend entirely on his own resources.

Thankfully, this was not difficult. Like all ferrets, Fritz had a natural taste for mice, voles, rabbits, and other small, furry creatures, and since his teeth were quite sharp and his sense of smell even sharper, he had no trouble making a decent living—at least as far as his meals were concerned. A large rabbit warren was conveniently located on one side of the road and Wilfin Beck lay at his door, so he never went to bed hungry or thirsty.

I am sure you are thinking that, having escaped into the wild and gained his freedom, this ferret must be very happy. He was decently fed, he lived under a bridge where people's comings and goings kept him amused, and he had a comfortable hole in the ground in which to sleep.

Within a few months, however, Fritz realized that mere survival was not enough. He missed the cultured life, the concerts and museums and art galleries. But he was an intelligent and resourceful ferret. The first thing he did was to move house, to a larger burrow farther downstream, where the Coniston coach rumbling overhead did not wake him in the mornings. The burrow had once belonged to a badger family and was quite extensive, needing only a little remodeling—a skylight in the central parlor, windows in the rooms on the side of the hill, that sort of thing. He furnished it with odd bits he borrowed from the village, and when that was done, he turned his attention to something he had long wanted to do. Ever since he and his master had visited Paris, where he had seen the work of Toulouse-Lautrec and Vincent Van Gogh, Fritz the ferret had wanted to be a painter.

It wasn't hard to contrive a painter's kit. He made a wooden easel, found scraps of canvas in the shed behind the Tower Bank Arms, and raided Miss Potter's collection of water colors and brushes at Hill Top Farm. His first two or three paintings were not very good, but it wasn't long before he began to feel at home with his art, and to work away at it in earnest. He settled into a routine, foraging at night, sleeping in the morning, and, when the early-afternoon light flooded his new burrow, settling down to paint. He even found some clay and began to create sculptures. He was perfectly happy, as well he might be. But I am sad to say that he was also perfectly lonely.

"*Ah,*" said Rascal, getting to his feet. "*Here's tea.*"

"*Sit down,*" Fritz said hastily. "*Mind your elbows and tails, everyone, or you'll knock something off the shelves.*" He busied himself with the tray as Tabitha handed out the cups. "*Sugar? One lump or two? Milk or lemon? I'm sorry to say that there are no scones—I wasn't expecting company—but help yourself to a biscuit.*"

When everyone was provided for, there were a few moments of silence, and then Rascal said, "*It looks like losing that footpath is going to be a bit of a problem to the villagers. We wonder—*"

"*We want to know,*" said Tabitha, taking charge, "*why Mr. Harmsworth stopped the path.*"

"*Mrs. Stubbs has threatened to put a rock through Mr. Harmsworth's front window,*" Crumpet put in, and Max said, in a low voice, "*The children will have to walk the long way round to school.*"

"*I agree that it's a problem,*" the ferret said. "*But I doubt very much that Mr. Harmsworth can be persuaded to open the path. He closed it because of the haystack fire.*"

Max stared at him. Of course. The haystack at the edge of Applebeck Orchard had burned a few nights before. To most of us, perhaps, a haystack is a small thing, just a heap of straw, and what's so important about straw, for pity's sake? It's just dead grass. But to a farmer, a haystack represents a considerable investment in time and labor, not to mention the farm animals' supply of winter food. When one catches fire, whether by lightning or spontaneous combustion or otherwise, it isn't a trivial loss.

"You're suggesting that someone using the footpath might have set fire to the haystack?" Tabitha asked, frowning. *"And that Mr. Harmsworth closed the path to keep it from happening again?"*

"If that's the case," Rascal observed, *"blocking the path is likely to make things worse. It won't be a haystack next time. It will be a toolshed or a cider shed or a barn."* His voice dropped. *"Or a house."*

"That settles it," Crumpet exclaimed, in an authoritative tone. *"This is a flammable situation. I think we should—"*

"We really don't care what you think, Crumpet," Tabitha interrupted loudly. *"I am the president of the Council and I will tell you what—"*

"No, you won't," Crumpet cried. *"And what's more, you can stop interrupting me. I am sick to death of—"*

"QUIET!" the ferret roared. When everyone was silent, he went on, in an irritated tone. *"I do wish that you would talk one at a time. And quietly, please. This shouting and quarreling is very uncivil. Where did you animals learn your manners? In a barnyard?"*

Everyone fell silent. Crumpet licked her paw carelessly, as if she did not feel rebuked, which of course she did. Tabitha glanced up at the ceiling, trying not to look embarrassed. Rascal hung his head. Max suppressed a chuckle, thinking what a surprise the ferret had been. They had expected a fierce, barbaric animal who, given half a chance, would tear them limb from limb. Instead, they had found one who could teach them lessons in deportment.

"That's better," Fritz said after a moment. *"Well, then, I will tell you what I know. I was coming home from dining at the rabbit warren on Friday night, when I saw Mr. Harmsworth. It was past dark, and he'd brought a lantern and his horse and a cartload of wood stakes and wire and a bucket of hot tar. He took*

down the stile and built the barricade across the path, all the while muttering to himself."

"Muttering? Muttering about what?" Tabitha asked. *"And what good is the tar supposed to—"*

"Do you want to tell this story," asked the ferret, frowning, *"or shall I?"*

Rascal coughed. *"Please go on, Ferret. I beg you."* To Tabitha, he growled, *"Do be quiet, Tabitha, or we'll never find out what happened."*

"The tar," the ferret said, *"sticks everything together so thoroughly that it can't be pulled apart. As he worked, he kept muttering about the haystack. From what I heard, he believes it was burnt by people using the path—ramblers or day-trippers or village folk, most likely ramblers. And he means it not to happen again."*

"That's all?" Tabitha looked dissatisfied. *"There's nothing else you can tell us?"*

The ferret sniffed. *"You expected more?"*

"I'm not sure that it's ramblers or day-trippers," Rascal said hurriedly. *"There's Auld Beechie, remember. He's got a grudge."*

"Auld Beechie?" Max asked.

"Thomas Beecham," Rascal replied. *"He used to live in the Applebeck cottage—until Mr. Harmsworth turned him out last year. Now, he's odd-job man at the pub. Lives in that tumble-down cottage beside Cunsey Beck, where Jeremy Crosfield and his aunt used to live."*

"You're suggesting that Mr. Beecham burnt that haystack?" Tabitha sniffed. *"Seriously, I doubt it. After he's swept the kitchen at the pub, he always puts out a saucer of milk for me."*

Crumpet hooted. *"And that makes him a good person? Just because he's kind to an old cat? Don't be silly, Tabitha. Whenever Auld Beechie drinks more than his usual half-pint, he says some very nasty things about Mr. Harmsworth. Blames him for losing his cottage. Swears he'll get even. If you ask me, Auld Beechie burnt that haystack."*

"Just who are you calling an 'old cat'?" Tabitha inquired icily.

"If the collar fits—" Crumpet purred.

"Girls!" barked Rascal. *"That's enough."* He paused. *"I have to say, though, that I agree with Crumpet. When Auld Beechie drinks too much, there's no predicting what he'll do."*

The ferret frowned. *"I can tell you this,"* he said slowly. *"Mr. Harmsworth is wrong if he's thinking that it was a rambler or a day-tripper who fired that haystack."* He drained his teacup.

"Well, then, who was it?" Crumpet demanded. She glared at Tabitha. *"Mr. Beecham, I suppose."*

At that moment, the clock on the mantelpiece began to chime. *"My gracious,"* the ferret said, putting down his cup. *"Just look how late it's got. I have work to do this morning, and I'm sure that you have other matters to attend to. Perhaps we can continue this conversation at another time."*

"Bother," Crumpet grumbled.

"But we want to know now!*"* Tabitha stamped her paw. *"Tell us!"*

"Ladies, ladies." The ferret gave a reproving tsk-tsk. *"You'll never get anywhere making demands."* He stood. *"When you arrived, you came in the back way. You'll be glad to know that there's another entry, much more direct. Come, let me show you."*

And with that, he led them through a hallway lined with more paintings and into an entrance foyer, which was furnished with an elegant table, a mirror, a vase of fresh flowers, and the sculpture of a ewe with her lamb. As usual, Max brought up the rear.

The ferret stopped him at the door. *"I admire uniqueness,"* he said. *"I believe I have an eye for it. And if you don't mind my saying so, old chap, you are truly unique. Common cats have tails. You don't. I should very much like to paint your portrait, if you would be so kind as to agree."*

Max was dumbfounded. *"Paint—paint my portrait?"* he gasped. It took a moment for Max to find his voice. *"I can't think of anything I would rather do,"* he managed at last.

"It won't take long," the ferret assured him. *"I work quickly, and I shouldn't impose on you for more than a few hours. Of course, we can do this at your convenience."* With a flourish, he bowed from the waist. *"I am your servant."*

Max pulled himself up, feeling as if the earth had suddenly shifted on its axis. *"Thank you,"* he said simply. *"Thank you."*

"Splendid! Splendid, old chap!" the ferret cried. *"I shall even get up early, so we can get a good start. You'll come tomorrow?"*

"Tomorrow," Max said, and left with his head high.

He would have carried his tail high, too, if he'd had one.

5

Another Conundrum

When Miss Potter of London purchased Hill Top Farm in 1905, the village of Sawrey was not pleased. The women feared that a city lady would be much too grand for village society, while the men were affronted by the idea that the nicest old farm in the district had been bought by an off-comer, a spinster with no experience whatsoever as a farmer. They laughed at her for paying too much for the old place, predicted that she'd fail by year's end, and laid bets on who would buy the farm when it came up for sale again.

But Miss Potter surprised the men by not only lasting the year but by making very wise and necessary repairs to the farm buildings, improving the Hill Top sheep flock by acquiring some fine Herdwick ewes, and expanding the cattle herd with the purchase of two Galway cows. She surprised the women by proving, as Bertha Stubbs put it, "as common as any t' rest of us, only more so." And for the next year or two or three, they became rather comfortable with

Miss Potter as their neighbor, and some even thought that her celebrity brought a certain . . . well, distinction to the village. It was a compliment to the village that a famous author had chosen Near Sawrey as her country residence, wasn't it?

The villagers were not so pleased, however, when Miss Potter bought Castle Farm, thereby becoming the largest landowner in Sawrey, next to Lady Longford. Oh, there were a few who pointed out that old farms were no longer bought by real farmers, for there was no money to be made in farming. If Miss Potter (most still didn't consider her a "real" farmer) hadn't bought Castle Farm, it might have fallen into the hands of a land speculator, who would have built cottages and perhaps even a hotel and shops. All of this would've meant a influx of day-trippers and fell-walkers and noise and traffic and an increase in the rates, which would have been bad for everyone. So it was lucky for the village that Miss Potter took the farm off the market.

But others pointed out (quite reasonably) that land development would also have brought employment, which would have meant steady money in everyone's pockets, and when this was said, many people found themselves nodding. A few more shillings a week would not be amiss, would it, now? I regret to say that the villagers, like most of us, wanted both the penny and the bun.

Beatrix, however, was not troubled by the villagers' opinions, for she was simply doing what she most wanted to do. She had paid for both farms from the royalties of her children's books, among them *Peter Rabbit, Mrs. Tiggy-Winkle, Jemima Puddle-duck, Ginger and Pickles*, and the latest, recently published, *The Tale of Mrs. Tittlemouse*. Her little books were very inexpensive (*Peter* had sold for just one-and-six) so that children could buy them from their pocket money. She found it hard to believe that all these tiny purchases had brought her enough money to buy not just one but two—two!—beautiful old farms, and some other small fields besides. She couldn't help thinking that the whole thing had happened entirely by magic, a feeling that possessed her every time she returned to Hill Top Farm, as she was doing this morning.

She got down from Mr. Heelis' gig and bade him goodbye. She watched him drive off, then stood for a moment on the path and surveyed the house, thinking once again how much she loved it and how astonishing it was that this magical place, on such a magical morning, actually belonged to *her.*

When you go to visit Hill Top (as you certainly may, since the house now belongs to the National Trust, which opens it almost daily to the public), you might not see immediately why Beatrix Potter loved it so much. The house is a traditional seventeenth-century, two-story North Country farmhouse, plain and unadorned by any kind of architectural fripperies. It had been long neglected when she bought it, and she put quite a lot of effort into restoring its original appearance, as well as building an addition for Mr. Jennings (the farmer who managed her animals) and his family. Like the other houses in the village, the exterior was plastered with a pebbly mortar painted with gray limewash. The eight-over-eight windows were lined up symmetrically, bottom and top, the sashes painted white. The house was roofed with local blue slate, and the chimney pots, like well-tutored schoolboys standing in a row, wore peaked slate caps. The porch was constructed of slate, four enormous blue slabs, two vertical pieces at the sides and two more for the peaked roof. The slate itself came from Outgate, just north of Hawkshead. It pleased Beatrix to know that her house—its timbers and slates and stones and mortar—was made entirely of materials that came from the land all around, and that her quarry also provided rock for road and bridge repair.

Just now, the front door was open—left so by Mrs. Jennings, who had been airing the place for her landlady's expected arrival. So Beatrix picked up her satchel and her hamper, went onto the porch, and through the door. And since I'm sure you want to know what the interior looks like, we will follow her. (Or you can go and see all the furniture and curtains and pictures and curios for yourself, for when Beatrix bequeathed Hill Top Farm to the National Trust on her death in 1943, she asked that it be kept exactly as she left it.)

At Beatrix's heels, we step directly into the main living area—the "hall," as it was called by the North Country folk. When she bought the house, there was a partition here that formed a dark hallway, but she pulled it down, bringing in light and opening the room to its original generous size. Looking over her shoulder, we can see that the walls and ceiling are papered in a flowery green print, and that the room is furnished with a gate-legged table and rush-seated chairs, and two dressers, one a dark antique with a date of 1667, the other a pale oak dresser that displays a collection of blue and white ware and two portrait bowls. (If you look closely, you can see that one bowl pictures George III and Queen Charlotte, while the other depicts Lord Nelson.) Next to the dresser, facing the front door, is a tall oak clock, its dial painted with pretty flowers.

Along the west wall is a cast-iron range that fits neatly into the fireplace alcove, and a kettle steams quietly on the range. The floor is dark slate, with a red-bordered sea-grass rug and a smaller, shaggy blue one. The curtains at the deep-set window are red, and there is a pot of red geraniums on the window seat. A row of brasses hangs under the mantel, an old spinning wheel stands beside the fireplace, and a rocking chair is waiting for Beatrix to take a moment and sit down. Her leather clogs, made for her by a cobbler in Hawkshead, are waiting for her to put them on and go out to the barn to see the cows and chickens and pigs—but they will have to wait for a while, for she has other things to do.

Beatrix smiled at the room, which seemed to smile back, as excited and pleased as she was that she had come home again. The other rooms in this small house smiled, too, and chuckled and said how glad they were to see her and hoped that she would be able to stay for a very long time. Downstairs, there was the parlor with its marble Adam-style fireplace, oriental carpet, and richly paneled walls. Upstairs, her very own bedroom, with its stone fireplace and a window overlooking the garden; and the treasure room where she kept her collections of favorite things—porcelain, pictures, miniatures, embroideries, everything arranged just the way she wanted it.

Indeed, as she stood still in the hall, taking deep breaths of the tranquil air, filled with country scents of summer-warm dust and fresh-cut hay and blooming flowers, Beatrix felt that the house was perfect in every way. Her parents' elegant home at Number Two Bolton Gardens might be filled with angry squalls, London might be bleak and gray and chilly, and all of England might be peering into an anxious and unsettled future, with labor strikes and rising prices and war clouds gathering on the horizon. But none of that troubled her here. Hill Top was a refuge, a sanctuary, a haven from every storm.

Because of this, when she came to Hill Top, Beatrix always tried her best to put everything out of her mind except the tasks immediately before her. She focused all her attention on enjoying the present and keeping as contented and busy as possible, and in my opinion, she was doing exactly as she should. Wouldn't you agree? The past was full of unhappiness. More important, it was the *past*. It was over and done with, so why make herself miserable by thinking about what could not be changed? It had been the best of times and the worst of times, both together. She had loved Norman Warne with all her heart, but he had died suddenly, too young, too soon, just a month after she had accepted his ring.

And even that short month had not been the happy time it should have been. Instead, every day had been a tempest. Norman was certainly respected and respectable—his family was well-known in the London publishing world—but he didn't belong to the Potters' social class. He worked for a living, and that, in Mrs. Potter's phrase, was "wretchedly vulgar." Marrying him would be an appalling mistake, and Mr. and Mrs. Potter simply would not allow it. (I wonder if Queen Alexandra said something like that to Princess Victoria, when Lord Rosebery offered. "Oh, but my dear, he's only an earl! We won't speak of it.") When the worst happened, and Norman had died, the Potters could scarcely hide their relief. Their daughter was no longer in danger of marrying the fellow.

Well. All that ugliness was in the past, and Beatrix was determined that she would not trouble herself by thinking of it. But now she was confronted by a present conundrum, and she could not put it out of her mind. Opening her satchel, she took out a paper-wrapped parcel and put it on the table. Then she went up the stairs to her bedroom to take off her travel things and change into her farm clothes. As she did this, she made herself think about Mr. Heelis, although she would really rather not. She was going to have to decide how to deal with the situation.

It was clear to her that he was beginning to care for her, not in a friendly, affectionate way, but more deeply. She had suspected this the last time they were together. Now, after this morning, she was sure about it. And since Mr. Heelis was the kind of man he was, honest, straight, and true, he deserved something honest, straight, and true. She was going to have to confront the issue directly. And soon, no matter how painful it might be.

Beatrix went into her bedroom, took off her blouse and skirt, and put on the simpler costume she always wore around the farm. She picked up her comb and glanced into the mirror to tidy her flyaway hair, pausing for a moment to wonder what Mr. Heelis—a handsome, eligible bachelor, who could have his pick of all the women in the entire district—saw in her. The mirror told her the truth: that she was plump, round-faced, and plain-featured, with a nose that was too big (that, at least, was what her father's friend John Millais, the famous painter, had said of her when she was a girl) and cheeks that were too pink. Her blue eyes were her best feature, and her mouth turned up naturally at the corners, but her brown hair was rather thin, the result of illness when she was younger. She gave the mirror an ironic smile. If Mr. Heelis cared for her, it was certainly not because of her great attractiveness.

But he did care for her, she was sure of that. Oh, not because he had told her in so many words, for he was a gentleman (although not in her parents' definition of that word) and extraordinarily shy. If it hadn't been for what had occurred between them when they were alone together one day last winter, downstairs in this very house, Beatrix might not herself have a very clear idea of what was going on.

If you and I had been there when it happened, we might not even have noticed, because it had happened so fast and seemed such a small thing, although certainly not to Beatrix. Mr. Heelis had been teasing her, in a friendly, light-hearted way, about solving mysteries. Then, fearing that he had offended her, he had reached out impulsively and taken her hand, as if in apology.

And instead of pulling her hand away with a laugh, as she should have done (as any other woman with a brain in her head would have done), her eyes had stupidly filled with tears, a choking sob had risen in her throat, and her fingers had tightened on his. She hadn't intended any of this; she simply couldn't help herself. She was remembering the moment when Norman had taken her hand in that way and what it had meant to both of them, both for good and for ill. She was torn between desperately wanting it to happen again, with Mr. Heelis, and not wanting it to happen again, ever, with anyone—especially not with Mr. Heelis.

No, not Mr. Heelis, of all people, for he could only be hurt by the inevitable consequences. At that very moment, she knew she should do something to stop it.

But she hadn't. She and Mr. Heelis had been together only twice more, and briefly, in public. A few days later, she had gone back to London, thinking (hoping, really) that by the next time she saw him, he would have forgotten all about what had happened between them and become interested in someone else. But when she got off the ferry this morning and saw him waiting, it was as if no time at all had passed. Certainly nothing had changed. One glance at his face told her that he felt the same way, and one look into her heart told her that her own feelings had not changed.

And therein lay the problem, the conundrum. Her attraction to Mr. Heelis felt to her like disloyalty to Norman. Of course, Norman had been dead for five years now—five years this very month—and he would be the first to tell

Beatrix to go on with her life and be happy in any way she could. But Norman's sister Millie was a very dear friend, and Beatrix's books were published by Norman's brothers, Harold and Fruing. Norman's mother was dead now, but the entire Warne clan, down to the nieces and nephews, treated her as a cherished member of the family. How would they feel if she became involved with someone else? Wouldn't they be hurt?

But these feelings of loyalty and disloyalty, painful as they were, were not the chief barrier to a friendship, or something more, with Mr. Heelis. No. There was one thing worse, a hundred times worse, for Beatrix knew with a sad, sick certainty that her parents would react to Mr. Heelis exactly as they had to Norman. And it would be even more terrible this time. Her father was in ill health and extremely irritable. Her mother was maddeningly determined to keep her with them. Any suggestion that Beatrix might be inclined to care for someone, might even consider marriage, would send them into paroxysms of anger and fear.

Beatrix could just imagine it, the shrill arguments, the shouting and pouting and weeping. "You are a selfish, thoughtless girl," her mother would sob bitterly, and require to be put to bed with lavender and salts. Her father would turn turkey-red and wave his arms and stamp around like a furious gorilla—funny, if it weren't so sad. And they would both point out, loudly and repeatedly, that they would be dead in just a few years, and surely she could manage to postpone her own selfish pleasures for a little longer. (Beatrix's father did die just four years after the time of this story, although her mother lived on for nearly a quarter of a century longer.)

And leave them for what? For whom? For a country solicitor?

"A country solicitor?" her father would growl with profound sarcasm. "A man who spends his time handling other people's real estate transactions instead of his own? A man who rides about the countryside surveying property and writing people's wills? It's out of the question, Beatrix. Out of the question, my girl! I will hear no more about it."

And her mother would snap, "Don't be ridiculous, Beatrix! Just look at you. You are too old to make a silly, romantic fool of yourself. And over a country solicitor, too."

And if she had been foolish enough to suggest that Mr. Heelis might be invited to tea so that they could meet him and see what a fine man he was, what an upstanding—

"Ridiculous!" her father would exclaim, and her mother would put her hand to her forehead and cry, "Beatrix, you are making me ill. You know you are, and you're doing it on purpose. I will not have that man in this house and that's all there is to it. Now, stop being such a goose and get me a cup of tea."

Oh, dear. I am sure I wouldn't want my mother and father saying things like that to me, and if they did, I would probably storm out of the house, and slam the door behind me. But that would not be Beatrix's way—at least, not yet. And if it seems to you that Beatrix's ideas of loyalty are far too limiting and idealistic (she has mourned for Norman for five years? five *years?*—really, isn't that long enough?), and that if Will Heelis really cared for her, he would come straight out and tell her so, well, do please remember that Beatrix and Will live in a world where people do not talk about such things with our readiness and ease. We speak of matters of the heart, our hearts and our friends', with a freedom that they would have found incomprehensible, and our willingness (should I say eagerness?) to trade touches and embraces and even kisses with people whom we barely know would have seemed cheap and immoral. This does not mean that Beatrix Potter and Will Heelis do not feel passion or deep emotion, for of course they do. It only means that they are not as quick to express it.

And if you think about it, perhaps the social conventions that keep them from falling into each other's arms might have an important result. Perhaps their feelings are the deeper and more passionate because they are stopped up, as with a cork in a bottle of champagne, and when those feelings can no longer be denied and must burst out, they are all the more powerful.

But it's not up to us to judge, is it? Miss Potter and Mr. Heelis are products of their time and place, just as you and I. If we want to understand them, we shall simply have to take them as they are: Mr. Heelis hopelessly shy and reserved (inhibited, we might say); Miss Potter impossibly tangled in a sticky spiderweb of obligations.

There was a knock on the door downstairs. Beatrix put down her comb. She hoped very much that it wasn't Mr. Heelis come back again. For if that was who it was, she was going to have to tell him that their friendship could never be anything more than just that—a friendship. Anything else, any kind of romantic attachment, was quite out of the question, now and in the future.

6

Bosworth Badger Is Perplexed

Miss Potter was not the only one to feel the magic of this beautiful morning.

A little distance away, on Holly How, Bosworth Badger had taken his midmorning tea out to the front porch of The Brockery, where he could sit quietly in his rocking chair and enjoy a wide view of green meadows and fell-sides.

The Brockery, one of the oldest badger setts in the Land Between the Lakes, is an animal hostelry known far and wide for its hospitality and good cheer. To keep the place in good order, there is a staff of six, including four badgers (Bosworth, the owner and manager; Primrose, the housekeeper; Hyacinth, Primrose's daughter and assistant; and Parsley, the cook), as well as two rabbits, Flotsam and Jetsam. There are several permanent residents, like the pair of orphaned hedgehogs and quite a few spiders and beetles, most of whom come and go as they please and don't bother to sign the guest register.

And of course, there are a great many wayfarers, like the fox who likes to pop in for a day or two, or the trio of long-tailed mice that spent a full week recovering from an attack by a vagrant cat. There's also the odd weasel and stoat, who are politely asked to please sleep at the far end of the burrow, close to an exit, because of the odor, you know. Most guests pay in kind, with services and food and other useful items, like the bar of soap brought by the fox (pilfered from the storeroom at the Tower Bank Arms), which Primrose immediately cut up into smaller bars and distributed among the guest rooms. But Bosworth is a softhearted fellow. Animals temporarily down on their luck—the red fox with a leg injured in a game-keeper's trap, and the family of rabbits whose burrow had been flooded—are permitted to stay at The Brockery even when they cannot pay their bill. (The Fifth Badger Rule of Thumb suggests that, since badgers usually inherit dwellings that are much too large for them, they should practice a generous hospitality and welcome all those who have temporarily fallen on hard times.)

Bosworth's morning work (reviewing the guest registry, going over Primrose's housekeeping accounts, and making an entry in the *History*) was finished, and he was glad to spend a few moments out of doors. The sun was smiling cheerfully, the breeze was of an easygoing temperament, and the sky was unambiguously blue, with only a few feathery clouds brushing the fells to the west and north. It was a fine time to be a badger, Bosworth thought as he poured himself a cup of tea and helped himself to a scone. And The Brockery at Holly How was undoubtedly the very best spot in all the world to be a badger *in*.

And I daresay Bosworth is right. Holly How is a rocky hill not far above the village of Near Sawrey. Wilfin Beck curls like a silver ribbon around its foot and Cuckoo Brow

Wood rises darkly at its back, climbing the steep slope of Claife Heights and spilling over the top and down all the way to Lake Windermere. From Holly How, Bosworth can look in several directions, toward the neat green pastures of Holly How Farm, where Jeremy Crosfield lives with his aunt (when he's not away at school, that is) and toward the darker shadows of Tidmarsh Manor, where Caroline Longford lives with her grandmother. He can't see Near or Far Sawrey, for they are tucked away behind other hills. But he knows the hamlets are there, for he's visited them many times on the nocturnal journeys that badgers like to take in search of brambles and gooseberries, unguarded hens' nests, and apples. As a matter of fact, Bosworth is well acquainted with Mathilda Crook's gooseberries, Bertha Stubbs' chicken coop, and Mr. Harmsworth's apple trees, although he always tries very hard not to take the very last of anything. He feels bound by the Twelfth Badger Rule of Thumb, you see: *When helping oneself in someone else's garden patch, one must not be greedy but mindful of others who depend upon the same food. It is only good manners to leave a little for the gardener.*

At the moment, though, Bosworth is not thinking of nocturnal adventures in the gardens of the twin Sawreys. He is drinking his tea, nibbling his scone, and trying to solve a problem—a very large and perplexing problem. We might even call it a conundrum, unless you're getting tired of that term, which seems to be coming up rather often in this story. If you are, we shall have to think of another word for it.

The puzzle is this. Bosworth is getting on in years, you see. His muzzle is graying, he is slowing down, and he is becoming more and more forgetful. Whilst he is still able to fulfill his basic obligations as host of The Brockery and official clan historian and keeper of the *History of the Badgers of the Land Between the Lakes* and its companion *Genealogy*, he knows that the time is coming when he shall have to turn these important responsibilities over to a younger badger. The trouble is that he is the very last badger in the long lineage of Holly How badgers. There is no younger badger to whom he might hand the task.

For this grim situation, Bosworth knew that he had no one to blame but himself. Things might have been very different if he had obeyed his parents' wishes, stayed on at The Brockery or settled nearby, and fathered a family. But as a youth, he had been restless and even a little reckless, eager to fare as far afield and enjoy as many adventures as any young badger could, giving no thought to having a family. He had returned from his journeys only when his father wrote that he was dying and wished to pass on the Badger Badge of Authority to his eldest son.

This Badge authorizes the holder to carry on the work of the badgers of Holly How. It is a round wooden disk suspended from a blue-and-gold woven ribbon and brightly emblazoned with the Badger Coat of Arms, twin badgers rampant on an azure field, with a shield inscribed in Latin with the family motto:

De Parbis, grandis acerbus erit.

In English: *From small things, there will grow a mighty heap.* Or as the local badgers put it: *Many littles make a mickle, Many mickles make a mile.* It refers, Bosworth understood, to the badgers' habit of excavating their burrows inch by inch, foot by foot, one generation after another generation, until there was a mile or more of intricate underground tunnels and great heaps of dirt piled outside the various doors. Which is why badgers inherit dwellings that are much too large for them, and feel obliged to share with others.

On official occasions, Bosworth wore the Badge proudly around his neck, and looked forward to passing it on to the next generation. But therein lay the rub, for Bosworth had no eldest son, no son, nor any children at all. Now, personally, this was not an issue for him. He did not feel the lack of a family, for he was affectionately viewed as a pater familias by the many animals who called The Brockery home, and he fondly considered all of them—even the rabbits and spiders and occasional vagrant fox—to be his true relations and friends. But he deeply regretted the lack of an heir where the *Genealogy* and the *History* were concerned, for it was unthinkable that these important documents—which consisted of some two dozen leather-bound volumes shelved in The Brockery's library—should come to an end for want of someone to maintain them.

However, there it was. Unthinkable it might be, but he had to think it. He had been putting it off for months, ignoring the nagging voice at the back of his mind reminding him that he had failed in one of his most significant duties: to identify a young male badger worthy of wearing the Badge of Authority and carrying on the great work of the *History* and the *Genealogy*.

This is not to say that he hadn't tried. Oh, no, not at all! For a time, Bosworth thought he had found exactly the right badger: Thorn, a strong, promising young fellow with a great intelligence and a willing heart, who had seemed to be all the things a badger could want in a son and heir. But Thorn, like Bosworth himself, was restless (this is in the nature of young male badgers, I suppose), and at the beginning of the year he had gone off to see the Wide World. He had promised to keep the badgers of Holly How (his mother,

Primrose, The Brockery's housekeeper; his sister Hyacinth; and Bosworth) informed of his whereabouts, for he knew that all of them would worry.

But nearly nine months had gone by and nothing at all had been heard of Thorn. No penny postcards, no wish-you-were-heres, no reassuring words brought by nomadic animals who had happened to meet the intrepid explorer deep in a tropical jungle or in an exotic foreign bazaar. Not a single word, which was very unlike young Thorn, who felt a strong tie to his mother and a great affection for Bosworth. If he had been able to communicate, he would have, and that was that.

The badgers tried to keep their spirits up, but their hopes were rapidly fading. All three were well aware of the Thirteenth Badger Rule of Thumb: *Animals are prone to accidents, and there are many traps and snares in this dark and uncertain world.* After all this time, they had to accept the sad truth. It was quite likely that they would never see Thorn again.

When confronted with such a hard truth, animals find it of no use to whine and complain—that is a human habit. So as Bosworth drank his tea and looked out over the green velvet valley of Wilfin Beck, he was trying to formulate a strategy for dealing with the vexing matter of the Badge, the *History*, and the *Genealogy*. He had thought of a solution, a rather creative solution. It had popped into his mind a few days ago whilst he was making an index of the last three dozen entries in the *History*.

But the solution was a radical one, very radical. Such a thing as Bosworth imagined had never before been attempted (or if it had, he had never heard about it), and he wondered what the other animals might think. What he needed was some expert advice. He should have to take up the matter with a certain learned friend who had a very good head where things like rules and precedents and so forth were concerned. His friend would no doubt be able to make a suggestion.

Bosworth closed his eyes for a closer examination of this perplexing problem (badgers always think better with their eyes shut). A moment or two (or perhaps a half hour) later, he found himself jolted awake by a rush of air and a solid *THWUNK*.

"Gooood mooorning, Badger," said the owl, for it was he who had just dropped down out of the sky: Professor Galileo Newton Owl, D.Phil., one of the largest (and certainly the wisest) tawny owls in the whole of the Land Between the Lakes. *"And how are yooou this fine mooorning?"*

The badger blinked. It was rather unsettling to be thwunked awake. *"I am well,"* he said, and picked up the teapot, which seemed to have grown a bit cool in its cozy during his nap. *"Do you have time for a cup, Owl? There is a question I should like to ask you."*

"B'lieve I dooo," agreed the owl, and pushed his daytime flying goggles (the ones with the dark lenses) to the top of his head. The professor had a wide reputation among the animals in the Land Between the Lakes and was known by a great many of the Big Folk, as well. He lived in a great hollow beech tree at the top of Cuckoo Brow Wood, where he studied the stars. He enjoyed an international reputation for his scholarship in celestial mechanics, and this with very good reason, for he spent the hours from midnight to dawn in his treetop observatory, searching the sky with his telescope and making notes in his celestial logbook. He was also an enthusiastic naturalist, taking a special interest in the nocturnal habits of the scaled, winged, and furred creatures who frequented the fells and dales. He carried out his investigations from dusk to midnight, generously inviting

his research subjects to be guests at his table. He therefore spent a great deal of time on the wing above the Land Between the Lakes, and since his eyesight was very sharp, there was not much that escaped his notice.

The professor took his cup and held it delicately in his wingtips. (I hope someday you will have the opportunity to see an owl do this, for it is quite an amusing sight.)

"Before you ask your question," he announced importantly, *"I have news."*

"Of Thorn?" Bosworth asked eagerly. This was quite natural, I suppose, since he had been thinking of that dear boy shortly before the professor dropped in.

"Nooo," the owl said, with a look that said he was very sorry. *"It is about the fooootpath throoough Applebeck Orchard."*

Bosworth sighed. If Thorn were anywhere in the district, the professor would know. So he must be elsewhere, or dead. *"What about the footpath?"*

"Mr. Harmswooorth has closed it with wire and wooood and tar. The villagers are deeply disturbed. Some—the Ramblers, particularly—are threatening to take the matter intooo their own hands. I predict perturbations," the professor added gloomily. *"Violent perturbations."* He was fond of big words.

Bosworth sat up straight. *"Closed the footpath!"* he exclaimed. *"That's very bad news, Owl. Very bad news indeed."* He shook his head, remembering other footpath controversies, at Ambleside two years before, in the Wythburn Valley, and at Keswick much earlier, where hundreds of people had come out to protest, owing to barricades that landowners had placed across the paths, all of which was recorded in the *History.* *"Any idea why Mr. Harmsworth is doing this?"*

"Why, tooo keep people off his land," the owl replied, and sipped his tea.

"I understand," Bosworth said impatiently. *"But why?*

People have been using that path for . . . well, centuries, I suppose."

"Ah," said the owl. "Yes. Well, I overheard him tooo say that *he's lost apples tooo the children and a haystack tooo fire, caused by a Rambler. 'Enough is enough,' he says."*

Bosworth looked away, thinking guiltily of the apples he had enjoyed the previous week. But surely he had not taken enough to—

"But those are not the real reasons," the professor went on in a knowing tone.

"Really?" asked Bosworth. "Well, then, what is?"

"It's very simple. He intends tooo sell Applebeck Farm, and the prospective purchaser has told him that there'll be more money if the public access has been cut off." The professor peered over his beak at the plate at Bosworth's elbow. "Are those raisin scones, by any chance?"

"I'm sorry," Bosworth said apologetically. "I should have thought. Yes, raisin scones. Parsley's finest. Do help yourself, old chap." Parsley was known far and wide as an excellent cook, and many animals stopped at The Brockery just to sample her cuisine.

"Thank yooou," said the professor, and did so forthwith. "Of course," he added, munching, "Mr. Harmsworth does not intend for anyone tooo know about the sale until the papers have been signed."

"Then how do you know?" inquired Bosworth.

"I have my methods," the professor replied tersely.

As there was no point in inquiring further along those lines, Bosworth asked instead, "And who is the prospective buyer?"

"I don't knooow," said the owl regretfully. "Yet." He bit into his scone. "I dooo know, however, that the haystack fire was not caused by a careless Rambler. I saw the culprit myself."

Bosworth put down his cup. *"Who was it?"*

"It was," said the owl importantly, *"a female person. Or a male person wearing a cloak and a bonnet and carrying a candle lantern. All very old-fashioned."*

Bosworth stared. *"You actually saw this person set fire to the haystack?"*

"If you mean, did I catch her—or him—in the very act, the answer is nooo. I noticed this person, as I say. But I had other things on my mind—specifically, a tender young vole whooose acquaintance I was eager tooo make. When the vole and I flew back toward my home, I saw that the haystack was burning. It is logical tooo assume, is it not, that it was she—or he, impersonating a she—whooo set it ablaze."

"But who?" Bosworth asked blankly. *"Who would have done such a thing?"* And then a possibility occurred to him. *"I wonder if Auld Beechie might've done it. He worked for Mr. Harmsworth until last winter. They did not part on good terms. At least, that's according to Miss Potter's Herdwick ewes, who heard them quarreling when they were working on the stone wall between Applebeck Orchard and Hill Top. Nearly came to blows, I understand."*

"Auld Beechie?" the owl asked. *"That would be Thomas Beecham? The fellooow has a ship on his shoulder."* He looked skeptical. *"The lantern I understand. I suppose it was the source of ignition. But why would he disguise himself in a cloak and bonnet?"*

"A chip," the badger amended.

"A cloak and bonnet," the owl repeated. *"I asked: why would he disguise himself in a cloak and bonnet?"*

"I mean, it's a chip that people have on their shoulders," the badger said gently.

"A ship," the owl insisted. *"A miniature, I suppose, like a ship in a bottle."* He smiled. *"I have always thought it a picturesque expression."*

Bosworth sighed. When the professor felt he was right, there was no arguing with him. *"Auld Beechie has certainly been nursing a grudge since he was turned out of his cottage. I can picture him putting a torch to that haystack, out of pure spite. But somehow I can't picture him wearing a disguise. So why the cloak and bonnet?"*

You and I are eager to know the answer to that question, aren't we? But I fear that we must wait for an answer, for the professor, while he is quite wise, does not know everything.

"I cannot say." The professor's tone was irritated, for he always hates to admit to not being fully informed on a topic of some importance, as he had been required to do twice in the last few sentences. *"It was dark, and I was flying quite high overhead. It is fair tooo say that I have spectacular vision, but even I cannot be expected tooo see through a cloak and bonnet, into a person's heart."* He fluffed his feathers crossly. *"You wished tooo ask me a question?"*

"What? Oh, yes." Bosworth recovered himself. *"I've been thinking about the* Genealogy *and* History. *I need to name a successor to wear the Badge of Authority and manage everything after I've gone. I thought it would be Thorn, but he seems to have . . ."* Bosworth swallowed the harder word. *"He seems to have disappeared."*

"Ah, Thorn," the owl said regretfully. *"A very fine lad. Yes, well, dooo gooo on, dear fellow. Whooo are you thinking of as a successor?"*

"Hyacinth," said Bosworth, and found as he said her name that he was quite happy with the idea, even though it was a radical choice. She would bring a female's insight to the historian's task, which was all to the good. And of course, she would be right at home managing The Brockery.

"Whooo?" the owl asked, turning his head to gaze at

Bosworth and opening his eyes very wide. *"Whooo was that yoooou said?"*

"Hyacinth. Thorn's sister," Bosworth explained. *"She is a very intelligent, diligent, thoughtful badger, and—"*

"But she is a female," the professor said definitively.

Bosworth shifted in his chair. *"Yes, of course,"* he admitted. *"But as I say, she is intelligent and diligent. There's no question that Hyacinth can do the work. It's only a matter of precedent and—"*

"Far be it from me," the professor intoned in an authoritative voice, *"tooo make pronouncements concerning the way yoooou badgers dooo business."* (That's exactly what he was doing, of course, but the owl was never one to shirk an important task.) *"However, the* History *is not just a history of badgers, as yoooou know. It documents all that goes on in the Land Between the Lakes. Hence, it must be compiled by the best qualified animal."*

"But what if Hyacinth is the best qualified?" Bosworth asked, perplexed. *"I've searched all through the* History, *and I can't find anything that says that the historian must be a male."*

Bosworth could not find a rule excluding females because nobody had thought to put one there. For the most part, badgers are open-minded animals who value the contributions of both sexes equally. In fact, the Tenth Badger Rule of Thumb states that all badgers, regardless of sex, age, and state of health, are important to the well-being of the badger clan and must be honored for the roles they play in maintaining a stable and productive community life. It would not have occurred to the badgers to even mention the issue of gender. But the professor saw it differently.

"It is not mentioned," said the professor grandly, *"because it is tacitly assumed. The question has not come up, yoooou see, because it does not merit examination."* He put down his cup and settled his feathers. *"This is because, as the French novelist Guy de*

Maupassant has said, 'The experience of centuries has proved tooo us that females are, without exception, incapable of any true artistic or scientific work.'" He paused, then added portentously, "*This is only tooo true, as I feel sure yooou will agree, Badger. It is an indisputable fact that females suffer from certain innate and irremediable intellectual deficiencies. The celestial flame that warms and sets fire tooo the masculine soul is simply—*"

"*Thank you, Professor,*" the badger said loudly, rattling his cup. Once the professor began to lecture, one had to plug a stopper in the flow however one could, or one was in for it. But it was already too late.

"*—Simply lacking in females,*" the owl went on, not noticing. "*Which is not tooo say that the fairer sex lacks the finer feeling. Oooh nooo, not a bit! It is only tooo say that our charming females lack the disciplined, deep understanding of fundamental truths that is granted tooo males, and are consequently unable tooo undertake abstract speculation in those intellectually demanding branches of knowledge, such as history or philosophy or the sciences. This was the view of the great Immanuel Kant (1724–1804) and I myself am of the same opinion, for which reason I am strenuously opposed tooo female suffrage. Females dooo not have the intellect required tooo cast a considered vote, nor dooo they—*"

He was (thank heaven!) interrupted by the opening of the front door. "*Parsley says to tell you that lunch is ready, Uncle,*" said a crisp young female voice. "*Cold cucumber soup and cress sandwiches.*" It was Hyacinth herself, an attractive badger with a gleaming black and silver coat, a long, delicate snout, and a very pretty black nose, as shiny as patent leather. Bosworth was not her blood uncle, but she (like Thorn) had adopted the term as an endearment, and he liked it.

"*Thank you, my dear.*" Gratefully, the badger stood and brushed scone crumbs from his fur. "*Will you join us, Owl?*

There's plenty, you know. And I should like to hear more about what you saw the night the haystack burnt."

Indeed, there was always plenty. The corollary to the Fifth Rule of Thumb (regarding hospitality) was that a badger's table should be spread in generous abundance, with enough food for any visitors who happened by at meal-time. As a consequence, a great many visitors made it a definite point to happen by at mealtime, and almost every seat was almost always occupied.

But the owl had another urgent appointment. *"Lunch!"* he hooted. *"My stars—is it that late already? My midday nap has been expecting me for the past quarter-hour, and I dooo not like tooo keep it waiting."* He pulled his flying goggles down over his great round eyes and raised his wings. *"Mind what I say, Badger. Surely there is an alternative tooo—"* He cast a significant look at Hyacinth. *"You take my meaning, I am sure,"* he added. And with that, he lifted himself heavily into the air.

The owl's precipitous departure leaves us rather dissatisfied, I should think. I for one would like to have heard more about the cloaked and bonneted person who might have been responsible for Mr. Harmsworth's haystack catching fire—although since she, or he, was carrying a lantern, perhaps it was accidental, rather than deliberate.

I would also like to give the professor a good, hard shake on account of his attitude toward females, although I know it wouldn't change a thing. This owl may be very learned, but he (like everyone else in this story; indeed, like all of us) is the product of his times and cannot help himself. And he is certainly no more bigoted and intolerant than that celebrated philosopher, the eminent Immanuel Kant, whose ideas he has borrowed. I must warn you that, in the course of our story, we shall hear more comments like these, and counsel you to keep your temper.

Bosworth sighed as he gathered up the cups and the empty plate and put them all on the tray. An alternative to Hyacinth? If there were, he had not yet come up with the name. And for the life of him, he couldn't think why there should be any serious objection to her.

But then, he was only a badger. The professor and Mr. Kant certainly knew better. It was a perplexing problem, a conundrum. Perhaps he should put off making a decision until he'd had time to think some more.

"Let me, Uncle," Hyacinth said, adding the teapot to the tray and taking it from him. *"I wonder if you've heard about the closing of the Applebeck Footpath."*

"The professor was just mentioning it," Bosworth said, holding the door open for Hyacinth. Really, she was such a capable badger. Surely— *"You've heard about the situation, then?"*

"I happened to run into Fritz the ferret last night, near the rabbit warren. He told me that the path was closed off. Wire and sticks and staves and tar, he said."

"Ah, Fritz," Bosworth remarked. They were walking down the hall. *"Not a very sociable creature, I'm afraid. Stand-offish."*

"Oh, he's just shy," Hyacinth said in a cheerful tone, over her shoulder. *"He's much friendlier after you've got acquainted. Did you know he's an artist?"*

"No, I must say I didn't know."

"He does very fine work, Uncle. And he's such a great source of information. You know how ferrets love to snoop. Regular detectives, they are—you can't keep a thing from them. Anyway, he told me that Mr. Harmsworth had closed off the path. He also

said that he had seen something mysterious on the night the haystack burnt."

"Mysterious?" Bosworth asked. *"What was it?"*

"A figure in an old-fashioned bonnet and cloak, he said, carrying a lantern—one of those old-time candle lanterns. I tried to get him to tell me more, but that was all he would say."

A cloak and bonnet? Why, that was what the owl had reported, Bosworth thought. So they had both seen the same thing. As an historian, he always appreciated confirmations. And confirmations from two unrelated sources were the very best.

Hyacinth was going on. *"Anyway, what Fritz said about the barricades made me curious about the path—how long it has been in use and all that sort of thing. So I took the liberty and looked it up in the* History. *I hope you don't mind."*

"Mind!" exclaimed the badger. *"Why, bless my stripes, I don't mind at all, my dear. You may make free of the* History *anytime you like. And what did you discover? The path has been in public use for a very long time, hasn't it?"*

"Oh, yes," Hyacinth replied. *"And what's more, I discovered an interesting mystery about that path—and about the orchard, as well."* She gave an excited little laugh. *"It appears that the orchard is haunted, Uncle! And I think it's entirely possible that the ferret actually saw the ghost!"*

Bosworth paused. *"Now that you mention it, I believe I do recall my great-grandmother speaking of a ghost—a human ghost, that is, the ghost of a woman—who occasionally appeared in Applebeck Orchard."*

Casting his mind back into the far distant past, he could see himself as a tiny badger, sitting at Great-Grandmother's knee in front of the winter fire and listening to her old, cracked voice as she told the stories her own great-grandmother had told her, many badger lifetimes ago. But it was no wonder that he had forgotten, for Great-Grandmother had told many stories and most of them had been ghost stories, in one way or another, since animals have a very strong sense of the immanent and pervasive realities of the spirit world. The Fourteenth Rule of Thumb states it very clearly: *Our badger ancestors have crossed the bridge to the Back of Beyond, but their spirits are constantly with us, in the form of what humans like to call "ghosts." The prudent badger is mindful of their presence, and always behaves as if he is in the company of watchful elders.*

"*That's the one,*" Hyacinth said excitedly. "*The ghost of Applebeck Orchard!*"

"*I'm afraid I don't remember the details of that particular ghost,*" Bosworth remarked ruefully. "*There have been so many.*" It was true. The Land Between the Lakes sometimes seemed peopled by ghosts, who were often said to take an active hand in human affairs. But in this case, Bosworth thought he ought to remember, and felt a twinge of worry. It was just one more sign of his growing forgetfulness.

"*Perhaps the ghost's story is recorded in the* History," he added. The dozen large, leather-bound volumes contained thousands of pages, all covered with neat, tiny writing. It was impossible for even the most devoted badger historian to have read them all.

"*It is, indeed,*" Hyacinth replied. "*And it's fascinating. Apparently, the ghost only appears when there's trouble in store for the village. In fact, I wonder if she might have something to do with—*"

But they had reached the kitchen. Parsley took the tray from Hyacinth and set her to work filling the soup tureen, while Bosworth was handed a plate of cress sandwiches and a stack of napkins to carry to the table. So we shall have to contain our souls in patience until lunch is over, the washing-up done, and Hyacinth and Bosworth can sit down together and read their ghost story.

And in the meantime, we have something else to do. When we left Miss Potter at the end of Chapter Five, she was on her way to answer a knock at her door. I think it is time to go and see who is calling at Hill Top Farm.

7

Miss Potter Accepts an Assignment

To Beatrix's great relief, the person knocking at the door was not Mr. Heelis. It was Margaret Nash, of Sawrey School. She was carrying a cloth-covered basket.

"Welcome back to the village, Beatrix," Margaret said with a smile, and held out the basket. "I've brought you a jar of jam and half a loaf of Annie's fresh-baked soda bread, as a special thank-you for the books you sent for the library shelf at school. The children practically read them to tatters last spring."

Beatrix stepped back. "How very kind of you, Margaret." She took the basket. "I've been thinking of you, as well. And your sister. Come in, won't you? The kettle's hot—we can have tea in just a moment."

"Why, thank you," Margaret said. "I'd love to." She was a slender, brown-haired woman with a high forehead, wide cheekbones, and a cheerful expression that gave her a youthful look and made her pretty, in a modest sort of way. Today, she was dressed in her usual working costume, a simple ivory shirtwaist and brown skirt, although since it was summer, her sleeves were rolled to her elbows and she wore a wide-brimmed cream-colored straw hat that shaded her face. Like Beatrix, Miss Nash was a spinster—married, everyone said, to Sawrey School and the children who passed through its doors and then went on to marry and have children of their own, who became her pupils in their turn. She was held in considerable esteem in the village, for (after many years of serving as the teacher of the infant class) she was now the school's headmistress, one of the highest positions an unmarried woman might hope to achieve in most of England at that time.

Beatrix undid the paper-wrapped parcel she had brought in her satchel and took out a packet of tea. "I've brought some Earl Grey. Would you like it?"

"That will be a great treat," Margaret said, taking off her hat and sitting down at the oak table. "The Hawkshead shops seem never to have it, and when I went over to Kendal, I couldn't find it there, either." Margaret could remember her growing-up years in a farming village not far from Liverpool, when China tea was still a luxury. Her mother, who knew all there was to know about herbs, brewed teas from their garden—peppermint and catmint and chamomile and medicinal teas, such as sage for stomach upsets and lavender for headaches. Now these old herb teas were nearly forgotten, replaced by China tea. Earl Grey was such a favorite that the shops could not keep it in stock.

"I'm curious," Beatrix said, pouring hot water from the kettle over the loose tea in the brown china teapot. "I've only just arrived, Margaret. How did you know I was here?"

Appreciatively, Margaret sniffed the delicious aroma of

bergamot and citrus that rose out of the teapot. "Why, Bertha Stubbs, of course. Who else?" During the school term, Margaret's next-door neighbor at Lakefield Cottages also did daily work at the school—mopping, cleaning, keeping up the stoves. She was in the habit of voicing her opinion about anything and everything as loudly as possible, and carried on until she herself was ready to stop, and not before. "I'm afraid . . . That is—" Margaret took a deep breath. "The fact of the matter is that she happened to see you and Mr. Heelis driving together and . . . well, jumped to conclusions. 'Contusions,' as she put it." Bertha was notorious for her unconventional use of language.

Beatrix gave a vexed sigh. "I'm the one who's likely to feel those 'contusions.' Stories about oneself—especially untrue stories—are as bad as a bruising." She shook her head. "Bertha Stubbs will have me married off within the month, I'm afraid."

"Within the week is more like it," Margaret said with a rueful laugh. "I am sorry to be the bearer of such news, Beatrix. But I did think you ought to know."

"I'm glad you told me." Beatrix squared her shoulders. "There's no help for it, I suppose," she added practically. "The villagers are going to say whatever they please. I don't suppose I need to tell you that there is absolutely nothing between Mr. Heelis and myself."

Now, you and I know that this is not quite true, strictly speaking. There is something between Beatrix and Mr. Heelis, about the size and shape (in our modern way of putting it) of a very large elephant in a very small room. The difficulty was that Beatrix wished the elephant would go away, and could not, under any circumstances, admit the existence of such a creature to anyone else, not even to Margaret, whom she liked very much.

Margaret shook her head quickly. "No, of course not," she said, although from the way Beatrix's cheeks had colored, she wondered whether Bertha Stubbs—who could be surprisingly perceptive, especially when one did not want her to be—might have glimpsed something close to the truth.

Margaret had had her own romantic hopes for many years, although I am happy to say that Mr. Heelis was not the target. No. Enshrined in Margaret's heart of hearts was Captain Woodcock. Not to put too fine a point on it, she thought him simply the most handsome, most intelligent, most reasonable, and kindest gentleman in all the world. In fact, there had been a brief time a few years before, when he had helped her gain appointment as headmistress of Sawrey School, that she had hoped . . .

No again. *Hoped* is too strong a word. Margaret had only allowed herself to imagine—for merely a moment or two, or perhaps not even as long as that—what it would be like to be loved by such a man, to live with him in a house as grand as Tower Bank House, with Elsa Grape to do the cooking and a tweeny and an upstairs girl and old Fred Phinn in the garden. And she would have the management of the house and make sure that everything was comfortable and convenient for the captain, and that there were always clean collars and cuffs in his bureau drawer. And perhaps there would even be children, if—

But that particular heaven was totally out of reach, not even worth the imagining, and Margaret knew precisely why. Captain Woodcock was a gentleman, and she was not a lady. She was a working woman, a school headmistress— not so very much different, when she thought about it, than being a schoolteacher. It scarcely mattered that he and she were of an age and both free, for he was a settled bachelor, quite handsome, and she was a spinster and plain. And of course, if she thought about it very long, she had to admit that she was not free at all. There was Annie, dear, dearest Annie, who could never in the world manage on her own, poor sweet soul, especially in the wintertime.

And that was all there was to it, as Margaret knew very well. She was a practical person. Hoping was of no use and imagining was an utter waste of time, so she wasn't going to indulge in either, at least for no more than a moment. But still—

"And how is your sister?" Beatrix rummaged in her parcel and took out two lemons, a packet of sugar cubes, and a small box of biscuits. She picked up a knife and began to slice the lemons. "You said in your letter that she is not well."

Beatrix and Margaret had begun to correspond rather regularly, and Margaret usually included a few snippets of news in her letters. As headmistress, she was acquainted with all the local families, and Beatrix loved to hear what was going on in the village.

"She's a little better," Margaret said cheerfully. "She's usually well in the summer, you know. It's the winter cold that does not agree with her."

Annie, two years younger than Margaret, walked with a limp due to an illness as a child, and had never fully recovered her strength. But she was always positive in her thinking and she worked as much as she was able. For a time, she'd been employed in the Far Sawrey post office. Now she gave piano lessons at home and led the local choral group and cooked and kept the garden (with a little help from Henry Stubbs) and the cottage, which was always as bright and tidy and snug as Margaret could wish. In fact, if Margaret had reflected on the matter, she might have seen how much she depended on Annie for all the comforts of home. But she didn't, and when she thought of it, it was always the other way round: Annie depended on her for love and strength and care. Not even the bit of money each of them had recently received from their father's estate made any real difference.

Beatrix put the sliced lemons on a plate. "Have you thought of moving to the south?" She lifted the cloth from the basket. "Oh, what a lovely loaf of bread! And shall we have some jam, as well?"

"Yes, let's," Margaret replied. "It's Annie's strawberry jam, you know. We divide the labor. I pick and Annie jams. She sells quite a lot of it now. Sarah Barwick has put it on the counter in her bakery, and Lydia Dowling has it in her shop." With a sigh, she folded her arms on the table. "The south would be much better for Annie, of course. But I should have to find a new position and we should have to up sticks and move and—"

She laughed helplessly, thinking what a hugely unmanageable task it seemed. And of how much she loved the village and hated the thought of living anywhere else, which made her feel quite guilty, of course, for Annie would indeed fare better in a warmer climate. (I understand these confused feelings all too well, and I daresay you do, too.)

"And school will be starting in just a few weeks," she went on, pushing her guilt away. "So a change is quite out of the question for this year, I'm afraid. P'rhaps next." Although they had been through this before, she and Annie, and Margaret knew very well that next year would be exactly the same, especially since Annie (whilst she sometimes expressed a vague longing for seeing the world beyond the village) had no very clear idea of where she wanted to move.

Beatrix cut a slice of bread. "But perhaps just Annie might go, by herself. That way, you wouldn't have to move house. Moving is always such a trial."

"By herself?" Margaret said, and chuckled. Annie would never go anywhere without *her*. Why, she'd be helpless, just helpless. Where would she live? *How* would she live? Of course, there was the money from their father's estate, but it wouldn't be enough. She should have to work, and—

"It's a nice thought," she added, trying to be tactful, "but I really don't think it would do, Beatrix."

To Margaret's surprise, Beatrix held her ground. "It might do, Margaret." She cut another slice of bread. "Actually, it might do very well. An acquaintance of mine, a nurse, has just opened a sanitarium on the south coast, near Brighton. She has been looking for someone to help with music and entertainments—it's important for the patients to keep their spirits up, of course, and she considers music to be highly therapeutic. I thought immediately of Annie and would love to recommend her. It would be the same sort of work she is doing here—teaching piano, leading a singing group—but in a warmer climate. And of course, she'd be meeting new people."

"Oh, but Brighton is so far away!" Margaret exclaimed. If there were difficulties—if Annie got low-spirited or sick, as she often did in winter—she herself should have to go and rescue her, and that would be very hard to manage during school term.

"It is far away," Beatrix agreed with a little laugh. She put the bread slices on a plate and opened the jam. "About as far south as one can get without falling into the Channel, wouldn't you say? Of course, the sun doesn't shine there every day of the year, but there's not the snow and ice we have here." She poured two cups of tea. "You know, it might be better for both you and Annie," she added delicately. "To spend some time apart, I mean. The winters here do feel rather . . . well, claustrophobic at times. Don't you agree?"

Margaret colored and looked away. Beatrix was a thoughtful, generous person, but she had a reputation for managing things in the village, and Margaret hated the idea of being managed. She supposed there was something in what Beatrix was saying, but she was reluctant to admit it.

She cleared her throat. "I suppose I do tend to be a bit protective. But in this case—" She stopped.

"And perhaps Annie depends on you just a bit more than she actually needs to," Beatrix said. She chuckled ironically. "But here I am, the pot calling the kettle black! My parents do rather keep me close, and I feel obliged to help them all I can. I know just how you must feel." She looked at the table. "Oh, milk. I knew I was forgetting something. Do you take it, Margaret?"

"Lemon for me," Margaret said, helping herself, and took the opportunity to change the subject. "Actually, I wanted to mention something important to you, Beatrix. It's about Mr. Harmsworth's niece, who's come to live with him. I'm always reluctant to interfere in family matters where the schoolchildren are concerned, but this is rather a special case."

"Mr. Harmsworth of Applebeck Farm?" Beatrix asked, surprised. "The man who closed off the footpath? I didn't know he had a young niece."

"It's a dreadful thing about that footpath, isn't it?" Margaret's mouth firmed. "I very much hope Captain Woodcock can get the path reopened. He's seeing Mr. Harmsworth today." She had heard this bit of news from Agnes Llewellyn at the village shop, when she went in to buy a sausage.

"I do, as well," Beatrix agreed. She frowned. "I know that some landowners are nervous about being invaded by great hordes of fell-walkers, who leave the gates open and drop greasy lunch wrappers along the way. But the path through Applebeck Orchard isn't a fell-path. It's a path used by local people, coming and going from one Sawrey to the other—and especially to church."

"And to school," Margaret said regretfully, thinking about how many extra steps she would have to walk next term, if the captain couldn't settle the business. She leaned forward. "But it was Mr. Harmsworth's niece that I wanted to tell you about, Beatrix. Gilly, her name is. She's fourteen and recently orphaned, and her uncle is apparently her only relative. She came to school for the last few months of term and finished with the other older children this spring. She was an excellent scholar. In fact, she took first prize in our spelling bee, and was awarded a copy of *The Tale of Jemima Puddle-duck*—the one you donated to the school."

"How nice," Beatrix said. "I'm glad the book was used in that way."

"Yes, but . . ." Margaret sighed. "Oh, dear. I'm not sure I know what I should . . ."

"Please," Beatrix said. "Do go on."

"Well, you see, Gilly spoke to me before the end of term about wanting to find employment, away from Applebeck Farm. She's unhappy, living there with her uncle and aunt. She's made to work very hard, apparently."

"I'm sure that Mrs. Harmsworth is glad to have some help with the household," Beatrix said.

"No doubt," Margaret said dryly. "Although it appears that 'some help' does not exactly describe what Gilly is asked to do. And whilst she didn't tell me so directly, it is my impression that both Mr. and Mrs. Harmsworth are stern disciplinarians. Mr. Harmsworth particularly. I worry that she's being ill-treated."

Beatrix's face darkened. "I saw the man once," she remarked in a low voice, "beating a dog. We had a few words about it."

Beating a dog. Margaret shuddered. It was her experience that if a man would beat a dog, he would strike a child. She took a deep breath. "As I understand it, in addition to the housecleaning and laundry and garden, Gilly also does the work of the farm's dairymaid, who was recently let go. And she's not being paid, of course. She would like to go into service elsewhere, and I promised to help. I wondered if you knew of a place coming open."

I am sure that you and I are horrified at the thought of a fourteen-year-old girl leaving school and taking on the adult responsibilities of cooking and cleaning, not to mention churning butter, and making cheeses. Most of our fourteen-year-olds spend their spare time in the malls, or sending text messages to friends on their cell phones. And of course, they are not even allowed to have a job until they are sixteen.

But in this era in England—and in America, too—girls of fourteen and even younger regularly left their homes and families (if they were lucky enough to have a family) and went into service. A fortunate few found positions on large estates where every member of the staff had his or her special duties and an able servant could look forward to what we nowadays think of as "career advancement," up the ladder of domestic service. The unfortunate many had a worse fate. They worked—and were appallingly overworked—in smaller private homes, where they were responsible for laying and lighting the fires, making the beds, mopping the floors and dusting the furniture, cooking the meals, and doing the washing-up. These "maids-of-all-work," as they were appropriately called, might earn nine pounds a year, including a room-and-board allowance. In today's American currency, considering inflation, this would amount to something like a $100 a month, $25 a week, $3.57 a day, or about 21 cents an hour.

Beatrix frowned. "But even if the girl could find another place, what makes you think the Harmsworths will let her go? As things stand, they are getting someone to cook and clean house and do the dairy work—and it's only costing them her room and board. In the circumstance, I'm sure they'd prefer to keep her."

Beatrix bit her lip with a troubled look, and Margaret wondered whether she was thinking of herself. Beatrix certainly didn't have to cook and clean and perhaps she wasn't overworked. But at the heart of it, her situation might not be so very different from Gilly's. Mrs. Potter seemed to treat her daughter as an unpaid servant, and it was clear that neither Mr. nor Mrs. Potter was willing to let her have a life of her own choosing.

Margaret gave a dispirited sigh, feeling that most women, no matter their social class, were destined to be unhappy. But she was one of the lucky ones, wasn't she? She couldn't marry the man she loved, but she had Annie to look after, and the school and the children as well. She sat up straighter.

"P'rhaps you're right," she said. "P'rhaps the Harmsworths won't let her go. But I feel I ought to give it a try, somehow. Do you know of anyone who's looking for a servant? I asked at the Tower Bank Arms—I thought Mrs. Barrow might be in need of a housemaid. But she is not."

Beatrix tilted her head to one side. "The last time I visited

Tidmarsh Manor, Lady Longford mentioned that she might be looking for an upstairs maid. I don't think there would be any dairy work, if that is not to Gilly's liking."

"Tidmarsh Manor would be perfect!" Margaret exclaimed happily. "Could you find out if the place is still open? I wouldn't want to get Gilly's hopes up—or open the subject with the Harmsworths—unless there was a real possibility."

Beatrix gave her a considering look. "I'm going to Tidmarsh tomorrow to see Caroline. If you like, I'll speak to her ladyship about the situation and let you know what I find out."

"Yes, I would like that, very much," Margaret said warmly. "How is Caroline? You've heard from her?" Margaret knew Caroline Longford from the months she had spent at Sawrey School, before Lady Longford had employed Miss Burns as the girl's governess.

"I had a letter from her a few weeks ago, and one from Miss Burns, as well. Caroline is advancing quickly in her musical studies. You know she's been studying piano with Mrs. King?"

Margaret nodded. "Annie says that Mrs. King is an excellent teacher. Caroline must be doing well indeed."

"So it seems," Beatrix said thoughtfully. "Mr. Heelis mentioned that he heard her play one of her own compositions and was quite impressed." She gave Margaret a direct look. "Caroline wrote me that she wants to study composition. She hopes to become a composer."

"A composer!" Margaret said blankly. "But there are no women composers!"

"There's Ethel Smyth," Beatrix reminded her. "And Dora Bright. Both of them have had their music performed—

although I'm sorry to say that I've never had the opportunity to hear it myself."

"Perhaps," Margaret replied doubtfully, remembering a newspaper article Annie had read to her. The writer (a man, of course) had been at pains to argue that women's genius is not creative, but reproductive; ergo, they could play someone else's music (a man's) but they could not compose. "But there certainly aren't many, and their work isn't widely performed," she added. "And where would Caroline study? I don't suppose musical composition is something one can teach oneself."

"The Royal Academy of Music has admitted women for many years," Beatrix replied. "Mrs. King has encouraged Caroline to apply there." Her voice became dry. "Women are not admitted to the study of composition, but Mrs. King apparently feels that Caroline's talent is so striking that the administrators might be persuaded to relax the rule. She has already written a recommendation."

"A recommendation!" Margaret gasped. "Does Lady Longford know?" She answered her own question. "Of course not. She would never have permitted it. There's the cost, for one thing." Lady Longford had the reputation of being the most parsimonious person in all of the Land Between the Lakes. She would never agree to pay Caroline's tuition at the Royal Academy—let alone her living expenses in London, where she would have to go to study. "And of course there's the question of a chaperone," she added. "Her ladyship would not permit her granddaughter to go to London by herself. Not in a hundred years."

"I'm afraid you're right on all counts," Beatrix said. She gave a rueful smile. "Lady Longford has no idea that any of this is brewing. Miss Burns and Caroline have both asked me to be there when they tell her. They apparently think my presence will blunt her ladyship's wrath." The smile became a chuckle. "I don't hold out much hope of that, I'm afraid."

"Nor do I." Margaret sighed. "You've taken on quite an assignment. Two, actually. Seeing about a position for Gilly and telling Lady Longford that her granddaughter wants to be a composer." She shook her head. "I certainly don't envy you, Beatrix. Her ladyship will not want to let Caroline go."

I find myself wondering (and perhaps you do, too) why Margaret does not see the similarity between her attitude toward Annie and Lady Longford's attitude toward Caroline. She might, for instance, have said something like, "I'm having the same difficulty imagining letting Annie go." But she didn't, and I don't suppose we can blame her. Margaret loves her sister very much. Perhaps she will hold on forever, thereby denying both Annie and herself the ability to live independent lives, which would be a very great pity, in my opinion.

Beatrix nodded. "I am sure you're right about Lady Longford," she said. "I foresee storms on the horizon." She smiled and picked up the teapot. "Let me pour you some more tea."

"Thank you, no," Margaret said, and stood. "I'm on my way to visit Mrs. Lythecoe." She smiled. "Now that the village has got Dr. Butters married, they're hoping for the vicar and Mrs. Lythecoe."

Beatrix accompanied her to the door. "You'll think of what I said about Annie?" she asked. "I'm sure your only consideration is what is right for her, but the sanitarium might be just the thing."

"I'll think about it," Margaret replied (rather stiffly, I'm afraid), and said goodbye.

And now that the vicar has come into our story, perhaps it is time we paid him a visit. We're in luck, it seems, for Captain Woodcock has just arrived to talk with him about the footpath situation that is troubling everyone in the village. And I for one would like to listen in.

8

The Captain and the Vicar Confer

"Good day, Vicar!" Miles called from the garden gate. He could see Vicar Samuel Sackett bending over a rosebush. He was wearing his old gray sweater, the one with both elbows out and two buttons missing, and he had his pruning shears in hand. "A fine morning, isn't it?"

The vicar looked up from the rosebush. "Why, good morning, Captain! Indeed, a fine morning, very fine. Do come in, won't you? I didn't hear your motor car."

"I walked," Miles replied. His blue Rolls-Royce—the only motor car in the district—attracted a great deal of notice when he drove it out, and was usually accompanied by a crowd of small boys and dogs. He was not so eager for attention this morning, and since the sun was shining and the sky was quite blue, he had decided that a pleasant walk on a summer's day would be just the ticket.

"Walking is a fine way to get about," said the vicar approvingly, who always went everywhere in his parish on foot, usually carrying one or another of his large collection of walking sticks. "What would you say to a cup of tea, Captain? Mrs. Thompson can bring it to my study."

"I would say yes, if we could have it in the garden," Miles said, a bit uncomfortably. Mrs. Thompson, the vicar's housekeeper, was known to listen at doors. He added, half-apologetically, "I should rather like our conversation to be private. If you take my meaning."

"Ah, yes." The vicar gave a rueful sigh. "I appreciate your concern."

In fact, the vicar was beginning to feel that perhaps he really ought to do something about Mrs. Thompson. She was taking a greater interest in his well-being than she had since she had come to work at the vicarage some eight or nine years before. This morning, for instance, she had almost insisted on getting her hands on his sweater, in order to repair the sleeves and replace the buttons. He had had a difficult time convincing her that he liked it exactly as it was, with the elbows out and the buttons gone, for he never buttoned it, anyway. And although Mrs. Thompson was a fine housekeeper and a reasonably good cook, she had begun to monitor his activities rather closely of late. She was always near at hand when he wanted something, nearer than was comfortable, and she seemed to anticipate his requests in a way he found disturbing. In a word, she hovered. The vicar had begun to think it was time to make a change.

But Samuel Sackett, who was gentle and scholarly and often rather vague, was not a decisive man. In fact, he was a ditherer. When his duty had to be done—that is, when he felt strongly about a certain issue or when matters were urgent—he was uncompromising in his pursuit of what he knew to be right and good. But the thought of sacking Mrs. Thompson because she listened at doors or hovered over him whilst he ate his dinner was enough to give him indigestion for a week, not to mention the profound alarm he felt at the thought of hiring someone to replace her.

But he did not have to face that particular calamity this morning. He went to the door, put in his head, and called, "Tea for two, Mrs. Thompson, if you please. We shall have it in the garden."

He returned to his guest and the two sat down at a table in a quiet corner, beside an extravagant cabbage rose laden with fragrant, luscious pink blossoms. They occupied themselves with conversation about various inconsequential parish matters until Mrs. Thompson brought a tray.

" 'Tis a bit chilly," she said, leaning over the vicar with a solicitous smile and speaking in the rather loud voice she had lately adopted, as though he were hard of hearing. "Windy, too. Wudn't tha rather have thi tea in t' study, Vicar?"

"It's quite warm enough, I believe," Miles put in, when the vicar hesitated. "Thank you, Mrs. Thompson." After she had departed, scowling, he added, diffidently, "I wanted to consult you about the Applebeck Footpath. I shouldn't like our conversation to get back to Mr. Harmsworth."

The vicar poured. "Ah, yes. The footpath. A bad business, to be sure, very bad. I saw the tangle of wire and staves, all tarred over, when I went to St. Peter's yesterday. The people of Near Sawrey will have farther to walk to get to church. And of course, the children, walking to school." He frowned as he set the teapot down. "Appalling, really. Not at all the sort of thing one likes to see happen in our village."

"Perhaps you could tell me something about the history of that path." The captain stirred two lumps of sugar into his tea. "If you know it, that is."

The vicar settled back in his chair, cup in hand. "As it

happens, I do. Several years ago, Major Ragsdale asked me to do a bit of research for his Ramblers on our local footpaths—in anticipation, I believe, of possible closings." He sighed. "It seems to be the thing to do these days, to close off public access to the wilderness. The commons were enclosed here over a century ago, in 1794, and there have been battles ever since."

"Applebeck Orchard is hardly the wilderness," Miles reminded him gently. "In fact, there's not much wilderness left hereabouts."

"You're right, of course," the vicar said. He added with an unaccustomed sarcasm, "Applebeck Path is merely an age-old pathway between our two settled hamlets. Which, some might say, makes it even more important than a footpath through a wilderness."

"Because it is the way to church?"

"As I read the parish records," the vicar replied, "the use of the path dates back long before the building of St. Peter's. It is mentioned in early records going back to the time of Elizabeth the First."

"And when was St. Peter's built?" Miles asked.

"Forty years ago. At the time—1869—many large houses were being constructed in the area, and it was thought that servants and their families would attend services." The vicar shifted uncomfortably. The vision of the builders, sadly, had been far too optimistic. His present congregation was much smaller than the four hundred for whom St. Peter's had originally been built. Some of the pews had already been taken out.

"At any rate," he went on, "when I began to look into the matter, I learned that the first trees were planted in Applebeck Orchard in 1802. The footpath was already in existence at the time, for users of the path were cautioned to be mindful of the young trees. The road between Near and Far Sawrey—a cart-track at the time, I suppose—made the same large dogleg that it does now. The path cut off a considerable distance."

"It's been in continuous use for all that time, then," Miles said thoughtfully, watching a red admiral butterfly open and close its wings on a branch beside the table. "And it was in use at the time when Mr. Harmsworth bought Applebeck Farm."

"Oh, yes," the vicar agreed. "That makes a difference, doesn't it?"

"It does indeed," Miles said. "Theoretically, a path becomes a legal right of way because the owner has dedicated it to public use. Practically speaking, only a few paths are ever formally dedicated. But the law assumes that if people are permitted to use a path without interference for some period of time, the owner intends to dedicate it."

"What period, exactly?"

"That varies. If there's been heavy use, and the landowner is aware of it, the court accepts a relatively short period. For example, there was a rather well-known case in 1790 where the court ruled that six years' use was sufficient time to establish the public's right of way."

"Then there's no question about the Applebeck path," the vicar replied.

"There's always a question," the captain said testily. "The matter will have to be heard in my court. And I shall have to rule on it."

"If testimony to the years of use is required, Dolly Dorking might be helpful." Dolly—Auld Dolly to the villagers—was the mother of the Near Sawrey postmistress. She was well past ninety, but her memory was still remarkably good. He frowned. "Of course, Mr. Harmsworth has owned the place for only ten years or so, and he's not from this area. He may not know how long the path has been in use. In fact, he may know nothing of the orchard's sad history."

"The orchard has a history?" Miles asked, cocking an imperious eyebrow.

"Of course it does," the vicar replied, mildly rebuking. "All places have a history, you know. This one is tragic. A drowned child, a mother gone mad, a husband who refused to allow her to be sent to an asylum. The poor woman was locked in the attic at Applebeck House for ten or fifteen years before she died—or so the story goes. I am told that her window looked out on the place where her daughter drowned, in Apple Beck."

"That is tragic," Miles agreed. "But in those days, the mother was probably better off at home than in a madhouse. One sympathizes with the husband, who lost both his daughter and his wife."

"Indeed. The villagers have embellished the sad tale with a ghost story, of course," the vicar added. "Every death, it seems, has to be followed by an apparition. And of course, the apparition's every appearance must foretell one sort of disaster or another. Such is the nature of ghosts. And villagers."

"You're not suggesting that this tale has any relevance to the closing of the path, are you?" Miles' voice was dry. "Has a ghost been seen?"

"Yes, according to Mrs. Thompson," the vicar replied with a small smile. "The night the haystack burnt." He sipped his tea. "Constable Braithwaite investigated the fire, I suppose."

"Quite thoroughly," Miles replied. "It was arson, definitely—a candle stub was found near the scene. Unfortunately, there was no clue to the identity of the arsonist, although Braithwaite questioned Tom Beecham first. Since Harmsworth sacked him last winter, Beecham has made no secret of his resentment."

"Yes, I've heard him, more than once," the vicar said ruefully. "He's quite bitter about his dismissal. I should hate to think he might be angry enough to commit such a reprehensible act, though."

The vicar always hated to think that anyone would step off the straight and narrow, Miles thought. Aloud, he said, "It's difficult to obtain a conviction to an arson charge, of course, unless there's a credible witness."

"Indeed," the vicar said. "Well, I certainly hope that the culprit can be found and brought to justice."

The captain changed the subject. "Will Heelis suggested that a committee be formed to look into footpath closures. It won't be named in time to help with this case, but it seemed a good idea to me." He paused. "Would you be willing to put such a committee together, Vicar? Heelis suggested that Miss Potter might be asked to serve. We both agree that she has a steady head. As to the other members, that would be up to you."

The vicar considered doubtfully. "I'm not sure I should like to actually lead . . . That is—"

Miles gave an internal sigh. If only the vicar weren't such a ditherer! "You could appoint yourself the committee's historian," he said, "and let someone else chair it."

"Historian! Of course." The vicar brightened. "And Miss Potter would make an excellent chair. If you like, I shall speak to her about it."

"Splendid!" Miles said emphatically. "But the present situation cannot wait on the formation of a committee. I'm going to see Harmsworth this morning. Not looking forward to it, I must say."

"I shouldn't think," the vicar agreed. Adam Harmsworth had a reputation as rather a difficult fellow. "I do believe," he added tentatively, "that it would be good if he could be persuaded to remove the obstruction before Major Ragsdale stages his protest. The major is rather vigorous when it comes to organizing things."

Miles put down his cup, frowning. "Ragsdale is staging a protest?"

The vicar cleared his throat. "He seems to have it in mind to encourage the Claife Ramblers to storm the ramparts, as it were. I encountered him yesterday evening at the post office, and that's what he told me. I'm not sure it will come to that," he added hastily. "Major Ragsdale may think better of his threat."

Miles shook his head. "Exactly what we need," he muttered. "A protest. Marches. People carrying signs and singing." He broke into a mocking verse. "'The Ramblers of Sawrey will break every chain and open the footpaths again and again.'"

"I always hate to hear a perfectly good hymn pressed into service as a protest," the vicar said with a sigh. Years ago, the Keswick Footpath protesters had adopted "The Lion of Judah will break every chain" as their marching song, and the thing had caught on. It was sacrilegious.

"I'm with you there," Miles said, but for a different reason. He did not like fusses. If there was a difference of opinion, it should be approached with logic and a cool head. Civil disorder broke the bonds of community and set people against one another. Marches and protests and singing and chanting led to brawls and fisticuffs.

"I think there was some mention of the newspaper, as well," the vicar said diffidently. "The major has also been in touch with a journalist from the *Westmorland Gazette*. He seemed to feel that a story might attract additional attention to the problem. I'm afraid he sees this as a good thing."

"Well, I'll soon put a stop to that," Miles said, with great firmness. "The village does not need this kind of disagreement—nor this sort of notoriety. I'll speak to Ragsdale as well as Harmsworth, and see if this matter can't be brought to a speedy conclusion." He paused, adding thoughtfully, "If not, I suppose a supervised trespass could be arranged."

"Trespass?" The vicar's eyes widened. "That sounds alarming."

"Not at all. Ragsdale or someone else—it doesn't matter who—would trespass, Constable Braithwaite would arrest him, and the matter would come before me. It is the way these things are usually handled. Thank you for letting me know what's afoot, Vicar."

"Not at all," the vicar replied, adding, "I'm glad you're taking action." He could hear the wistfulness in his tone. He admired men who could take a decision and act on it with speed and effectiveness. He wished that he were one.

Miles chuckled wryly. "I hope you're still glad when this is over." Of course, he had no doubt as to the eventual outcome. He would hear the case, and if matters were as the vicar had outlined them, he would rule that the path had to be reopened and dismiss the trespass charges. A very simple bit of business.

Or at least, so he thought. Of course, things aren't always as simple as they seem, are they? Solutions turn out not to solve everything, and life has a way of landing us in the middle of some very difficult dilemmas. But perhaps our justice of the peace—a man of law and order—may be forgiven for thinking that the law is capable of righting any wrong and solving any disagreement between people.

There was a silence, as another butterfly—a blue one—briefly visited the tea table, then flew off in the direction of the rosebush. The men drank their tea in silence, each one occupied with his own thoughts.

"Does it seem to you," the vicar said at last, "that the world is all at sixes and sevens just now? King Edward has died, and nobody knows whether King George is up to the task. And there's all that business about women wanting the vote and laborers wanting to work shorter hours, and the Germans wanting God only knows what." He gave a distressed sigh. "One wishes for the old days, when Queen Victoria kept the Kaiser under her thumb."

"And when women and workers were happier with their lot in life?" the captain asked, with a wry lift of one eyebrow.

The vicar sighed again. "One doesn't like to hold others back from opportunity, does one? I suppose change is always unsettling, even when it's change for the good. And change for ill—" He put down his cup. "There was an article in the *Times* recently, predicting hard times ahead for us all. Wars and rumors of wars, you know. All those dreadnoughts our navy is building, fourteen since 1905, according to the *Times*. Imagine that! Fourteen of those monsters. And the Kaiser's navy, too. Both trying to get the upper hand." The vicar took a breath. "And the comet didn't help, either. It's superstition, of course, but people took it as a bad sign, coming so near the King's death. And now this business with the footpath."

"Speaking of which." Miles drained his cup and put it down. "I don't suppose I could persuade you to go with me to visit Mr. Harmsworth, could I?"

On this, the vicar did not dither. "I would if I thought I might be of service, Miles," he said firmly. "But I doubt that I could make any contribution. I do wish you good luck," he added.

"Thank you," Miles said, and took his leave.

9

The Captain Lays Down the Law

The captain's interview with Mr. Harmsworth did not, I am sorry to say, conclude very satisfactorily, at least from the captain's point of view. Mr. Harmsworth, I believe, thought differently of it. By the time it was ended, in fact, he probably felt he had come out the winner.

Applebeck House was a traditional seventeenth-century farmhouse with thick, gray roughcast walls and a blue slate roof. It sat against a low hill overlooking the large apple orchard, while not far from the back garden, a small stream—Apple Beck—rippled between green banks overhung with willows, its waters sparkling gaily in the midday sunshine. It didn't seem deep enough, Miles thought, for a drowning. But perhaps the child had fallen into the water and hit her head on a rock. Accidents like that happened too often. He glanced up at the window at the gable end of the house. Was that where the mother had sat, year after year, leaning on the windowsill, staring out at the place where her daughter had died? No wonder the poor woman went mad.

Miles knocked several times, and then resorted to shouting, "Is anybody at home?" The door was opened at last by a slender, pale young girl of thirteen or fourteen. Her yellow hair was parted in the middle and plaited in two thick braids. She wore a plain dress of dark gray stuff, a dirty white apron, and clogs that seemed a size too large for her. Miles thought that she looked frightened, as if she were not accustomed to strangers coming to the house.

Saying as little as possible, the girl directed him out to the barn, where he found Adam Harmsworth bent over the broken wooden shaft on a farm cart. He was a thickset, swarthy man with a heavy black beard, broad shoulders, and muscled forearms. He dropped his wooden maul and scowled as the captain greeted him. The two had met only once, when the captain had ruled against him in a dispute over a horse. Neither had forgotten.

"Why've thi come?" Harmsworth growled, his face and neck reddening.

"I'm sure you know," the captain said mildly.

" 'Tis about t' footpath, ain't it?"

"Exactly. I have had a preliminary look into the history of the Applebeck Footpath, Mr. Harmsworth. Parish records show that it has been in continuous public use since before the first trees were planted in the orchard over a hundred years ago. You yourself have permitted its use every day during the ten years you have owned this property. I should therefore like to request that you take down the barricades and—"

"I ain't takin' down those barr'cades," Harmsworth said flatly. He bent over and picked up a long, narrow piece of wood meant to serve as a shaft, and brandished it. "Just last week, t' haystack was burnt down to t' ground by trespass-ers in t' orchard. If they'd stay on t' path and behave like decent folk, that 'ud be one thing, an' I'd leave 'em to it. But they left t' path an' put a match to me haystack. T' constable sez he doan't have a clue as to who dunnit." He flailed the air with the shaft as if he were fending off drag-ons. "Well, I know who dunnit, I do. 'Twas Major Ragsdale an' his rabble o' Ramblers."

"If you have evidence—" the captain began, but was cut off.

"I doan't need no evvy-dence!" Mr. Harmsworth cried, dancing an irate jig. "What I need is for Ragsdale an' his gang to be locked up in gaol for burnin' me haystack. Why ain't they, I wants to know! Why?"

Now, if you suspect that Mr. Harmsworth is a man of limited aptitudes (and perhaps even a little comic in his enthusiasms), I must caution you. His schooling ended early, he reads little beyond an occasional newspaper, and his imagination is confined to what is in front of him. But he is clever with his hands, he understands the needs of his farm and orchard, and he has a very strong sense of the rightness of his cause. He must not be underestimated.

Not liking the wild way Mr. Harmsworth was swinging the shaft, the captain stepped back. "I appreciate your con-cern," he said in a conciliatory tone. "The burning of a hay-stack is a serious crime, and it is regrettable that the constable has not yet been able to identify the culprit." He thought briefly of old Thomas Beecham and wondered if it would be a good idea to interview him again—himself. Beecham was really the most likely suspect, in spite of what Harmsworth said.

"I've stopped up t' path an' it stays stopped until Rags-dale an' his mob are in gaol," Mr. Harmsworth snarled.

"An' even then I may not feel like unstoppin' it. Folks can just go round by t' road. Won't hurt 'em to walk a few steps farther. Ol' Bertha Stubbs can walk off some of her fat." He straightened. "Now, I'll thank thi to get out of my barn, Cap'n Woodcock. There is nae more to be said. Be off."

Mr. Harmsworth might be full of bluster, but behind his rant the captain heard a dangerous menace. It was time to lay down the law.

"There is certainly more to be said," he replied firmly. "And more to be done. You cannot take the law into your own hands, Mr. Harmsworth. It would be in your own interest and in the best interest of the community if you would remove the barrier."

Mr. Harmsworth thrust out his chin defiantly. "And if I doan't?"

"Then you can expect trespassers," the captain said regretfully. "Sooner, rather than later, I should expect. The constable will be here to maintain order, but—"

"Trespassers," snorted Mr. Harmsworth contemptuously. "That 'ud be Ragsdale's hooligans, I'd reckon." He narrowed his eyes. "They 'ud love to try an' take down me blockade, they would."

"The constable will be here to maintain order and make any necessary arrests," the captain said stiffly. "When the case comes before me, as justice of the peace, I will review the matter and make a ruling." He paused. "I am giving you fair warning, Mr. Harmsworth. As things stand now, and unless you can show cause to the contrary, I am inclined to reopen the path."

Mr. Harmsworth spit on the ground. "And I'm givin' thi fair warnin', Mr. Captain Justice of t' Peace Woodcock, *sir*." He raised his fist. "If anybody comes onto me land to take down me fence, he'd better come ready fer trouble. I was a keeper onct, and t' son of a keeper, and I've got m'self a good shotgun. I knows how to use it, too. So if tha values thi health, keep off. An' that goes for t' constable, too."

Captain Woodcock frowned. A former military man himself, with more experience of war than he liked to remember, he hated it when someone threatened to take up arms against other men. But he only said, coolly, "You're attempting to intimidate a representative of the Crown?"

"I sart'nly am." Mr. Harmsworth smiled with grim satisfaction. "An' it gives me a great deal o' pleasure to do it, that it does." He picked up his wooden maul in one huge fist and the board in the other. "Be off!"

The captain left, shaking his head at the stubbornness of the man and wishing that the whole matter would simply evaporate.

Adam Harmsworth, quite satisfied that he had won this battle, if not the war, went back to his work on the farm cart.

Neither man noticed the slender girl in the dark gray dress who had crept to the back of the barn and stood there, her ear pressed against a crack in the wooden boards, listening, her eyes widening and her breath coming faster at the mention of the gun. And when the captain left, she followed him a little way, keeping to the shadow of the shrubbery, but keeping close, as if she might be hoping to catch him up.

The captain was walking with angry strides, and she had to run. She was nearly within reach of him by the time he came to the dooryard gate and was opening her mouth to call out to him. From our vantage point, watching beside the path, I can't help but wonder. What would have happened had she spoken, had he turned, had they talked?

Would she have told him something that would have

kept everyone from being involved in actions they could not resist but would inevitably come to regret?

Does she know anything that might keep a gun from being fired, and someone from being hurt—or even possibly killed?

And most important, what sort of courage is required for a girl so young to step forward and speak to a stranger— to a justice of the peace, an official representative of the Crown, the symbol of law and order in the land? Does she have it in her? If not now, will she be able to find it?

These questions certainly deserve an answer, but I'm sorry to tell you that we're not going to hear it—at least, not at the moment. But stories are often like this, aren't they? The entire outcome of a tale can hang on a single word, spoken or withheld. And life—well, it's just the same. One movement, one smile, one shake of the head—a very small thing can change the course of an event, or a nation, or history, or what have you, in a very large way.

And that is exactly what happened at this moment. For just as the girl was stepping forward to call out to the captain to please stop, she was prevented by the sound of a window flung open and a shrill, strident voice shouting: "Gilly! Stop that hangin' about like a gawky goose! Whyn't tha in here moppin' t' floor, like tha'rt told?"

If the captain heard the woman's shout, he did not give a sign. Perhaps he was too occupied with his angry thoughts to hear anything else but the words in his head—what he should have said to Mr. Harmsworth, what he was going to say the next chance he got, and so forth. I'm sure you can imagine all that he was thinking, for it's very much the same thing we've all thought after we've been in a heated argument with someone and find ourselves thoroughly out of temper.

But the girl heard. She bit her lip angrily, narrowed her eyes, and with dragging feet, went into the house.

And whatever she was going to say went unsaid—at this moment, at least, which I think is a great pity. It's clear that Gilly has something on her mind and wants very badly to talk to someone. It's too bad she isn't able to talk to Captain Woodcock.

10

At Applebeck Farm

If you don't mind, let's follow the girl into the house. Gilly Harmsworth is an important character in our story, and I think it's time we got acquainted with her, and with her uncle and aunt as well. What we know so far is only what we have heard from Margaret Nash, who had the girl as a student. Gilly is an orphan, Miss Nash said, and hopes to find another place to work—and presumably, to live—away from Applebeck Farm.

It's not hard to think why she wants to get away. The old farmhouse, while it may once have been a comfortable home to a loving family, is not that kind of house now. Sadly neglected, it is in dire need of painting, the windows require repair (one pane is broken, another is mended with cardboard), and the cracked roof slates and chimney caps should be replaced. I subscribe to the belief that the exterior of a house tells us much about the condition of life within, so I don't hold out high hope for the Harmsworths.

The inside is just as dark and gloomy and forbidding as the outside. A meager coal fire burns in the stone fireplace, under an iron kettle half-filled with potato-and-mutton soup, the main course for today's dinner. The blue slate floor is bare of rugs or carpets, the wallpapered walls are dingy and smoke-stained, and the furniture—awkwardly placed and either too large or too small to fit comfortably into the room—looks as if it would like to run away somewhere and hide. There is a scrap of curtain at the window to filter the western sun, but no pictures on the walls nor pretty china on the shelves, no vases of flowers nor pieces of framed fancywork nor polished brasses. There are no books except for the Bible—no, that's wrong, for there is one other, although it is hidden away. *The Tale of Jemima Puddle-duck*, by Miss Beatrix Potter, which Gilly won in the school spelling contest, is a dearly loved possession, almost as dear as the photograph of her mother and brother, in a tarnished silver frame beside her bed. But she has never told her uncle or aunt about Miss Potter's book, fearing it might be taken away from her. So she keeps it under the straw pallet that serves as her mattress.

The stairs are steep, narrow, and uncarpeted. Upstairs are two bedrooms, each with a single window: Mr. Harmsworth sleeps in one room, Mrs. Harmsworth in the other. On the upstairs landing is a wooden ladder to the attic, where Gilly sleeps, in the narrow room, scarcely wider than her narrow cot, that was once occupied by the unfortunate madwoman, locked away by her husband. I doubt if Gilly knows about that poor mother, or about the child who drowned. If the Harmsworths know, they wouldn't likely have told her. And if she wonders who carved the desperate words in the wooden windowsill or drew the ugly pictures on the wall of her tiny attic room, she hasn't asked.

But you and I, looking at those words and drawings, might very well understand why the villagers believe that Applebeck Orchard is haunted, if not by unquiet spirits, then by failed dreams, sad recriminations, and a despairing sense of loss. But the ghost itself must be real, for a great many people have seen it, including Gilly. She doesn't always go to sleep when she is bid to bed, you see. On nights when the moon is bright, she reads her book beside her casement window, or simply looks out and marvels at the moon turning the orchard to a shimmering silver.

So whenever Gilly sees the ghostly figure in a black bonnet and long gray cloak drift out of the willows along the beck and move gracefully, almost floating along the footpath, carrying an old-fashioned candle lantern, she is less afraid than intrigued, feeling that the spirit is as much a part of the orchard as the moon and the silvery trees. She watches the figure—a woman, surely—as it becomes completely transparent, then takes form again, and at last fades formlessly, silently into the rising mist, like a waking dream. Gilly imagines that there is a certain sadness about her—the Gray Lady, she calls her—and loneliness. Yes, loneliness and deep regret, as if she is searching for a thing she has lost and still dearly loves. Once, when the Gray Lady raised her bent head and looked straight up at the window where Gilly crouched, she fancied that she glimpsed a faint, wistful smile in the shadow of the bonnet. And when one black-mitted hand was raised in a gesture of greeting, Gilly raised her own in return, as though there were a bond between herself—the lonely child alone in the attic—and the lonely creature in the gray cloak.

Perhaps Gilly is not afraid because she knows, she can feel, that the Gray Lady means her no harm. Or perhaps she is not afraid because she is a self-contained young person who watches and observes and keeps her feelings hidden deep within herself. She finds herself angry much of the time— can you blame her?—but she is not one who is easily frightened, even by a ghost she can see through, like a will-o'-the-wisp. (Some grownups may scoff at the idea of ghosts and fairies and dragons and suchlike, but I confess that I am not one of them, especially when it comes to the Land Between the Lakes, which is an undeniably magical place. Here, almost anything can happen, and generally does. Ghosts that you can see through are not out of the question.)

And whether Gilly knows that the Gray Lady once lived in her attic room makes no difference at all, for what Gilly knows or doesn't know about the Applebeck past has nothing to do with her present life there. Her mother died when she was four. She lived with her father and younger brother in Liverpool. When her father died, her brother went to live with their mother's sister on a small farm in the Midlands, and Gilly was sent to live with her father's brother and his wife at Applebeck Farm.

Mr. Harmsworth would have preferred to have taken her brother, of course—boys are always at a premium on farms—but he was only eleven and sickly. Upon inspection, Gilly proved to be both strong and tall, and Mr. Harmsworth decided that she could probably do the work as well as an ailing boy, who (he said) might take it into his head to die at any moment. He was right. The boy died of consumption not long after he went to live with his aunt, whereupon Mr. Harmsworth congratulated himself (in Gilly's hearing) upon his astute judgment. I am sure you can understand Gilly's bitterness when she heard this callous remark, for she loved her brother very much.

The work, of course, was Mr. Harmsworth's chief consideration in all of this, since neither he nor Mrs. Harmsworth was inclined to give a home to a homeless child out of the goodness of their hearts. No, indeed. The girl should have to work for her living, like the rest of the world. The Harmsworths did not even mean her to finish school, but changed their minds when Miss Nash called at the house and made it clear that the school officials expected all children in the district to complete their educations. When the term was done, that was the end of that.

So, like most girls and boys in England at this time (and in America, too, for that matter), Gilly went to work. And very hard work it was—or at least, we would think so. In fact, we might find this kind of life very hard to imagine, since our own boys and girls are asked, at the most, to clean their rooms and keep their toys picked up. Gilly got up before dawn and milked the three Applebeck cows while it was still dark outside, then did the breakfast washing-up, made beds, swept the floors, and dusted. After that came the work of the day, overseen by Mrs. Harmsworth: washing on Monday, ironing on Tuesday, mending on Wednesday, marketing on Thursday, cleaning on Friday, and baking on Saturday. The Harmsworths were chapel and observed a strict Sabbath on Sunday, which meant that there was no reading (unless it was the Bible) nor amusements of any kind. But while meals were eaten cold, the milking and washing-up still had to be done.

In addition to her household duties, Gilly was also expected to work in Applebeck's separate buttery, a stone building with a wooden roof, where much of the household's work—baking, washing, pickling, churning, and cheesemaking—went on. This was also where the great oak casks were kept, holding oatmeal and barley. There was a stack of wooden buckets and a cheese press, too, and cheese-rims and shelves full of cheeses, and a large wooden up-and-down butter churn (old-fashioned by this time and replaced in most households by the box churn and oval churn, but still in use at Applebeck). It was Gilly's job to milk the cows, separate the milk from the cream by pouring it into flat pans and skimming off the cream that rose to the top, then churn the cream into butter, and make the cheeses.

In her spare hours (they must have been few!), she was sent to work in the garden—by itself, a demanding job, since all the potatoes, cabbages, beans, and greens that appeared on the table were grown on the farm. Mrs. Harmsworth prepared breakfast, dinner, and tea (like many farm families, the Harmsworths ate their main meal at noon and had a hearty tea, something like what we would call an early supper), but Gilly did the washing-up. Every evening was spent beside the fire, mending, darning, and knitting socks. Bedtime was early, for they were all very tired. (I don't wonder at this, do you?) And since Gilly was not allowed to take a candle to the attic—candles were expensive, and there was always the danger of fire—she could not read her book, except (as I said) on nights when there was a very bright moon.

In our time, children asked to do even a fraction of this work would certainly rebel and go about pouting all the time or threaten outright to run away from home. But it was not the work that made Gilly want to leave Applebeck. No, not at all. Children who lived on farms worked on the farms, and children who lived in factory towns worked in the factories, and both girls and boys grew up expecting to live a life built around work. What's more, Gilly had a special affection for the Applebeck cows, and enjoyed making butter and cheese from their milk, a magical process, or so it seemed. Dairy work, she thought, was a very pleasurable occupation. If she could choose, she would gladly spend all her time at it. No, it was not the work that troubled her, but the people she worked for, of whom I will have more to say a page or two further on.

As I write this, I find myself feeling very sorry that our story must include Gilly's unhappy circumstances at Applebeck Farm. I would find it far more pleasant to write (and you to read, I am sure) about cheerful Deirdre Malone at Courier Cottage, who has just been promoted to help Mr. Sutton manage the accounts in his veterinary practice. Or about Caroline Longford, Lady Longford's granddaughter, who has almost no work to do at Tidmarsh Manor, and should (one might think) be the most cheerful of these three young women. But Caroline is not, as we shall see shortly, for she has immodest ambitions and her life seems strewn with insurmountable challenges. In sum, I believe that Margaret Nash—who is herself not the happiest of women—can be forgiven for her suspicion that most women of her time, no matter their social class, were destined to be unhappy.

Mrs. Ernestina Harmsworth of Applebeck Farm was certainly amongst the unhappy ones. Born Ernestina Westgate, daughter of a penniless country parson, she had met and married Mr. Harmsworth (on very short acquaintance) just two years before, in the city of Manchester where she was working and Mr. Harmsworth had taken his apples to sell. She was already a spinster when Mr. Harmsworth came into her life, for reasons having mostly to do with her own lack of physical attractions (she was gaunt and bony, with a great beak of a nose and thinning hair eked out with hairpieces fore and aft) and a certain selectivity where men were concerned.

It is perhaps ironic that, after exercising such particular care in the choice of a husband, Miss Westgate should so passionately fasten her affections on Mr. Harmsworth, who was neither wealthy nor handsome nor learned nor a gifted conversationalist. But he may have presented himself somewhat differently to her than he has to us. And when we are in love (or think we are), we often see the object of our desire through rose-colored glasses.

I am not at all sure that it was love, however, that led Miss Westgate to agree to become Mrs. Harmsworth. Perhaps I am being overly mistrustful of the lady's motives, but I rather suspect that the greater attraction was the prospect of leaving the haberdashery where she was employed as a shopgirl and moving to her very own home, where she would be in full charge of her very own household, which at the time of the proposal included a young maid-of-all-work named Prunie and a dairymaid named Fancy. (Miss Westgate had never enjoyed working in that haberdashery, and in any event would have had to find a new place, because the shop burned, together with the whole block of adjacent shops, the day she gave notice. Miss Westgate had watched the enormous conflagration from a distance, and had felt quite satisfied at the sight.) A great many marriages have been made for reasons other than love, however: marriage for financial gain, for social status, for security, for comfort. If Miss Westgate had other motives, they were her business entirely, and I for one will not criticize. I am sure that you would not want anyone second-guessing your decision to marry.

But whatever Miss Westgate's motives, they may not have served Mrs. Harmsworth well. When she agreed to marry Mr. Harmsworth, you see, she had the idea that she was coming to a better situation—taking a step up, as she put it to herself. This is not to say that Mr. Harmsworth intentionally deceived her, but rather that she deceived herself, hearing only what she wanted to hear about the farm he owned and the tiny village where it was situated. As a result, Miss Westgate had developed a rather romantic notion of the place, imagining it to be much grander, more substantial, and more inviting than Mrs. Harmsworth found it to be.

By the time of our story, I am sorry to report, her heart was filled with a bitter disappointment, for she had come to recognize Applebeck for what it was: a bleak, neglected, and unhappy Lakeland house attached to a poor garden, an old orchard (from which Mr. Harmsworth made just enough money to live on), and pasture enough for only three thin cows. In fact, when she first arrived, the new Mrs. Harmsworth was sorely tempted to pack up her things and return to Manchester forthwith—although that (for reasons known only to herself) did not seem like a very good idea. She had been further deterred by the fact that she had not a penny of her own, not even enough to buy a train ticket. And of course, there had been nothing to return to. The haberdashery was gone, the room she had lived in was let, and she would have to look for a new place and somewhere to live—all on no money.

This was indeed a dark moment, but things were about to get darker. Mr. Harmsworth had not chosen his new wife for her beauty or her dowry, or because he had fallen desperately in love with her. His motives were much simpler than that, and he made no effort to disguise them. He had watched Miss Westgate at her work and felt that she was a strong and capable woman. And because she expressed such a firm interest in his apple business, he had got the notion that she would willingly join him in his efforts to make a success of Applebeck. I think you can see that there was more than a little self-deception on both sides.

At any rate, when the newly married Mrs. Harmsworth arrived at Applebeck, she discovered that her husband had discharged both the maid-of-all-work and the dairymaid and had used their wages to buy a cider press. You can imagine the effect of this decision on Mrs. Harmsworth, who was not consulted. Any illusions about her new husband were quickly dispelled, and Mrs. Harmsworth realized that Mr. Harmsworth was every bit as bleak and unhappy as his house.

Mrs. Harmsworth was not of a cheerful nature to start with, and these experiences only embittered her further. It was not long, then, before she began taking matters into her own hands. She blamed her husband for her present circumstances and took pleasure in finding little ways to get even with him, such as pouring out a quart of good milk or loosening the bung on an apple cider keg or smashing a nest of eggs. She wrung every penny she could from the inadequate household allowance that her husband gave her (which no doubt accounts for the perennial shortage of candles, matches, sugar, and tea at Applebeck Farm). She even pilfered his pocketbook from time to time, especially after he'd just got back from the pub and was in no condition to recall how much he had spent. She tied this hoard of money into a blue kerchief and hid it under a floorboard in her bedroom upstairs, thinking ahead to the day when she would have enough to go somewhere—to Liverpool, perhaps, since it wasn't a good idea to go back to Manchester—and set herself up in business as a seamstress. It wasn't that she was particularly skilled in needlework, or that she had any very practical plan for her future. It was just that she needed to imagine herself doing something, anything, other than living at Applebeck.

Things became a little more comfortable for Mrs.

Harmsworth when Gilly arrived and was given many of the housekeeping tasks. She kept a sharp eye on the girl and a sharp tongue, too, with a shrill, "Gilly, do this," and "Gilly, do that," and "Hurry up, Gilly!" every few moments. And on the occasions when Gilly did not move smartly enough or did not follow her orders exactly, Mrs. Harmsworth would give her a lash or two with a small riding crop she kept for this purpose. Perhaps the mistress thought she was doing her duty by minding the servant. But I think it more likely that she was merely taking out her frustrations on someone who was lower in the Applebeck pecking order than herself.

Unfortunately, having Gilly to order about did nothing to ease Mrs. Harmsworth's resentments against her husband. In fact, her anger had become volcanic, constantly steaming away under the surface, sometimes erupting violently, lava-like. She had stopped speaking to her husband, glowered at him across the table, banged the dishes and plates whenever he was in the room, and flew into frequent fierce rages. And since Mr. Harmsworth paid no attention at all to his wife, it was easy for Mrs. Harmsworth to turn her wrath on Gilly, who had learnt to duck when the crockery came whizzing through the air.

Mr. Harmsworth, for his part, did not notice whether Mrs. Harmsworth loved him or hated him. If he was disappointed in his wife's refusal to join in his efforts to make the apple business pay, he didn't reveal it. He was the same stolid, unmoving creature from one day to the next, keeping his eyes on his work, speaking only to give an order or complain that something was not done right. In all the months Gilly had lived there, she had seen him aroused to excitement only once. That was the night the haystack burnt, when he had rushed out across the field with a bucket to put it out, which was of course very silly, for by that time the fire was roaring away, and nothing but the heaviest downpour of rain could have doused it, and perhaps not even that.

After that night, he lapsed back into his usual gloomy silence, although Gilly could sense a simmering anger inside him, as if the fire that had burnt the haystack had somehow gotten inside the man and could not be put out. She was not surprised when he put up the barricades, or when he threatened Captain Woodcock with his shotgun. She would not be at all surprised if he fired it, either, and the idea frightened her nearly to death—which, I suppose (although I don't know for certain), is the reason she wanted to talk to the captain.

I think you will agree that the situation at Applebeck Farm must have been a terribly unpleasant one. For Gilly, it was intolerable, and her resentment was growing by the day. What's more, she suspected that her uncle intended to keep her working at Applebeck for as long as he could—for her whole life, if she did nothing to keep that from happening. After all, he was getting a very good bargain. He paid her nothing, not even the few pence a day she had asked for. She ought to be glad, he said, that someone had been willing to take her in, so that she didn't have to go to the parish poorhouse—that was payment enough, by itself. And he was doing his duty just by providing her with clothing, a bed, and food. Why, he had even allowed her to finish school. She should be grateful for that!

In the circumstance, it is no wonder that Gilly thought of running away. But she was a practical girl, and knew that unless she could get her hands on enough money to tide her over, she might find herself in an even worse situation. Or she could take out her resentment (which was every bit as fierce as Mrs. Harmsworth's) by some other means. Embittered servants often engaged in criminal acts, like the young woman who stole a large sum of money from the wealthy lady who employed her and went off to Paris to live on the Rue d'Artistes. Or the odd-job boy who was convicted of setting fire to his master's barn and stealing his master's silver whilst everyone was engaged in fighting the fire.

So now you know what is going on at Applebeck Farm, with Mr. and Mrs. Harmsworth, and with Gilly, and why Gilly is so anxious to find somewhere else to live and work.

But when we followed Gilly into the house, the captain went off up the hill. I don't think we should let him get too far away before we catch up to him.

11

The Captain and the Major
Make a Plan

After Captain Woodcock left Applebeck Farm, he walked up the hill and down the road, striding fast, staring straight ahead, scarcely paying attention to where he was going. But while he was angry (as much at himself for having lost his temper as at the man who had provoked him), he had not lost his ability to focus on the problem and formulate a plan. And when he calmed himself enough to look up and take a breath, he saw that he had arrived at the very place he had meant to visit next: Teapot Cottage, the tiniest dwelling in the village.

Teapot very much resembled a cozy Cotswold stone-built cottage, but with slate rather than thatch for the roof, and was screened from the lane by a virtual forest of hawthorn. Inside, this miniature hideaway was blessed with all the hand-hewn beams, secret crannies, and odd little inglenooks that any Romantic's heart might desire. And outside—well, there was Major Roger Ragsdale in his garden, the sleeves of his shirt rolled to the elbow, his collar open. He was hoeing the soft earth around his cabbages, which were aligned with military precision in the straightest of straight rows. The garden was small, like the cottage, but the major's cabbages were amongst the largest in the district, and sweet and juicy as well. They always took top honors at the Harvest Festival held in Far Sawrey in late September. They had better, if they knew what was good for them.

The captain stopped beside the green-painted gate through the neatly trimmed hedge. "Good day, Ragsdale," he called, not quite sure whether it was morning or afternoon and not wanting to pull out his watch to see.

"Ah, Woodcock," returned Major Ragsdale, looking up. He was a short, slender, and very brisk man with a military manner and a neatly trimmed pencil mustache. He spoke in clipped, military tones. "I say there, old chap, you've come along just at the right moment. Hoeing cabbages is hungry work. I was thinking of going in and having a bite of sandwich. Would you care to join me?"

Which is why we find Captain Woodcock taking off his tweed jacket and hanging it on the chair in the tiny kitchen of Teapot Cottage, where Major Roger Ragsdale (Ret.) lived all by himself. It was a good thing he did, too, for there wouldn't have been room for a Mrs. Ragsdale, or anything larger than a cat. (And a cat would certainly have served, for the cottage was plagued by a gang of mice which had grown rather too familiar with Major Ragsdale's larder.) The cottage was called Teapot because its tiny sitting room had once served as a tiny tearoom, operated by a very tiny and very old lady who always wore a mobcap and a black dress with a lace fichu. She served crumpets and scones and tea to weary day-trippers who were glad of a bite and a sip, even if they had to practically sit on one another's laps to get it.

"I've come on an errand, actually," the captain said, sitting down at the narrow table, which was wedged between the wall and the door with barely room for a pair of chairs. He watched Major Ragsdale cut precise slices from a loaf of fresh-baked bread and cover them with exactly sliced cold beef and mustard, rings of silver onions arranged carefully on top. "It has to do with the Applebeck Footpath, as you might have guessed."

"Ah," said Ragsdale. "Right ho. Yes, I did guess, I must say." He pursed his lips and pulled his neat black brows together. The effect may have seemed rather comic, but you would not want to laugh at Major Ragsdale, who had served with distinction in the Boer War and had been with Baden-Powell at the Siege of Mafeking.

"I understand that you're planning something," the captain said.

"Ah, you've heard about our march, then." The major beamed. "Capital response from the Ramblers, capital, Woodcock. Exactly what I would have expected of the chaps, eh, what?"

He gestured toward a wall hung with framed photographs of men dressed for a climb in the Alps: tweed knickers, stout boots, woolen socks, and felt hats, leather kit bags slung over their shoulders. The photos showed them climbing steep fells, negotiating narrow tracks, and happily posing in front of pubs, tankards in one hand, walking sticks in the other. Above the display was a large framed photograph of Major General Baden-Powell, in full regimental dress.

"Look at them, Woodcock," the major said fondly. "Like the finest British soldiers, these men. Always up for a stirring challenge, in war and in peace. Superb lot. Superb. Baden-Powell would be proud of them." He topped both sandwiches with a crisp spear of pickle and poured them each a cup of strong, hot tea.

"I have heard about your march," the captain agreed— rather diffidently, since the major outranked him. But they had both left the Army some time ago, he reminded himself, so the matter of rank (a habit that was hard to break) was neither here nor there. He squared his shoulders. "I have heard," he repeated, more firmly. "And I am asking you to call it off."

"Call it off?" Chuckling, Ragsdale pulled out his chair and sat down. "Sorry, Captain. Not for anybody's money. The march is on for eleven hundred hours tomorrow. Seventeen Ramblers have pledged to attend. Tonight, we're to meet at Tom Patchett's house to make placards and signs. Mrs. Patchett and several ladies have volunteered to paint a banner, bless 'em." He picked up his sandwich in both hands. "And I have arranged for a reporter to be here, from the—"

"There'll be no march, Major Ragsdale," interrupted the captain, very firmly. "By eleven hundred hours, you will be in the custody of Constable Braithwaite, charged with attempted trespass."

The major stared. "Trespass!"

"Trespass," the captain replied.

The major put down his sandwich. He tilted his head, narrowing his eyes and studying the captain as if he was not sure that he had heard the word correctly. "By Jove, Woodcock," he said at last. "I do believe you're serious."

"I am."

"But an arrest won't— That is to say, it isn't the thing to—"

"It is the very thing," the captain said, now with great firmness. "I want you at the north end of the footpath at nine in the morning, Major. The constable and I will meet you there. You will attempt to take down the barricade—"

The major shook his head. "It'll take more than one man to pull down Harmsworth's barricade. I've had a close look. Bloody stout, it is. Built like the barriers Baden-Powell laid down before Mafeking to foil the Boer attack—wire, wood, tar, the lot."

"I didn't say—" the captain began.

"Won't do, Woodcock," the major said authoritatively. "One man won't do. You want that barricade down, you want my chaps, that's who you want. All I have to do is say the word, and they'll have it away in a tick. And then they'll march down the path to the south end and pull that one down, as well. The thoroughfare is reopened, the village restored to order." He smiled. "The unpleasantness is over and done with in a hurry, old man. Right ho. Chop-chop." He picked up his sandwich again.

"I didn't say you would take it down," the captain explained patiently. "I said you would attempt to take it down. It comes to the same thing, in the eyes of the law, you see, but without the bother. You make the attempt— no more than putting out your hand and shaking a bit of wire. The constable arrests you. No unpleasantness, no exertion. The whole business is over in a jiffy, and all very simple. No marches, no songs, no protest." He paused for emphasis. "And no journalists."

"Nonsense. Never been arrested before, never will be arrested. I will not submit to arrest for any reason. Looks bad on the record. If you want those barricades down, you want my men. Got it?" He added, with significance, "Captain."

The captain sighed. "I appreciate your point, Major. But it really is a simple—"

"An arrest on one's record is not simple," the major said with great firmness.

"It won't be on your record." The captain leaned forward. "Look, Ragsdale. I've had a quick look into the history of that footpath. I'm going a bit out of bounds here to tell you this, of course. But it's very likely—in fact, I believe that I can promise to dismiss the attempted trespass charges against you and order Harmsworth to reopen the path. Of course, I'll hear whatever evidence the fellow pleases to offer, but at the present time, I see no merit in his case. None at all."

"Dismiss the charges?" The major frowned. "Nothing on the record? And the barricade will come down?"

The captain took a deep breath, feeling that he had gone farther out than he liked on a very thin limb. "You have my word, Ragsdale."

"And what if Harmsworth objects to my 'attempted trespass'? What if he defends his barricade?"

The captain remembered Harmsworth's shotgun, then as quickly dismissed the thought from his mind. "I will be there. The constable will be there."

The major gave him a dark look. "When we Ragsdales put our hand to the plough, we do not readily sheathe the sword, Woodcock. If I am assaulted, I shall return the blow in kind."

"You won't be assaulted," the captain said confidently. He frowned. "One thing we ought to clear up, though. I take it that none of your Ramblers had anything to do with that haystack being burnt."

"Of course not!" Ragsdale exclaimed heatedly. "My men are gentlemen. None of them would do such a cowardly thing. And anyway—"

"And anyway, the haystack being burnt is no defense for

the closing of the footpath. Although that is precisely the reason Harmsworth gives for doing it."

"You've talked to him, then?"

"Before I came here." The captain chuckled darkly. "Not an altogether prepossessing fellow, I should say. Surly."

"Well, then," began the major.

"Well, then," the captain preempted him. "There will be no need for signs or banners, and I will greatly appreciate it if you will tell your Ramblers to keep to home tomorrow. I don't want anyone inciting to riot, on either side. I don't even want Harmsworth on the scene, if we can help it. So. We shall meet at nine o'clock. You will put your hand on that barricade. Braithwaite will arrest you. I'll take you in custody and the constable can fetch Harmsworth to my house, where we'll hold the hearing. With luck, the whole business will be over and done in a matter of an hour or two. When the reporter arrives, you can tell him that it's all been taken care of."

"Well, then," said the major again. He picked up his sandwich in a gesture of capitulation. "Shall we have our lunch, Captain?"

"Very good," said the captain, feeling that he had accomplished this entire bit of business about as well as it could have been accomplished. He took a bite and chewed appreciatively. "Jolly good," he said. "Splendid sandwich, Major. Simply splendid."

And with that, the two men stopped talking about the campaign they had laid out for the morrow and began talking about the major's cabbages and the captain's plans for a fishing trip to Derwentwater with Mr. Heelis. And in another twenty minutes, lunch over, the captain was on his way home.

We shall follow him for a bit, as he strides, jauntily now,

along the Kendal Road, across the bridge over Wilfin Beck, past Hill Top Farm and the Tower Bank Arms and the village shop, which Miss Potter immortalized in *Ginger and Pickles*. He is swinging his walking stick with a great flourish and whistling tunelessly between his teeth, entirely satisfied with his plan for tomorrow's trespass. Law and order, that was the ticket. Devise a strategy, develop a plan, carry it out with good sense and sound judgment, and peace and harmony will be restored in the land. All will be well. All will indeed be well.

Ah, Captain Woodcock, Captain Woodcock. Wouldn't it be nice if everything worked out exactly as we planned? Life would be so simple, and we should all be so very happy.

But of course it doesn't.

And it isn't.

And we aren't.

12

In Which We Hear a Ghost Story

We could ask almost anyone in the village to relate the tale of the ghost of Applebeck Orchard. Agnes Llewellyn and Mathilda Crook mentioned it at the very beginning of our story, and would be delighted to tell us all about it, I'm quite sure. The vicar certainly knows it, at least in outline. And old Dolly Dorking would undoubtedly be glad to serve it up to us with great relish, in eerie detail. In fact, there is nothing the Sawrey villagers like better than a good story, especially when it is told in front of a dancing fire on a cold winter's night, and accompanied by a cup of hot mulled cider.

And ghost stories are the very best stories of all. The tale-teller speaks in a hushed voice that inspires shivers and shakes and half-frightened silences, whilst the conjured spirits lurk, listening, in the dark corners of the room. At last, the fire burns down, the cider is drunk up, and the storyteller and the audience creep off to bed, where they hurriedly say their prayers and pull the covers over their heads very fast, before the fairies or ghosts or trolls can come out of their corners and carry them off.

But when we left The Brockery at the end of Chapter Six, Hyacinth and Bosworth were planning to have a look at the *History*, where the story of the ghost of Applebeck Orchard—together with a great many stories about animal spirits—is recorded. And since badger historians are a great deal more reliable than the villagers (who love to embroider every ghost story with their own particular experiences of ghosts and positively relish a bit of exaggeration here and there), I should rather hear about the Applebeck ghost from the badgers, if you don't mind.

So we will leave Captain Woodcock to enjoy his illusions, walk up Market Street and Stony Lane and across the meadow to Holly How and then up the hill to The Brockery. But we don't have to hurry, because—what with one thing and another—it isn't until nearly teatime that Bosworth Badger and Hyacinth can sit down with the *History* and read the ghost story that Hyacinth discovered buried in its pages.

They had intended to do this right after lunch. But that meal had become rather complicated. Three visitors had come over from their home at Briar Bank: Bailey Badger, his guinea-pig friend Thackeray, and Thorvaald, the young dragon who lived with them. Thorvaald (whose unusual story you can read in *The Tale of Briar Bank*) had been away for several weeks, flying around England to visit a number of his fellow dragons who were assigned to guard ancient hoards of treasure. This was part of a survey Thorvaald was conducting, and he wanted to tell Bosworth all about it so that his research could be recorded in the *History*. He also had an interesting story to relate about a close encounter he had had with a petrol-powered flying boat over Lake Windermere.

"*A flying boat!*" exclaimed Bosworth, wide-eyed and disbelieving. "*A boat that* flies? *Are you sure that's what you saw, Thorvaald? Why, I've never heard of such a thing!*"

If you find it odd to hear a badger marveling to a dragon about a flying boat, I don't suppose I can blame you. However, as I said, almost anything can happen in the Land Between the Lakes, and generally does. And in this case, the flying boat that Thorvaald almost ran into (quite literally, I'm afraid—it was a very near miss) is a real thing, not a fiction invented by me or Thorvaald or anyone else. A certain gentleman had taken it into his head to build a hydroplane factory at Cockshott Point on Lake Windermere, and the local people (as we overheard Mr. Heelis telling Captain Woodcock) were all up in arms about it. This is the flying boat that the dragon saw. And since Bosworth considered that a flying boat was a great deal stranger than a dragon— he was, after all, acquainted with a dragon, but had never seen a flying boat—he was utterly engrossed in the dragon's story, although he was a good deal confused when the dragon happened to mention that the boat had wings and a tail.

Meanwhile, Primrose and Parsley kept Hyacinth busy with the regular after-dinner and housekeeping chores. So it was not until an hour before tea, when the Briar Bank trio had departed for home, that Hyacinth and Bosworth could find a moment to sit down in front of the fire in the library with the *History* open before them and glasses of cold lemonade beside them.

"*This is the story?*" Bosworth asked, turning to the page that Hyacinth had marked.

"That's it, Uncle," Hyacinth said. *"I found the tale enormously intriguing—but then, I'm rather fond of ghost stories. I wonder what you'll think."*

"I think," said Bosworth, leaning back, *"that I should like to hear you read it aloud."* He smiled at the young badger. *"If you don't mind, that is."*

"I'd love to," Hyacinth replied warmly.

And so Bosworth reclined comfortably in his leather chair with his feet on his ottoman, sipping his lemonade and listening as Hyacinth read aloud in her musical voice. And whilst he very much wished that her brother could have been there to share the story with them, he could only be quite happy that *she* was there in Thorn's place and feel very much put out at the owl for making such an enormous to-do over the possibility that a young female might be awarded the Badger Badge of Authority and appointed as the official Badger historian.

Not that Bosworth had fully made up his mind to do this. The question was still under consideration. But the more he considered it, the more confident he became that this was what he ought to do, Owl or no Owl. Of course, he might live for a very long time, happily continuing to carry out his appointed tasks. But if he should die or become incapacitated, Hyacinth—with a little training and encouragement along the proper lines—could certainly take his place. As far as he was concerned, the fact that she was a female was neither here nor there.

Hyacinth (who had no idea that her future was under such serious consideration) took the book, cleared her throat, and began. Should you care to read the story for yourself, you will find it on pages 113 and 114 in Volume 11 of the *History*, to the right of the fireplace in the study, third shelf from the top. The page is dated December 12,

1873, and the record is written in a minuscule hand in a crisp, no-nonsense style. Should you prefer to hear, rather than read, it, I invite you to join Bosworth and me. The leather chair opposite the fireplace is empty and waiting, and I believe there is an extra glass beside the pitcher of lemonade. Would you care for a cool drink?

The Ghost of Applebeck Orchard

In 1837 (the same year that the young queen Victoria ascended to the throne), Applebeck Farm and Orchard were owned by John Fowles. He and his wife, Elizabeth, had one daughter, Hester, who at this time was twelve years old. She was a pretty child with golden hair and blue eyes, the very dearest thing in the world to her mother and father. It was a great tragedy, then, when the child drowned in a willow-fringed pool of Apple Beck. Hester's mourning parents buried her in the churchyard.

Hester's father went back to work in his orchard, tending silently to his trees. But her mother blamed herself for the child's death and grieved violently, spending every day beside the brook where Hester had drowned, scattering wildflowers over the water and carrying on conversations with her daughter. One day she ran to her husband where he was working amongst his apple trees. She was laughing and happy, for she had seen Hester, she said, gathering flowers in the meadow on the other side of Apple Beck. "She's not dead!" she cried. "I know she isn't dead!"

So every morning, the mother would go out into the meadow and search all day long for Hester, and every evening, she would walk through the twilight along the public footpath, carrying a tin candle lantern and calling for the child. There was no stopping her, even on the most inclement of winter nights, when she would put on her black bonnet and wrap herself in a long gray cloak and tramp through the snow with her candle lantern.

John Fowles was distraught. His neighbors, the vicar, and everyone in the village counseled him to put his wife in an asylum, where she could be cared for and perhaps get well. But John loved Elizabeth very much and could not bear to have her sent away from him, especially to such a dreadful place as an asylum for the insane. Instead, he confined her to the house for fear she would injure herself, and when she still managed to make her way out, locked her in the attic. From her window, she could look down on the pool where Hester had drowned. Because he loved her, John took very good care of her, making her meals, ensuring that she had everything she needed or wanted.

But of course, what she wanted was Hester. And so, when Elizabeth died in 1852, she was buried next to her little girl. But that was not the end of her story. Her ghost was seen for the first time the very evening of her burial, dressed in a flowing gray cloak and walking along the Applebeck Footpath, carrying a tin candle lantern and calling out for Hester. The next day, a horse ran away with a carriage and two people were killed on the road. The villagers were sure that the ghost of Elizabeth Fowles was a portent of this misfortune.

And so it may have been, for as time has gone on, the ghost of Applebeck Orchard has appeared before many sad tragedies. She was seen walking along the footpath on the eve of Prince Albert's untimely death of typhoid in December 1861; a day prior to a horrendous train wreck in Wales in which many were killed; the night before a terrible storm took the lives of six fishermen on Lake Windermere; and other similar occasions.

These sightings were reported by respected villagers,

whose word, it would seem, could be trusted. In one case, she was seen by two persons walking together: the owner of the Sawrey Hotel and the village butcher. Sightings were also reported by trusted animals: by a pair of elderly Herdwick ewes at Hill Top Farm, by three rabbits from the warren across the road from Applebeck Orchard, and by the senior badger from the Applebeck badger sett, amongst others. Human sightings cannot be completely verified (and since humans are frequently known to exaggerate and embellish their reports, and even to lie), but the animal sightings are testimony to the true existence of this spirit.

"An entirely satisfactory ghost story," said Bosworth, when Hyacinth had finished reading. *"Sad, of course, but most ghost stories are."*

Hyacinth closed the book with a sigh. *"Yes, sad."* She leaned forward. *"But there's more, Uncle. Fritz the ferret claims to have seen the ghost—at least, he saw a mysterious figure with a lantern, wearing a bonnet and cloak."*

"He's not the only one," replied Bosworth. *"Professor Owl also saw that figure, although he didn't identify it as a ghost. He told me he thought that she—or a male dressed as a female—set the haystack afire, although he didn't actually see her do it."* The badger chuckled. *"He was on his way to dinner at the time, I believe, so he may not have been paying attention."*

"Do you suppose a ghost could cause a fire?" Hyacinth asked doubtfully. *"Perhaps her appearance was simply a portent of the fire."*

"I'm afraid I don't know," Bosworth confessed. *"You might have another talk with the ferret, now that you've read the story."* He paused. *"Have you a moment, Hyacinth? There's something important I would like to discuss with you."*

"Of course," Hyacinth said, putting the *History* on the table. *"What is it, Uncle?"*

Bosworth smiled. An idea had come to him, perhaps the answer to his dilemma. He could name Hyacinth to an interim post as Historian-and-Genealogist-in-Training, with the possibility of accepting the Badger Badge of Authority when the time came—if Thorn had not returned by that time. He and Hyacinth could work together for several hours a day. He could teach her everything he knew about the *History* and the *Genealogy*—everything he would have taught Thorn. And if Thorn came back before he was ready to turn over the Badge, Bosworth felt confident that Hyacinth would willingly, even happily, step aside and let her brother wear it.

Now, I don't know how you see the matter, but if I were Hyacinth, I think I should be offended by this offer, which seems patronizing and condescending. "You can learn to do the work, and you might even have the honor of wearing the Badge—but only if your brother doesn't come back. How's that, my dear girl?" If Bosworth made that proposal to me, I should tell him that he could put it right back into his pocket. But of course, he isn't *my* uncle, and Hyacinth might be more tolerant than I.

But Bosworth did not get the opportunity to offer this dubious honor, at least, not at this moment. The bell rang for tea, and since nobody at The Brockery likes to keep Parsley waiting, he only said, regretfully, *"Well, then, tea. We shall have to take up our discussion later, my dear."*

"Of course," Hyacinth said, in an understanding tone. *"I'll just go and see if I can help lay the tea. I'll tell Parsley you'll be along when you're ready."*

Our badger picked up the *History* and returned it to its place between Volumes 10 and 12 on the third shelf, which is where you should look for it if you decide to read that ghost story for yourself. Then he picked up the empty lemonade glasses and ambled toward the library door, thinking what an amiable companion little Hyacinth had turned out to be and what a pleasure it would be to train her. And if the professor wanted to put up a squawk about it, well, let him.

The owl, important as he might be, was only an owl, after all. It was badgers who hosted the inn and badgers who kept the *History* and the *Genealogy*, and a badger who would make the final decision.

When the time came. Of course, it hadn't, yet.

13

An Unlucky Chapter

I sometimes think the thirteenth chapter ought to be left out of books, just as the thirteenth floor is sometimes left out of hotels, and the thirteenth row is occasionally omitted from theaters, and some hostesses invite twelve or fourteen guests to their dinner parties but never thirteen. But of course, when you are telling a story and there are unhappy or misfortunate or even tragic events to relate, they have to be told, no matter what chapter they are put into. So the fact that it is in Chapter Thirteen that our story takes an unlucky turn does not make that chapter itself unlucky. Nor is Captain Woodcock's plan for the arrest of Major Ragsdale turned topsy-turvy solely because it takes place in Chapter Thirteen. No, that is superstitious foolishness. What happens, happens. And whether the chapter is thirteen or fourteen or some other chapter altogether makes not one bit of difference.

Except that there is no getting around the fact that the

whole affair was entirely unlucky, from start to finish. And if you like to attribute these misfortunes to the fact that they take place in Chapter Thirteen, well, I suppose I can't stop you, can I?

Here is what happened. Since it is rather complicated, I must ask you to pay special attention to the sequence of events.

Miss Potter got out of bed very early in the morning, as she always did when she came to Hill Top Farm, throwing open her window to greet the green meadow and the hill that rose above the house and the sweet blue sky and the wood thrush singing from the highest branch of the tallest apple tree. Except that it was raining—well, misting, with intermittent showers of rain. And if you have ever visited the English Lake District, you know that it is every bit as beautiful, and perhaps even more so, when the sky is pewter-gray and the cool morning mist curls through the trees and hovers over the summer meadows like a blessing.

But Beatrix, whilst she enjoyed the mist almost as much as she loved the sun, had things to do and did not like to do them in the rain. She dressed in the blouse and skirt she had worn on her arrival, pinned up her hair, and break-fasted, then made a quick tour of inspection through the barn, the barn lot, and the garden. She paused to say good morning to Kitchen, the Galway cow; Blossom, Kitchen's calf; Winston, the husky farm pony; Aunt Susan and Dor-cas, the fat Berkshire pigs who lived to eat; Mustard, the old yellow dog; and Kep the collie, her favorite of the farm dogs. The chickens (Mrs. Boots, Mrs. Bonnet, and Mrs. Shawl) were too busy teaching their chicks to look for bugs amongst the rhubarb to say hello, and the Puddle-ducks had already gone to Esthwaite Water for their morning swim. But the Herdwick sheep, Tibbie and Queenie and their sisters and all the spring lambs (now very handsome in their summer fleeces), bleated a greeting to Miss Potter from the rocky hill above the farm, for they were very glad that she had come home. And the lettuces and marrows and runner beans all looked lush and happy in the garden, and very pleased indeed to wake up and find their leaves all wet.

Having assured herself that all was well in her small farming world, Beatrix knocked at the Jenningses' door and asked Mr. Jennings if he would be so kind as to fetch Winston and hitch him to the pony cart (freshly painted red just the week before) so she could drive out. She found that Mr. Jennings was not in a very pleasant mood, because the rain had come on the day that he planned to finish the haying, and all farmers know that wet hay is not a good thing. But he went out to find Winston and she went back to her own part of the house to put on her mackintosh and rain hat and collect the baby bunnies—Peaches and Cream— she had brought with her. She glanced up at the tall clock with the painted face, which showed that it was fifteen minutes before nine, early for a morning visit, but Beatrix had several things to do that day, and she wanted to get an early start.

What's that you say? I haven't mentioned the bunnies until now? Oh, dear. Well, you're right. You see, Peaches and Cream (two small white bunnies with pink eyes and see-through ears) were in that wicker hamper that Beatrix carried across Lake Windermere. They have not yet figured in our narrative, so I suppose I just forgot about them. It's hard to keep track of every single detail when you're telling a story.

But these bunnies, small and innocent as they are, are about to become important, for they are the reason that Beatrix is preparing to go out at such an early hour on a drizzly morning. They are promised to Dimity Kittredge's two children, who are nearly old enough to have the care of pets, especially when they are supervised by Emily, their nanny. Once the bunnies have been delivered to Flora and baby Miles at Raven Hall, Beatrix plans to drive up Cuckoo Brow Lane to Tidmarsh Manor to call on Lady Longford and have a conversation about—well, you know. Beatrix feels she ought to get a start on the assignment she accepted the day before from Miss Nash.

And that is why we find Beatrix Potter, dressed for rain, carrying her wicker hamper and her umbrella out to the pony cart, where Winston is waiting. He has company, too, for Rascal (the fawn-colored Jack Russell terrier we met earlier in our story) had been calling on Mustard and Kep when Mr. Jennings came out to fetch the pony and had decided he wanted to go wherever Miss Potter was going.

"*Good morning, Miss Potter!*" Rascal barked, jumping with stiff-legged joy at the sight of his favorite person.

"Why, it's Rascal!" Beatrix exclaimed, latching the hamper firmly and stowing it safely under the seat. "How very nice to see you." She smiled down at the little dog. "Would you like to go with us? Winston and I are driving to Raven Hall, and then on to Tidmarsh Manor. We'll likely be back before lunchtime." She looked up at the sky. "Of course, since it's raining, you might want to stay here and stay dry."

"*Oh, but it's not raining that hard!*" Rascal exclaimed. "*Who cares about a little bit of wet?*" He leapt onto the seat in the cart. "*Of course I want to go. I was hoping you'd ask, Miss Potter.*"

Alarmed, Winston looked back over his shoulder. *"Raven Hall?"* He shook his brown mane, whinnying loudly. *"Naaay! Isn't there somewhere else you would like to go, Miss Potter?"*

Beatrix climbed into the cart and took up the reins, clucking to the pony. "Winston is never happy about taking me to Raven Hall," she confided to Rascal. "That hill is rather steep, you know." She raised her voice. "But our Winston is certainly the strongest pony in the village, so I'm sure he'll be able to manage the hill without any difficulty at all. And I've some fresh carrots in my pocket that he can munch on when we get there."

At this, Winston pricked his ears. It is always pleasing to hear that one is the strongest pony in the village. And fresh carrots to munch on—well, perhaps that hill isn't so terribly steep, after all. So he picked up his neat little hoofs, leaned into his harness, and trotted forward with a right good will, down the lane toward the Kendal Road.

And that is how Miss Potter, in the company of Winston and Rascal, came to be crossing the bridge over Wilfin Beck a few minutes after nine on a misty, drizzly morning, right in the middle of Chapter Thirteen.

At ten minutes to nine, just as they had planned, Captain Woodcock and John Braithwaite, the village constable, set up station at the barricade that Mr. Harmsworth had erected at Applebeck Footpath. The past few days had been warm and bright (perfect haying weather, if you happen to have a hayfield that wants cutting), but this day promised to be chilly and rainy. The sun was just as anxious as we are to see what's going to happen at this important juncture in the history of the Applebeck Footpath, but he was thwarted by the curtain of rain that hung between him and the scene below. So he dawdled a bit, hoping that the clouds would go away before he had to get on with the rest of his day's appointments. There was very little breeze, although the leaves on the willows beside Wilfin Beck quivered slightly, as if the trees anticipated that something . . . well, unlucky was about to happen.

Under the nearby bridge, Max the Manx and Fritz the ferret were wondering why the captain and the constable were hanging about at the barricade, in spite of the wet. The ferret and the cat had gone out together at first light (before it began to rain), so that Fritz could make sketches of Max while nobody else was out and about. Max was a bit self-conscious about posing and had to be coaxed, so he was glad of the chance to do it privately, as it were. It had already been a companionable sort of morning, for the ferret felt that he was capturing the image of quite a unique cat, and Max felt enormously complimented at the thought that his tailless self was deemed significant enough to merit an artist's attention.

Max watched as Captain Woodcock consulted his watch once again. *"What do you suppose they're up to?"* he mused, as the captain looked once more at his watch and said something to the constable.

"I have no idea," said the ferret. He put his sketchbook and pencils into his kit bag to keep them from getting wet. *"But if they're looking for the ghost, they missed her. She was out last night. Before midnight, it was."*

"The ghost of Applebeck Orchard?" Max asked in surprise.

The ferret chuckled. *"There's more than one ghost around here?"*

"I can think of several," Max replied, for he had once set about collecting all the local ghost stories. They suited his

gloomy outlook on life. *"There's the ghost that walks in St. Peter's cemetery on All Hallows Eve. There's the ghost that appears at the ferry once or twice a year. There's the Claife Crier, there's—"*

"The orchard ghost," the ferret said in a definitive tone. *"Old-fashioned black bonnet, gray cloak, lantern—the usual ghost costume. The Herdwicks tell me she's haunted the orchard for sixty-some years now, so she's nothing new. Portends calamity, they say. Tibbie, the oldest sheep, told me the ghost was seen on the night before the Queen died, back in '01. And I know for a fact that she was out on the night the haystack burnt, because I saw her."*

Max twitched his whiskers anxiously. He had heard about this ghost, and if she had been seen last night, trouble must lie ahead. *"I wonder what calamity is looming now,"* he muttered. I don't think Max knows that this is Chapter Thirteen, or he might be even more anxious.

However, Max had no time to think further about the ghost of Applebeck Orchard, for just at that moment a man in uniform came striding purposefully along the road toward the barricade. *"Look, Fritz,"* he exclaimed. *"It's Major Ragsdale. How splendid he looks!"*

"Doesn't he just!" said Fritz admiringly. *"He looks like he's going to a parade."*

"He looks like he is a parade," Max said, and sighed. He had always admired the major, whose cabbages were the stuff of legend and whose garden was the neatest in Far Sawrey. And just the day before, he had heard that a cat might be wanted at Teapot Cottage, to clear out a gang of mice from the larder. Now, seeing the major, he remembered that he had thought of applying for the position. But of course he wouldn't get it, he reminded himself gloomily. Nobody wanted a cat who had no tail.

It was indeed Major Ragsdale, and he looked like a

parade because he was wearing his service uniform: a smart wool jacket, khaki-colored, with epaulettes on the shoulders and a colorful array of campaign ribbons pinned above the left breast pocket; khaki wool riding trousers, carefully brushed; Sam Browne leather belt and holster and brown leather boots, polished to a fare-thee-well; officer's cap with a shiny visor, set at a cocky angle. The rain pattering down on the visor beaded up into tiny droplets.

"Ah, Captain!" the major cried, and brandished his swagger stick. "And Constable Braithwaite! The troops are assembled, then, and ready for battle, rain or no. Prepared to storm the barricades, eh, what?"

John Braithwaite glanced at the captain and cleared his throat in an embarrassed sort of way. He was a burly, red-faced man, whose village constable's uniform was slightly shabby with patches on the elbows and tarnished buttons. "Er, g' mornin', Major," he said.

"Egad," muttered Captain Woodcock, with barely disguised amusement. This was not what he had planned. Aloud, he said, "Ah, Ragsdale. You're punctual. And in full kit, no less."

"Thought our campaign maneuver merited a bit of the old dress-up," the major said in his brisk military way. He squinted at the sky and held out a hand. Several drops splatted into his palm. "Unlucky weather, eh? But nothing like the downpours we had at Mafeking. Mud so deep the horses mired in it up to their fetlocks." He smoothed his mustache with his little finger. "Now, then, gentlemen. Are we ready?"

"I believe we are ready," said the captain, still amused. He had not planned anything on the order of a military expedition and found the major's getup rather silly. "If you will just put your hand on—"

But the major was already advancing. He raised his swagger stick over his head, struck a pose as if he were engaging a fencing opponent, and cried, at the top of his lungs, "Dread tyrant fall! Down with the barricades!" With that, he smacked his swagger stick across the top of the pile of twisted wire and wood staves.

What followed has been the subject of much dispute. Mr. Harmsworth claims that he shouted a warning from behind the clump of willows where he had been waiting since the first gray light of dawn. What he said (he said) was, "Git off me proppity, or I'll shoot!"

The captain, the major, and the constable all claim that they heard no warning. (Max the Manx and Fritz the ferret were not asked to give evidence, but if they had, they would have testified that they didn't hear it, either.) So perhaps Mr. Harmsworth only meant to shout and never quite managed to get the words out.

But it is certainly not disputed by either party that Mr. Harmsworth fired his shotgun (aiming high, as he later claimed, so as not to injure but merely to frighten the trespassers and persuade them to leave his property).

And if causing great fright was his purpose, Mr. Harmsworth certainly achieved it. The captain, the constable, and the major, hearing the blast, threw themselves flat on the ground behind the barricade as the birdshot went whizzing over their heads.

"Take cover!" cried the major—unnecessarily, since all three of them had already done this. In great excitement, he fumbled at the button on his holster and pulled out his Webley. "Never fear. I shall return fire!"

"Put that gun down, Ragsdale!" the captain shouted and, since Ragsdale showed no signs of doing so, yanked the revolver from the major's hand. He got to his knees behind the barricade and raised his head to peer over it, trying to catch sight of their attacker. "Hold your fire, Harmsworth!" he shouted. "Fire again and I'll have you charged with—"

Afterward, Mr. Harmsworth claimed that he heard the major cry, "Return fire!" and the captain call, "Fire again!" And so he fired his shotgun once more.

Now, if you will glance quickly at the map at the front of this book, you will see that the spot where this armed altercation took place—the north end of Applebeck Footpath—is no more than a few yards from the Kendal Road, just to the east and south of the bridge over Wilfin Beck. As it happened, Miss Potter, driving Winston the pony, with Rascal on the red pony-cart seat beside her and the two bunnies in a hamper underneath, was traveling east on the Kendal Road, in the direction of Raven Hall and Far Sawrey. Unluckily, she happened to drive onto the bridge at the very moment Mr. Harmsworth happened to fire his first shotgun blast. Winston (normally a mild-tempered pony who is slow to react to strange noises) was so terrified by the sudden, ear-splitting BLAM that he reared up on his hind legs, whinnying loudly, as Miss Potter pulled on the reins, struggling to regain control.

"Ayyee!" Winston cried. "Somebody's shooting at me! Ayyee! Ayyeeeee!"

And as it further happened, a farmer's wagon, loaded with four stacks of wooden crates filled with live chickens and pulled by an old, slow draught horse named Nellie, was approaching from the opposite direction, headed for the poultry market at Hawkshead, where the chickens were destined to be sold for slaughter. Nellie, like Winston, was so startled by Mr. Harmsworth's shotgun blast that she, too, reared up on her hind legs and pawed at the air, something she had not done since she was a filly. The young farmer's boy who was driving the wagon first thought that he himself had been shot, then thought that the horse had been shot, and then feared that Nellie (who was standing up, as tall as a house) was going to fall straight backward, into his lap. Quite properly, the boy did not want a lapful of heavy horse, so he threw up the reins and dove over the side of the wagon.

Then came the second **BLAM**, which seemed even louder and more terrifying than the other. First Winston, then Nellie stopped pawing the air and came down hard on their front feet. And both horse and pony, each equally terrified and having nowhere to go but forward, ran full-tilt toward each other, with the predictable result.

And that is why I say that books, like hotels and theaters, ought perhaps to leave out the thirteenth chapter altogether.

14

Miss Potter Puts on the Brakes

Well. Since we have arrived at the fourteenth chapter, I may now tell you that neither Winston nor Nellie was badly hurt when they ran together, for (and this is very good luck, I would say) they managed at the last possible moment to avoid a direct collision.

The farmer's boy, having dropped the reins and dived out of the wagon, had left his horse to her own devices. But this turned out not to be a bad thing, for Nellie is an old, slow creature who ought to have been retired years ago and is still on the job because she is the farmer's only horse. She does not in any circumstance like to run, even when (as she thought in this case) she is being fired upon. And she most certainly does not like to bump into another horse, or even a pony. Something might get broken—some part of Nellie, that is.

So Nellie breathed a sigh of relief when Winston veered to the left at the very last minute. She stopped running as soon as she could and stood there, head down, sides heaving, taking in huge gulps of air. But Nellie is a big horse (about the size of the Clydesdale horses you may have seen on television) and she didn't come to a full stop quite soon enough to keep the farmer's wagon from tipping onto two wheels, first one side and then the other. It did not tip over altogether, just far enough to slide those four tall stacks of wooden chicken crates onto the road, where they broke wide open, scattering dozens of squawking chickens. (There were so many loose white feathers that, afterward, the village children ran down to the road and pretended that it had snowed.) The farmer's boy, badly scratched from having taken a nosedive into a bramble patch but not otherwise damaged, scrambled to his feet and began to give chase to the chickens, who ran off to hide under the farthest bushes. (Chickens are not nearly so brainless as people say. They understood full well that if they got to Hawkshead Market, the next stop would be the stew pot.) The boy found a few, but more found new homes in the village, at Belle Green and Castle Farm and Hill Top and Low Green Gate, thereby postponing their date with the dumplings for another year or two.

And what of our Miss Potter? Well, she did not drop the reins and dive over the side of the pony cart, like the farmer's boy. She stayed on her seat, held on to the reins, and gave Winston the firm, expert guidance he needed, which probably explains the fact that Nellie and Winston only brushed past each other, and that the wheels of the pony cart and the wagon did not lock together (as sometimes happens in this sort of collision), wreck both vehicles, and seriously injure both horses and occupants.

Safely past the danger of collision, Miss Potter put on the brakes. "Whoa, Winston!" she cried, bracing her feet against the front of the cart and pulling back on the reins with both hands. "Whoa, there!"

"*Naaayy!*" whinnied Winston. He tossed his mane, flicked his tail, put back his ears, and kept on running. "*Naaayy!*"

"Stop, Winston!" Rascal barked frantically, trying hard to keep his balance as the pony cart lurched from one side to the other.

"*Whyyyy?*" whinnied Winston, who by this time had stopped thinking that he had been shot and was running because . . . well, just because. You know how some ponies are.

"Because I said so!" Miss Potter shouted, and yanked back on the reins with all her might.

Winston stopped so abruptly that Miss Potter and Rascal were flung forward. "*That hurt!*" he exclaimed in a self-pitying tone. He felt the bit with his tongue. "*That reallyyy hurt, Miss Potter!*"

"*Serves you right, you rogue pony. We could have been killed!*" Rascal was breathing heavily, his tongue hanging out. "*Miss Potter, that was an amazing feat—keeping your seat, holding on to the reins. You kept us from turning over!*"

"Are you all right, Miss Potter?" cried Captain Woodcock, running up to the pony cart.

"Jolly good horsemanship, Miss Potter," shouted Major Ragsdale, right behind the captain. "By Jove, Baden-Powell should have liked that!"

Miss Potter fixed her rain hat more firmly on her head and scowled at the gun in Captain Woodcock's hand. "Were you shooting at us, Captain?" she asked frostily.

"No. No, oh, no," said the captain, and hastily returned the Webley to its owner, who buttoned it into his holster. "Mr. Harmsworth did the shooting. At us. That is, at the major and myself. And the constable," he added, as Constable Braithwaite appeared. He had seized the reprobate Mr. Harmsworth and now had the shooter in one hand and his shotgun in the other.

"Tha wast trespassin' on me private proppity!" shouted Mr. Harmsworth angrily, struggling to free himself from the constable. But while Mr. Harmsworth was broad-shouldered and stocky, he was much shorter than the burly constable, who had him firmly collared and was holding him so high that his feet barely touched the ground. "An' I wasn't shootin' at thi—nor at tha, Missus," he cried to Miss Potter. "I was shootin' over t' men's heads, where they was on me footpath." He kicked his heels so fiercely that the constable set him down.

"Well, I was on the *public* road, Mr. Harmsworth," Miss Potter said with asperity. "And since the road is higher than the footpath, I was your target, however unintended. I consider myself lucky not to be picking birdshot out of myself or my pony."

"*Or me!*" Rascal barked. He shuddered, thinking how his handsome fur could have been tattered by birdshot.

"Apologize to the lady," the major growled. "Just think of the damage you could have caused." He glanced back to where the farmer's boy had crawled out of the bramble bushes and was making his way toward his waiting horse and wagon. "And have caused," he amended. "That boy will never catch all those chickens. Their owner has sustained a considerable property loss, I'd say."

Mr. Harmsworth looked down at his feet.

"Apologize to Miss Potter," the captain ordered. "You understand that she can press charges against you, don't you?"

At the words *press charges*, Mr. Harmsworth looked up.

"Sorry, Missus." His voice was low and sullen. "Din't mean no harm."

Miss Potter considered this for a moment, remembering what Miss Nash had told her, and also recalling the occasion when she had come upon Mr. Harmsworth beating the dog.

"I will accept your apology," she said crisply, "on one condition."

"Condition?" Mr. Harmsworth said dubiously.

"Yes. On condition that your niece be allowed to spend the afternoon with me. Tomorrow."

"Gilly?" Mr. Harmsworth gaped. "Wot dost tha want wi' Gilly? Her be but a poor girl, an' not much of a hand at workin' in the house, 'cept wi' t' butter 'n' cheeses, which tha dusn't need."

If Miss Potter heard and took note of this, she gave no indication. "What I want with the girl is of no concern to you, sir," she said, raising her chin. "I shall call at Applebeck Farm at half-past one tomorrow to fetch her. Please see that she is ready. She will be returned before tea."

Mr. Harmsworth appealed to the captain. "But I doan't see why Gilly should—"

"Consider it done, Miss Potter," the captain said, paying no attention to the man's protests. "If you like, I should be glad to accompany you to make sure that your request is carried out."

"*I'll go, too,*" Rascal volunteered, curious to know what Miss Potter wanted with the young girl. Not for dairy work, surely. At Hill Top, as everyone knew, Mrs. Jennings was a dab hand at butter and cheese. For a dairy worker, there was none better than Mrs. Jennings.

"I think there will be no difficulty," Miss Potter said, and picked up the reins. "Mr. Harmsworth, I accept your apology. Please tell Gilly to expect me tomorrow. Half-past one." She clucked to the pony, and Winston, having repented of his rash behavior, accepted her instructions, picked up his hoofs, and began to trot.

At Raven Hall, Peaches and Cream (who, since they were very young rabbits, had napped throughout the entire ordeal) were delivered without further incident and were promptly carried off to the nursery, where little Flora and baby Miles fell immediately in love with them. Nana, the nursery dog (named for Nana, the Darling children's Newfoundland nurse in Mr. Barrie's play *Peter Pan*), was also enchanted with the bunnies, but was prevented by Emily (the children's real nanny) from close acquaintance with them. Beatrix gave each of the children a hug and a kiss and pronounced them the most beautiful babes there ever were, which pleased Mrs. Kittredge mightily, although it did not surprise her in the slightest, for she said the very same thing to herself every single time she looked at them, which was as often as possible. Like Mrs. Darling, she was frightfully proud of her children.

Leaving the bunnies to the tender mercies of Emily, Nana, and the children, Mrs. Kittredge took Beatrix downstairs, where she served tea in fine china cups and scones and bramble jelly on fine china plates in the conservatory overlooking the Raven Hall garden. You remember, I expect, that Mrs. Kittredge is the former Dimity Woodcock, Miles Woodcock's sister, whom he forbade to marry Major Kittredge but had to relent when Dimity absolutely put her foot down on the subject. Dimity has been the mainstay of Vicar Sackett's parish for many years, and though she does not have as much time to spend on parish work as she would like these days, she keeps informed. So this morning, as she poured tea and handed out scones, she brought Miss Potter up-to-date on the village gossip.

When it was her turn, Miss Potter recounted the events of her travels that morning, with an emphasis on its comic (rather than the potentially tragic) aspects, giving special attention to the heroism of Mrs. Kittredge's brother, Captain Woodcock. And then she added, rather thoughtfully, "I am to meet a young person tomorrow, Mr. Harmsworth's orphaned niece, Gilly. Miss Nash tells me that the girl would like to find a new place, away from Applebeck Farm. Of course, one does not like to meddle in family matters, but I confess that I do not find Mr. Harmsworth to be a very nice fellow."

"Not very nice indeed!" Dimity exclaimed. "Closing off the footpath and firing at Miles and Major Ragsdale! And the house at Applebeck is a dreadfully gloomy old thing. Are you helping the girl find a new place?" She picked up the teapot. "Another cup?"

Beatrix accepted both the tea and another spoonful of bramble jelly for what was left of her scone. "I thought first of Lady Longford," she said. "She had an upstairs position— but that was some months ago. And when I spoke with Mr. Harmsworth about the girl this morning, he said that she had a special liking for dairy work. I thought I would just mention it to you, in case you might know of something."

"As it happens," Dimity said thoughtfully, "our dairyman is looking for a helper. The girl would have to be able to milk, as well as do the butter and cheeses." She smiled crookedly. "Our dairyman is a very nice person. I think the child might find it easier to please him than Lady Longford."

"You might be right," Beatrix said, for Lady Longford's

reputation as a difficult mistress was widely known. "As to milking, and butter and cheeses—I'll see what I can learn when I meet the girl tomorrow. If her experience and attitude seem suitable, might I bring her over?"

"Of course," Dimity said. "Now that's settled, what shall we talk of next?"

Beatrix put down her plate. "Miss Nash told me that now that Dr. Butters has married, the village expects that the vicar and Mrs. Lythecoe will soon follow." She laughed. "The village usually has it wrong, of course, but I hope in this case they're right. Is there a chance, do you think?"

Dimity's answer was interrupted by a greeting.

"Miss Potter!"

Beatrix looked up. It was Major Christopher Kittredge, Dimity's husband. He had once been a good-looking man, but had come back from the Boer War without an arm and an eye and with a disfiguring scar on one side of his face, which had been horribly burned. But his cheerful manner and amiable temperament made it easy to overlook his appearance. In fact, people who knew him constantly forgot about it, and were often surprised when it was brought up. "Oh, yes, I suppose he is rather the worse for wear," they might say. "But that's what war is all about. One scarcely notices, does one?"

"Hello, Major," Beatrix said warmly, and held out her hand. "How nice to see you!"

"Mr. Heelis told me you had arrived," the major said, as Dimity poured him a cup of tea. "I saw him yesterday. We're both working on the flying boat business." He raised an eyebrow. "You know about that, do you, Miss Potter? It's the kind of thing you'd be interested in, I'm sure. Heelis is taking quite a hand in the affair."

"No, I don't know about it," Beatrix said, frowning. "Flying boats?"

"Oh, let's don't talk stuffy old business, dear," Dimity begged, handing her husband a cup. "Miss Potter has a thrilling tale to tell you—all about being shot at on the Kendal Road. Her pony ran away and nearly collided with a draught horse pulling a wagon loaded with chickens. It's lucky that someone wasn't killed."

"Shot at, Miss Potter?" the major exclaimed. "Who shot at you? Why?"

So Beatrix told her story. When she got to the part about the chickens flying every which way, and the constable holding Mr. Harmsworth so his feet barely touched the ground, and Roger Ragsdale looking as if he were marching in a dress parade, the major laughed so hard he had to put his cup down. But he sobered almost immediately, remembering that Miss Potter, as well as the boy driving the farmer's wagon, had been in serious danger.

"I hope Woodcock deals sternly with that fellow," he growled. "Closing off a public footpath, firing a shotgun in the direction of a heavily traveled road—Harmsworth must be out of his senses!"

"I wonder if all this has something to do with the haystack being burnt," Dimity mused. "I understand that Mr. Beecham has been implicated. At least, that's what my housekeeper told me. Her son works at the Sawrey Hotel and hears all the local gossip."

"Haystack?" Beatrix asked, frowning. "Mr. Beecham?" Which necessitated the telling of *that* story, as well. "Oh, dear," she said, when she had heard it. "Old Thomas has done garden work for me since early spring. I rather like him, you know, even if he is a crusty sort." Crusty, and not quite trustworthy, for she had caught him in a lie about the work. A lie, and a small theft, since he had put some seed potatoes in his pocket and taken them home with him. Still, she understood that he had little money. She didn't begrudge him a few potatoes, although she would much rather he had asked.

She glanced at the clock and put down her cup. "If that clock is right, I really need to be on my way. I have an errand at Tidmarsh Manor this morning, and if I don't hurry, I shall be late."

Beatrix was getting into the pony cart when she remembered that Dimity had not finished telling her about the vicar and Mrs. Lythecoe, and that Major Kittredge had not related the business with the flying boats.

15

Hyacinth Takes a Test

"If yooou insist on goooing throoough with this training business," intoned the owl, slowly and deliberately, *"I suggest that yooou at least administer a test."*

"A test?" Bosworth asked uncertainly. *"What sort of test?"*

The two friends were sitting on the lower sun porch of the professor's home, in the copper beech at the top of Claife Heights, enjoying glasses of the professor's favorite ginger beer, which he himself made from a recipe passed down on his mother's side of the family. It had stopped raining a little while before, and the air was mild and sweet-smelling.

"A test tooo see if your Hyacinth has the proper aptitudes," the professor said. *"Just because yooou think she can dooo all the things required of a wearer of the Badge does not mean she can, yooou know."* He sipped his ginger beer, frowning over his beak. *"It would be rather inconvenient tooo appoint her tooo the post, only tooo discover that she is incompetent."*

"Incompetent!" The badger bristled. *"That's ridiculous. Of*

course she's not incompetent! Hyacinth is a most able, most talented badger. She is observant and thoughtful and resourceful. She reads and writes with great skill and—"

"If that is the case," the owl said sententiously, *"yooou shouldn't object to giving her a test. And then yooou will be sure. Before you invest a great deal of time in training, that is."*

Bosworth turned his glass in his paws. With a sigh, he said, *"I suppose you're right."* If nothing else, the test might silence the owl. When Hyacinth passed it, the professor would have nothing more to complain about.

"Of course I'm right," said the owl complacently. *"I am always right. And it's only logical. Hyacinth should be tested."*

The badger considered this for a moment. *"What kind of test are you thinking of, Owl?"* How does one measure agility of thought, or the ability to deal with challenging situations, as those confronted in The Brockery every day? Or ingenuity, or resourcefulness? Keeping the *History* was only one of the tasks Hyacinth would have to carry out.

The owl smiled his owlish smile. *"I should think it would be something having tooo dooo with memory and recall, shouldn't yooou? Dates are of supreme importance. And lexical skill, as well—an historian must know how tooo spell. As tooo the rest of it—well, yooou can leave the details tooo me, my dear Badger."* The professor reached out with his wing to pat the badger's shoulder in a comforting sort of way. *"Testing is something at which I am an expert, yooou know. I have studied and taught extensively, and my work often involves tests of one kind or another."* He smiled again, smugly. *"That is why they call me Professor."*

"Just don't make it too hard." The badger sighed again. Without thinking, he added, *"I don't want her to fail."*

The owl turned his whole head to give him a long, hard look. *"That, my stripy friend,"* he said in his most professorial tone, *"is exactly the problem I am trying tooo illustrate."*

Pondering the implications of this, the badger was silent for a moment. Finally, he said, *"I haven't yet spoken to Hyacinth about the possibility of training her. I didn't want to get her hopes up, in case . . ."* His voice trailed off. He hated to admit that he was still hoping to hear something, anything, from the missing Thorn. *"Well, just in case,"* he said finally, and added, *"How do you propose to administer a test to someone who doesn't know why she's being tested?"*

"That is an interesting question," the owl said. *"I shall have tooo think about it for a moment."* And with that, he fluffed his feathers, settled his wings, and closed his great, round eyes, first one eye, then the other.

Ten minutes later, the badger realized that the owl had been waylaid by a nap, something which often happened at this time of day. He cleared his throat. When the owl didn't move, he got up, took his friend's glass, and set it quietly on the table. Then he leant over the owl and said, into his ear, *"I'm going back to The Brockery, Professor. When you've come up with an answer, that's where you'll find me."*

As Bosworth made his way down the tree-trunk ladder that the owl kept for the convenience of his four-footed friends, he could hear the professor snoring.

Bosworth ambled home through the pleasant summer woodland, pausing here and there to investigate a promising community of earthworms or grubs in the rich, moist soil, snacking as he went, feeling the warmth of the sun and the kiss of the breeze on his black fur.

But he was not a happy badger. In fact, the more he thought about it, the more troubled he became by the professor's proposal to test Hyacinth. Oh, he could see a certain wisdom in the idea. One did not want to invest a great deal of time and energy in attempting to train an animal who proved in the end to be unsuited to the task. But the professor's plan also seemed to him to suggest a certain lack of confidence in the young badger. After all, his father had not proposed a test when he offered the Badge of Authority to Bosworth, nor had his father been tested, nor his grandfather, nor his great-grandfather, nor his great-great—

And then Bosworth was struck by an insight that was so astounding in its simplicity and clarity that it almost knocked him over. *"Why, it's because we are all males, that's what it is!"* he thought, flabbergasted at this sudden and unexpected understanding.

"My father just assumed that his son had the ability to do the job, as did his father and grandfather before him. None of them would ever have considered choosing any of their daughters. And Owl would never have suggested giving Thorn *a test to see whether he was competent."* Bosworth kicked angrily at a clod of dirt. *"But a female—now, that's an entirely different kettle of fish, isn't it? A female ought to be tested to see if she's up to the job."* He sniffed in growing disgust. *"Why, I call that arrogant, I do! I call that supercilious and condescending, and I don't like it. I don't like it, not one bit!"*

And the more the badger thought about it, the less he liked it. It seemed to establish one set of rules for males, another for females. What was more, it seemed to put Hyacinth—whom Bosworth knew to be every bit as bright and energetic and resourceful as her brother—at a distinctly unfair disadvantage, and (if one were to generalize from this situation to others) to give male badgers a serious edge in any competition.

Now, this may seem to you to be rather ironic (it does to me), since Bosworth had certainly been patronizing enough when he considered suggesting to Hyacinth that he train her for a job that she could turn over to her brother, in the event of his return. And this sudden insight about male badgers having the advantage—well, I'm sure it's old news to you, for the issue of discrimination has been openly debated in our society for several decades, at least.

But Bosworth, who had never before been called upon to consider the question, found it deeply troubling. Was it possible . . . Could it be . . . Had he risen to his comfortable and authoritative place in the world entirely upon his *gender*? Had he gone through life with the idea that he had earned his success—and indeed, his triumphs—when all along these had come to him solely because he was a *male*?

Bosworth was still thinking these troublesome thoughts when he arrived at The Brockery. He had lingered so long in the woods that he had missed lunch, and Parsley, Primrose, and Hyacinth were in the kitchen, doing the washing-up. Bosworth put in his head, said hello, and quickly withdrew, because the sight of them made him oppressively aware of the way The Brockery's duties were divided.

And then, as a kind of punishment, Bosworth set himself to a task that he truly detested and which, every year, he put off as long as he could. He donned a gray dust-smock to keep his fur from getting dusty, took a lighted candle-stick in one paw and a notebook in the other, and put a pencil behind one ear. Then he struck off down one of the many corridors that angled away from the large dining hall, the central room in the occupied part of The Brockery. He would conduct his annual Survey of Renovation Requirements, an onerous and boring task and a very dirty one, to boot. It was something he needed to do, as manager of The Brockery, but he always put it off until he couldn't put it off any longer. And today, this tedious job seemed a perfect retribution for all the privilege that he—a male—had enjoyed over the years.

To carry out the survey, Bosworth had to inspect every chamber in the sett, including all the hallways and corridors and inglenooks and crannies and parlors and bedsits and alcoves, in order to see what renovation and refitting might be needed. Since The Brockery had been excavated by many generations of badgers (none of whom ever bothered to draw a room plan or develop a decorating scheme), most of it was a bewildering labyrinth of rooms that were connected by dark, dusty corridors where few animals (other than the original badger-digger) had ever set foot. And no matter how thorough Bosworth had been when he made the previous surveys, he always managed to find himself in some remote part of The Brockery he'd never visited before. Many times, he would have been thoroughly lost had he not possessed the sketch map that had been drawn by his father after getting himself thoroughly lost on one of *his* annual inspections.

For the next hour, Bosworth stumped about, walking up and down steeply sloping passageways, climbing wooden ladders (for the rooms were on various levels), poking into corners, making notes in his notebook. Some of the rooms were low-ceilinged and cellar-like, with nothing much to recommend them, while others were vaulted and very grand and might serve for a conference of mice or a Sunday congregation of voles. Many had never been occupied, except by itinerant spiders and beetles who had come in the back way to get out of the weather. Some required whitewashing, some needed new carpets, others were in want of furnishings. By the light of his flickering candle, Bosworth could see that almost all were in need of a good turning-out.

But the badger was not paying the proper sort of attention to his task, for his mind was occupied with the unpleasant business that the professor's proposal had brought up. Now that he had begun to understand the extent to which female badgers were restricted in their advancement by certain prejudices, what was his proper course of action? Should he permit the professor to test Hyacinth? Or should he—

Whilst he was thinking, he was trudging along the corridor. He came to Room 428 and opened the door, noticing that rainwater had dripped into the room, traveling along a large root that had grown through the ceiling. The floor was rather muddy. He was making a note to this effect when he heard a faint voice calling in the distance, *"Uncle, Uncle, where are you?"*

Bosworth brightened. Well. It was always good to have company when he was doing this kind of work, and in this case— Perhaps he could take the opportunity to talk over the situation with her.

"I'm here, Hyacinth," he called.

After a moment, the voice came again, more distant this time. *"Where, Uncle? Where are you?"*

"You're going in the wrong direction, Hyacinth," he shouted, much more loudly. *"I'm in Room 428."*

"Where is Room 428?" the voice called. It was even fainter. Hyacinth was moving away from him.

"Bother," grumbled the badger. He should have to go and look for her. But it wasn't a bother, really. He was tired of making inspections and taking notes. It was time for a cup of tea and a nice warm scone with lavender honey. Yum. Yes, that was exactly what he wanted. He would find Hyacinth and they would sit down together over tea and a scone, with a spoonful of lavender honey, and talk about . . . well,

about all the things he had been thinking. So he put his pencil behind his ear, tucked his notebook under his arm, and took up his candlestick. He stepped out of Room 428 and turned right.

But that was wrong, he realized, having gone some distance along the dark corridor. To get back to the main corridor, he should have turned left. So he went back and tried again.

But this time, he went past Room 428 (the plate on the door was too tarnished to be easily read), and found himself in a strange corridor. Recognizing his error, he turned around and tried to retrace his steps. But he must have gone too far again, for now he found himself confronted by three corridors, one leading straight ahead, one angling off to the right, and the other angling off to the left.

Well. This was easily solved. He should only have to consult his handy-dandy map and—

But when Bosworth opened his notebook to look for the map, he saw to his breathless horror that it was not there. It must have dropped out somewhere along the way.

And by this time, of course, poor Bosworth was thoroughly befuddled. He had not the foggiest notion which of these corridors would take him back to familiar territory. But even this would not have been an insurmountable problem, I suppose, except that our badger's candle, which had been burning for quite some time now, had burnt all the way down to a very short stub. It flickered and flared as candles do when they are trying to tell us that they are about to go out, and that if we want more light, we shall have to fetch another candle. And in the space of a breath, the candle did just that. It went out, plunging Bosworth into a sudden and total blackness—for he had quite thoughtlessly failed to bring a spare candle. (Please take note of this, gentle reader. When you go underground, or wherever it promises to be thoroughly dark for an extended period of time, take not one candle but two, or perhaps even three. One can never have too many candles.)

Of course, an absence of light would not ordinarily be a problem for badgers, who spend most of their lives underground and can see in the dark just as well as we can see in the light. What's more, they have very reliable noses, which can lead them anywhere they want to go, particularly when there's something to eat at the end of the trail—a fresh scone, say, warm, with lavender honey. I daresay a healthy badger can smell lavender honey a mile away.

But our badger had been suffering for several days from a bothersome cold, so even if Parsley took the lid off the honey-pot and held it under his nose, he could not have smelled it. Even worse, his eyes had been giving him trouble lately—it was all that tedious writing, of course—and he had brought the candle to help himself out. Now the candle was gone and he was stranded, thoroughly lost in the great earthen labyrinth of The Brockery, whose corridors twisted and turned and curled and coiled for miles and miles under Holly How.

"Oh, dear," the badger muttered. *"This is not a good thing."* He pushed down the sudden wish that he had had the foresight to pack a picnic lunch, just something to tide him over, for it was possible that he would not get back in time for tea, or perhaps tomorrow's breakfast, or lunch, or the next day's dinner. He might even be lost forever.

Perhaps you are thinking that this is highly improbable, but I am sorry to say that such things have happened before and—given the haphazard design and construction of the sett—are quite likely to happen again. Indeed, Bosworth's great-great-uncle Benjamin (an elderly badger, but still quite spry, who used a cane with a curiously carved head) had gone off one afternoon to visit an invalid hedgehog who was staying in one of The Brockery's farthest guest rooms. When he did not return for tea, a rescue party was sent out. But in spite of their efforts, Great-Great-Uncle Benjamin was never seen or heard from again. His sudden disappearance was one of The Brockery's great mysteries.

Bosworth thought of this with a shiver. But then he reflected that it would not do to lose his spirit, for that would only make things worse. He stood very still, trying to think. Then it occurred to him that he could think just as well sitting as standing and perhaps even better, and anyway, his legs were telling him that he should sit. So he sank down on the ground with his back to the wall.

This was no time to panic, of course, and normally Bosworth was a very levelheaded badger who could meet any threat with a chipper, *"Oh, there you are, silly old thing. Let's see what can be done."* He had always tried hard to practice the Fifteenth Rule of Thumb, expressed thus: *It is the better part of wisdom to keep one's head when one is confronted with catastrophe, calamity, or cataclysm. Losing one's head never solves anything.*

But when a substantial amount of time had passed (hours and hours, Bosworth thought, although of course it was too dark to see his pocket watch) and he had not yet thought of anything he might do to save himself, he had to acknowledge the panic that was clenching a fist in the general region of his breastbone. What was more, the air had begun to seem rather warm and close, and he realized that he must be in an area of the sett which was closed off from the outside and therefore had no ventilation. It wasn't likely that he would suffocate—or at least, he didn't think so— but the lack of fresh air was making him frightfully drowsy.

It was all he could do to keep his eyes open, especially since there was nothing to look at but black, black, and more black.

And worse, he had begun to feel that he was not quite alone. Spiders, perhaps, or was it beetles (he couldn't see which in the dark) were creepy-crawling along the floor and across his paws. And then up his legs and over his shoulders and his face, tickling him with their little beetle feet, or spider feet, as it were. There were only a few at first, and then, just as he was telling himself sternly to stop imagining things, there were hundreds of them, dancing the fandango in his fur, investigating the recesses of his ears, tiptoeing out to the tip of his nose. And then he began to hear their conversations—whistlings and whisperings and murmurings and rustlings—and he got the impression that the spiders in the lot (or perhaps the beetles had gone away and they were *all* spiders!) were plotting to spin their sticky webs around him. If he didn't do something, he would find himself wrapped like Gulliver and tied with Lilliputian threads into a tidy bundle so that he couldn't move, breathe, couldn't—

He shook himself. This would not do! It would not do at all. He could not just sit here and let the spiders package him up, as if he were a butcher's parcel. He would get up and walk on a bit, hoping to find a more congenial place to have a rest. Or perhaps, if he was lucky, he would come to the end of the corridor and find that he could push his way out into the open, where he could take big, deep gulps of fresh air and—

Yes. He would walk on, that's what he would do. He got painfully to his feet and began to feel his way along the wall. Walking was a dangerous business, because the sett was constructed on various levels. Some of the corridors took rather sudden plunges, and there were stairways and ladders that led up or down quite unexpectedly. If one were not extremely careful, one might find oneself stepping out into thin air.

Just as the badger was thinking this thought, it happened. The corridor suddenly became a steep incline, and the floor fell away under his feet. He dropped his notebook and candlestick and scrabbled for some sort of handhold, a root or a stone sticking out of the earthen wall, grabbing at anything that would keep him from sliding and skidding and slipping over the edge. But there was nothing, nothing at all, to hold him back. Before he could even cry *Help!* or *Save me!* or even *Bless my stripes!* he was falling, toppling, tumbling tail over teakettle through the empty air.

THun**K**!

For a very long moment, Bosworth could only lie there, flat on his back, trying to get his breath, feeling the hard hammering of his heart as he looked into blackness, the thickest, darkest, murkiest, most sinister blackness he had ever seen. He had hit bottom. Or at least, what he thought was bottom.

But perhaps it wasn't *the* bottom, he thought, in a muzzy sort of way. Perhaps he had only fallen onto a ledge, and if he moved or tried to roll over, he might roll straight off and down, and heaven only knew how FAR down it was to the real bottom. He tried to put out his right paw to feel for the edge. But the paw was pinned under him, and it hurt. The pain was like fire, running up his wrist, to his elbow. Broken, probably. Oh, dear. A broken leg. That complicated things. It complicated things a very great deal.

He took a deep breath, lifted his left paw, and wiggled it. Well, good. At least that one wasn't broken. He reached out as far as he could, feeling flat earth, earth covered with inches of dust. He sneezed. He might be lying on a ledge, but at least it wasn't a narrow one. He kept reaching, kept feeling, and then he felt something else. It was a heap of something, a pile of old clothing, perhaps, or an old fur coat that somebody had tossed into his pit.

He patted it. Yes, fur, that was what it was. It was something furry, and dry, very dry, and dusty. And there was a stick of some kind lying across the heap.

But it wasn't exactly a stick, was it? No. Bosworth felt it with his paw. It was . . . It was a cane. A cane with a curiously carved head.

Bosworth had found Great-Great-Uncle Benjamin.

And that was when the bleak reality of his situation struck him. He squeezed his eyes shut and sucked in his breath, trying to quiet his hammering heart. Bosworth had found himself in some prickly patches, especially back in the days when—footloose and fancy-free—he had roamed the world. But this was the most terrible, most grave, most potentially deadly difficulty he had ever fallen into, never mind the pun. Here he lay in pitch blackness, one foreleg broken, at the bottom of a very deep pit in an unused corridor in a forgotten corner of his very large house, beside his deceased great-great-uncle, who had perished many years before. No one knew where he was—not Parsley nor Primrose nor Hyacinth nor any of the others. It was entirely possible that he could suffer poor Great-Great-Uncle Benjamin's fate, and no one would ever be the wiser.

If that was what happened, our badger would not be very happy about it, of course. But animals have rather a different view of death than we do. The Thirteenth Rule of Thumb reminds every badger that animals are prone to accidents and that there are many traps and snares in this world. One must be prepared to depart from this life (when it is time) in the same way that one arrives in it, without fuss or fanfare, with all one's business in good order. Unfortunately, however, Bosworth's business was not quite in good order, for he had not yet named anyone to wear the Badger Badge of Authority when he was gone.

"And why not, is what I want to know."

Bosworth's eyes popped wide open against the darkness. He had heard the words as clearly as if . . . as if they had come from the pile of fur and bones that lay within arm's reach.

"And why not? I ask you," came the voice again, a little louder and testier. *"Why have you put off doing the most important thing a wearer of the Badge ought to do? I tell you, boy, I am very disappointed in you."*

This time, Bosworth was sure. He was in the presence of the spirit of Great-Great-Uncle Benjamin, who had himself been a wearer of the Badge and had every right to chastise him. The Fourteenth Rule of Thumb came into his mind, and he shivered. Great-Great-Uncle Benjamin had crossed the bridge to the Back of Beyond, but his spirit lingered behind. He, Bosworth, was in the company of one of his watchful elders.

In the company of watchful elders. Of course! That was why he was here. Great-Great-Uncle Benjamin had arranged events in such a way that Bosworth would tumble into the very same pit where the elder badger had lost his life! But why go to all that trouble? Surely, as a spirit, Great-Great-Uncle Benjamin could talk to Bosworth whenever and wherever he chose. He did not need to engineer a twenty-foot drop to tell Bosworth to get on with the business of naming his successor.

Cradling his injured foreleg, Bosworth pulled himself into a sitting position. Of course Great-Great-Uncle Benjamin could talk to him—and perhaps he had. Perhaps it had been *his* voice that had been nagging at the back of Bosworth's mind these past few weeks!

And Bosworth had ignored him. Well, not exactly *ignored*, perhaps, but he hadn't moved very speedily to get something done. Suppose Great-Great-Uncle Benjamin had nagged and nagged and kept on nagging, until he realized that Bosworth was not really *listening*? Suppose he decided, then, that the only way to make his great-great-nephew come face-to-face with the decision he had to make was to put him into an entirely helpless position, flat on his back at the bottom of a very deep, very dark pit, with a broken foreleg.

Bosworth was covered with chagrin. He could see now that he had dragged his feet, held his fire, delayed, deferred, procrastinated, and postponed. Unforgivably, he had put off doing the most important thing a holder of the Badge ought to do, his last, his most important task. If he died here beside Great-Great-Uncle Benjamin—and he very well might, since no one knew where he was—there would be no one to carry on the work. There would be no one to take responsibility. What would happen to The Brockery, and all the animals in it? What would happen to the *History*? The *Genealogy*?

At this thought, Bosworth began to feel deeply ashamed of himself, which I perfectly understand. Don't you? Just imagine for a moment how you would feel if you were lying with a broken arm at the bottom of a pit filled with the darkest, heaviest blackness you had ever experienced, in the company of a long-dead relative who was reminding you of something you were supposed to do that you had failed to do, something so urgent, so important, that the continuing life and health of your family depended on it.

I know how I should feel. I should feel dreadful. I should feel frightened, of course, and panicked. In fact, I should feel terrified. And I would most likely start screaming.

Afterward, Bosworth said he wasn't screaming, exactly. *"I was calling out,"* he explained, when it came to telling this part of the story. *"I was shouting, just in case there might be anyone nearby who could hear me and come and fetch me out of that hole."*

But to tell the plain, unvarnished truth, Bosworth was screaming. Not to put too fine a point on it, he was bellowing at the top of his lungs, and there is no shame in saying so, none at all. Indeed, I think it was a very good thing that our badger did bellow, for if he had not made such a very great commotion, he might not have been heard.

But I am happy to tell you that he was heard.

Hyacinth heard him, and this is how it happened.

When she could get no answer to her own shouts for directions to Room 428, Hyacinth had gone back to the main living area to fetch a large torch. And because she had an intuition (a *female* intuition?) that something very unpleasant had happened to her uncle Bosworth, she also fetched with her Parsley's nephews, who had dropped in for a brief visit. These young badgers—Paolo and Pedro were their professional names, although they had been born Tom and Dick—were trapeze artists. They starred in a traveling circus called ALEXANDER AND WILLIAM'S CIRCUS, on its way to Carlisle for an upcoming series of performances.

There were a great many small circuses in those days, and they traveled all over the country in their gaily painted caravans, bringing exotic entertainments to rural people. Miss Potter herself wrote about this particular circus in her book *The Fairy Caravan*, noting that it featured a "pigmy" elephant (that was Paddy Pig with a moss-stuffed black stocking for a trunk and a howdah made of a bright-colored tea caddy), a dormouse named Xarifa, Jane Ferret (no relative to Fritz), and Tuppenny, a long-haired guinea pig. She neglected to mention the badger trapeze artists, I'm sorry to say. But she did tell all about the clever caravan, which was no doubt just like the ones she had seen touring the Land Between the Lakes. She described it as a tiny four-wheeled caravan, painted yellow and red. It had windows with muslin curtains, just like a house, and outside steps up to the back door, and a chimney on the roof. All the animals could be invisible at will, because they carried fern seed in their pockets. (If you want to know what happened when the pony lost his fern seed, you will have to read Miss Potter's book.)

Now, Paolo and Pedro were muscular, agile, and entirely fearless young badgers, especially when it came to ropes. In fact, they were exactly the sort of fellows one would want to take on a rescue mission, and it was a very good thing that they just happened to drop in the very afternoon that they were needed.

It was also a good thing that Bosworth went on shouting (or screaming or bellowing or roaring or whatever you want to call it), because it was the sound of his cries that guided Hyacinth and his rescuers—and not a moment too soon, either, for he had shouted himself hoarse and was beginning to run out of steam. Another ten minutes, and I doubt that he would have been able to summon so much as a whimper. And then of course, it would have been Bosworth and Benjamin, together for eternity.

So it was one very relieved badger, as you can imagine, who looked up and saw a flickering beacon of light—a beacon of hope—many feet above his head. It was Hyacinth's torch.

"Hullo up there!" he croaked. *"I'm here. Down here! Very far down,"* he added to himself. *"I doubt you'll be able to get me out."*

Hyacinth leant over the edge. *"Uncle!"* she cried anxiously. *"Uncle Bosworth, are you all right?"*

"More or less," Bosworth called. *"Can somebody fetch a rope?"* He tried to move. *"Or Parsley's laundry basket, p'rhaps? My right foreleg appears to be broken. I don't think I can climb a rope."* To be truthful, he wasn't sure he could manage to get into Parsley's laundry basket, either.

"Don't worry, Uncle," Hyacinth shouted in a comforting voice. *"Pedro's gone for a rope. Someone will be down to get you very soon."*

And someone was. He proved to be an extremely strong and agile badger, who came paw-over-paw down a rope, which was secured at the top end by another extremely strong badger. A moment later, a second rope came down, with Parsley's large wicker laundry basket fastened to the business end. There was some difficulty getting Bosworth into the basket—his foreleg hurt him very much, of course—and he was really too big for the basket.

But once he was in, hauling him out of the pit was duck soup, as the Americans say. After all, Paolo and Pedro were used to handling ropes and swings and the like, and they brought up the basket with a minimum of swaying and bumping against the sides of the pit, although the ascent made Bosworth feel quite airsick. Once he was safely out of the pit, the circus performers took turns carrying Bosworth on their backs through the labyrinth of passages, back to the main part of The Brockery. Getting back wasn't difficult at all, either, because Hyacinth (clever lass!) had taken the precaution of mapping their route as they went along. Please remember that the next time you're about to enter a badger sett. Making a map is infinitely better than finding yourself lost.

With the aid of Hyacinth's map, the rescue crew returned safely, and it was no more than half an hour after his rescue that Bosworth was sitting in his rocking chair beside the kitchen fire, his feet soaking in a wooden tub of hot water and Epsom salts, his poor injured foreleg expertly splinted by Parsley and wrapped with a poultice of boneset leaves, to speed healing. There was a glass of restorative nettle beer at his left elbow, and a plate of fresh, hot scones, slathered with lavender honey and freshly churned butter, at his right. The talk, of course, was all about how Bosworth had managed to fall into the pit and what he found at the bottom (the details of which you have already heard), and how other animals might be prevented from getting lost and falling into it.

And all the while, Bosworth kept his eye on the handsome trophy he had brought back with him—well, not a trophy, exactly, but certainly a reminder of his grueling and very nearly fatal experience, letting him know that there was something he needed urgently to do. It was Great-Great-Uncle Benjamin's cane, cut from a length of the sturdiest oak, polished to a deep, rich gleam, and topped with a head that was carved into a crown-like shape, so that the whole affair looked rather like a scepter.

And Bosworth was ready to do it—more than ready, in fact. He was tired of procrastinating, postponing, deferring, and delaying. He didn't give a hoot what the professor thought, and whilst he wished fervently that Thorn would come back, he was confident that Hyacinth was the very best choice of a badger to wear the Badge. As far as he was concerned, she had already passed the most significant test, expressed in the Fifteenth Rule of Thumb: *It is well to keep one's head when one is confronted with catastrophe, calamity, or cataclysm. Losing one's head never solves anything.* And also in the Sixteenth: *The prudent badger assesses the situation, determines a course of action, and speedily gathers the appropriate resources. Such badgers should be called upon for leadership whenever the clan is in need of help.*

Hyacinth had kept her head, had brought help, and a torch and ropes and a map, and had gotten them all back safely.

"*It's time,*" Great-Great-Uncle Benjamin whispered, at the back of his mind.

It was time, and Bosworth knew it.

He held out his undamaged paw. "*Come and sit beside your old uncle, Hyacinth,*" he said. "*I would like to talk with you.*"

16

Miss Potter Lets Something Slip

Tidmarsh Manor was a large, forbidding-looking house, built entirely of stone and overshadowed by ancient pines and yews, at the edge of Cuckoo Brow Wood. Its windows turned blank, empty eyes onto the world, and its chimneys rarely showed a trace of smoke, because Lady Longford believed that fires (except on the coldest of days) were a fine way to burn up money. Generally speaking, the house wore the same grim, cheerless look as did its longtime owner—which might prompt us to wonder whether her ladyship was perpetually out of temper because she lived in such a bleak house, or the house was always sullen and cross because her ladyship lived in it. Also at the manor with Lady Longford: her granddaughter Caroline, now sixteen; Caroline's pretty governess, Miss Burns; and Mr. and Mrs. Beever, gardener and cook, respectively. Oh, and Dudley, her ladyship's fat, snappish spaniel, who was named for her ladyship's departed husband and was much too fond of sweetmeats. There is even a certain resemblance between the deceased master and his surviving dog, evident when you study the oil painting of his lordship that hangs in her ladyship's drawing room.

This morning, Dudley was sitting by the gatepost as Miss Potter and Rascal drove up. With an effort, he hoisted himself to his feet and bared his teeth at Rascal. *"Well, if it isn't the town mongrel, come to visit the gentry. Who invited you, mutt?"*

"Why, it's Dud the Chub," Rascal barked sarcastically, jumping out of the pony cart. *"You've got to stop eating all that candy, Dudley, old chap. You've put on at least three pounds since the last time I saw you."*

"Dudley!" Miss Potter exclaimed. "You are a rude, unpleasant creature. Be quiet at once!" To Rascal, she added, "And if you can't be civil, you shall have to stay here at the cart with Winston."

Winston tossed his head. *"Whyyy am I always the one who's made to look after that dog? I have better things to do."* He was eyeing a patch of fresh green grass by the gatepost, where Miss Potter had just tied him.

"I'll be civil, Miss Potter." Rascal wagged his stump of a tail. *"If you don't mind, I'll just come inside with you."* And he began to follow Miss Potter up the path to the door.

"You'll do no such thing, sir," Miss Potter said sternly, pointing. "Go round to the kitchen and see if Mrs. Beever might be willing to part with a bone."

"Jolly good idea," Rascal agreed. *"I'll tell her you sent me. Ta, old boy,"* he added to Dudley, and trotted off.

It was not a coincidence that Beatrix had chosen to call at Tidmarsh Manor on this particular morning. As she told Margaret Nash, Caroline and Miss Burns had written to ask her to come, and even named the day. Mrs. King would also be there, for Caroline was giving a debut performance of one of her own compositions for her grandmother. Further, Mrs. King intended to tell Lady Longford (or so Miss Burns had written) that the girl's talent was so outstanding that she had recommended her admission to the study of composition at the Royal Academy of Music. Beatrix was not looking forward to today's visit. She did not like rows—her own with her parents were upsetting enough—and this might be a battle royal. But she had promised Caroline and Miss Burns, and she would do her best.

Some moments later, Beatrix was seated beside Lady Longford on the velvet sofa in the manor's drawing room, with Miss Burns and Mrs. King in adjacent chairs, listening to Caroline play an original étude. The girl was dressed in an old-fashioned white dress with a pink sash (selected, no doubt, by her grandmother), and her hair was tied back with a matching pink ribbon. Beatrix thought how grown-up and poised she seemed, very different from the shy, self-conscious child who had come from the sheep station in New Zealand where she had lived until the deaths of her parents. Lady Longford had disowned Caroline's father when he refused to marry the person she had chosen for him, gone off to New Zealand, and married for love—a sheep herder's daughter, and much beneath him.

Her ladyship, an elderly autocrat who believed that everyone in the world should instantly obey her orders, had at first refused to take in her orphaned granddaughter. But once she had grown accustomed to having the girl around the house, she had become very possessive, telling her what to wear and how to behave. As Caroline wrote in one of her letters, "Grandmama has been very kind to me, taking me in when I had nowhere else to turn. I am grateful, but I'm afraid it will be difficult for her to allow me to grow up and lead my own life."

Caroline's performance was, Beatrix thought, quite lovely. She herself was no musician, of course, but to her ear, the composition did demonstrate a remarkable talent. As she listened, she hoped very much that Lady Longford could be persuaded to allow her granddaughter to enter the Royal Academy, although she feared that this was not likely. As Lady Longford listened, she kept time with her ivory-headed cane, thumping it on the floor. If this was a distraction to the pianist or to the rest of the audience, no one mentioned it.

Caroline finished her piece and stood with one hand on the piano, blushing as her listeners applauded.

"Bravo!" cried Miss Burns excitedly, jumping up. "Bravo, bravissimo!"

"That was lovely, Caroline," Beatrix said, smiling.

"An excellent performance, Miss Longford," Mrs. King said approvingly.

Lady Longford pursed her lips. Never one to praise, she only said, "Acceptable, child, quite acceptable." She dabbed her white lace handkerchief to the corner of her eye, suggesting the possibility of a tear. "I daresay your grandfather, Lord Longford, would very much have enjoyed your playing." She glanced in the direction of the oil portrait of her husband (which, as we have previously noticed, bears a striking resemblance to Lady Longford's spaniel). Although his lordship had been dead for many years, the portrait remained heavily draped in black crepe, and a large vase of black silk flowers sat on a table beneath it, tied with a black satin bow. Lady Longford herself—a tall, very thin lady with formidable black brows and a thin, pinched mouth—always wore black. The Victorians demonstrated an immense enthusiasm for mourning.

Another dab with the handkerchief. "His lordship was a patron of the arts, you know," she added.

"Was he, indeed?" Beatrix asked quickly. She had heard this story many times before, but she thought perhaps it might offer an opening for what was to come.

Lady Longford lifted her pearl-handled lorgnette to peer at Beatrix. "Oh, yes, Miss Potter. He always admired young ladies who were accomplished in the arts, especially the musical arts."

"Then he would have good cause to admire his grand-daughter," Mrs. King put in smoothly. She was a buxom lady with porcelain skin, beautiful hands, and very black hair piled in intricate coils on the top of her head. She wore a loose, flowing garment of gold, purple, and red, testimony to her artistic temperament and her reputation as a re-nowned pianist. She spoke in a deep, almost masculine voice, with a trace of a German accent. "If I may say so, Miss Longford has an extraordinary talent for composition. Quite extraordinary," she added, with emphasis.

"Caroline," her ladyship said sternly, "you may go to your room now. Young ladies should not be present when their accomplishments are being discussed."

Beatrix put her hand on Lady Longford's arm. "Oh, but I think we must make an exception in this case."

Her ladyship frowned. But (although she almost never listened to anyone, especially when they were saying some-thing that contradicted her own point of view) Lady Long-ford usually paid a reluctant attention to Miss Potter, for whom she held a grudging admiration. Several years before, Beatrix helped her ladyship to escape from the deadly clutches of her personal companion, Miss Martine, who defi-nitely did not have her mistress' best interests at heart. (If you do not know the full story, you can read it in *The Tale of Holly How*. It will help to explain what is about to happen.)

"Oh, very well," Lady Longford remarked petulantly. "If

you're going to stay, child," she said to Caroline, "you can make yourself useful. Fetch my shawl. There, on that chair." Obediently, Caroline brought the shawl and draped it over her grandmother's shoulders.

Mrs. King cleared her throat. "As I was saying," she said authoritatively, "your ladyship's granddaughter has an extraordinary talent. I have taught for many years—indeed, I may say that I have had experience with a very large number of talented and capable pupils. But I have seen only a very few persons who are endowed with Miss Longford's native ability—her gift, that is—of composition. She seems to hear the music in her mind, and needs only to learn the mechanics of transferring what she hears to the page and to the instrument. This is all the more remarkable," she added, "because she has had so little opportunity, in this remote place, to hear music performed."

Lady Longford, perhaps somewhat cowed by the confidence in Mrs. King's voice, made an unusual attempt to be gracious. "I am glad to hear that you think so highly of the girl," she said, inclining her head toward Mrs. King with what can only be described as a simper. "A talent for music is one of the greatest gifts a wife can bring to her husband. She can provide his entertainment in the long winter evenings. And her children will—"

"Oh, tut-tut." Mrs. King waved her hand dismissively. "I am not speaking of that sort of gift. In my opinion, Miss Longford is born to the composition of music." She lifted her chin imperiously. "That is why I have written a letter recommending her—*strongly* recommending her, I must add—for admission to the study of composition at the Royal Academy of Music. My letter was sent together with a portfolio of her work."

Lady Longford's mouth dropped open and her eyes went

wide. "The Royal Academy—" she gasped. Then she recovered herself, pressed her lips together, and scowled. "Absurd. Ridiculous. The Royal Academy. It is the most nonsensical thing I have ever heard."

"But, Grandmama," Caroline cried in a pleading tone. "I do so want—"

"Be still, child!" Lady Longford commanded sharply. She turned her gaze on Miss Burns, a slender, pretty young lady with blond hair and blue eyes. "I hold you responsible for this folly, Miss Burns. You have encouraged Caroline to raise her sights to impossible heights. You have too many foolish notions about what is possible." She gave a scornful wave of her hand. "The Royal Academy of Music would never admit a girl."

"Your ladyship is in error." Mrs. King's deep voice cut through Lady Longford's rebuke. "The Royal Academy of Music has admitted women to the performance program for many years. It is true that women have not previously been admitted to the study of composition, for it is felt—by the men, I should say—that women have neither the creative genius nor intellectual capacity and strength necessary for that work." Her voice sharpened. "This is utter nonsense, of course, which I have told them on several occasions. Women's musical talents must be encouraged!"

"Yes, indeed," Miss Burns cried bravely. "Yes, indeed! They must!"

Mrs. King continued. "In fact, I believe Miss Longford's talent to be so clearly worthy of nurture that the administrators might be persuaded to admit her." She smiled. "I am sure that your ladyship will be gratified to learn—"

"Well, she won't be," Lady Longford said frostily. "You say so yourself, Mrs. King. 'Women have never been admitted—'"

"Oh, but that was before!" Miss Burns burst out. She flung out her arm in such excitement that she knocked a framed photograph from the table next to her chair.

Lady Longford narrowed her eyes. "Before what?"

"Before they saw Caroline's work and heard from Mrs. King how very good she is. Caroline has been admitted, Lady Longford!" Miss Burns retrieved the photograph from the carpet and replaced it on the table. She turned to Caroline. "Show her the letter, my dear."

Caroline pulled a folded letter out of the pocket of her skirt. "Here, you see, Grandmama? I'll read it to you." She stood and cleared her throat. " 'We are pleased to acknowledge Miss Longford's superior potential and to accept her into our program.' " She gave a little skip. "They've let me in, Grandmama. I'm to be the first! The very first!"

There was a silence. All eyes were on Lady Longford.

Her ladyship folded her hands over the head of her walking stick, scowling darkly. "I should have been consulted on this matter before now, Caroline. You seem to be extraordinarily talented, I will grant you that, and it is very kind of the administrators to make an exception and admit you. Your admission is neither here nor there, however. You are far too young to live alone in the City, and I refuse to remove myself there. It is out of the question."

"But I won't be living alone, Grandmama," Caroline said breathlessly. "That is the great beauty of it. You see, Miss Burns has taken a teaching position at a very fine girls' school—Mrs. Alton's School for Young Ladies—not far from the Academy. I can board at Mrs. Alton's, and Miss Burns will look after me. And Mrs. King—" She clasped her hands. "Oh, Grandmama, this is the very best part!"

"I shall be teaching at the Academy during the coming year," Mrs. King said genially. "I am willing to keep an eye on Miss Longford while she is there. I am also well acquainted with Mrs. Alton, where Miss Burns will be teaching. I can vouch for the school's excellence. Boarding there will be ideal. As well as the supervision, Caroline will have the advantage of friendships with girls of her age, something she lacks here."

"Miss Burns has taken a position elsewhere?" Lady Longford's mouth had turned down at the corners and her voice was sepulchral. "She is *leaving* Tidmarsh Manor?"

"If your ladyship will recall," Miss Burns said tactfully, "you were quite firm about engaging me on a year-to-year basis only, since you wanted the opportunity to look for a replacement, if you chose to do so."

This is quite true, but very foolish on Lady Longford's part, I have always thought. Adding to the bother of finding a suitable governess for a sixteen-year-old (the position would ordinarily end when the pupil approached eighteen) was the even greater nuisance of finding someone who would agree to come to such a remote place as Tidmarsh Manor, where there is practically no society worth mentioning and certainly no opportunity to escape to the opera or a museum. Had not Miss Potter strongly recommended Miss Burns and had not Miss Burns wanted an opportunity to see the Lakes, her ladyship might still be searching.

"I reminded your ladyship last month," Miss Burns added in a deferential tone, "that our agreement would conclude in a fortnight. You said——"

"Oh, *bother* what I said," Lady Longford snapped. "You cannot leave us, Miss Burns. I forbid it. Did you hear me? I forbid it!"

There was another silence. Mrs. King coughed. Miss Burns looked down at her fingers twisting in her lap. Caroline caught her breath.

"Miss Burns is correct, Lady Longford." Beatrix spoke decidedly, since she had been in on this plan for several weeks—had in fact given a very strong character to Mrs. Alton on behalf of Miss Burns. "She is a teacher. When she understood that her contract was not to be extended here, she had a perfect right—in fact, she was obligated—to seek employment elsewhere."

"But her contract will be extended here," Lady Longford insisted. "Caroline *is not going to London.*" She thumped her walking stick on the floor, emphasizing her words. "I am delighted"—this, even though she didn't sound one bit delighted—"that you, Mrs. King, have seen fit to recommend Caroline to the Academy, and that you are willing to look after her. It is gratifying to know that Miss Burns is so highly thought of that she has easily found other employment." She sighed, putting on a falsely pained expression that wouldn't fool anybody for a minute. "Of course, now that you have made all these careful arrangements, you are all probably expecting that I shall be forced to give my permission. But I shan't. I cannot. And that's all there is to it."

"There is another reason, then?" pressed Beatrix.

Lady Longford sighed again, with even more pretended pain. "As you very well know, Miss Potter, I am not made out of money. In fact, I am nearly destitute. I scarcely have one penny left to rub against another penny. I may even be forced to sell some property." She closed her eyes, adding piteously, "I am sorry to tell you this, but I simply cannot afford the tuition, not to mention the boarding expenses, and the traveling back and forth. It is all much too expensive." Her eyes came open and her voice sharpened. "And it is not fair to badger an old, penniless lady for money. I don't want to hear another word about it."

Mrs. King frowned. "If Miss Longford's tuition proves a

hardship, the Academy may be able to grant her a scholarship."

"And I think that the boarding costs might be negotiated," Miss Burns said, "in view of the circumstance."

"There, Grandmama!" Caroline said triumphantly. "Do you see? It needn't cost so very much after all, especially since Miss Burns will no longer be my governess."

"Charity!" Lady Longford pulled down her mouth. "A scholarship is charity, Caroline. I will not allow you to accept it. And since I cannot possibly afford the expensive tuition—"

"It is not so costly as your ladyship might think," Mrs. King said.

"Excessive," Lady Longford snapped, glaring.

"Not so much." Mrs. King's voice hardened.

"Exorbitant!" The two ladies were glowering at each other.

"Reasonable," Mrs. King said loudly, "especially considering all the many advantages Miss Longford will—"

Lady Longford pounded her cane on the floor. "I shall not have my granddaughter going to school in London! It is far too costly, and accepting charity is entirely out of the question. Do you hear me? Does *everyone* hear me?"

Another silence. Out in the hallway, the clock struck twelve. Somewhere, a door slammed. From a distance came the sound of hammering.

Adroitly, Beatrix seized the chance. "Well, then," she said brightly. "If cost is the only reason your ladyship is hesitating, I am sure that Caroline will be willing to pay her expenses herself, out of the funds from her parents' estate."

Lady Longford gasped. Miss Burns made a small noise. Mrs. King gave a dry chuckle.

"My . . . parents' estate?" Caroline asked blankly. "I don't understand. There was no estate. There are no funds."

"Why, of course there are, my dear," Beatrix replied. "Mr. Heelis told me so himself, just yesterday. The legal knots have all been untied and the money invested. I am sure that the principal will yield enough interest to—"

"Hold your tongue, Miss Potter," Lady Longford commanded in a threatening tone. "Not another word." If it had been anyone but Beatrix, I'm sure her ladyship would have boxed her ears.

Beatrix frowned. "I don't understand," she said perplexedly. "Have I let something slip? You mean, Caroline doesn't know about the money? She doesn't—" She put her hand to her mouth, letting her eyes go wide, the very picture of embarrassment. "Oh, dear! If I've spoken out of turn, I really must apologize. I didn't know . . . I didn't mean . . ."

Caroline pushed herself out of her chair. "Is it true, Grandmama? Did Papa and Mama leave money for me?" Her voice rose. Her hands were clenched, her cheeks were glowing red. "Money for my *education*?"

All eyes were fixed on Lady Longford.

Her ladyship cleared her throat. "It is true that a . . . a certain sum remained in your parents' estate after all the property was sold up. It has been invested for your future." She looked up at the ceiling. "There is no provision for withdrawals, however, so I did not see that you needed to be informed."

"Informed!" Caroline drew herself up, her eyes flashing. "Of course I needed to be informed! And just how long did you plan to wait before you told me, Grandmama? Until you were ready to find a husband for me, as you tried to find a wife for Papa? The money was to be my dowry, I suppose.

It would go to my husband when I married." She tossed her head scornfully. "Well, what if I don't choose to marry anyone, ever? What if I choose to have a career in music?"

Beatrix was uncomfortably reminded of her bitter confrontations with her own parents about her engagement to Norman—and since then, about the time she spent away from them, at Hill Top. But she was also impressed by the girl's willingness to stand up for what she wanted.

Lady Longford pressed her lips together. "I am only trying to do what is best for you."

Beatrix almost smiled. Her parents had said those very same words to her.

"What is best for me," Caroline said resolutely, "is to study at the Royal Academy. Since you do not have the funds to help, I shall go to Mr. Heelis and tell him that I will use my own money to pay my tuition, as well as my board and room and travel expenses."

Beatrix felt like exclaiming, "Well done, Caroline!" But instead, she only winked, and got a slight smile in return.

Lady Longford cleared her throat. "I wish," she said petulantly, "that you would not go leaping to conclusions in such a hasty way, Caroline." She glared at Miss Burns. "And that you had consulted me before you made other employment plans or—" She turned her attention to Mrs. King. "Or recommended my granddaughter to the Academy. However—" She stopped.

Everyone looked at her.

She cast her eyes toward the portrait of Lord Longford. Her voice became pious. "However, I believe that Lord Longford would be excessively gratified to know of his granddaughter's acceptance, and that my poor darling would much prefer it if I—" She paused here, and regarded Beatrix with a reproving glance. "If *I* were the one who supported Caroline. Therefore, in deference to his lordship's wishes—" She paused for effect. "I will pay the first term's tuition and board and room. If Caroline distinguishes herself, she may continue. If not—" She looked down her nose at her audience and her tone became imperative. "If not, my support will be withdrawn and she will come home. Is that clear to everyone?"

Everyone knew, of course, that the good Lord Longford had nothing to do with her ladyship's change of heart. It was Caroline's threat to ask Mr. Heelis for her money that had forced her ladyship's hand. And everyone knew that her ladyship, once committed, would continue to support Caroline. So everyone was pleased, and all showed it.

"Oh, thank you, Grandmama!" Caroline cried, and flung her arms around the old lady's neck.

"Splendid decision," said Mrs. King.

"I am so very glad," Miss Burns added warmly.

Beatrix, for her part, leaned forward and whispered something in Lady Longford's ear. Her ladyship looked up quickly. It seemed at first she would scowl, but then she actually smiled.

What Beatrix had said was, "And now we see you in your true colors."

17

In Which We Are Surprised

While Beatrix was at Tidmarsh Manor, Captain Woodcock was presiding over a hearing into Mr. Harmsworth's armed assault on the officers of the law and the general public, as well as the closure of Applebeck Footpath. The hearing was held in the library at Tower Bank House. Mr. Harmsworth appeared in the custody of Constable Braithwaite. Major Ragsdale, still in full kit, also attended, to face the charge of trespass.

The discussion of the issues was at times loud and heated (especially on the part of Mr. Harmsworth). The captain considered the question of the footpath, declared that its long history of public use warranted its continued use as a public thoroughfare, and instructed Mr. Harmsworth to immediately remove the barricades that were obstructing the path. Since the footpath was a public thoroughfare, the charge of trespass against Major Ragsdale was dismissed. Mr. Harmsworth was found guilty of armed assault and, after a stern lecture, placed on two years' probation. The removal of the barricades was one of the conditions of his probation, which also required him to yield up his gun.

Mr. Harmsworth was surly. "And if I doan't give up me gun? Or take down t' barriers?"

"Your probation will be revoked. You will be remanded directly to gaol and your case put before the magistrate—who is a good deal less lenient than I. Constable Braithwaite will accompany you to see that my order is carried out."

"But wot about me haystack?" Mr. Harmsworth glared at Major Ragsdale. "'Twas t' Ragsdale ruffians wot burnt it down. They ought to pay me for t' damage."

"I say, now!" the major exclaimed, in high dudgeon. "That is entirely uncalled for! The Ramblers are gentlemen, to a man. They would never stoop to—"

"Who says they stooped?" Mr. Harmsworth demanded truculently. "They cud've stood on t' road and tossed a burnin' brand onto t' haystack. No need at all to stoop."

The constable stifled a chuckle.

The major hooted. "Of all the foolish—"

"I will have order in this court!" The captain banged his wooden gavel smartly on the library table. "Major, there's no need for name-calling. Constable, escort Mr. Harmsworth to the footpath and see that the barricades are removed."

When they had gone, he said to the major, "I imagine you are contemplating some sort of public victory celebration. But I hope you will not further inflame the situation." He chuckled wryly. "Perhaps 'inflame' was not a good choice of words. All I meant to say was—"

"I quite take your point, Captain Woodcock," the major said with a small smile. "I shall let the Ramblers know that their celebrations, if any, ought to be private. And between you and me, I believe you handled the case admirably. I congratulate you, sir."

For a moment, the captain thought that the major was about to salute him. But he only pumped the captain's hand and left, saying once again how very glad he was that the business had been concluded satisfactorily.

The captain went to stand by the window with his hands in his pockets, whistling tunelessly and staring out at the summer garden. It had stopped raining, and old Fred Phinn was stooped over, weeding the phlox, while Mrs. Stubbs' cat watched him impassively. The captain had the uneasy suspicion that this was not the end of this affair, and I must tell you that he was right, but not for the reasons he supposed.

He wasn't planning to go out again for a time, and since it was rather warm, the captain took off his coat, unbuttoned his collar, removed his cuffs, and rolled up his shirtsleeves. He was thinking, and not very happily, that he should have to go to the kitchen and find himself something to eat. Elsa had been called away so suddenly that she had not prepared anything for him, which meant that he had eaten last night at the pub. He would have to eat there again tonight, and a pub lunch was not appealing. Perhaps a sandwich, although he was not sure there was any bread left and he had no idea where Elsa kept—

But someone was knocking at his front door. He stopped whistling and went to see who was calling.

"Why, Miss Nash!" he exclaimed in some surprise, for that was who it was. "Good afternoon!"

I am surprised that Miss Nash has come calling, especially since I know a little of the history of her heart. Of course, the captain knows nothing at all of her affections, for she has successfully kept them hidden from everyone, and most particularly from him. Indeed, he has not even seen her since the graduation of the junior class, at which (as one of the school trustees) he presided. He is vaguely aware that she looks pretty today, in a pink-and-white crepe de chine blouse and gray serge skirt, with pink two-button gloves and a neat, narrow-brimmed straw boater with pink velvet ribbons perched on top of her rich brown hair.

(If you are thinking that this is rather detailed description for a man who is only "vaguely aware" of the way the lady looks, you are right. Even a man who is acutely aware might not be able to tell you that her ribbons are velvet and that her blouse is made of crepe de chine, let alone number the buttons on her gloves. This is *my* description, since I want you to see what the captain is seeing, even though he could not begin to tell you the details himself. Authors have a way of slipping in bits like this, so you need to be wary.)

"Good afternoon, Captain," Miss Nash said primly. "If you have a moment, I should like to talk to you about the need for some repair of the two stovepipes at the school. I feel it should be done before the term begins, to avoid any unnecessary interruptions. The money is available, but we shall need the trustees' approval."

"Of course, of course," the captain said, wishing urgently that he had not taken off his cuffs and rolled up his shirt-sleeves. He led the way to the library. "Would you like a cup of tea? Elsa is out for a few days and the maid is off, but I'm sure I can manage."

"Tea would be lovely," Miss Nash replied, seating herself and taking off her pink gloves.

The captain paused on his way out of the room, remembering that there was something that Dimity always asked when it came to tea. "Milk or lemon?" he ventured.

Miss Nash smiled. "Milk, as long as it isn't any bother."

"No bother at all," he assured her gallantly.

But of course the whole thing was an enormous bother, from start to finish. The fire in the kitchen range had not been tended all morning, so it had quite naturally gone into a sulk, and the water in the iron kettle that sat on the back of the stove was not nearly so hot as it ought to have been. The captain had no idea where Elsa kept the tea, and some determined rummaging through the cupboard was required to find it, cleverly hidden in a green metal canister labeled TEA. He couldn't find the tea ball, so he put the loose tea in the teapot and filled it from the kettle (sadly, the water was only lukewarm). He was hoping the tea leaves would settle, although it's been my experience that they never do. If there's a tea leaf in the pot, it will find its way to my teeth and be displayed for all to see.

Another few minutes were required to find the sugar, cups, saucers, and spoons, and longer to locate the biscuits— only four of them, unfortunately, but perhaps that was enough, since they seemed a bit stale. He was elated to find the milk exactly where Mr. Llewellyn had put it on the kitchen table. It was warm (owing to sitting out all morning) and the thick cream had risen to the top, plugging the neck of the glass bottle. When he tried to pour the milk into a pitcher, the cream-plug stuck, then abruptly came loose, resulting in a flood on the kitchen table. There was only enough milk left in the bottle to half-fill the little pitcher, and not enough time (of course) to mop up the puddle on the table, so he left it where it was.

And all the while the captain was thinking, with rising irritation, that his sister Dimity would never have allowed both Elsa and the maid to go off on the same day, so by the time he located the tray and everything was on it, he was feeling thoroughly put-upon. Being a bachelor was all well and good, he reflected, as he shouldered open the kitchen door and carried the tray down the hall toward the library, and he certainly enjoyed his privacy. It was very pleasant to prop one's stockinged feet on the fender on a cold winter evening whilst reading the newspaper, and gratifying to smoke an offensively odiferous cigar without being frowned upon. But he had to admit that there were certain matters—such as breakfast, lunch, tea, and dinner, as well as collars and cuffs—that were not well managed unless they were managed under the careful supervision of the lady of the house.

The captain was still thinking these thoughts as he went into the library. "Sorry it took so long," he said, with an apologetic smile at his guest. "I'm not accustomed to looking for things in the pantry and—"

But that was as far as he got in his explanation, for in placing the heavy tea tray on the library table, he misjudged its position (or was perhaps smiling at Miss Nash when he might better have been looking at what he was doing). He missed the table, just, and the tray tilted abruptly, taking the teapot with it, and the cups and saucers and spoons and sugar bowl, milk pitcher, and plate of biscuits, **CRASH!** in a shatter of china and cascade of tea and milk on the library floor—the wood floor, thankfully, and not the rug.

"Oh, blast!" the captain muttered, staring helplessly down at his trousers, which were gaily decorated with splashes of tea and milk, whilst the puddle grew all around him like a small ocean lapping at his boots, the biscuits like little brown rafts (they were chocolate), sailing on a sea of creamy foam. He was a dolt. He was a clown. He was a clumsy idiot.

"Oh, dear," exclaimed Margaret. "Oh, my goodness gracious, I do so hope you're not burnt!"

"No, no," the captain said, touched that her first thought was for his welfare. "But I've certainly made a mess."

"Not at all," she replied. And then (over her shoulder, for she was already halfway to the library door), "Don't move. I'll just go and get a mop and some rags."

Now, we may want to ask how it was that Margaret knew that the cleaning supplies were stored in the closet under the stairs. Or we may just assume that since everyone keeps their mops and buckets and dusters and cleaning rags in that particular closet, most women would look there first. (I would—and I daresay you would, too.)

In the event, Margaret went straight to the closet. When she came back to the library, she was carrying a mop in one hand and a bucket and several clean rags in the other. She set them down and rolled up her sleeves. Since she still had on her neat straw boater (with the pink velvet ribbons), she might have looked a bit incongruous, but as far as the captain was concerned, she looked like an angel. An angel of mercy, that is, bent on mercifully mopping up the mess he had made.

By this time, Miles had somewhat recovered his equanimity. Margaret wielded the mop and then got down on her knees to finish the job with a handful of rag. Wanting to show that he could be useful, he also got down on his knees and began picking up the smashed crockery pieces and putting them on the tray.

"There," Margaret said, surveying their work with satisfaction. "Elsa will never know what happened—unless she misses her teapot. Although I must say, it isn't the prettiest teapot I've ever seen." She looked up at him and giggled.

We have known Captain Woodcock for—let's see, how many books now? Six, is it? During the whole of our acquaintance with that gentleman, I don't believe that we have ever found him to be seriously flustered. He is a man of cool and level head, who takes pride in knowing exactly what to do in every situation, whether it is dealing with an illegal gathering of badger-baiters or an angry man wielding a shotgun—or even a foundling baby that appears in his house as if by magic. He meets all with equanimity and a calm self-assurance.

But Margaret's sweetly girlish giggle and her direct look completely undid him. Or perhaps it was the fact that she was kneeling beside him on the floor of his library, in her lovely pink-and-white crepe de chine blouse (although he couldn't have told you what sort of blouse it was if his life depended on it) with the sleeves rolled to the elbows, and that little curl of rich brown hair just in front of her pretty ear, and the sweet, soft scent of violets (the violet toilet water that Annie had given Margaret for Christmas and which she saved for very special occasions), and the depths—the mysterious, luminous depths—of her gray-green eyes, ravishingly long-lashed.

Well. Whatever it was, Captain Woodcock was suddenly robbed of the wit to ask himself what under the sun he was doing or why he was doing it or whether it was the right thing to do, which was a very good thing, in my estimation. Both the captain and the headmistress are thoroughly Victorian, although they are living in an Edwardian age, and neither often acted on impulse, especially where the heart was concerned. Which makes the present scene so delightfully surprising, to me and I hope to you and I am sure to Captain Woodcock and perhaps to Margaret as well. (I say "perhaps" because I am not entirely sure what she had in mind when she came calling, although I suspect that she didn't, either.)

For once in his life, the captain was moved by a genuinely human impulse so strong and powerful that he could not resist it. Slowly, as if mesmerized by Margaret's nearness, he put his hands on her shoulders, and then, bending toward her, kissed her on the mouth. His arms went around her and he felt her sway toward him and he drowned in her sweetness—

But only for an instant. I am sorry to tell you that the Victorian gentleman he was, top to stern and fore and aft, took control of the situation. He released her and wrenched himself violently away, rocking backward.

"Please forgive me, Miss Nash," he exclaimed. "I am so very, very sorry! How can I ever—"

But if he had become the ultimate Victorian once more, Margaret, to her enduring credit, had not. She put out her hand and touched his cheek. "Nonsense," she said very bravely, and smiled a tremulous smile, although her eyes—ah, those luminous gray-green eyes—were wet with tears. "I should like you to kiss me again, Captain Woodcock, if you please."

Of course Captain Woodcock was pleased, very much pleased, to do as she asked. He was charmed, in fact: no lady had ever before asked him to kiss her in such an artlessly enchanting way. I suppose this was what won the captain's heart, this simple, guileless request for a kiss. And because they were both on their knees beside the mop bucket, their kiss somehow seemed . . . well, even more innocent, perhaps.

And since what happened next is a very private and intimate thing between two grown-up people who do not go around indiscriminately kissing everyone they see, we will step away and leave them to their enjoyment of each other. A very proper enjoyment, I hasten to add, for while they were not exactly behaving as Victorians, their passion (which was quickly and mutually discovered, to the astonishment of both) was constrained within Victorian bounds. I daresay that even Victoria herself could not have been more pleased, especially when the captain heard himself murmuring, much to his own amazement, "Oh, my dear Miss Nash, my very dear Miss Nash. I have been so blind, such a complete and utter fool! I find—" He swallowed. "I find that I love you, that I have loved you for a very long time. Is it possible . . . May I hope . . . Can it be that you care for me?"

To which Margaret heard herself replying, with bewildered shock, "Oh, yes, Captain Woodcock. I do care, very much!"

At this point, I imagine our good queen (who was happily and romantically in love with her darling Albert, to whom she bore nine children in seventeen years) would have smiled her blessing and tactfully turned her back, so as not to embarrass her royal self or them. And so, my dears, shall we.

Well, of course we *should*—although I don't mind saying that I am no Victorian, and neither are you. And since you and I have watched people kissing in the movies and on television thousands of times, we are not embarrassed in the slightest by what is going on. So I shall linger behind to watch and listen and share the romantic pleasure, and if you don't care to join me—well, I'm sorry.

The captain, entirely unable to be either sensible or rational and feeling himself quite out of his depth, took a deep gulp of air (exactly as if he were about to go down for the third time, which I suspect he was), and uttered those four words that have the potential to change one's life forever. Of course, since he was the captain, and a Victorian, there were a few more than four words and he saved the most important until the very end.

"Miss Nash, I am sure this is appallingly precipitous, but I cannot wait another hour, another minute, another second. Can you find it in your heart to make me the happiest of men? Will you marry me?"

Miss Nash's cheeks were every bit as pink as her blouse, her eyes were wet and shining, and she had no words to waste. She whispered, sweetly and simply, "Yes. Yes, with all my heart."

Which quite naturally leads, as it should, to another round of kissing and caressing and whispering. And if you think the captain's marriage proposal is rushing things a bit, please remember that he and Miss Nash have been acquainted for going on a dozen years now, during which time they have lived in the same very small village, participated in the same parish activities, attended the same school celebrations, and dealt together (he as trustee, she as headmistress) with a myriad of problems concerning the school. Not to mention that Miss Nash has secretly dreamed of the captain for a great many years, and that the captain has resisted his sister's earnest urgings that he should court Miss Nash for another good long time—although of course it could not happen until it was *his* idea, now, could it?

If I were waxing poetic (and isn't a love scene just the place for a little poetry?), I might say that their regard for each other, astonishing as it is to them (and perhaps to us), is like a plant that grows quietly and contentedly in a dark corner of the parlor, until one day—when we had altogether forgotten that it was there and in fact have often neglected to water the poor thing—it surprises us with an incredibly lovely blossom. Love is like that, sometimes, I am glad to say, growing steadily along in secret, as it were, and then suddenly bursting forth like the sun coming out from behind a bank of gray clouds, where it has been all along, even though we couldn't see it.

So. Now that they have finished kissing and saying, "Are

you sure?" and "Yes, very sure. Are you?" and "More sure than I have ever been in my whole life," we shall follow them to the kitchen, since both of them now feel very much in need of that cup of tea they didn't get when the captain dropped the tea tray, and a very good thing that was, if you ask me. Margaret (whose hat had fallen into the mop bucket during the romantic interlude and had been rescued and brushed off by the captain) saw at once that the fire had sulked itself away to nothing, so the captain brought in some kindling and a bucket of coal, and it was not long before the fire was cheerful again and the kettle was hot and the tea properly brewed. In the meantime, Margaret wiped up the spilt milk on the kitchen table, sliced a loaf of fresh bread she found in (who would have thought?) the breadbox and a joint she located (quite reasonably) in the cooling cupboard, and put out butter, mustard, lettuce, and sliced onions. She also found two pieces of apple pie, which no doubt Elsa Grape had meant for the captain.

"Quite remarkable, Miss Nash," Miles said as he sat down to his sandwich and pie, thinking how astonishingly changed was his situation since the last time he had visited his kitchen, less than a half hour before, and realizing that he was completely and entirely happy for the first time in his whole life. "Quite remarkable," he said again, picking up his sandwich. (Whether he meant not having to go out for a pub lunch or his being in love with Miss Nash, I shall leave it to you to decide.)

"Margaret," she said shyly, equally amazed at the way her life had changed—had completely turned upside-down and inside-out—just since she had walked through the front door. She handed him the mustard. "I should like you to call me Margaret, please."

"Miles," he said, and smiled at her, trying out "Miles

and Margaret" in his mind a time or two and thinking that the names sounded very well together. Then he tried, "Mrs. Miles Woodcock," and liked that just as much. Then his smile faded abruptly, for the captain was by nature a cautious man and had just remembered something he really ought to have thought of before he asked Miss Nash to be his wife. Not that he would object to her sister coming to live with them, since there was certainly room in the house, now that Dimity had married and left him. But still—

He put down his sandwich. "There is something we need to discuss."

"You're speaking of Annie, I suppose." Margaret met his eyes without hesitation.

Miles felt a thrill at being so well understood. It spoke well for their future together. He reached out and put his hand over hers.

"I hope you don't think I . . . Of course, your sister is welcome to live here with us. More than welcome. I just . . ." His voice trailed off. He pressed her hand and released it.

"Thank you." Margaret began to butter her bread. "However," she added in a careless tone, "it doesn't look as though that will be necessary. Annie is strongly considering Brighton for the winter. If she likes it, perhaps she will stay."

Brighton? Well, my goodness gracious. Are you surprised? I certainly am, and a bit put out, too. I mean, I had no idea that Margaret had already spoken to her sister about the situation at the sanitarium! I couldn't have guessed that Annie had expressed an interest in trying it out, and perhaps even making it permanent. I had expected, since this seemed to be an important part of our story, that we would know about it so that we could listen in on their discussion. But now we discover that we have been deprived. Margaret and

Annie have talked about this question behind our backs, as it were, not even letting us know that the subject was about to come up so that we could hurry over to Lakefield Cottages and listen in. I call that rude, I do. If I were in full charge of this story, it would certainly be better managed.

"To Brighton!" the captain exclaimed, every bit as surprised as we are.

Margaret put down her knife. "Miss Potter tells me that a friend of hers, a nurse, is opening a sanitarium there. She is looking for someone to help with the music therapy program."

"Ah," the captain said knowingly. "Miss Potter is in it, is she?" He'd had enough experience of Miss Potter to understand that when she saw a need for something to be done, it was generally done, in one way or another.

Margaret nodded. "Miss Potter suggested to me that Annie might be a suitable candidate, and I brought it up with her last night. I admit to being a bit surprised myself when she said she was interested." (You see? We are *all* surprised!) "Actually, Annie was more than interested. She seems terribly enthusiastic about the idea of spending the winter where it is warm and seeing new sights and meeting new people. I think it is very brave of my sister to want to leave her home and go off on her own. And of course I want to support her in any way I can."

Oh, but I can hear you now! You are saying, "Do come on, Miss Nash. Tell us the truth! You had that discussion with Annie last night, and you expected her to say no. You were shocked to hear that she was delighted to have the chance to leave you and make a new life somewhere else. In fact, it probably upset you dreadfully, since it meant that you were losing your sister and would have no one to care for—and no one to care for you, for the rest of your life, perhaps. And so this afternoon, you appear at Captain Woodcock's door, wearing your smartest little hat and prettiest blouse and toilet water and spouting that tall tale about the school needing some sort of repair. And all the time you were hoping that he—"

But the repair really does need to be done, I assure you. Miss Nash (who taught the juniors) and the teacher of the infant class have been talking about it since the end of the previous winter, when both the stovepipes proved to be far too smoky for everyone's good, especially the children's. And if a lady wishes to wear her favorite hat and gloves and blouse and dab on a bit of violet toilet water when she goes out to make a call, who are we to criticize? How often have you done the very same thing? And quite innocently, too, without any intention of making some poor hapless fellow fall in love with you.

Or perhaps you might wish to say, "Come now, Captain Woodcock, tell us the truth! Your cook-housekeeper has left you and the maid is off and it has been suddenly and forcefully brought to your attention that your house is in want of a mistress and that you are in want of a wife (collars and cuffs are a necessary thing in this world, after all). And here is Miss Nash on your doorstep, quite pretty in pink and very adroit with a mop. And your romantic passion suddenly overwhelms you, to the point where you are moved to ask her to marry you? Oh, come now, Captain. Let us be honest with each other. What you are after is a *housekeeper*."

So you see? There are two sides to every story, especially a romance. And if Miss Nash needs someone to take her sister's place in her heart and Captain Woodcock needs someone to take his sister's place in his home . . . Well, perhaps there is a certain mutually beneficial symmetry here.

But there is also a compelling mutual need, and I for one

am unwilling to find fault, especially since our two lovers seem to have the wish and the will and the wherewithal to make each other happy. There is more than enough sadness and loneliness in this world. A little love goes a very long way toward mending both.

Miles took charge of the situation. "My dear girl, of course we shall support Annie," he said warmly, "financially, if you like. And if the sanitarium doesn't suit, if Annie wants to come back to Sawrey—" He took a bite of his sandwich. "She will be welcome here," he said with his mouth full.

Margaret was glowing. "Thank you," she whispered. "Thank you very much, Miles."

And so, since there is much to discuss—the wedding and the honeymoon, and whether Mrs. Woodcock will continue in her position at Sawrey School (probably not), and when they will make their happy announcement to their family and friends (as soon as possible)—we shall wish them well and leave them to it.

Anyway, some very exciting—and disturbing—events are about to happen at The Brockery, and we will not want to miss a moment.

18

The Lost Is Found, and Then Some

It was rather rude of me to drag you away from The Brockery at the end of Chapter Fifteen, just as Bosworth was about to tell Hyacinth that she had passed the test—a test that not even Owl, in his superior wisdom, could have devised—and that he felt she was qualified to hold the Badge of Authority. So we shall return straightaway to The Brockery and rejoin the group in the kitchen—Bosworth, Hyacinth, Parsley, and Primrose (Hyacinth's mother), Parsley's nephews having taken themselves off to rejoin their circus, carrying with them Bosworth's hearty thanks and a basket of savory pies packed by Parsley.

You will notice that we have come back into the scene just where we went out, and that nothing at all has happened while we've been absent. Writers and readers of stories, you see, enjoy special privileges. In books, we are not limited to the arrangement of events as we are in the world of railway timetables and appointment calendars, which are organized chronologically and require one to be in the appointed place at the appointed time or all is lost. This, when you get right down to it, is a very tedious sort of ordering, and I for one am glad we're not limited by it.

Therefore. We have returned to the kitchen just as Bosworth propped Great-Great-Uncle Benjamin's cane against his rocking chair and held out his paw to Hyacinth. *"Come and sit beside your uncle, Hyacinth. There's something I've been meaning to ask you. Something rather important."* He chuckled wryly. *"And after what happened today—my falling into that pit, I mean—I think it might even be rather urgent. I've been thinking of it for a while, and should like to get on with it."*

On the other side of the room, Primrose paused in her mending. Parsley, who was mixing the batter for the steamed ginger-and-treacle pudding she was making for supper, gave Bosworth a questioning look. Reading her glance, he nodded briefly. Primrose sighed, Parsley smiled sadly (both were thinking of Thorn, I am sure), and then went back to their work.

Hyacinth sat down beside the badger, listened gravely as he spoke, and then was silent for a moment, looking into the fire. At last she said, in a very low voice, *"Thorn was meant to have the Badge, wasn't he?"* It really wasn't a question.

"It is given to the badger with the greatest promise," Bosworth replied firmly. *"I want you to have it, Hyacinth."*

"And when Thorn comes back?" she pressed.

Bosworth spoke with resolution. *"We will welcome him with open arms and rejoice with full hearts. And you, my dear, will go on wearing the Badge."*

She gave him a direct look. *"You're sure?"*

"I am very sure. If you agree, we'll work together to train you to take over the History *and the* Genealogy. *There's not that*

much to it, of course—just a bit of documenting. As to managing The Brockery—" He chuckled again. *"Well, I think you know all you need to know about that already, don't you?"*

"She certainly knows a good deal," Primrose said, looking up from her mending. *"But I do wish you wouldn't make it sound like you're on death's doorway, Bosworth. You have a great many good years left in you yet, my friend."*

"I may," Bosworth agreed cheerfully, *"but then again, I mayn't. Who knows, in this world? Animals come and animals go, but life goes on, you know."* There were other things he might have said about how nearly losing his life had made him realize that he really ought to name his successor, or how (while work was all well and good and ought to be done) every animal ought to leave some time in his life for enjoyment. But this wasn't the time to be philosophical. It was a time for practicalities. *"Given all the accidents that may befall us,"* he added, *"it's best to be prepared."*

"But still—" Parsley said, giving her pudding batter a few extra-hard strokes, which Bosworth took to mean that she expected him to live forever, which of course was impossible.

"I am thinking of myself, you know, and my own pleasures." He smiled merrily. *"Why, who knows? I might just go off on holiday, now that I can count on Hyacinth being here to manage things in my absence. I have long threatened to go and visit my very dear old friend, the badger who lives in the Wild Wood and sends me stories about Rat and Mole and some rapscallion named Toad. But what with one thing and another, I've never quite found the time to go."* He looked at Hyacinth. *"You'll accept the position, won't you, my dear?"*

"I really think we ought to wait," Hyacinth said in a low voice. *"When Thorn comes back—"*

"When Thorn comes back," Bosworth said quickly, *"I'm sure*

he will applaud what we've done and wish you the very best in your new position. Please say you'll do it, Hyacinth."

Hyacinth's eyes were wet, and Bosworth knew she was thinking of her brother. But she raised her head, straightened her shoulders, and said, in a clear, firm voice, *"Yes, I accept. I am honored, Uncle, that you think me worthy to wear the Badge. Thank you."*

Perhaps you can imagine all the things that were going through Hyacinth's mind. I can, anyway. She was thinking, I am sure, that this honor should belong to her brother—whilst at the same time she was enormously flattered that Bosworth Badger had chosen her. She knew she could do the work, but there was something else beneath that confidence: a worry, not well defined but certainly very real, that accepting this responsibility might keep her from doing other things that she wanted to do in her life.

Find a mate, for instance, and have a family. How would a male badger feel about a female who was in charge of such a complex operation as The Brockery, the largest and best-known animal hostelry in the Land Between the Lakes? Might he be . . . well, afraid of her? Or worried that she might try to manage him the way she managed the hostelry? And if she did find a mate who respected her commitment to her work, how would she find time for her children? She knew how busy Bosworth kept, from early in the morning until late at night—and he didn't have babies to attend to. She would be constantly juggling first one thing, then another. Would that make her happy?

But these were private questions, and Hyacinth kept them to herself, in part because they had no answers, in part because, if she voiced them, she might be misunderstood.

"I'm so glad you've accepted, my dear," her mother said tremulously. *"Thorn will be very happy for you."*

"*Yes, Mama,*" Hyacinth murmured, although in the past few weeks, she had begun to lose hope that Thorn would ever return. And if he did, she suspected that he would not be quite as pleased as their mother thought. Thorn expected to assume the Badge, she knew that much. Would he—

Parsley interrupted her thoughts. "*We are all very proud of you, Hyacinth.*" She scraped the batter into the pudding basin and wiped her paws on her apron.

"*Well, there's no time like the present, my dear,*" Bosworth said. "*Why don't we have our little ceremony here, in front of the fire? Later, we can invite a few friends and have something more official. But I'll feel better, knowing it's taken care of.*"

"*I'll fetch the Badge,*" Parsley said, and left.

"*I have something to give you, Hyacinth,*" Primrose said, and followed Parsley out of the room.

Bosworth leaned back in his chair. His broken foreleg was throbbing, his head ached, and he was inexpressibly weary. But all in all, he felt very good. Hyacinth had shown her mettle, and he had made his choice. And once he had made up his mind, he was not the sort of animal who changed it.

A few minutes later, Parsley was back, carrying the Badge in its velvet-lined case. It was a carved wooden disk ornamented with the Badger coat of arms and family motto, suspended from a woven blue-and-gold ribbon, designed to be hung around the neck. The Badge was worn only on state occasions, of course—it would get in the way of one's everyday duties. The rest of the time, it was displayed on the fireplace mantel in the library, beneath the portraits of other holders of the Badge. Thinking of this, Bosworth frowned. His portrait had not yet been painted. It should, for the sake of tradition. And so should Hyacinth's. He should have to arrange it with Fritz the ferret, who was quite remarkable at capturing likenesses.

A moment after, Primrose returned, trailed by the two young rabbits who helped with the housework and opened the door to guests. *"I thought our girls ought to be with us for this occasion,"* she said. *"Flotsam, Jetsam, take off your aprons and caps. We're having a ceremony."*

"Oooh!" squeaked Flotsam ecstatically. *"I loves ceremonies, I do!"* And Jetsam, always the thoughtful one, said, *"It's true, then? Hyacinth is getting the Badge, even though she's a girl?"*

"Yes, it's true," Parsley said definitively. *"Now, take off those aprons and smarten up, girls. And no chattering. This is serious business."*

Primrose was carrying a wooden box. She put it down on the table and opened the lid, taking out an ornamented silver pen and inkwell. *"This belonged to your father, Hyacinth. He wrote all his letters with this pen. I'm sure he would want you to use it when you're working on the* History.*"*

"But it's meant to be Thorn's!" Hyacinth cried tearfully, scrambling to her feet. *"He's expecting to have Father's pen and inkwell, just as he's expecting to have the Badge!"* She put her paws to her face and began to weep as if her heart would break. *"Oh, Uncle, I don't think we should do this. We ought to wait for Thorn to come home!"*

"But then we won't get our ceremony," mourned Flotsam.

Jetsam said sternly, *"You have to do this, Hyacinth. For us. To show all the other animals that a girl can do things just as well as a boy."*

Primrose put her arms around the girl's shoulders. *"Your uncle needs the assurance of knowing that the Badge is settled,"* she said in her daughter's ear. *"It means a very great deal to him, my dear. Please don't disappoint him."*

Hyacinth straightened and gulped a deep breath. *"All*

right, then," she said, and wiped the tears from her cheek with her paw. *"I'm ready."* She smiled shakily.

Bosworth hoisted himself out of his chair as Hyacinth came to stand before him, with Primrose and Parsley right behind. All wore solemn faces, befitting the important occasion—an occasion with absolutely no precedent, as everyone knew. The badger hadn't given any thought to what he ought to say, and his own investiture was so distant in time that he was having difficulty remembering it. But when he opened his mouth, the words seemed to come unbidden, perhaps from that place at the back of his mind where Great-Great-Uncle Benjamin had spoken. He found himself saying this:

"From time out of memory, we badgers have lived together in communities with badgers and other animals, linked by bonds of family and friendship. But even though we are all equal in our care and respect for one another, we must choose one of us to be our leader, to manage our day-to-day affairs and record our recollections before they pass into the remote and unremembered past. Our leader is one to whom we owe not obedience, but deference and a special regard, for he—" Badger caught himself with a cough. *"For she holds our needs in her heart, and is ever mindful of our concerns. It is my duty and great privilege to choose our next leader and the wearer of our Badge. I am proud to name you, Hyacinth, to succeed me as the wearer of The Brockery's Badge of Authority, the very first female badger ever to do so."*

Parsley handed him the badge. Hyacinth stepped forward and bent her head, and he gently draped the ribbon around her neck. As she straightened, he saw that she was smiling through her tears.

"I will do my very best," she said in a firm voice, *"to earn the trust you have placed in me, and to use the soundest judgment in*

making choices and taking decisions. I hope I won't disappoint you, Uncle."

"You won't," Bosworth said confidently. *"You'll do a fine job, Hyacinth, I'm sure. I—"*

There was a clatter in the hallway, the sound of footsteps, and a voice calling, *"Mama! Mama, it's me! I'm back!"*

"Thorn!" Primrose cried, as the door burst open and Thorn came into the room. *"Oh, my son, I had almost given you up!"* She flung her arms around him and buried her face against his fur. He was much more substantial than he'd been when he left, taller, heavier, and (to judge by his scarred ears and muzzle) a badger to be reckoned with.

"Thorn!" Bosworth shouted with joy. *"My boy, my boy, how wonderful to see you!"*

"Don't believe your mother," Parsley said stoutly. *"She never gave you up, not for a single moment. None of us did! Welcome home, Thorn."*

"Brother," whispered Hyacinth, her large dark eyes bright with tears. *"I can't believe—"* She began to pull the Badge off over her head and ears, but Bosworth caught her paw.

"No," he said sternly. *"You wear the Badge now, Hyacinth, and ever shall, until you are ready to pass it on to your son—or your daughter."*

But she could not respond, for she was already engulfed in her brother's warm embrace.

A moment later, Thorn let her go, stepped back, and looked down on her, his eyes wet and shining. *"Well, sister,"* he said (wasn't his voice deeper now, and richer?), *"I see that you've been promoted. Congratulations! It couldn't happen to a worthier badger."*

"You really think so?" Hyacinth asked tremulously. *"You're not upset?"*

"Upset?" Thorn threw back his head and laughed. *"I'm*

delighted, and so proud. The Brockery is lucky to have you." He turned to Bosworth. *"I hope, sir, that this doesn't mean that you're thinking of retiring altogether."* He looked down at the badger's bandaged foreleg and frowned. *"An accident? I trust it wasn't too serious."*

"A lucky tumble," Bosworth said, and kissed Thorn on both cheeks. *"Good you're home, boy. Where in the world have you been?"*

Thorn looked around at each one of them. *"Well, to tell the truth,"* he said, *"I've found a new home, a new happiness, and a—"* The door opened. *"And a new bride,"* he said, as the door opened again and a strange badger shyly entered into the room.

Everyone gasped. All the other badgers in the room were black, but this badger was different. Her thick, rich coat was almost pure white, shading to cream along tail and ears, and she had no stripe.

No stripe! Imagine that—a badger without a stripe!

But her eyes were the color of glittering rubies, her nose a gleaming alabaster, her claws polished ivory. Bosworth thought he had never seen a more beautiful, more striking female in his life. For a moment, he envied Thorn with his whole heart. If only he were younger—

Now, if you think I'm making this up, I assure you that I am not, not at all. Albino badgers are very rare, it is true, and they seem to be concentrated in a small number of locations, such as Kent and Dorset and Somerset. But they do exist, for I have seen pictures of them, and have even seen one stuffed and mounted. (Oh, dear.) And if you are trying to imagine what this one might have looked like, picture a miniature polar bear.

This strange white badger went up to Primrose. *"Hello, Mama,"* she said in a sweetly melodious voice, holding out a paw. *"My name is Buttermilk."* She smiled. *"Thank you for raising such a wonderful son."*

Well. I daresay you can guess what happened next—all the greetings and huggings and kissings and congratulatings and the general all-round happiness that was so full and frothy and fizzy that it threatened to overflow and spill in jubilant rivulets of joy and delight, like a bottle of bubbly with the cork popped, all over the kitchen floor. But it wasn't long before everyone was seated in front of the fire, where Parsley's ginger-and-treacle pudding was steaming merrily away in a pot of boiling water. All had cups of tea and plates of scones with plenty of butter and lavender honey, and Primrose and Buttermilk and Thorn were sitting as close together as three badgers could possibly sit, all of them looking unspeakably happy.

"And now you'll tell us your story, won't you, Thorn?" Bosworth pressed. *"You've been gone for months and months. We have to hear all about it—where you've been, how you met Buttermilk, the whole lot of it. And don't leave anything out—not a single word!"*

Now, each badger holds in his heart the Eighth Badger Rule of Thumb: *Every animal's story is one of the most important things about him (or her), for animals are storying creatures and live by their tales and the tales they have learnt from others. One's stories are as important to one's self-esteem as are one's fur and whiskers and ought to be admired in much the same way.*

That's the badgers' rule, yes. But I don't think anybody would mind if I took the liberty of summarizing Thorn's tale for you, since the telling went on for the entire rest of the day, Buttermilk often chiming in to tell one part or another, and Thorn interrupting Buttermilk, and questions from everyone. So here it is, a (very brief) summary. I hope

I haven't left out anything important; if I have, no doubt Thorn will be the first to correct me.

Thorn's Tramp Abroad

When Thorn left The Brockery, he intended to travel only as far as the south of England—it was winter, and all he was after was a bit of sun on his fur. But then he got the chance to cross the Channel on a ferry, and it wasn't long before he found himself in the south of France, and from there it was only a short hop to the Mediterranean. Of course, even a short hop may be a very great distance for a badger, whose legs are rather stumpy and who can only run fast in brief sprints. A brainy badger bent on reaching a distant destination, however, is always able to find some means of transport, and Thorn encountered no difficulties.

In Rome, he met an adventurous French badger named Pierre, and after a week of sightseeing, the pair headed north to the Swiss Alps, and then west to Paris. Pierre fell in love with a Parisian badger (we are leaving out a great lot of ooh-la-la here), so Thorn said goodbye and caught a train to Calais, where he went back across the Channel on a packet-boat. There were hair-raising adventures and thrills and chills all along the way, of course, escapes from this and that and the other thing, but we won't go into those. We'll hurry on to the serious romance, for that's when the story really gets interesting.

By this time, it was late April and Thorn had decided he had been away long enough. He had been traveling the whole time and, like many young badgers, had not taken the time to write home and let the family know where he was, so he was feeling urgent and (well, I should hope so!) a little bit guilty. He got off the packet-boat at Dover and struck off to the north, catching rides on hay wagons and beer lorries, foraging for his meals (an enterprising young badger can always find something to eat), and sleeping out under the stars.

All this was rather a lark, and Thorn was having a good time of it, until he fell in with a gang of . . . well, not very nice badgers, young toughs out to make a name for themselves in the badger world. This gang of thugs (yes, Thorn included) raided a sett called Brockmoor Manor on the outskirts of Underbarrow, a village a few miles west of Kendal, where Buttermilk lived with her family. (If it's just occurred to you that there is a similarity between the names of the badger setts—*Brockmoor Manor* and *The Brockery*—please know that it is no coincidence. From ancient times in England, badgers went by the name *brock*, as in the Helmingham Manuscript from 1398: "The black raven is friend to the fox, and therefore he fights with the brocks.")

Anyway, none of the hoodlums had ever seen such a white badger before, and one of them had the bright idea that they should take this stunning creature hostage and hold her for ransom. Her parents would probably pay dearly for her release.

"And that's where it all came crashing down," said Thorn, hanging his head. *"Seeing what they were about, I suddenly saw what I had become—a rogue, a renegade, a rascal. I was ashamed of myself. I couldn't be a party to that awful business."*

"He rescued me," Buttermilk said with a smile, snuggling up against him. *"He saved me from those beastly animals. If it hadn't been for him—"* She shook her head somberly. *"Something dreadful would have happened, I'm sure of it."*

Having extracted Buttermilk from the clutches of her captors (through trickery and with only a minor skirmish or two), Thorn returned her to her grateful parents. He was invited to stay at Brockmoor, so of course he did. One thing led to another, as it always does in romances, and very soon, Thorn was engaged to the most beautiful badger in the world. They had married a few days ago, with the blessing of her parents and the hearty approval of all the residents of Brockmoor. Which, like The Brockery, was an extended family of sorts, with rabbits and ferrets and itinerant voles and moles and rats and the like, all living together or coming to visit for a while and then leaving and dropping in again whenever they found themselves nearby and in need of a bed or a bowl of soup.

"Why, you're on your honeymoon!" breathed Flotsam, clutching her paws to her breast, her eyes round. *"How utterly romantic!"*

"Married!" exclaimed Hyacinth. *"I'm so happy for you, Thorn. And you, Buttermilk!"*

"You're coming back to The Brockery to live, I hope," Primrose put in eagerly. *"I should love to be able to hold my first grandchild."*

Thorn gave her a long look. *"Actually, that's what we've come to tell you, Mama. Buttermilk's father is getting on in years and needs someone to help him with Brockmoor Manor. I am now the wearer of the Brockmoor Badge, and I must return to do my duty."*

There was a stunned silence. Of course, Underbarrow was only twenty-some miles away across Lake Windermere—not very far at all to you and me. Why, we drive that distance, or more, to work or to school every day. And after Thorn's long tramp abroad, it probably didn't seem all that far to him. But to our stay-at-home badgers, Brockmoor might have been the moon.

Bosworth was the first to speak. *"The Brockmoor Badge,"* he said heartily. *"Congratulations, Thorn!"*

"Oh, yes!" Hyacinth cried. *"That's wonderful!"* She clapped her hands. *"Two badges in one family! What do you think of that, Mama?"* (I imagine that Hyacinth must have felt at least some relief, don't you? If Thorn wore the Brockmoor Badge, he certainly wasn't likely to feel put out that the Brockery Badge had been given to her.)

Primrose took out a white lace hanky and blew her nose. *"Why does it have to be so far?"* she asked plaintively.

"We know it's a long way," Buttermilk said consolingly. *"That's why we'd love to have you come and stay with us, for as long as you want."*

"At least until the first litter is born," put in Thorn. He grinned. *"I'm sure there'll be more than enough looking-after to suit both grandmothers."*

Primrose gasped and her hands flew up to her mouth. *"Oh, my gracious!"* she cried. *"The first litter! What good news! Why, of course I'll come!"* She looked at Bosworth. *"If I can be spared here, that is."*

"Of course you can be spared," Bosworth said firmly. *"We'll miss you, of course, but we'll manage. Won't we, Hyacinth?"*

"We will, indeed," said Hyacinth.

Parsley got up from her chair. *"Well, now, how do we feel about supper? We're having cheese and mushroom omelets and our ginger-and-treacle pudding."*

"Yippee!" cried Flotsam. *"I loves cheese and mushroom omelets!"*

"And ginger-and-treacle pudding is my very favorite," Thorn exclaimed. *"Parsley, old dear, you must have known I was coming. You certainly must give Buttermilk your recipe."*

"And I shall uncork that bottle of elderflower champagne that the fox brought the last time he came for a visit," Bosworth said. *"We shall have a celebration!"*

Of course they shall, as should I or you if we were in

their place. And since they have so much to celebrate—the return of the prodigal son, the introduction of his new bride, the announcement of the first litter, and *two* wearers of the Badge in one family—they're likely to be at it all night.

So we shall leave them to their domestic delights and go on to see whether anything is afoot in the village.

19

Mr. Beecham, a Conundrum, and Another Surprise

It is our Miss Potter who is afoot at the moment.

Over the years that she had owned Hill Top Farm, Beatrix had come to love nothing better than her regular evening walk. Winter, spring, summer, fall, walking was one of her greatest joys. But there was a special joy about late summer, when the land was burnished with the bronze glow of harvest, the skies were the color of the bluest of blue robin's eggs, and the sun, having almost finished his daily journey across the heavens, was at last content to drop into a billowy bed of lavender clouds, spread with rose-colored sheets. Coniston Old Man, the fell on the other side of Esthwaite Water, was also ready for bed, having drawn folds of diaphanous silver curtains about his burly head and shoulders and settled down to watch the stars and the moon put on their usual entertaining display, reflected in the lake that was spread out at his feet.

Tonight, as Beatrix walked down the hill toward Esthwaite Water, she was accompanied as usual by Rascal. He was quite fond of Miss Potter and would happily have run away from George and Mathilda Crook to come and live with her, except that there were already two dogs at Hill Top—Kep the working collie and Mustard, who was getting on in years. (Each of them thought that two dogs were one dog too many already, although they were of differing opinions as to which one ought to go.) So Rascal contented himself with going along with Miss Potter whenever he could, leaving the farm dogs to do their jobs: Kep to keep the Herdwicks in line (definitely not a chore Rascal fancied, being a fox hunting dog himself) and Mustard to look after the Puddle-ducks and the barnyard chickens. Rascal looked after Miss Potter, which he thought was a very good arrangement, indeed.

Contentment draped around her like a friendly woolen shawl, Beatrix walked slowly along the path at the edge of the lake, planting her oaken walking stick in the soft soil with every step. Esthwaite Water was the prettiest lake in all England, she had always thought. The grass along the shore was emerald green and velvety, clipped by the cows who grazed it and whose milk was sweet with its taste. The rushes grew tall in the shallows, and the lake itself lay calm and still, a luminous mirror reflecting the earliest glittering stars. A small wooden rowboat floated on its surface, as if suspended between water and sky, the fisherman a dark silhouette hunched over his fishing rod. Terns sailed on the water, gulls sailed through the air, and a pair of stately cranes stalked with silent dignity along the shore. A gaggle of water hens, small black birds with bright red bills, had entered into a heated discussion of where they would spend the night, some advocating one spot, others another, and all very positive in their opinions. A half-dozen ducks were busy getting their dinners, turning tails-up, heads-down among the green rushes and having quite a fine time of it indeed.

"Ducks are a funny sight, aren't they?" Rascal barked softly, trotting along beside her.

"Mmm," said Beatrix, agreeing with what she understood to be her companion's appreciation of the land and all its many creatures. She sighed with a touch of regret, and her contentment began to slip away. This trip would be too short—her visits to Hill Top always seemed to fly past in a flash—and she should soon have to go back to Helm Farm to look after her parents. She hated the thought, for returning always meant being blamed for all that had gone wrong in her absence. If she had stayed at Helm Farm, she could have done this or that to remedy the situation and her parents would have suffered no inconvenience. But as it was— well, of course it was all her fault. Naturally.

But what troubled Beatrix even more was the conviction that she ought to have a frank talk with Mr. Heelis about . . . well, about their friendship. The trouble was, she had no idea what she should say, or how she should say it. She frowned. Should she try to be clever or funny? Or perhaps she should be firm. Yes, perhaps it was best to be firm.

She cleared her throat and spoke aloud, resolutely. "Mr. Heelis, I believe I know something of your feelings for me and I must tell you that the situation is utterly impossible. It is out of the question that we should ever be more than friends."

"I beg pardon?" Rascal looked around, perplexed. Mr. Heelis? But there were just the two of them.

Beatrix shook her head. Far too firm, she thought, and too hurtful. He was a fine man and she had no desire to hurt him. She tried again. "My dear Mr. Heelis." Yes, that was better, but softer. It should be spoken more softly. "My dear Mr. Heelis," she said again, gently, "I am sorry to say that, while I have every respect for you, it is impossible that we should ever be more than friends."

"*Ah,*" Rascal said, understanding. "*You're rehearsing, poor thing.*" He always felt sorry for humans, who seemed to lead such complicated emotional lives—when it was all so simple, really. One did, or one didn't. If one did, the rest followed quite naturally, almost without thinking of it. If one didn't—well, one just went on one's way. No explanation, no rationalizations, no regrets.

"Thank you, Rascal," Beatrix said, smiling down at the little dog. It was nice to have an audience that didn't ask questions or offer advice. She paused, reflecting. Yes, the softer tone was certainly better, but her words were . . . Well, they verged on the dishonest. She should make it clear that her feelings were based on more than respect, shouldn't she?

"My *dear* Mr. Heelis," she said, getting down on her knees and looking into Rascal's eyes. "I have learnt to care for you, truly I have. But I must tell you that our friendship can be only that: a friendship." Ah, yes, that felt better. But surely some explanation was needed. She looked down at the gold ring on her finger. "You see, I still love Norman, and there's no room in my heart for anyone else."

"*Norman.*" Rascal put up a paw. "*It's always Norman, isn't it?*" He coughed cynically. "*Well, I suppose he'll do, as an excuse.*" That was another difference between humans and dogs. Every dog understood that when his mate died, it was a good idea to find another, even if only because it was so comfortable to curl up next to a warm body on a cold winter night, when the winds were howling and the snow was flying. Of course, *he* had not looked for another companion

after his Lady died, but that was because his village responsibilities kept him so busy, and because there was no one
that he truly fancied. (And if you're thinking that Rascal
might be just a bit hypocritical here—well, yes, I agree.
But he is not the main character in our story, and besides,
he's only a dog, so we will let that go.)

Beatrix took the proffered paw, frowning at the little
terrier, who seemed to have a skeptical expression on his
face. But was it true? Did she? Love Norman, that is.

Yes, yes, of course she still loved him. But the urgent,
unruly passion that had once been a burning flame seemed
so long ago, so far away. It was now only a gentle warmth.
Was it right to lead Mr. Heelis to believe that she could not
care for him because her heart was still too full of someone
else? And of course, there were other reasons—or rather,
another reason.

"My very dear Mr. Heelis," she said, still holding the little dog's paw, "I must tell you that—though I have come to
care for you deeply—our friendship must remain a friendship. It's my parents, you see." Yes, that was truthful. "My
parents expect me to remain with them for their lifetimes.
They have no one else, and I feel I owe it to them to—"

She stopped again. But it wasn't just that, was it? There
was more to it than that, of course, and she would just have
to be blunt about it. "I am sorry, Mr. Heelis," she said, "but
my parents would no more approve my marrying a country
solicitor than they approved my marrying a London book
publisher. That's dreadful, I know. But it's a fact, and I have
to face it."

Rascal retrieved his paw. *"Bully for you, Miss Potter,"* he said
softly. *"We've come to the heart of it at last, haven't we?"*

"Yes," she said, and sighed. "Now we have come to the
heart of it. I can lie to him and let him think I don't care. Or

I can let him know that I care, but that my parents are . . . bigots." She chuckled sadly. "It's a quandary. A conundrum."

"But you do care for him, don't you?" Rascal reminded her. *"I mean, all these 'dear' and 'very dear' Mr. Heelises—sounds to me as though you care rather a lot."*

Beatrix was silent for a moment. "I suppose," she said at last, "that if I were brutally frank with myself, I should have to admit that I do care for him. Deeply." It was true. He was the most admirable man she knew, always courteous, kind, and generous. A man that any woman might love—and choose to marry.

Rascal eyed her thoughtfully. *"And if you could have your way, you would marry him, Miss Potter?"*

She sighed, feeling that she was now in very dangerous territory, indeed. "I suppose I should also have to say that, if I could choose freely in the matter, I would choose . . . him." She got to her feet, speaking with determination. "But I cannot choose freely. And so I must choose between telling him an untruth and telling him that my parents are bigoted and intolerant."

"I'd go with the truth, on both counts," Rascal said. *"If it were me."* Of course, he had never been in this kind of situation. He was just a dog, and love was very much simpler for dogs. And cats and birds and—

Beatrix sighed again, more despondently this time. "I suppose I shall have to—" She broke off, turning. "Isn't that Mr. Beecham, just getting out of that rowboat?" The fisherman had pushed his rowboat onto the shore and was looping the painter around the trunk of a willow tree.

Rascal gave a startled yip. *"Yes, that's Auld Beechie."* He moved closer, pressing himself against her skirt. *"You want to be careful, Miss Potter. It doesn't do to provoke this fellow. If you ask me, he's the one who put a torch to Harmsworth's haystack."*

But Beatrix ignored the warning. "Good evening, Mr. Beecham," she called. "Lovely evening, isn't it?"

Thomas Beecham was nearing seventy, gray-haired and gray-bearded. He was missing most of his front teeth and the ones that were left were stained with tobacco, but he was nonetheless stocky and strong-shouldered. Squinty but shrewd gray eyes that missed nothing brightened his wrinkled face. He was dressed in a patched jacket, green corduroy trousers held up with a leather belt, a battered felt hat, and worn leather shoes. He carried a string of a half-dozen silvery fish in one hand and a fishing pole in the other.

"Hullo, Missus," he growled in a gravelly voice. He had come from the south of England years before, and had little of the local speech. "Didn't know ye'd come down from London."

"I'm over from Helm Farm, actually," Beatrix said. "That's where my parents are staying for their holiday." She smiled. "I was thinking of you today, and wondering when we should dig the potatoes you helped me plant."

"Another fortnight, or more," Mr. Beecham said. He did not return the smile. "Nights needs to git a mite cooler." He held out his string of fish. "Want some fresh trout, do ye, Missus? I'll sell it cheap. Thruppence a fish."

Beatrix cast an approving glance at the lake trout, which were plump and silvery and so fresh they were still wriggling. "I'd like that, indeed, Mr. Beecham," she said enthusiastically. "I'll take one—just the thing for tomorrow's dinner. Walk up to Hill Top with me and I'll get your money."

"Nah," he said. "I live right over there." He nodded in the direction of a cottage not far away, the small place, a stone hut, really, where the Crosfields—Jeremy and his aunt—had dwelled for a time. "Not near as nice as t' other cottage I had, but 'tis all I kin git for wot lit'le I kin pay." He did nothing to disguise the bitterness in his voice. He picked up a slender green willow stick, pulled a fish off the stringer, and thrust the stick through the gills. "Carry it like this," he said. "I'll stop fer my money tomorrow."

"Why, thank you," Beatrix said, and took the fish. She paused. "I wonder . . . I know this is a delicate matter, but I heard something today that troubled me very much."

"*No!*" Rascal yipped. "*Let's just go, Miss Potter. You don't want to offend this old rascal.*"

Beatrix took a deep breath. "I don't mean to be offensive, but—"

"*This man,*" Rascal said urgently, "*he flies off the handle. You never know what he might—*"

"Has t' do wi' that haystack o' Harmsworth's, don't it?" Mr. Beecham demanded sharply. He raised the fishing pole in a threatening gesture.

"*You see?*" Rascal barked, inserting himself protectively between Miss Potter and Mr. Beecham. He growled low in his throat.

"That's quite enough, Rascal," Beatrix said sternly. "Yes, it does have to do with the haystack," she said. "I shouldn't like to think—" She stopped, half-wishing she hadn't begun. The haystack was a police matter.

"Then don't," Mr. Beecham said roughly. He pulled his fierce gray brows together and thrust his head forward. "No biz'ness o' yours, Missus."

"*I'll defend you, Miss Potter!*" Rascal cried. "*This fellow won't lay a hand on you. Not so much as a finger!*" He planted his forelegs on the ground, baring his teeth and snarling fiercely.

"Rascal!" Beatrix exclaimed, irritated. She stepped in front of him. "If you don't stop, I shall send you home. Do you hear, sir?"

Rascal put his ears back, intimidated by Miss Potter's stern tone.

Beatrix returned to the subject. Since she had broached it, she ought to go on and not leave the matter hanging. "I was sorry to hear," she said quietly, "that some think you might have been involved."

Mr. Beecham clenched his fist. Rascal stiffened warily but was silent.

"I had nothin' to do wi' it, Missus," the old man growled. "Harmsworth's a fool and a cheat, and if somebody burned him out, I fer one wudn't shed no tears. I wuz fishin' that night, with a gent'lman from over acrost the lake, a charcoal burner. We wuz out here on the water when it happened. He'll testify to that hisself, he will. And that's wot I told the constable, when he asked me." He grinned bleakly, showing broken yellow teeth. "So ye kin jes' put the biz'ness right out o' yer mind, Missus. Yer haystacks is safe wit' me."

"Don't believe him, Miss Potter," Rascal urged. *"Everyone knows that this man is a liar!"*

Now, Beatrix was an avid reader of newspapers and understood very well that people sometimes fabricated an alibi, even going to the trouble of bribing a friend to testify on their behalf. She knew better than to place much confidence in an alibi. Mr. Beecham's angry, artless response seemed to ring with deep sincerity, but the old man had lied to her once before. What's more, he had stolen those seed potatoes.

"I see," she said cautiously. "Well, then, I shall rest easy about my haystacks. But I am told there were no storms that night, and no lightning. It seems that someone must have set that fire. Do you have any guesses as to who might have done it?"

"Guesses?" Mr. Beecham gave a sour chuckle. "Well, yes, I reckon I do, Missus. I'm guessin' it was Harmsworth hisself, the scallywag."

"Harmsworth?" Rascal yipped incredulously. *"Burnt his own haystack? That's nonsense!"*

"Mr. Harmsworth?" Beatrix asked in some surprise. "What reason would he have?"

"Wants to close that footpath, don't he?" The old man snorted. "What better excuse fer closin' the path than some-body puttin' a torch to his haystack? The fool prob'ly figgered he could get away with it." He grinned wisely. "He don't know Bertha Stubbs, though. She's mad enough to put a rock right through his window—or put a match to his barn." He gave Beatrix a significant look. "Anything else burns down at Applebeck, my money's on Bertha Stubbs."

Beatrix frowned, not liking the way Mr. Beecham was trying to shift responsibility. Bertha Stubbs made plenty of noise, but she was more bluster than bite. And anyway, Captain Woodcock had said that the footpath was being reopened, so Bertha would have no cause. But there was another question in her mind.

"Why would Mr. Harmsworth want to close the foot-path, though?" she persisted. "It doesn't make any sense."

"You ain't heard, Missus?" Mr. Beecham cackled. His breath smelled richly of garlic and beer, and Beatrix stepped back.

"Heard what?" she asked.

"Oh, forget it, Miss Potter," Rascal said. *"There's nothing to hear."*

"Noisy lit'le feller, ain't he?" the old man said, scowling down at Rascal. "Well, maybe the news ain't got round the village yet." He clicked his tongue against his teeth. "Harmsworth's got an offer to buy that orchard, y' see. But only if he closes that path first. The person who's after buyin' it told him there ain't no deal 'less'n the path's closed. The buyer aims to put in some new trees and don't want people treadin' back and forth crost the orchard."

So that's it! Beatrix thought. She should have guessed. Footpath closures always seemed to come when a property changed hands, or was about to. "And who wants to buy it?" she asked.

Mr. Beecham gave her a shrewd look. "Aha. Happen *you'd* like to have it fer yerself, eh, Missus?"

"Yes, of course, I'd like to have it," Beatrix said, being quite candid. "But I don't want the upkeep of an orchard, and anyway, I can't afford it. I purchased Castle Farm last year, and I have my hands full with new fences and drains and a barn roof."

"Aye." Mr. Beecham hitched up his trousers. "Ye're known here'bouts as a canny farmer, Missus. Somebody who takes good care o' her proppity. Ye're a careful mistress but fair to yer workers, as I know very well fer meself."

More than fair, Beatrix thought, remembering those potatoes. Anybody else would've made him turn out his pockets. "Thank you, Mr. Beecham," she said. "I do my best." She leaned closer and lowered her voice. "Who wants to buy it?"

Mr. Beecham laughed rudely. "Why, who else in t' world but her right royal ladyship, Missus?"

Beatrix stared at him disbelievingly. "Lady Longford?"

"*Lady Longford!*" Rascal barked. "*What would she want with an apple orchard?*"

"T' very same," Mr. Beecham said. "Offered to pay cash fer it, an' a right purty price, too—long as t' path is closed. Says she means to go into t' apple biz'ness."

Beatrix was silent for a moment, thinking about the claim that Lady Longford had made that very morning, as an excuse for not being able to send Caroline to study at the Royal Academy. She had maintained that she was nearly penniless, so destitute that she might be forced to sell some property in order to survive. But that had been a lie. She couldn't be so very destitute if she could afford to buy Applebeck Farm—with cash.

"How do you know all this?" Beatrix asked, at last.

" 'Cause Beever is my cousin," Mr. Beecham said promptly. "Ye know Beever, d'ye?"

Beatrix nodded. She knew the Beevers very well. Mr. Beever was Lady Longford's gardener and coachman. His wife was her cook-housekeeper.

"Tells me all sorts of things 'bout Tidmarsh Manor, Beever does." Mr. Beecham shook his head disapprovingly. "Now, there's a place I'd nivver work. Her ladyship pushes old Beever hard as a mule and don't pay him near 'nough for all he does."

Privately, Beatrix agreed, for Lady Longford was known far and wide as a demanding employer. But she did not want to say so out loud. "Thank you for telling me about the offer to buy the orchard," she said instead. "I'm glad to have the information."

But what should she do with it, now that she had it? she wondered, as she walked back up the hill to her farmhouse. Could Mr. Beecham be right? Was it possible that Mr. Harmsworth had burnt his own haystack to give himself an excuse for closing the footpath through the orchard, which Lady Longford wanted to buy? Or was this a clever ruse on

Mr. Beecham's part, designed to throw her—or anybody else who asked the question—off the track?

At Hill Top, she took the trout to the buttery at the back of the house, wrapped it in a damp towel, and put it on the cooling shelf. She glanced at the clock. It was only half-past eight and still light outdoors. This conversation with Mr. Beecham—perhaps it would be a good idea to discuss it with Captain Woodcock. She tidied her hair, put on the hat with the blue velvet ribbon, and set out down the hill behind the Tower Bank Arms—alone, this time, for Rascal had gone back to Belle Green to see whether dinner was ready. She had crossed the Kendal Road in front of Buckle Yeat Cottage when she saw Margaret Nash coming out of Captain Woodcock's front door. Her cheeks were the same pink as her blouse, her hair was in slight disarray, and she was smiling dreamily to herself.

Now, you and I know how quickly Margaret's life has changed and how astonished she is by everything that's happened on this momentous day. Our Beatrix, of course, doesn't know a thing—but she is about to find out.

"Beatrix!" Margaret cried, and hurried toward her, arms outstretched. "Beatrix, I have the most wonderful news! You'll never in the world guess what has happened!"

Beatrix stared. Surely it had to be good news, for Margaret was smiling with such a happy excitement. "Why, no," she said. "I don't think I can. Tell me."

Margaret's eyes sparkled. "Miles—Captain Woodcock—and I, we're to be married!"

"Married?" Beatrix stood still, feeling her eyes grow wide. "But how . . . when . . . ?"

"Today! It happened today! Isn't it marvelous? And we've just come back from Raven Hall, and telling Dimity and the major, who had us both to dinner. And Dimity is as thrilled as I am and absolutely insists on having the wedding in their lovely garden. It turns out that she has been secretly hoping Miles would ask me and I never guessed a thing!" The words were pouring out in a happy torrent. "Oh, Beatrix, it's too wonderful! And it's all thanks to you!"

"To me?" Stunned, Beatrix could not think what in the world she might have done to bring Captain Woodcock and Margaret Nash so precipitously together.

"Yes, you!" Margaret laughed delightedly. "In fact, it's all owing to you, every bit of it. If you hadn't suggested that Annie go to Brighton to the sanitarium—"

"Annie likes the idea?" Beatrix broke in.

"She absolutely loves it! She'll be coming to see you to get the particulars. She is terribly keen on going, which at first was something of a let-down for me, since . . . well, you know. It's a little hard to let her go. And of course I had no idea that she was hoping to find a way to leave the village."

"I understand," Beatrix said. "But I still don't see how Annie's going to Brighton is connected to your marrying Captain Woodcock."

"Well, it is," Margaret said. "I was thinking of Annie's going, you see, when I came here to talk to Miles about repairing the school stovepipes. He made us tea, but he dropped the tea tray, and I helped him clean it up, and he—" Her pink cheeks grew even pinker, and she looked away. "That's when he asked me to marry him, when we were both on our knees picking up the broken crockery and I was mopping up the mess." She giggled helplessly. "We must have looked very silly. But we didn't think of that at the time. It just seemed so right and natural."

"So you love him, then?"

"I have loved him for longer than I dare to think," Margaret said. "Of course, I could not have told him that, or even imagined—" She stopped, then said in a wondering tone, "How could I have even dared to imagine?"

Beatrix smiled. "But I still don't understand how—"

"Well." Margaret took a deep breath. "After he asked me to marry him and I had said yes, we went to the kitchen to make another pot of tea, because the first one was broken, and he asked if Annie would be coming to live with us and I said no, because she is going to Brighton, and he said how glad he was she is able to be independent and live her own life."

"Oh," Beatrix said, and suddenly understood why Margaret had connected Annie's move to Brighton with her own marriage. If Annie had insisted on staying here in the village, Margaret would not have felt free to encourage the captain's proposal. When he brought it up, she might have discouraged him, or rejected him. And once discouraged or rejected, he might not have persisted.

Beatrix laughed again. "Well," she said in a knowing voice, "that explains why you are wearing your best pink blouse and your lilac toilet water, I suppose."

"I suppose it does," Margaret acknowledged, "although I had no idea when I set out . . . I mean, I couldn't have guessed that he . . ." Her voice trailed off and her cheeks grew even pinker. "I hope you don't think—"

"I don't." Beatrix took Margaret's hands. "And however it came about, I am so pleased—especially if I have played a tiny role. Captain Woodcock is a fine man. I am sure he will make you very happy."

Margaret leaned forward and kissed Beatrix's cheek. "I will do all I can to make *him* happy," she whispered. "Now, please forgive me. I must run and tell Annie this news. She will be utterly astonished! And so pleased."

Beatrix watched her go, thinking that Annie could be no more astonished than she was. Margaret and Captain Woodcock—to be married! It was a shocking surprise, sure to set the village on its ear the minute it was known. Why, the tongues wouldn't stop wagging for months!

And who could blame Beatrix if, mixed into the surprise, there was a certain amount of envy? I could not, nor could you, I'm sure. First Dimity Woodcock had married Christopher Kittredge, the love of her life. And now Margaret Nash, the spinster schoolmistress, was marrying Captain Woodcock, whom she had loved, by her own admission, longer than she dared to think.

And I could not blame Beatrix, either, if there was a certain amount of sadness, mixed with the envy.

Could you?

20

At Applebeck

Of all the difficult days Gilly had spent at Applebeck, to-day had been the very worst. After breakfast, her uncle had taken his shotgun down from its hooks on the wall and stormed out of the house, muttering under his breath about the footpath. A little later, as she churned butter in the buttery, she had been startled to hear the rattle of gunfire from the direction of the footpath. She had left her churn and run toward the house, where Mrs. Harmsworth was standing at the door, staring out.

"What's happening?" Gilly cried, frightened. "Who's that shooting?"

"Who cares?" Mrs. Harmsworth said, and lifted her chin. Her eyes were glinting. "Mebbee t' fool has shot his-self. Now, git on back to t' buttery and finish thi churnin'. When 'tis done, there's t' floors to be scrubbed and t' stove to be blacked." And with that, she turned and went back into the house.

Gilly knew that the Harmsworths were not happy together, but it was a shock to hear Mrs. Harmsworth talk about Mr. Harmsworth in that way, especially since Gilly doubted very much that Mr. Harmsworth had shot himself. It was more likely, angry as he was, that he had shot someone else.

There was nothing she could do about the situation, however, so she went back to the old stone buttery—a drafty place and cool, very pleasant in the summer but appallingly cold in winter—and tried to lose herself in the pleasures of sweet milk and rich cream and thick golden butter. She also took refuge in her favorite daydreams, which were her chief comforts through the long days—daydreams where she found employment elsewhere, with amiable people, in a clean and agreeable place, where she could have an hour to herself every day to read, and perhaps a little gray cat who would come and drink from the saucers of milk she would put out for him. But they were only daydreams, and Gilly was realist enough to know that, whatever happened to Mr. Harmsworth, there would be no escape for her. She would still have to live with Mrs. Harmsworth, who would continue to demand that she do all the work. All she could do was run away.

Mrs. Harmsworth refused to wait the noon meal for her husband, saying that whatever fix he'd got himself into was no business of hers. She and Gilly had just sat down to bowls of potato soup and sausage and brown bread and cheese when they heard a clatter outside, and the sound of voices. It was Mr. Harmsworth, come to fetch some tools. With him was Constable Braithwaite, very stern, who had apparently come to see that the barriers at either end of the footpath were taken down. An hour later, Mr. Harmsworth was at the table, greedily tucking into his dinner, sullen and silent. In spite of Mrs. Harmsworth's shrill questioning, he would not say a word about what had happened, or who or what had been shot, or why. His only words, at the end of his meal, were addressed to Gilly, who at Mrs. Harmsworth's command, had already started the washing-up, in a basin at the far end of the table.

"Wot dost tha know 'bout Miss Potter, girl?" he demanded roughly.

Gilly turned to stare at him, her hands dripping. "Who?"

"Miss Potter." He got up from the table and came toward her. "Owns Hill Top Farm."

"I don't know her," Gilly said, and went back to her washing-up. Strictly speaking, this was true, although you and I know that upstairs, hidden under her straw mattress, is the book that Gilly won in the school spelling contest, written by Miss Potter. At the moment, Gilly is glad that she had not mentioned the book to her aunt or uncle.

"Then why dost she want to see thi tomorrow?" He seized her arm, his face ugly, his eyes narrowing to slits. "What nonsense hast tha told her aboot us?"

"See me tomorrow?" Gilly asked blankly. Why would a famous author want to see *her*? Did Miss Potter mean to take her book back?

"What all this?" Mrs. Harmsworth demanded. "What's this aboot Miss Potter?"

Mrs. Harmsworth had never met Miss Potter, but she had heard plenty about her from the people at the butcher's shop in Far Sawrey, where she queued up once a week for a joint. Miss Potter was a wealthy lady from London, who made books for children and who owned two of the best farms in the area—one of them, Hill Top, just on the other side of the beck.

"What dost Miss Potter want wi' our Gilly?" she asked

suspiciously. (You will notice that it is "our Gilly," now that someone else seems to have taken an interest in the girl.)

"Dunno," her husband muttered. "But she's to come for t' girl up tomorrow after dinner."

"Come for her?" shrilled Mrs. Harmsworth. "Miss Potter is takin' our Gilly away? Why? How could'st tha let her do such a thing?"

"Hold tha tongue, woman." Mr. Harmsworth glared at his wife, but did not answer her question, no doubt because he did not want to admit that he had endangered Miss Potter and her pony and that an afternoon with Gilly was the price to be paid for his reckless behavior. "See that she's got a clean pinny, one that ain't patched." He turned his glare on Gilly. "And see that tha keeps't a curb on thi tongue, girl. Miss Potter's got no need to know nothin' aboot us or what goes on in this house. Not a word, dost tha hear? Not a single word. And be sure that tha'rt back afore tea."

And that was all that could be got out of him for the rest of the day.

Mrs. Harmsworth now had another reason—a very good reason, to her way of thinking—for being angry at Gilly, who had been singled out by their wealthy neighbor for who-knew-what kind of attention. She kept after her for the rest of the day, shrilling demands and lashing out furiously when the work was not done to her specifications. As it could not be, for she never gave the same instruction twice, always wanting something different, until Gilly was dizzy with her demands and had never felt so angry and resentful in her whole, entire life.

For her part, Mrs. Harmsworth could not contain her rage, both against her husband, who had clearly had some sort of run-in with the law and would not tell her about it, and against Gilly, who must have had some sort of secret

communication with Miss Potter. Why else would that
lady insist on seeing a mere girl? Was she going to try to
take Gilly away and put her to work at Hill Top Farm?

Of course, that was nonsense, Mrs. Harmsworth told herself. Gilly was a good dairy worker, to be sure, but she wasn't
that good, and anyway, Mrs. Jennings, who did the dairy
work at Hill Top, was known to be amongst the very best in
the district. Gilly wasn't pretty, either, with that milky face
and pale hair. Or smart—why, she rarely said a single word!
So no doubt this was just some sort of silly, half-baked
scheme on the part of Miss Potter, and didn't mean a thing,
although why Mr. Harmsworth would consent to let Gilly
have a full afternoon off, she couldn't understand for the life
of her. And when Mrs. Harmsworth couldn't understand
something, it made her very, very angry.

This puzzling business went round and round in Mrs.
Harmsworth's mind for the rest of the day, until she felt
herself spinning out of control and knew almost nothing
except for her rage at Gilly, who was somehow at fault for
everything. And since Mr. Harmsworth absented himself
in the orchard and barn and Gilly was the only available
target for Mrs. Harmsworth's wrath, Gilly was scolded over
and over again.

This sad state of affairs continued until tea was finally
over, the darning basket was emptied of its socks, and at
last, both Mr. and Mrs. Harmsworth went to bed in their
second-floor bedrooms. Gilly climbed the narrow ladder to
her attic room—as usual, with no candle. The moon was
bright, and since she was half-afraid that Miss Potter might
require her to return *The Tale of Jemima Puddle-duck*, Gilly
took it out from under her straw pallet and carried it to the
open casement, wanting to read it one more time. Perhaps
winning it had been a mistake, after all, and Miss Nash had

really meant to give it to someone else. Or perhaps Miss Potter (who had donated it to the school) had found she needed this one and meant to take it back. Gilly sighed, turning the pages and thinking how she should hate to give it up, for it was the only book she had ever owned and she was very, very fond of it.

She had just got to the part where Jemima had met the fox and was being shown by that gallant gentleman to a private place where she might lay her eggs, when she heard a noise outside. She lifted her head. Someone was coming around the back of the barn, moving slowly through the moonlight. It was the figure in a black bonnet and long gray cloak, carrying an old-fashioned tin candle lantern.

Gilly was not afraid; as I said, she had seen the ghost before, on more than one occasion, and knew that it was not an invention of her overcharged imagination. She knew that others had seen it, as well, over many decades. The children at school had told her that, so she had no reason to doubt the ghost's reality—as a ghost, that is. She had seen for herself the way it floated, the way it dissolved, took form, and then dissolved again, as if it were not a thing of this earth and not subject to natural laws.

But as Gilly watched, she saw that there was something different about this ghostly figure—about the way it moved. This figure did not gracefully dissolve into a transparent mist and then re-form. It had a certain solidity and strength, a certain . . . well, clunkiness.

Gilly put down her book, frowning. She hesitated a moment longer, watching the figure make its way along the path. And then, glad that she had not yet changed into her nightgown, she pulled on her shoes and climbed back down the ladder, then crept down the creaky stairs to the kitchen, and silently, silently out the door and into the moonlit night.

21

A Modest Proposal

Will Heelis had business at the bank in Windermere that afternoon, and had stopped off to have a look at the property on Cockshott Point, on Lake Windermere, where the flying boat factory was about to be built. As far as he could tell, everyone in the surrounding farms and villages was opposed to the scheme, but whether their opposition would do any good or not, it was too soon to know. The owner of the factory seemed to be moving full steam ahead, convinced that Lake Windermere was the perfect site to experiment with his new aeroplane, which was already fully operational and had already made a flight or two over the lake.

When Will arrived at the ferry, he found that there was a long queue ahead of him, for the boat was temporarily docked for repairs to the boiler. He was forced to sit and twiddle his thumbs for several hours, so it was twilight when he was finally aboard and on his way back across the lake, in the company of a number of disgruntled passengers, local folk who were heard to say, with bitter sarcasm, " 'Tis nivver a boat, 'tis a conundrum."

Will had lived for some time at Sandground, in Hawkshead, with Cousins Fanana and Emily Jane. These two spinster ladies usually made an early night of it. Not wanting to inconvenience them by asking for a late supper or disturbing them when he made something for himself, he stopped at the Tower Bank Arms to eat. No, not at Captain Woodcock's house, which is also called Tower Bank, but at the inn, which offered (in Will's opinion) quite a good pub meal.

Now, if you are thinking that it is rather confusing to have both an inn and a house called Tower Bank in a village as small as Near Sawrey, I will fully agree. You see, before Captain Woodcock bought the house (which is largish and somewhat grand), it belonged to the village squire. The squire was also the owner of the village pub, which bore the amusing name The Blue Pig. Feeling that "The Blue Pig" did not have quite the dignity he was after, the squire decided to call his pub the Tower Bank Arms, in honor of his house. The villagers were not pleased (they were accustomed to The Blue Pig, as it had been called for as long as anyone could remember) and off-comers were terribly befuddled. Strangers who intended to take a room for the night at the Tower Bank Arms found themselves on the squire's doorstep, whilst people who came to do business with the squire were often discovered lingering over a half-pint at the pub.

But Will Heelis knew just what he wanted and where to find it. He had stopped at the Tower Bank Arms because Mrs. Barrow (the pub owner's wife) served a fine Cumberland sausage with a sauce of apples and onions, along with boiled potatoes and cooked red cabbage, and he made a splendid meal of it. This was a good thing, and soothing, for our Will had been troubled the entire day, not only by the flying boat controversy, but by a certain concern that chased itself around and around in his head whenever he was not thinking of flying boats.

This concern had to do, as you have most certainly suspected, with Miss Potter. The fact was that Will had not been able to get her out of his mind since he had let her out at Hill Top Farm the day before. Over his Cumberland sausage, and after a great deal of backing and forthing and toing and froing in his mind, he had come at last to a conclusion, a momentous one. It was time to have a frank and candid talk with the lady, who lived not a stone's throw from where he was eating his dinner. (Indeed, the fact that she lived so close by had probably influenced his choice of a place to dine. He might, after all, have chosen to eat at the Sawrey Hotel, where he could have gotten a perfectly good piece of fish or a rare roast of beef.)

Will understood that there were very good reasons weighing against a conversation with Miss Potter. She was still very fond of her dead fiancé, and felt a great loyalty to Warne and his family, whom she counted as her dear friends. But Will also felt that she was growing fond of *him*, although she might find that difficult to acknowledge, especially since her parents would be strongly opposed to any suggestion of a match between them.

Still, he knew, beyond a shadow of a doubt, how he felt about her. And even though he was generally mild-mannered, slow to speech, and sometimes slow to action, he had a remarkably stubborn streak—some might even say a certain doggedness. Will Heelis had never considered himself a man of grand passions or even a very romantic person (he

was far too sensible for that), but he was a man of firm con-
victions and (when it was necessary) of unwavering courage.
When he made up his mind that he wanted something, he
would not let anything in the world stand in his way. And
now that he clearly understood that he loved Miss Beatrix
Potter and could never be happy with anyone else, he knew
that he had to act on that knowledge.

It was as simple as that—and it was why he needed to
talk with her. He didn't care (he told himself as he dis-
patched his sausage) that her parents would never agree to
their marriage. It didn't matter (he thought as he paid his
bill) how long he would have to wait. He could wait as long
as necessary (he concluded, taking his hat and leaving the
pub), if Miss Potter would only promise him that, somehow, someday, she would be his wife.

His wife. Mrs. Will Heelis. Beatrix Heelis.

These words wrapped themselves like a loving embrace
around his heart and would not let go. They were still ringing in his mind when he went down the front steps into the
darkening evening and turned to the left to climb the hill to
Miss Potter's house, which stood directly behind the pub.
They were still ringing like bells in his heart, not a half-dozen
steps later, when he bumped squarely into the lady herself,
who had not five minutes before left Captain Woodcock's
house, having told him what she had learnt from old Mr.
Beecham.

"Mr. Heelis!" she exclaimed, snatching at his arm to
keep from falling on the uneven ground.

"Miss Potter!" he cried, steadying her. "Oh, forgive me! So
clumsy—I'm sorry. Are you all right?" He dropped his hand
and snatched off his bowler hat. "You're not hurt, are you?"

"No, of course not," she said breathlessly. "I'm afraid I
wasn't looking where I was going. I didn't expect—"

"Nor did I," he said. The determination that had filled him while he was eating his Cumberland sausage now seemed to have seeped away, and he thought it might be a good idea to say good night and be on his way back to Hawkshead. But since she was not running away up the path, and since he did want so very much to talk with her, he found himself suggesting, "Perhaps you would like to go for a walk, Miss Potter. The moon is rising, and it will be very bright. I shouldn't think we would need a lantern."

She took a tremulous breath, hesitated, then said, "Yes. Thank you, Mr. Heelis."

Which is why, a few moments later, we can see the pair of them, walking down the Kendal Road in the direction of Wilfin Beck, Mr. Heelis tall and thin and lanky, in his usual brown suit and brown bowler hat and with his hands in his pockets; Miss Potter short and rather plump, in her Herdwick tweeds, with her straw hat (the one with the blue velvet ribbon) and oaken walking stick. And since we very much want to hear their conversation—at least I do—we will follow along behind. Of course, if you are not inclined to eavesdrop on what promises to be a private and intimate discussion, you are certainly free to wait at the gate, where there is a convenient bench. I shan't hold it against you, and will be glad to tell you everything that has happened when we meet again. You will stay behind? Ah, but I see that you are just as eager to listen as I, so we shall hurry to catch up.

There is a certain self-conscious distance between our two friends, and for a long time, a silence, not quite comfortable. Then, when they speak, they both speak at the same time, and in a rush.

"I have been hoping to talk with you, Miss Potter—"

"There are some things that need to be said, Mr. Heelis—"

This choral unison strikes neither of them as funny, of course. They are both far too serious for that. After a moment, they try again, with (naturally) the very same result.

"I have been thinking all day—"

"It has been much on my mind—"

Gallantly, Will smiles down at her. "You first, Miss Potter."

Beatrix shakes her head. "No, you, Mr. Heelis. I insist."

And with this, of course, they are at another impasse.

But at last, just as they reach the bridge over Wilfin Beck (the very same spot where Winston was frightened by the gunshot and ran away with the pony cart that morning), Will summons his courage, takes off his hat, and opens his mouth to utter the words that have been going round and round in his head all day. The night has grown dark by this time. He is grateful for the shadows, and although the moon shines brightly enough to see Miss Potter's face, he turns his head to one side and looks down at the ground instead. He finds that he has just enough courage to speak, but not quite enough courage to look at her.

"Miss Potter, I care for you. I care deeply. I don't suppose this is any secret to you—I am sure it has been increasingly apparent each time we've been together this last year, and perhaps even before. Please do believe me when I say that I am not insensible to your feelings for Mr. Warne, nor to your . . . difficulties with your parents. But I must tell you truly, and from my heart, that if your circumstances change—"

He swallows. The words sound too blunt, too forceful to his ears. Has he said too much? Is he too arrogant? Is he frightening her? But having gone this far, he cannot see how to get back, and feels as if he has somehow crossed a bridge of enormous consequence into a land of unfathomable mystery. He takes a deep breath and stumbles on. The words sound inadequate and clumsy, and he wishes he'd taken the time to rehearse them. But (he tells himself) at least they are sincere.

"I know your parents believe me unworthy. It is true—I *am* unworthy, and I should never wish to cause you a single moment's unhappiness on my account. But if . . . if your circumstances can ever permit you to consider having me, Miss Potter, my heart . . . my heart is yours." He gulps. "Truly, honestly, and eternally yours."

Oh, my dears. If a very tall and lean man, handsome and well mannered (and a man of whom you were already more than fond) made this speech to you, could you resist? Tell the truth—honestly, now. I do not think I could, especially when he had got to the part where he was truly, honestly, and eternally mine. I don't know about you, but I'm sure I should crumble. I should simply fall into his arms and wait for the wedding bells.

But our Beatrix is made of sterner stuff. She hears what we have just heard and is profoundly moved by it. What woman could fail to be moved by such a humble, self-effacing, sweetly modest proposal? Yes, of course she is already aware that Mr. Heelis harbors feelings of affection for her, but she could not have expected a proposal so soon, or so eloquently framed, or spoken in a voice that rings with such passion. If she were able to freely choose (as a certain sagacious little dog has put it), she would probably do what I would have done. Her resolve—to be true to Norman, to respect her parents' wishes, to remain a spinster for the rest of her life—would have crumbled.

But it doesn't. Beatrix gathers all her strength, straightens her shoulders and firms her voice, and speaks the speech that she had practiced, or something very like, although she is uneasily aware that it does not quite fit the circumstance.

"My dear Mr. Heelis, I must tell you that—though I do care for you—our friendship must remain a friendship. I still have an enduring fondness for Norman, and my parents present a substantial obstacle to my living my life as I would choose to live it."

Well, there it is. As clear and emphatic a "no" as any woman might reasonably be expected to give a man who has just confessed that he is eternally hers. Not only that, but she has given reasons, to boot. A previous affair of the heart, parents' objections. Sound reasons, I should think. Irrefutable. I'm curious to see how our Will is going to respond.

But Will has not thought beyond his first speech. In fact, it has taken so much courage to put his feelings into words, and his words were so spur-of-the-moment, that he has not given any consideration to what he should say after. After she says "yes" or "no," that is. And her definitive "no" has rather considerably narrowed the possibilities, wouldn't you say?

The polite response, of course, the one we should expect him to offer, is the murmur of some sort of brief, apologetic phrase: "Thank you, my dear Miss Potter, and do please forgive my impetuousness. I fear I am not quite myself this evening. Shall I see you home?"

To which Beatrix might be supposed to reply very politely—something on the order of, "Oh, please do not apologize, Mr. Heelis. It is of no consequence, no consequence at all. We shall not speak of the matter again. And I beg you not to trouble yourself. I can walk home easily from here. Good night."

But Will has long since left the familiar country of

formulaic phrases and conventional actions and has crossed the border into that bewildering no-man's-land where people do the strangest, wildest, most utterly unpredictable things. Perhaps you have found yourself in this sort of situation before, where it is absolutely impossible to know what you are going to say or do until it is actually said or done, and then you are astonished at yourself.

And so is Will. He is amazed to find himself taking Beatrix's hand, looking directly into her face, and asking a completely irrational question in an entirely rational tone: "My dear Miss Potter, how is that?"

"I beg your pardon," she says, and is so startled by this unexpected question that she lifts her eyes to his.

"Tell me how you would choose to live your life—if you were free to choose."

And with this impertinent, insolent, and terribly cheeky request, Will Heelis has opened a whole new chapter in his life, and in Miss Potter's.

"Please." She tries to retrieve her hand and can't. "I don't . . . I can't possibly . . . I'm not sure . . ."

He refuses to relinquish her hand. "I think you are sure, Miss Potter. I *know* you are." And of course he is right.

"It doesn't matter what I would choose, Mr. Heelis. I *can't*. Really," she adds rather crossly, "it's out of the question. It's pointless to talk about it, so let's not. And if you don't mind, I should like you to let go of my hand."

Perhaps you are thinking that Miss Potter should have rehearsed her second act. I most certainly agree. If I am ever put into this awkward position, I will be sure to have given some thought to what I will say after I have said "no," for sometimes even a very firm "no" is not the last word.

Mr. Heelis thinks so, and is not going to take no for an answer. As I said earlier, he is a persistent man, even a stubborn man, when his feelings are aroused. And they have been corked up for so long that, now that they are loose, they refuse, like Aladdin's genie, to be stuffed back into that ridiculous bottle. They emerge with a power and eloquence that astound him and catch Beatrix completely off her guard.

"I believe we must talk about it," he says firmly, and continues to hold her hand. "I love you, Miss Potter—Beatrix—and I believe that you love me. Do you not?"

Beatrix turns her head aside. "I admit to a certain . . . deep fondness for you, yes," she says reluctantly. "But our friendship must remain a friendship. I—"

"You have already said that." He is impatient. "If you are deeply fond of me—if you love me, if you would choose to marry me if you were free to choose . . ." He stops, feeling that there might be one too many *ifs* in his sentence, but not sure which one should come out. "If you *would* choose to marry me, Beatrix, you should say yes, now. I am content to wait until your circumstances change, however long that may be."

Uncertain, startled, she turns to look at him. "Wait?"

"Yes. Wait. Of course. What did you think? That I would carry you off to Gretna Green to be married next fortnight? I know that your parents prefer you to—"

"Mr. Heelis—"

He touches his finger to her lips. "Will, please. Call me Will, Beatrix."

She pulls back, as if his touch is electric. Perhaps it is. How long has it been since a man touched her lips? Norman is said by all who knew him to be as shy and diffident as she, and they were so rarely alone—I wonder, did he ever even kiss her? Or even hold her hand? Or did their love affair take place only in their letters?

She takes a deep breath and steadies herself. "My parents will never consent to our marriage, Mr.—Will. It's pointless even to speak of it."

"Your parents—" He stops. He was going to say that her parents would not live forever, which is certainly true but sounded cruelly blunt. He settles for something quite different, and hits upon—perhaps by accident or perhaps even by some sort of divine intervention—the one thing that might move her.

He says: "Let's not consider your parents, or their consent or refusal, not at the moment. Can we not simply agree that we love one another, and that we would like to be married, if, and when, the circumstances permit?"

She frowns. "I don't believe—"

"I do. I believe it very much." He pulls her hand against his chest, his eyes holding hers so that she cannot look away, his words urgent. "I believe that we love one another, Beatrix, and that we would like to be married—someday. Not today, not tomorrow or next week, but someday. And that's all I need to believe at this moment."

She tries to pull away, but is captive. "It's too soon, Will. Let's not—"

"Too soon?" He laughs lightly. "We have known one another for five years, Beatrix. Five years. And I have loved you almost since the beginning. Since that afternoon we drove back from Ambleside in the rain. Remember?"

And as he hears himself say these surprising words, he acknowledges their truth to himself. Five years. He has loved this woman for five years. He just hasn't *known* it, that was all.

And if you think it is impossible for a person to love another person for five years and be entirely unaware of it, please consider that the Victorians made it a practice to imprison their disruptive, unruly feelings in the cellar of Dr. Freud's unconscious until those feelings became so strong that they fought their way out and clamored relentlessly for acknowledgment. Which is what has happened here, I suspect. Mr. Heelis might have been slow out of the gate (five years!), but there is no stopping him now. He has the bit in his teeth, and this is the home stretch. He sees the finish line not far ahead, and he is having a strong go at it.

"Yes, I remember that afternoon." She pulls in her breath. "Five years? It has really been that long?"

"That long. And it can be longer, as long as need be," he says earnestly. "If only I have your promise, Beatrix."

She bites her lip. "Just a promise? That's all you want from me?"

"Yes, a promise. That's all." But a promise is everything, isn't it? Especially for a woman like Beatrix and a man like Will. Once spoken, the promise is binding.

She seems to consider. The moment stretches on, lengthening until the nighttime silence is broken at last by a querulous *Whooo-who-whooo?*—Professor Owl, I am sure, inquiring as to the possibility of a dinner guest. Or perhaps, in some metaphysical way, he is posing a question to Beatrix. If not Norman Warne, my dear, who? If not Will Heelis, who? Who, who?

She deliberates a moment longer, and then another. And finally she lifts her chin, meets his eyes, and speaks quite firmly, as if she has at long last made up her mind. "Well, then, here is my promise. I promise not to marry anyone but you, Will Heelis." She pauses, and her eyes glint in wry amusement. "There. That is my promise, and I freely give it. Will it do?"

He frowns. She hasn't promised to marry him, now or in the future—has she? No. She has promised not to marry anyone *but* him. His frown deepens. Is she teasing? Is she having sport with him? Does she intend never to—

"There, you see?" she says with relish. She at last succeeds in reclaiming her hand and steps back. "It is not enough for you, after all your pretty speeches. I *knew* you wanted something more from me. Well, that's all you are going to get. You are free to take back your proposal."

"No, no," he says hastily, feeling himself caught and bowled, and very handily so. His respect for Miss Potter rises even higher, if that were possible. "It is enough. It is more than enough. I am entirely satisfied. I—"

He stops, heartened. Really, it is all very logical. She *has* promised. And he knows Beatrix Potter well enough to know that she is a woman of her word. She will never break a promise. She will marry him, or she will never marry. Isn't that what he wants? Well, not exactly, perhaps. But he knows it is the best he's going to get, and he is content. His spirit suddenly lightens, and the moon seems to smile on them warmly and sweetly and with the fullest possible approval.

"Very well, then," he says. "You have given your promise, and I accept it, with all my heart. Now you shall have mine."

Her eyes widen, and he knows that she has not thought this far. "Oh, but, I don't want— No, please, Mr. Heelis— Will! No promise! You really must look for someone who can make your home happy and comfortable and give you children and—"

He overrides her protest. "I promise to marry no one but you, Beatrix Potter." The words are as sacred to him as if they were said at St. Peter's, before Vicar Sackett and the entire congregation. He steps back. "There. Your pledge, and mine. We have agreed. To an engagement."

"An engagement?" she whispers, and pales. "Oh, *dear.* This isn't what I meant to do. Not at all!"

"Too late for that, my dear," he says with a chuckle. "Renege, and I shall sue you for breach of promise. And since I know my way around a courtroom, Miss Potter, you shall surely lose."

"But I don't want— I can't possibly— My parents—"

"Yes, you do want," he says firmly, putting his hands on her shoulders. "And whether you can or you can't doesn't enter into it in the slightest, not at the moment. Nor do your parents. It is only the two of us, Beatrix. No one else. And no one else needs to know. It is our secret."

I'm afraid he is wrong, though. You know, and I know. And someone else knows—someone, indeed, two someones—for they are watching and listening at this very moment, and are likely to tell the exciting news to everyone they know.

He smiles down at her. "And now that we are well and truly engaged, I would like to kiss my fiancée. If she doesn't mind, that is."

And since the moon has discreetly retired behind a convenient cloud and the darkness wraps them like a cloak, this is the ideal moment for their kiss. About time, too, wouldn't you say? I (and perhaps you) have been waiting for this moment through several books now, and had just about given up hope that it was ever going to happen. And here it is at last, hooray! We can stand back and watch and smile and enjoy it—not as much as our Beatrix and her Will, perhaps (it is their first kiss, after all, and aren't first kisses always wonderful?), but enjoy it we certainly shall.

Except that we shan't.

For Will doesn't get to kiss his new fiancée, although this is not his fault. Just as he is bending to claim that most pleasurable privilege, he catches sight of something out of the corner of his eye. Beatrix sees it at the same moment, points, gasps.

"Fire!" she cries. "The buttery at Applebeck—it's burning!"

Will wheels to look. Yes, fire! Flames are shooting out of the windows of a stone building a hundred yards down the footpath.

"I'll run to the pub and get help," Beatrix says breathlessly. "You go and see if there's anyone in that building."

And without another word, she is racing up the hill in the direction of the Tower Bank Arms. Will sprints in the other direction, toward the burning building.

He is nearly there when he remembers that he has not gotten his kiss.

22

In Which All Conundrums Are
Resolved—Or Are They?

The Great Applebeck Fire, as it came to be called, took
hours to subside. It was not extinguished by the impromptu
fire brigade that turned out as soon as Miss Potter raced into
the pub and raised the alarm. No—in spite of the stout efforts of the valiant men and women who formed a human
chain and passed pails of water from Wilfin Beck and tossed
them onto the burning building, the fire was doused by an
opportune thundershower that happened by. It was kind
enough to pour buckets of rain onto the burning building,
and also managed to drench all our intrepid fire fighters before it went on its way, chuckling at the fine joke.

But by that time, I am sorry to say, the ancient timbers,
rafters, and joists that supported the old slate roof had all
burnt through. Whilst the stone walls still stood fairly
firm, the roof caved in and the interior was completely gut-
ted. The embers continued to smolder for long hours after
the thundershower had wandered off into the western fells

and everyone, exhausted with work and excitement and wet from head to toe, had gone home to indulge in a hot toddy, a good toweling, and bed. As they went, they speculated (naturally) about the cause of this second fire at Applebeck Farm within the space of a few weeks.

" 'Twas t' Ramblers!" cried Mr. Harmsworth, who had appeared at the fire in his trousers and muslin nightshirt, which he had not taken off when he was woken and told that the buttery was burning. "They set fire to t' haystack, and they're back again to burn me out!"

"Ridiculous," snorted Major Ragsdale. He had heard the alarm and run over from Teapot Cottage. "Likely, your dairymaid left a candle burning. Happens all the time." He shook his head reprovingly. "Careless dairymaids. Never look what they are doing."

"Ask me, 'twas Bertha Stubbs," whispered Agnes Llewellyn to Mathilda Crook, as they started up the path toward the village. "Her threatened to put a rock through his window, to get even fer closin' t' footpath. Reckon her figured a torch 'ud do a better job."

Bertha Stubbs, too far behind them to hear what they were saying, had her own opinion. " 'Twere t' lightnin'," she claimed loudly, although it was an indisputable fact that the storm had not arrived on the scene until the building was entirely engulfed in flames. "Reet dang'rous, that lightnin'."

" 'Twas Auld Beechie wot done it," said Dick Llewellyn, confidentially, to Constable Braithwaite. "Who else has a reason fer wantin' to cause Harmsworth grief? Had to be him."

The constable, who agreed with Mr. Llewellyn's assessment of the situation, left the scene of the crime and went directly to Mr. Beecham's cottage on Cunsey Beck. He pounded on the door and called loudly, but nobody answered except an old yellow cat who screeched at him from the shed. Then, just as the constable was about give it up as a bad job and go home and dry off, Mr. Beecham came around the corner of the cottage, smelling of smoke and smudge and wet right through to the skin, like everyone else, and carrying a very nice wooden cheese ring under one arm and a wooden churn under the other. He had seen the fire from his cottage window, he explained, and hastened to fight it, as any good neighbor would.

The churn and the cheese ring? Oh, he had bagged—er, he had *found* them—just outside the burning building, and not wanting either to be damaged, had brought both along home with him, to be returned later. As for how the blaze began, it was his considered opinion that Mr. Harmsworth had set it, although he was at a loss to explain, now that the footpath was closed, why he would do such a thing, especially if (as Mr. Beecham claimed) the property was about to be sold.

And when Constable Braithwaite pointed out that Mr. Beecham himself had a jolly good reason for burning down the building, Mr. Beecham became indignant. He? Why, he had nothing to do with the fire! Nothing at all, and anybody who said anything else was either a liar or a bloody fool. He was only an innocent bystander who had done his very best to put out the flames and rescue valuable property, and had anybody thanked him for his strenuous efforts? No, of course they hadn't. And with that, he told the constable to go on about his business, for it was getting on past midnight and he, Mr. Beecham, intended to pour himself a stout tot of rum and go to bed.

The constable was frustrated and out of temper. But there was little he could do, for it was as Captain Woodcock reminded us earlier: unless there is an eyewitness to an arson, or unless the arsonist stupidly leaves a piece of incriminating evidence behind, it is very difficult to gain a conviction. So the good John Braithwaite had to content himself with confiscating the churn and the cheese ring and telling Auld Beechie to keep well away from Applebeck. If there were any more fires, anywhere, he—the constable—would know where to look first, by Jove.

But in this case, there *was* an eyewitness, although this fact was not known until the following day.

Miss Potter spent the morning seeing to her various farm duties. She went out into the hay field to inspect the haystacks; went into the garden to pick three bunches of grapes and some plums; discussed the acquisition of a new tup for her flock of Herdwick sheep with Farmer Jennings; and reviewed Mrs. Jennings' reports of the milk, butter, and eggs produced by the cows and hens, as well as the vegetables produced by the garden. These were pleasant tasks, and she always enjoyed them.

And since it was a day of blue skies and mild breezes, she saw no reason why the fire at Applebeck should keep her from meeting Gilly, as she and Mr. Harmsworth had agreed. So after the noon meal, she drove Winston the pony (with Rascal coming along for the ride) to Applebeck. When she arrived, Mr. and Mrs. Harmsworth were nowhere to be seen. But Gilly was waiting at the gate, wearing a patched white pinafore over a plain gray dress, her blond hair plaited into two braids. She had a book in her hand.

"Please climb in," Miss Potter invited, after she had introduced herself.

Gilly, feeling deeply troubled, complied. "Is this what you've come for?" she asked, holding out the book. "It's the one Miss Nash gave me for winning the spelling contest. I've loved reading it, but if you want it back—"

"Why, no," Miss Potter said, smiling. "The book is yours to keep, of course. I am glad you won it, and very glad you like it." She picked up the reins and clucked to the pony, who flicked his tail and tossed his head in a lively way, as though he was pleased to be out and about on such a pretty afternoon. "I have come just for *you*, my dear. I thought we might go for a drive. Should you like that?"

Gilly would like that very much. Other than her walks back and forth to school and to chapel on Sunday, she had been nowhere else but Applebeck, and she knew there was a great deal more to see. She felt rather shy as they drove off, but Rascal climbed into her lap and licked her face, and Miss Potter drew her out very quietly and skillfully, and before long Gilly found herself telling the story of her young life, where she had lived before she came to Applebeck, why she had come there, and what sort of work she did—keeping the buttery and making the cheeses, and doing the garden and the housework.

"It sounds quite a lot," Miss Potter commented. "You must work very hard."

"I enjoy most of it," Gilly said truthfully. It wasn't the work itself she minded, and the buttery had been a pleasant, quiet place—a place where she was usually left alone. "I don't know what's to be done now that the buttery has burnt, though," she said sadly. She cast a sidelong look at Miss Potter. "Did you see the fire?"

"I did," Miss Potter said. "It was quite a blaze."

Gilly sighed. "It's really too bad. I suppose all the dairy work will have to be done in the kitchen now." Which meant that she would be under Mrs. Harmsworth's thumb all day long. There would be no escape.

"Miss Nash has told me that you might be interested in finding another position," Miss Potter said. "Is that still the case?"

"Another position?" Gilly turned to stare at her, not sure she had heard correctly. "Oh, yes," she said, quite passionately. "I should love to leave Applebeck." And then, thinking she might have gone too far, smoothed her pinafore and added, in a more careful, grown-up tone, "That is, I would like to consider another place, if there's one available."

"I wonder, then," Miss Potter said, "whether you would like to drive up to Raven Hall." She pointed with her pony whip. "It's just up there, in Claife Heights, and not very far. Mrs. Kittredge tells me that her dairyman is looking for a helper. Perhaps the two of you might have a talk and see if it is a position that would suit you."

Gilly was astonished. "Do you mean it?" she cried, clasping her hands and abandoning all pretense of being grown-up. "Oh, Miss Potter, that would be wonderful!"

So Gilly spent the next hour meeting Mrs. Kittredge and Mrs. Kittredge's dairyman, and the dairyman's cows, and the cows' calves, and showing the dairyman how she churned butter, and answering his questions about how she made cheese, until everyone (even the cows, although their opinions were not solicited) professed themselves quite satisfied that Gilly Harmsworth was a good choice for the position of dairymaid. Miss Potter enjoyed a pleasant tea with Mrs. Kittredge, and Rascal discovered a satisfyingly meaty mutton bone in the kitchen waste, and Winston had a satisfying spot of very green grass to munch on while he was waiting.

Now, all that was left was to tell Mr. and Mrs. Harmsworth that their niece would be taking a place at Raven Hall, and that she would be leaving at the end of a fortnight. Miss Potter was not looking forward to this, because she was sure that there would be some sort of unpleasant confrontation. She also worried that it was not a good idea for Gilly to stay on at Applebeck for a whole fortnight. Still, the girl really ought to give notice, even though she was not a paid employee.

But that was not what happened. After they left Raven Hall, Gilly—who was now sure that she could trust Miss Potter to give good advice—opened her heart and confided what she had seen the night before. You remember, don't you? Gilly was sitting at the window of her attic when she saw the ghost in the gray cloak and black bonnet going down the path, except that the figure didn't exactly move in the way the ghost had moved—and she had seen the ghost before and was sure. So Gilly crept down the stairs and followed.

Only it wasn't a ghost, of course. It was a real person, and Gilly had been so shocked when she saw who it was and what that person was up to that she was frozen for a few moments, watching. Then she ran back to Applebeck and raised the alarm, although by that time, of course, it was already too late, because the fire had been lighted in a box of rags and the entire interior of the buttery was in flames.

Miss Potter heard Gilly's story with increasing alarm and acted decisively. Instead of turning Winston onto the Applebeck lane, she drove straight up the Kendal Road to Tower Bank House. There, she introduced Gilly to Captain Woodcock, who (in his capacity as justice of the peace) listened carefully to the girl's story, asked her a number of questions, and wrote down all her answers.

"You realize, of course, that you may very well be called upon to swear to what you have seen in a court of law," he told her when they had finished.

"Yes, sir," she said quietly. "It's all true, sir, every word of it."

"We shall see," he said. He looked at Miss Potter. "I think it would be best if you would go to Applebeck with us," he said. "We will go in my motor car," he added.

"Of course," Miss Potter said, and sighed, for she was not fond of riding in Captain Woodcock's motor car, which went very fast (a bone-rattling eight miles an hour!) and made so much racket that it frightened the village animals. But she knew that the captain wanted to make this an official visit, and of course, his motor car had a very official look.

That is why a short while later, the captain's shiny teal blue Rolls-Royce pulled up in front of the Applebeck farmhouse, and four people—Captain Woodcock, Constable Braithwaite, Gilly, and Miss Potter—climbed out. When they arrived, Mr. Harmsworth was in the barn, milking. Mrs. Harmsworth was upstairs, packing her bags.

Yes, packing. She thought she might go to Liverpool, where she had a cousin. Returning to Manchester didn't seem like a very good idea, for she was afraid that someone might recognize her. Anyway, she was very glad to have the little hoard of money that she had wrung out of the household accounts (and stolen from her husband's pockets), which amounted to enough to set her up as a seamstress—at least until her customers discovered that she couldn't so much as darn a sock.

As it turned out, however, Mrs. Harmsworth did not go Liverpool. Two hours later, Constable Braithwaite had installed her in the Hawkshead gaol, charged with two counts of the crime of arson. Confronted by Gilly's low-voiced accusation, the stern countenance of Captain Woodcock, and the sullen acquiescence of her husband, who by this time knew very well what she had done, she had broken down and confessed. She had put on the gray cloak and black bonnet she'd found in the attic and had taken the old tin candle lantern she found in the barn, and had burnt down both the haystack and the buttery, out of pure spite against Mr. Harmsworth.

But that isn't all. Perhaps it will come as no surprise to those of you who are careful readers, and suspicious, to learn that a week later, when Constable Braithwaite went to Manchester to investigate Mrs. Harmsworth's background, he discovered that Miss Westgate (her name at the time) had been discharged from her haberdashery position just hours before a fire destroyed not only the haberdasher's firm but a whole block of merchants' firms as well. She had been suspected of this arson at the time, but had disappeared before the investigation was complete.

Well, now. This was a good piece of work, I must say, and Captain Woodcock can perhaps be forgiven for thinking that Miss Potter—who had brought him the necessary eyewitness—had pulled yet another rabbit out of her very capacious hat.

"I do not understand how she does it," Miss Nash heard him mutter later that evening, as he was telling her about the capture of the village arsonist, and the mystery that Miss Potter had solved. "I simply do not understand."

But Miss Potter was not quite finished.

The next morning, Vicar Sackett came to call. He had heard the news about Mrs. Harmsworth and wanted to congratulate Beatrix for her part in identifying the arsonist. Like many others, he felt that if she had not been caught, she might have gone on burning things down, just to give herself a sense of importance. He dithered for a few moments, and then finally voiced his other reason for coming. Captain Woodcock had suggested that there be a committee to oversee any other footpath controversies. The vicar wondered . . . That is, he hoped . . . He was very anxious for Beatrix to serve on the committee.

"I'm glad to help out," Beatrix said. She liked the vicar, although she sometimes wished he were a bit more definitive. "Being asked to serve—it makes me feel as though I belong here."

"Oh, but you *do* belong here, my dear Miss Potter!" the vicar cried, in the most definitive tone Beatrix had ever heard him use. "Why, you are a very important part of our little village. The fires at Applebeck might have gone unsolved, if it hadn't been for you."

Beatrix shook her head. "I'm sure that Gilly would have told someone what she knew, sooner or later. I only—"

"No, Miss Potter," the vicar said authoritatively. "You will not evade my thanks. You befriended the girl and earned her trust. It might have been months or years—or never!—before she felt able to tell someone else what she told you. Indeed, you do belong here, my dear. We wouldn't know what to do without you!"

And with those encouraging words still ringing in her ears, Beatrix drove Winston back to Tidmarsh Manor, where she spent a little time with Caroline and Miss Burns. Both of them were terribly excited about their upcoming move to London, where Caroline would attend the Royal Academy and Miss Burns would teach at Mrs. Alton's School for Young Ladies.

"I'm worried about my guinea pigs, though," Caroline said, looking at the trio of energetic little animals—Nutmeg, Tuppenny, and Thruppence—who lived in a hutch in one corner of the schoolroom. "I don't know who will look after them while I'm gone."

"Would you like me to keep them for you in London?" Beatrix asked. "I'll give them walks in the garden and you can visit them whenever you like."

"Oh, Miss Potter!" Caroline cried, and flung her arms around Beatrix. "That would be wonderful. Thank you! And thank you so much for all you've done."

"Indeed," Miss Burns said. "I'm quite sure that our situation would not have turned out so well if you had not intervened."

"I don't know about that," Beatrix said. "But I'm glad to have done what I could. And I shall look forward to seeing you both in London soon and to hearing that you are having a very successful year at your schools."

Then she went down to the drawing room, where Lady Longford was sitting in the gloom, with all the draperies pulled shut. Her ladyship (having heard from Mrs. Beever that the buttery at Applebeck had burnt the night before) was pouting.

Beatrix wasted no time getting down to business. She seated herself directly across from Lady Longford. "I recently learnt," she said briskly, "that you and Mr. Harmsworth have been discussing your purchase of Applebeck Farm."

Lady Longford scowled. "I don't know what you're talking about."

"Oh?" Beatrix raised her eyebrow. "Then you are no longer interested in the property?"

Lady Longford eyed her guest warily. She had been very upset when she learnt, the previous year, that Miss Potter had bought Castle Farm. She had not wanted Castle Farm until she discovered that Miss Potter had bought it, of course, but she had regretted it ever since. After that experience, I don't blame her for suspecting that Miss Potter might be casting an acquisitive eye on Applebeck. Her ladyship, who hates to be bested at anything, hates it most of all when someone buys an attractive piece of property out from under her nose.

"I didn't say I wasn't interested," she muttered.

"Ah." Beatrix gave her a prim smile. "I understand that your purchase is on condition that the Applebeck Footpath will be closed."

"Indeed it is," said her ladyship haughtily, lifting her chin. "And it is a firm condition. I have no wish to have people of all sorts trekking across my land, damaging young trees, picking fruit, and leaving their greasy lunch wrappers to blow about. The path must be closed."

Beatrix spoke in a tactful tone. "Then I fear that your ladyship may wish to withdraw your offer of purchase. Captain Woodcock has ruled that the Applebeck Footpath is to remain open, as it has done for longer than anyone can remember. It will not be closed." She folded her hands. "In any circumstance. No matter who owns it."

"Remain open!" Lady Longford cried, half-rising from her chair. "Why, I never heard such nonsense. Miss Potter, this is . . . this is—"

"This is how it must be, I fear," Beatrix said, with a little smile. "I am very sorry for your disappointment." She allowed her smile to widen just perceptibly. "And if you are no longer interested in the property, I might consider making an offer. I understand that Mr. Harmsworth is quite anxious to sell."

There was a silence, as Lady Longford, who was stewing inside, considered the implications of this. At last she spoke.

"If you think," she said between clenched teeth, "that a little thing like a footpath is going to stop me from buying that property, you can think again, Miss Potter. I have made an offer for the property, and my offer will stand. Footpath or no footpath."

Beatrix pulled a long face, although in her heart she was delighted. She had told Mr. Beecham the truth: she could not afford to buy Applebeck, no matter how much she might want to own a producing orchard. And she knew that Lady Longford, for all her faults, was a capable landlord with a care for good farming practices. She would let the orchard and the old farmhouse to a capable farmer and orchardist who could make the most of both. Under her stewardship, the land and its creatures would prosper.

Pleased at having outwitted her rival, Lady Longford gave a smug laugh. "I see, Miss Potter, that you are bitterly disappointed at not being able to purchase Applebeck yourself. Well, well. These things happen, my dear. Life's little frustrations. We must just learn to live with them."

"I suppose," said Beatrix, putting on a sorrowful face. She rose and took her leave, and she and Winston drove home through the dappled shade of morning, the sun blessing the lane ahead, the meadows spread like a green comforter around her. Her time at Hill Top was growing short, and there were a great many things she wanted to do. She was glad that the next few days were free of any other obligations, and she could simply relax and enjoy them— enjoy her garden and fruit trees, her Herdwick sheep and the cows and pigs and chickens, enjoy a few hours for sketching and another few hours for walking at Moss Eccles Tarn and Esthwaite Water.

But enjoy, most of all, the secret she held warm and close to her heart: the pledge she had exchanged with Mr. Heelis the night before. It was lovely to know that she was loved. And while she knew that Mr. Heelis would come to regret his moonstruck promise and take it back when he had had some time to think, she would hold on to the memory of that night as long as she lived.

The pledge that Beatrix and Will had exchanged the night before was not as secret as they thought, of course. You and I witnessed this momentous event, although I don't believe we are likely to tell anyone, are we? But two others saw it, as well, and they are not quite so discreet as we. In a few days, the news will be all over the village—at least, among the village animals. The Big Folk may have to wait a little longer to find it out.

The witnesses, as you might have already guessed, were Max the Manx and Fritz the ferret. They may seem an odd couple, perhaps, but many people keep cats and ferrets together and find that the two are quite companionable. This amiable pair had spent a very pleasant day together whilst Fritz put the finishing touches on Max's portrait.

When it was done and the canvas unveiled, Max was astonished, for there he was, portrayed in all his tailless splendor. He suddenly saw himself in a whole new light. *"Why, it's me!"* he cried. *"And I'm . . . I'm quite handsome!"*

"Of course you are," said Fritz warmly. *"Didn't I say so? Didn't I say that you are unique among cats? An impressive beast? Well, here's the portrait to prove it!"*

Max sat staring at himself, purring deep in his throat and feeling himself grow proud and strong. Miss Potter had made pictures of some of the other cats in the village— Tabitha Twitchit and Crumpet and that lot—but Fritz had not chosen to paint them, for they were just ordinary cats.

And in Max's opinion (although I'm not sure that his view is to be trusted, since he is, after all, quite flattered by this artistic attention), Fritz's talents were superior to those of Miss Potter. Why, just look at that expression! And the way those whiskers gleamed. And those amber eyes, and that glistening black fur . . . No, Miss Potter had never done anything as fine as *this*.

After the portrait was properly hung in Fritz's gallery (where Max could come and look at it anytime he liked), they had celebrated with fresh-baked scones that Max borrowed from Sarah Barwick's bakery, thick yellow cream Fritz had fetched from the Applebeck cow, and strawberry jam from the ferret's pantry. Fritz, who had traveled in Cornwall, added a treacle topping and called the whole affair "Thunder and Lightning," which he said was quite the Cornish treat.

When they had finished, Max took one last look at his portrait. And then, feeling quite emboldened and pleased with his unique self, had gone out to look for a new job.

Which was why, when Major Ragsdale returned to Teapot Cottage from fighting the fire in the buttery late that night, he discovered Max the Manx on his doorstep. At his feet were not one but *two* dead mice, both of them quite large. Max had met them at the hole under the pantry window, where the Teapot mice were accustomed to come and go. He had slaughtered them quickly, but let one go, with instructions to tell the others that there was now a cat on the premises and they had better watch their step.

"*I understand that you are in want of a cat,*" Max said, offering a polite paw. "*I brought these fellows to demonstrate my mousing talents. I am quite skilled,*" he added. "*And I have references. My most recent employment was at Hill Top Farm. Miss Potter would be willing to vouch for me, I'm sure.*"

The major was so delighted to see Max—and those two very dead mice—that it never even occurred to him that he ought to ask for a character.

"My dear fellow," he cried ecstatically, bending over for a better look. "*Two* mice? Bravo! By any chance are you a stray?"

"*I am not a stray,*" said Max, bristling. "*I am merely a cat in search of employment. I do have one condition, however. I should like to be free at the weekend to visit the ferret who lives in Wilfin Bank. He is my dearest friend.*"

"Well, whatever you like, you shall have," said the major, casting another delighted look at the mice. "I say, old chap, you have made a most admirable beginning. I shall follow your progress with the keenest interest. And you may have employment here as long as you like." He stood aside so that Max could come in. "Now, how about a saucer of milk and a bit of liver to go along with those mice?"

"*Thank you,*" said Max warmly, and followed the major inside.

A few days later, Miss Potter walked through Far Sawrey on her way to catch the ferry. She was returning across the lake to Helm Farm and her parents, and in a few weeks they would all take the train back to London. (And in case you are wondering, yes. Yes, the Potters did hire a special train car for their horses and carriage.)

Leaving made her feel sad and regretful. Her heart belonged in the Land Between the Lakes, with the farm and, yes, in spite of all her reservations, with Mr. Heelis. She had seen him only once since they exchanged those impulsive pledges, on the night of the Great Applebeck Fire. But once was enough for him to reiterate his promise, remind her of hers, and claim that missed first kiss. (I'm sorry we weren't there to see it, but we can't be everywhere, can we? And it is good, after all, for our Beatrix and her Will to have a little privacy. Heaven only knows how long they will have to wait before they can be alone together again.)

Miss Potter was passing Teapot Cottage when she heard a sharp *Meow!* She looked up to see Max the Manx, sitting under Major Ragsdale's dahlias, his front paws folded under his black bib.

"Why, Max!" she exclaimed. "What are you doing here in Far Sawrey? Quite a distance from home, aren't you?"

"I am *home,*" purred Max, quite comfortably. *"I now hold the position of chief cat here at Teapot."*

"Why, hello, Miss Potter," said Major Ragsdale, coming toward her, rake in hand. "Fully recovered from that accident, have we?"

"Fully," Miss Potter assured him. She gestured at Max. "I see that you have a new cat."

"Splendid fellow, splendid," barked the major proudly. He bent over to stroke Max's ears. "I must say, I'm rather keen on the chap. Since he's been here, the mice have all but disappeared."

"They've moved to the Sawrey Hotel," Max explained, sotto voce. He gave Miss Potter a conspiratorial smile. *"I keep a few around for entertainment, and for show. Don't want the major to think he doesn't need a cat, you know."* And with that, he got up and began to wrap himself around the major's ankles.

"I am very glad to hear that," Miss Potter said. "There's nothing more comfortable around the house than a good mouser."

The major's voice softened. "Y' know, I've always wanted a Manx, ever since I was a lad," he said reflectively. "Always seemed to me to be distinctive. A different sort of cat. Out of the ordinary."

"Oh, I'm different, all right," Max agreed happily. "And very out of the ordinary." He arched his back, purring loudly. "Extraordinary, I'd say."

Miss Potter sighed. "Well, I must be on my way. I mustn't miss the ferry. My parents are expecting me to tea."

"With luck, you'll get there tomorrow," the major said, and saluted with his rake. "Remember, that's not a ferry; that's a conundrum. Farewell, Miss Potter."

"Goodbye, Miss Potter," meowed Max, as she turned to leave.

"Goodbye," Miss Potter said. "Until the next time."

Historical Note

꧁꧂

1910

Nineteen-ten was another busy year in Beatrix Potter's life. Early in the year, she was involved for the first (and last) time in her life in national politics, for free trade was on the political agenda, and it was something she cared about very much. If this issue sounds familiar, there's a reason, for Britain had done away with important tariffs in an effort to "globalize" its trading arena, and the arguments for and against free trade were just like those we hear today.

Beatrix took a personal view of the matter. A nationalist and protectionist, she had hoped to have her Peter Rabbit dolls made by a British dollmaker, but the Germans offered the cheapest bid, so her dolls—much to her distress—were being produced in Germany. At the rate things were going, she feared, Warne might even find it cheaper to have her books printed in the United States and shipped to England! Beatrix did her bit against the cause of free trade by contributing some sixty hand-drawn, hand-colored posters, including one that portrayed a Peter Rabbit doll with a costly price tag, displaying the legend "Made in Germany" and a note that German warships were being built on the profits of Germany's trade with England.

The Liberals carried the day, though. Free trade marched on, and Beatrix returned to drawing "pigs and mice," as she wrote to Harold Warne. She spent the spring putting the finishing touches on *The Tale of Mrs. Tittlemouse*, which was scheduled for October publication, and managing (from a distance) both Hill Top Farm and her 1909 purchase, Castle Farm. In this story, Applebeck Orchard is my own invention; there is no such property in the area of the Sawreys, Near and Far, and the only orchard that Beatrix cared about was the little orchard she planted at Hill Top. "There are quantities of apples, very few pears, & plums," she wrote to Millie Warne during her visit there in August 1910, and added that she had picked three bunches of grapes from her vines.

Beatrix's visits to Hill Top, though, were few and fleeting in this year, for her parents claimed almost all her attention and most of her energy. They spent their summer holiday at Helm Farm, in Bowness, an unlikely place for them, but all they could find at the last moment, the arrangements having been delayed (as Beatrix tells Will in this book) because of her father's health. She was less active creatively at this time, and the time she could spare for herself was focused on her farms. As Linda Lear remarks, in *Beatrix Potter: A Life in Nature*, by 1910, "the balance of [her] creative energy had shifted," and she was more interested in her real animals at her farm in the Lakes than the fictional creatures in the "little books." From now on, she would write and draw less for her own creative pleasure and more to earn money to support Hill Top and Castle farms.

Other Lakeland issues—such as footpaths and flying

boats—interested her, too. While I have invented the footpath incident for the plot of this book, Beatrix was a longtime advocate of open footpaths, like her friend Canon Rawnsley, one of the founders of the National Trust. In 1912, she was elected to a Sawrey footpath committee, a testimony to her acceptance as a farmer and countrywoman who understood issues of boundaries and rights of way. The hydroplane factory mentioned by Will Heelis, however, is a real one; only hinted at in this book, it will be a major part of the next book in this series.

Nineteen-ten may also have been a time of romance, as well. It is not clear from the existing records (chiefly Beatrix's letters) exactly when she and Will Heelis first acknowledged their love for each other. It seems that there was no official engagement until 1912, although in 1913, she wrote to her friend Fanny Cooper, "He has waited six years already." Whatever the chronology of their relationship, it was a friendship that evolved into love over time, in the context of Beatrix's continuing loyalty to Norman's memory. Linda Lear writes:

> *Beatrix had fallen in love with William Heelis in much the same way as she had with Norman Warne: slowly and companionably. . . . In the same way she had come to love Norman, Beatrix discovered the satisfaction and security that came from William's knowledge of the Lake District and its customs, and she relied on his advice about her properties in the same way as she had trusted Norman's expertise in publishing. . . . Beatrix had loved Norman for his imagination and his humour, and she similarly delighted in William's love of nature, his knowledge of the countryside and his zest for being out in it, whether he was fishing, shooting, golfing, bowling, boating or country dancing.*

And so I think it is appropriate for their engagement (albeit a secret one) to begin in this book, even though the time frame isn't quite consistent with the few known facts we have about their relationship.

I hope you think so, too.

Susan Wittig Albert
Bertram, Texas, September 2009

Resources

Beeton, Isabella. *Mrs. Beeton's Book of Household Management, 1861.* Facsimile edition. Farrar, Straus and Giroux, New York, 1969.

Denyer, Susan. *At Home with Beatrix Potter.* Harry N. Abrams, Inc., New York, 2000.

Lear, Linda. *Beatrix Potter: A Life in Nature.* Allen Lane (Penguin UK), London, and St. Martin's Press, New York, 2007.

Potter, Beatrix. *Beatrix Potter's Letters.* Selected and edited by Judy Taylor. Frederick Warne, London, 1989.

Potter, Beatrix. *The Journal of Beatrix Potter, 1881–1897.* New edition. Transcribed by Leslie Linder. Frederick Warne, London, 1966.

Rollinson, William. *The Cumbrian Dictionary of Dialect, Tradition and Folklore.* Smith Settle Ltd, West Yorkshire, UK, 1997.

Taylor, Judy. *Beatrix Potter: Artist, Storyteller and Countrywoman.* Revised edition. Frederick Warne, London, 1996.

Recipes from the Land Between the Lakes

Mrs. Beeton's Best Soda Bread
(from Mrs. Beeton's Book of Household Management, 1861)

To every 2 pounds of flour allow 1 teaspoonful of tartaric acid, 1 teaspoonful of salt, 1 teaspoonful of carbonate of soda, 2 breakfast-cupfuls of cold milk. Let the tartaric acid and salt be reduced to the finest possible powder; then mix them well with the flour. Dissolve the soda in the milk, and pour it several times from one basin to another, before adding it to the flour. Work the whole quickly into a light dough, divide it into 2 loaves, put them into a well-heated oven immediately, and bake for an hour. Sour milk or buttermilk may be used, but then a little less acid will be needed.

Dimity Woodcock's Bramble Jelly

In her journal, Beatrix describes the blackberry as "a kindly berry, it ripens in the rain." After she and Will Heelis were married in 1913, they lived at Castle Cottage. In her book *A Tale of Beatrix Potter*, Margaret Lane describes their dining room table, where "a law book and papers and deed-boxes" occupied one end, and "bramble jelly and toasted teacakes" the other. Perhaps the bramble jelly Miss Lane mentions was made from Dimity Woodcock's recipe. Bramble jelly is also used as a glaze for cheesecakes, pies, and flans, and as an accompaniment to mutton, pork, ham, duck, and goose.

> 2½ quarts blackberries
> ¾ cup water
> 3 cups sugar

TO PREPARE JUICE
Sort and wash the berries; remove any stems or caps. Put in a pan with the water, cover, and simmer gently for about 20–25 minutes, until soft. Place in a jelly bag and hang over a large bowl to strain out the juice.

TO MAKE JELLY
Measure 4 cups juice into a kettle. Add sugar and stir well. Boil over high heat to 110°C (220°F), or until mixture sheets from a spoon and jelly has reached the setting point. Remove from heat; skim off foam. Pour jelly immediately into hot containers and seal. Makes about 5 six-ounce glasses.

The Professor's Grandmother's Ginger Beer Recipe (an old recipe)

Ginger beer was brewed in England from the 1700s on. Its predecessor was mead, which dates back to Anglo-Saxon times. A honey beverage, it was naturally carbonated and yeast-fermented, often including ginger, cloves, and mace. In ginger beer, which was popular through the early 1900s, sugar replaced honey, and fresh Jamaican ginger root, with lemon, became the dominant flavor.

2¼ pounds sugar
1½ ounces cream of tartar
1½ ounces gingerroot
2 lemons
2 tablespoons fresh brewer's yeast
3 gallons water

Bruise the ginger, and put into a large earthenware pan, with the sugar and cream of tartar; peel the lemons, squeeze out the juice, strain it, and add, with the peel, to the other ingredients; then pour over the water boiling hot. When it has stood until it is only just warm, add the yeast, stir the contents of the pan, cover with a cloth, and let it remain near the fire for 12 hours. Then skim off the yeast and pour the liquor off into another vessel, taking care not to shake it, so as to leave the sediment; bottle it immediately, cork it tightly; in 3 or 4 days, it will be fit for use.

Parsley's Ginger-and-Treacle Pudding

Treacle is the word used in Britain for syrup made in the process of refining sugarcane. It can range from very light to very dark. The lighter syrup (produced from the first boiling of the sugarcane juice) is called light treacle or golden syrup. The second boiling produces a much darker syrup, which British cooks call treacle (or dark treacle) and Americans call molasses (or dark molasses). The third boiling produces what both British and Americans call blackstrap molasses, which is very dark, with a slightly bitter edge.

In this recipe, Parsley uses dark treacle (molasses). She also uses the shredded suet that is traditional for sweet and savory puddings and mincemeat. Suet has a high melting point that results in a light and smoothly textured pastry, whether baked or steamed. If you can't find this British specialty, freeze 4 ounces of butter and grate it.

> ¾ cup flour
> pinch of salt
> 1 teaspoon baking soda
> 2 heaping teaspoons ground ginger
> 1⅓ cups fresh breadcrumbs
> 4 ounces shredded suet or grated frozen butter
> 2 tablespoons dark treacle
> ¼ cup milk
> ¼ cup chopped crystallized ginger

Sift the flour, salt, baking soda, and ginger into a mixing bowl. Stir in the breadcrumbs and suet (or butter). In a small saucepan, warm the treacle until it liquefies, then add the milk. Pour into the dry ingredients, mixing well. Add the chopped ginger and mix again, adding a little more milk if necessary. Turn into a greased 1-quart pudding basin and cover with foil. Steam for 2–2½ hours, or until well risen and firm. Serve hot with custard or cream.

Mrs. Barrow's Cumberland Sausage, with Apple-Onion Sauce

Traditional Cumberland sausages are heavily flavored with pepper, nutmeg, and mace. Each butcher had his own recipe, but all were made in continuous coils up to four feet long. Sausage is most easily made with a meat grinder (hand or electric) with a sausage stuffer attachment. Cumberland sausage, served to this day at the Tower Bank Arms in Near Sawrey, may be accompanied by an onion and apple sauce.

SAUSAGE

½ cup hot water

¼ cup stale breadcrumbs

1 pound pork shoulder, boned and ground

6 ounces fat pork, ground

4 strips bacon, ground

1 teaspoon salt

1 teaspoon pepper

½ teaspoon nutmeg

½ teaspoon mace

sausage casings (ask your butcher or purchase
    online)

Add the hot water to the breadcrumbs and set aside. Mix the ground meats, salt, pepper, and spices. Add the breadcrumb/water mixture and mix very well, using your hands. Fry a spoonful of the sausage and taste to adjust the seasoning. Rinse the salt from the sausage casing. Using the sausage stuffer, fill the sausage casings, prick in several places, and refrigerate overnight. Bake in a greased baking dish at 350°F. Turn after 20 minutes, and raise the heat to 375°F. Serve with warm Onion-Apple Sauce.

ONION-APPLE SAUCE
  ½ onion, chopped fine
  Clove garlic, crushed
  2 tablespoons olive oil
  1 pound apples (Granny Smith or another tart apple)
  2 tablespoons water
  2 tablespoons apple cider vinegar
  Bay leaf
  Salt, pepper to taste

Sauté the onion and garlic in the oil until golden brown. Peel, core, and chop apples. Add to the onion. Add water, vinegar, and bay leaf and simmer for 15–20 minutes, until soft. Remove the bay leaf and puree the sauce in a blender. Add salt and pepper to taste.

Glossary

Some of the words included in this glossary are dialect forms; others are sufficiently uncommon that a definition may be helpful. My main source for dialect is William Rollinson's *The Cumbrian Dictionary of Dialect, Tradition and Folklore.* For other definitions, I have consulted the *Oxford English Dictionary* (second edition, Oxford University Press, London, 1989).

Along of. On account of, because of, owing to. "Along of the Applebeck ghost."

Auld. Old.

Awt. Something, anything.

Beck. A small stream.

Betimes. Sometimes.

Bodder, bodderment, boddering. Trouble.

Chapel. One who attends worship in a non-Anglican church.

Character. Letter of recommendation.

Dusta. Doest thou, do you?

Goosy. Foolish.

How. Hill, as in "Holly How," the hill where Badger lives.

Mappen. Maybe, perhaps.

Nae. No.

Nawt. Nothing.

Off-comer. A stranger, someone who comes from far away.

Pattens. Farm shoes with wooden soles and leather uppers.

Pinny. Pinafore.

Reet. Right.

Sae. So.

Sartin, sartinly. Certain, certainly.

Seed wigs. Small, oblong cakes, like tea cakes, flavored with caraway seeds.

Sumbody. Somebody, someone.

Summat. Somewhat, something.

Trice. Very quickly, all at once, "in a trice."

Trippers, day-trippers. Tourists, visitors who come for the day.

Tup. Ram.

Verra or varra. Very.

Wudna, wudsta. Would not, would you.